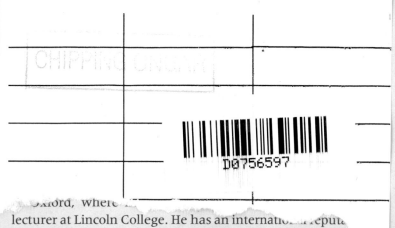

D0756597

...xford, where ...
lecturer at Lincoln College. He has an internatio... ...eput...
as a scholar, having published widely on ancient warfare,
classical art and the cultural history of the Roman Empire.

Iron & Rust is the first book in a major new series, *Throne of
the Caesars*, and follows his acclaimed and bestselling series,
Warrior of Rome. He divides his time between Oxford and
Newmarket in Suffolk, where he lives which his wife and
two sons.

www.harrysidebottom.co.uk

ALSO BY HARRY SIDEBOTTOM

FICTION
The Warrior of Rome Series
Fire in the East
King of Kings
Lion of the Sun
The Caspian Gates
The Wolves of the North
The Amber Road

NON-FICTION
Ancient Warfare

THRONE OF THE CAESARS
IRON
&
RUST

HARRY SIDEBOTTOM

HARPER

Harper
HarperCollins *Publishers*
1 London Bridge Street,
London SE1 9GF

www.harpercollins.co.uk

This paperback edition 2015
1

First published in Great Britain by
HarperCollins *Publishers* 2014

Copyright © Harry Sidebottom 2014

Harry Sidebottom asserts the moral right to
be identified as the author of this work

Maps © John Gilkes 2014

A catalogue record for this book
is available from the British Library

ISBN: 978-0-00-749987-8

While some of the events and characters are based on historical
incidents and figures, this novel is entirely a work of fiction.

Typeset in Meridian by Palimpsest Book Production Ltd,
Falkirk, Stirlingshire
Text design by Ben Gardiner

Printed and bound in Great Britain by
Clays Ltd, St Ives plc

MIX
Paper from
responsible sources

FSC C007454

FSC™ is a non-profit international organisation established to promote
the responsible management of the world's forests. Products carrying the
FSC label are independently certified to assure consumers that they come
from forests that are managed to meet the social, economic and ecological
needs of present and future generations, and other controlled sources.

Find out more about HarperCollins and the environment at
www.harpercollins.co.uk/green

To Ewen Bowie, Miriam Griffin
and Robin Lane Fox

*Our history now descends from a kingdom of gold
to one of iron and rust*

CASSIUS DIO LXXII.36.4

*There have never been such earthquakes and plagues,
or tyrants and kings with such unexpected careers,
which were rarely if ever recorded before*

HERODIAN I.I.4

CONTENTS

THE ROMAN EMPIRE
IN AD235–8

·············· Provincial borders
1. *ALPES GRAIAE*
2. *ALPES COTTIAE*
3. *ALPES MARITIMAE*

Dvina

Marcomanni
Quadi

Borysthenes

Iazyges

PANNONIA
INFERIOR

Mursa

Viminacium

Sirmium

Naisus

MOESIA
SUPERIOR

Serdica

DACIA

ROXOLANI

Durostorum

Novae

THRACE

Byzantium •

MACEDONIA

EPIRUS

ACHAEA

Athens •

GOTHS

Olbia •

KINGDOM OF THE
BOSPORUS

• Tanais

Panticapaeum •

Black Sea

MOESIA
INFERIOR

Sinope •

• Phasis

COLCHIS

IBERIA

Artaxata •

ARMENIA

PERSIAN
EMPIRE

Tigris

BITHYNIA-PONTUS

Cyzicus •

ASIA

Ephesus •

GALATIA

CAPPADOCIA

CILICIA

Samosata •
MESOPOTAMIA

Antioch •

SYRIA COELE
• Emesa

Euphrates

Palmyra •

SYRIA PHOENICE

LYCIA
PAMPHYLIA

nean Sea

SYRIA PALESTINA

Alexandria •

ARABIA

CYRENAICA

EGYPT

Nile

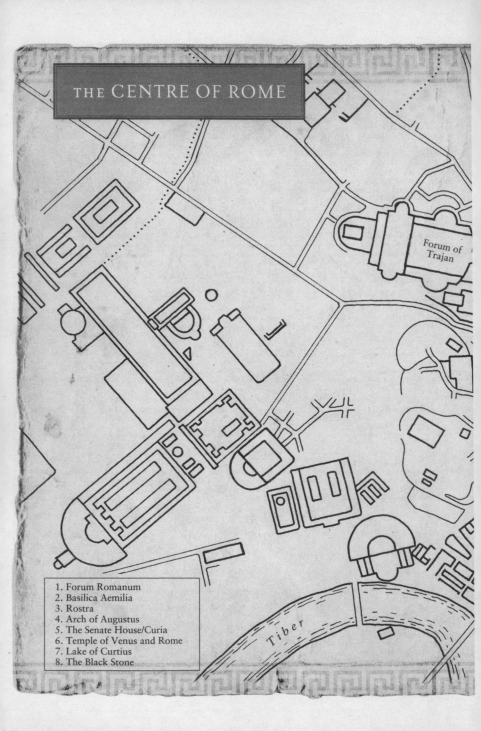

THE CENTRE OF ROME

Forum of
Trajan

Tiber

1. Forum Romanum
2. Basilica Aemilia
3. Rostra
4. Arch of Augustus
5. The Senate House/Curia
6. Temple of Venus and Rome
7. Lake of Curtius
8. The Black Stone

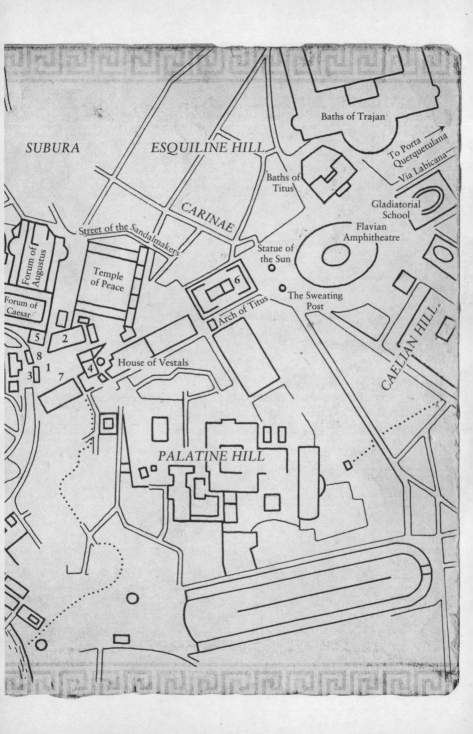

SUBURA

ESQUILINE HILL

Baths of Trajan

To Porta
Querquetulana
Via Labicana

CARINAE

Baths of
Titus

Gladiatorial
School

Street of the Sandalmaker's

Flavian
Amphitheatre

Statue of
the Sun

Forum of
Augustus

Temple
of Peace

6

Forum of
Caesar

The Sweating
Post

Arch of Titus

5

2

8

CAELIAN HILL

1

4

House of Vestals

3

7

PALATINE HILL

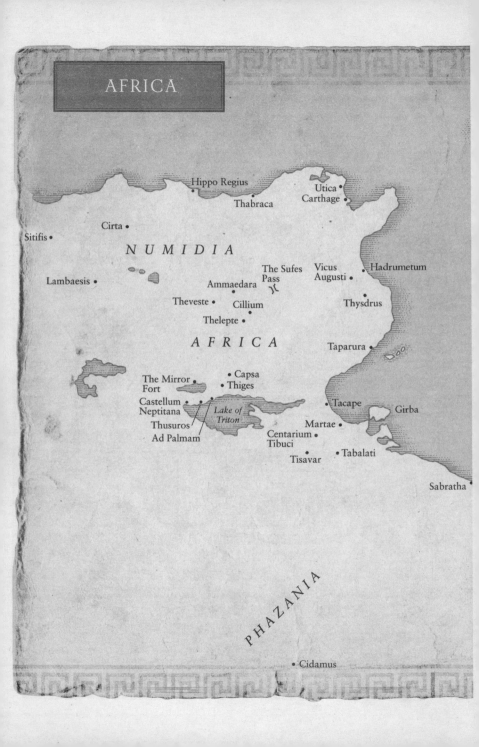

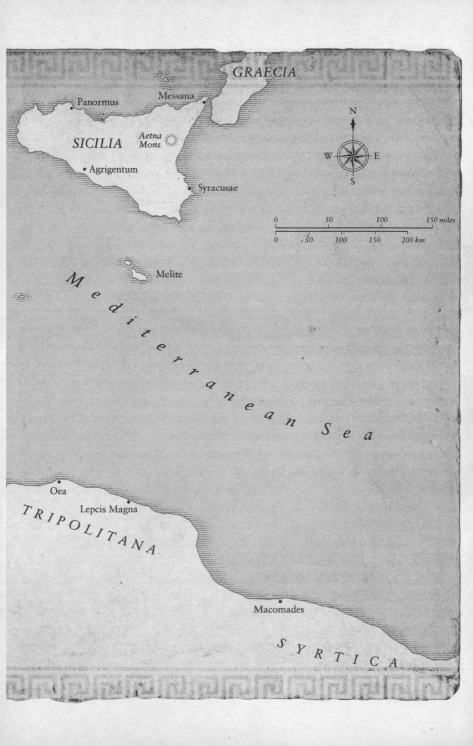

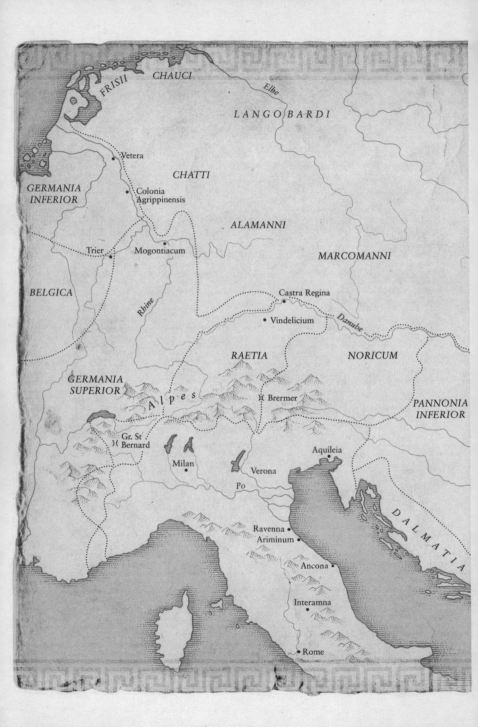

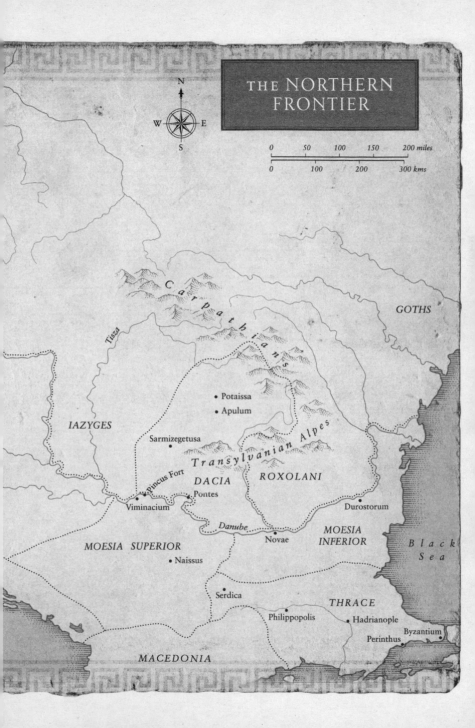

THE NORTHERN
FRONTIER

N

W   E

S

| 0 | 50 | 100 | 150 | 200 *miles* |

| 0 | 100 | 200 | 300 *kms* |

C a r p a t h i a n s

GOTHS

Tisza

IAZYGES

• Potaissa

• Apulum

• Sarmizegetusa

T r a n s y l v a n i a n   A l p e s

Pincus Fort

DACIA

ROXOLANI

• Pontes

Viminacium

• Durostorum

Danube

MOESIA
INFERIOR

• Novae

*Black
Sea*

MOESIA SUPERIOR

• Naissus

• Serdica

THRACE

• Philippopolis

• Hadrianople

• Byzantium

Perinthus

MACEDONIA

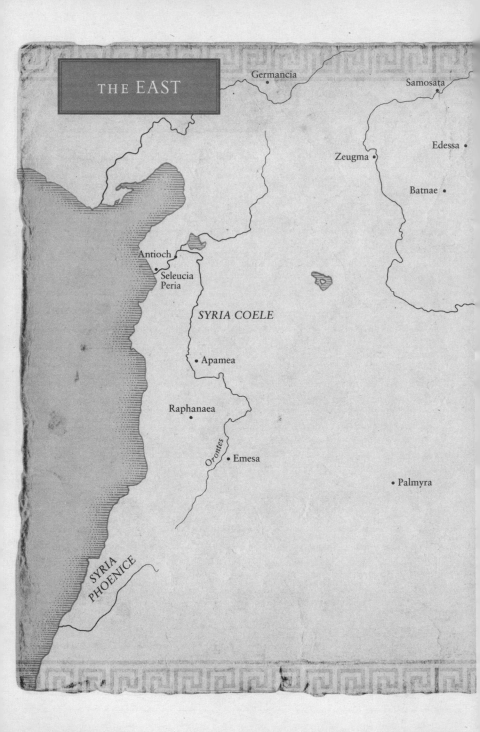

THE EAST

Germancia

Samosata

Edessa •

Zeugma •

Batnae •

Antioch
• Seleucia
Peria

SYRIA COELE

• Apamea

Raphanaea
•

Orontes

• Emesa

• Palmyra

*SYRIA
PHOENICE*

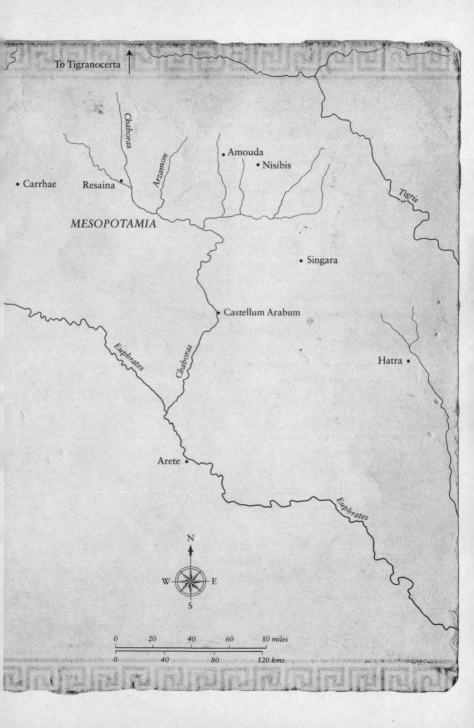

Cast of Main Characters
(a comprehensive list appears at the end of the book)

In the North

Alexander Severus: The Emperor

Mamaea: His mother

Petronius Magnus: An imperial councillor

Flavius Vopiscus: Senatorial governor of Pannonia Superior

Honoratus: Senatorial commander of the troops detached from Moesia Inferior

Catius Clemens: Senatorial commander of the 8th legion in Germania Superior

Maximinus Thrax: An equestrian army officer

Caecilia Paulina: His wife

Maximus: Their son

Anullinus: An equestrian army officer

Volo: The commander of the *frumentarii*

Domitius: The Prefect of the Camp

Julius Capitolinus: Equestrian commander of 2nd legion *Parthica*

Macedo: An equestrian army officer

Timesitheus: Equestrian acting-governor of Germania Inferior

Tranquillina: His wife

Sabinus Modestus: His cousin

In Rome

Pupienus: The Prefect of the City
Pupienus Maximus: His elder son
Pupienus Africanus: His younger son
Gallicanus: A Senator of Cynic views
Maecenas: His intimate friend
Balbinus: A patrician of dissolute ways
Iunia Fadilla: A young widow, descended from Marcus Aurelius
Perpetua: Her friend, wife of Serenianus, governor of Cappadocia
The die-cutter: A workman in the Mint
Castricius: His young and disreputable neighbour
Caenis: A prostitute visited by both

In Africa

Gordian the Elder: Senatorial governor of Africa Proconsularis
Gordian the Younger: His son and legate
Menophilus: His Quaestor
Arrian, Sabinianus, and Valerian: His other legates
Capelianus: Governor of Numidia, and enemy of Gordian

In the East

Priscus: Equestrian governor of Mesopotamia
Philip: His brother
Serenianus: His friend, governor of Cappadocia
Junius Balbus: Governor of Syria Coele, son-in-law of Gordian the
    Elder
Otacilius Severianus: Governor of Syria Palestina, brother-in-law
    of Priscus and Philip
Ardashir: Sassanid King of Kings

OUR HISTORY NOW DESCENDS
FROM A KINGDOM OF GOLD
TO ONE OF IRON AND RUST.

CHAPTER 1

The Northern Frontier
A Camp outside Mogontiacum,

Eight Days before the Ides of March, AD235

Hold me safe in your hands.

The sun would be risen, well up by now, but little evidence filtered through to the inner sanctum of the great pavilion.

All you gods, hold me safe in your hands. The young Emperor prayed silently, his mouth moving. *Jupiter, Apollonius, Christ, Abraham, Orpheus: see me safe through the coming day.*

In the lamplight the eclectic range of deities regarded him impassively.

Alexander, Augustus, Magna Mater: watch over your elect, watch over the throne of the Caesars.

Noises, like the squeaking of disturbed bats, from beyond the little sanctuary of the domestic gods, beyond the heavy silk hangings, disrupted his prayers. From somewhere in the further recesses of the labyrinth of purple-shaded corridors and enclosures came the crash of something breaking. All the imperial attendants were fools – clumsy fools and cowards. The soldiers had mutinied before. Like those disturbances, this one would be resolved, and when that happened the members of the household who had deserted their duty or taken advantage of the uproar would suffer. If any of the slaves or freedmen were stealing, he would have the tendons in their hands cut. They could not steal then. It would serve as a lesson. The *familia Caesaris* needed constant discipline.

The Emperor Alexander Severus pulled a fold of his cloak over his bowed head, placed his right palm on his chest, composed himself again into the attitude of prayer. The omens had been bad for months. On his last birthday the sacrificial animal had escaped. Its blood had splashed on his toga. As they marched out from Rome an ancient laurel tree of huge size suddenly fell at full length. Here on the Rhine, there had been the Druid woman. *Go. Neither hope for victory, nor trust your soldiers.* The words of the prophecy ran in his memory. *Vadas. Nec victoriam speres, nec te militi tuo credas.* It was suspicious she had spoken in Latin. Yet torture had not revealed any malign worldly influences. Whatever her language, the gods needed propitiating.

To Jupiter an ox. To Apollonius an ox. To Jesus Christ an ox. To Achilles, Virgil and Cicero, to all you heroes . . .

As he made every vow, Alexander blew each statuette a kiss. It was not enough. He got down on his knees, then, somewhat encumbered by his elaborate armour, stretched full length in adoration before the *lararium*. Close to his face, he noticed the gold thread in the white carpet. The fabric smelt slightly musty.

None of this was his fault. None of it. The year before last in the East he had been ill. Half the troops with him had been sick. If he had not ordered the retreat to Antioch, the Persians would have destroyed them all; not just the southern force which was left behind, but the main Roman field army as well. Here in the North the frontier had been breached in numerous places. Opening negotiations with some of the barbarians

2

was not weakness. There was no profit in fighting them all at once. Judicious promises and gifts could induce some to stand aside, maybe even join in the destruction of their brethren. It did not mean their punishment was waived, merely deferred. Barbarians had no concept of good faith, so promises to barbarians could not be considered binding. Such things could not be stated in public, but why did the soldiers not see these obvious truths? Of course, the northern soldiery, recruited from the camps, were little better than barbarians themselves. Their comprehension was equally limited. That was why they could not understand about the money. Since Caracalla, the Emperor who may have been his father, had doubled the pay of the troops, the exchequer had been drained. Veturius, the treasurer appointed by his mother, had taken Alexander to the *fiscus*. There had been nothing to see except rank after rank of empty coffers. As Alexander had tried to explain more than once on various parade grounds, donatives to the army would have to be extracted by force from innocent civilians, from the soldiers' own families.

A rush of light as a hanging was pulled back. Felicianus, the senior of the two Praetorian Prefects, marched in. No one announced him and no one closed the curtain. Through the opening, past the Prefect, flew innumerable tiny birds. They darted everywhere around the chamber, flashing bright yellow, red and green as they passed through the band of light. How many times had Alexander told their keepers about the trouble and expense in collecting them? At every dinner when they were released to hop and flutter about entertainingly one or two were lost or died. How many would be left after this?

Felicianus swiped with futile aggression at those that veered and banked near his head as he walked towards the pale gleam of the twin ivory thrones. The Emperor's mother was seated there in the gloom. Granianus, an old tutor of

Alexander's, now promoted into the imperial chancery, stood by Mamaea, whispering. The secretary of studies was always to be found by the side of the Empress, always whispering.

Alexander returned to his devotions. *What you do not wish that a man should do to you, do not do to him.* He had had the phrase inscribed over his *lararium*. He had heard it in the East from some old Jew or Christian. An unwelcome thought struck him. He raised himself on to his elbows. He looked for the court glutton. Alexander had seen him eat birds, feathers and all. It was all right. The omnivore was in a corner beyond Alexander's musical instruments. He was huddled with one of the dwarves. Neither was paying any attention to the ornamental birds. They were staring blankly into space. The mutiny seemed to have drained all their vitality.

'Alexander, get up, and come here.' His mother's voice was peremptory.

Slowly, not to appear too craven, the Emperor got to his feet.

The air was thick with incense, although the sacred fire burnt low on its portable altar. Alexander wondered if he should tell someone to get some fuel. It would be terrible if it went out.

'Alexander.'

The Emperor turned to his mother.

'The situation is not irretrievable. The peasant that the recruits have clad in the purple has not arrived yet. His acclamation will attract few supporters among the senior officers.'

Mamaea was always good in a crisis. Alexander thought of the night of his accession, the night his cousin-brother died, and shuddered.

'Praetorian Prefect Cornelianus has gone to fetch the Cohort of Emesenes. They are our people. Their commander Iotapianus is a kinsman. They will be loyal. The other eastern archers also. He will bring the Armenians and Osrhoenes.'

4

Alexander had never liked Iotapianus.

'Felicianus has volunteered to go back out to the Campus Martius. It is brave. The act of a man.' Mamaea lightly ran her fingers over the sculpted muscles of the Prefect's cuirass. Alexander hoped the rumours were untrue. He had never trusted Felicianus.

'The greed of the troops is insatiable.' Mamaea addressed her son. 'Felicianus will offer them money, a huge donative. The subsidies to the Germans will end. The diplomatic funds will be promised to the soldiers. And they will want those they believe their enemies.' She dropped her voice. 'They will demand Veturius' head. The treasurer must be sacrificed. Apart from the four of us, Felicianus can surrender anyone to them.'

Alexander looked over at the glutton. Among all the court grotesques, the *polyfagus* was Alexander's favourite. It was unlikely the mutineers would demand the death of the imperial omnivore.

'Alexander.' His mother's voice brought him back. 'The soldiers will want to see their Emperor. When Felicianus returns, you will go out with him. From the tribunal you will tell them you share their desire for revenge for their families. You will promise to march at their head against the barbarians who killed their loved ones. Together you will free the enslaved and exact awful vengeance on those who inflicted such terrible sufferings. Give the soldiers the proper address of an *imperator*: fire and sword, burning villages, heaps of plunder, mountains of enemy corpses. Make a better speech than you did this morning.'

'Yes, Mother.'

Felicianus saluted, and left the tent.

It was monstrously unfair. He had done his best. In the grey light of pre-dawn he had gone to the Campus Martius. Clad in his ornamental armour, he had ascended the raised platform, stood and waited with the troops who had renewed their oaths to him the night before. When the mutinous recruits had emerged out of the near-darkness, he had filled his lungs to address them. It was never going to be easy. Latin was not his first language. It had made no difference. They had given him no chance to speak.

Coward! Weakling! Mean little girl tied to his mother's apron strings! Their shouts had pre-empted anything he could have said. On his side of the parade ground, first one or two then whole ranks had put down their arms. He had turned and run. Pursued by taunts and jeers, he had stumbled back to the imperial quarters.

With the Prefect Felicianus gone, Mamaea sat as immobile as a statue. Granianus tried to whisper. She waved him to silence. The small birds fluttered here and there.

Alexander stood, irresolute. An Emperor should not be irresolute. '*Polyfagus*.' The fat man lumbered up and waddled after Alexander to where the food was set out. 'Amuse me, eat.'

Alexander pointed to a mountain of lettuces in a basket. The glutton started to eat, his jaw chewing steadily, his throat bobbing. He ate with little enthusiasm.

'Faster.'

Using both hands, the omnivore stuffed the green leaves into his mouth. Soon there were none left.

'The basket.'

It was made of wicker. The *polyfagus* broke it, and began. Although piece by piece it disappeared into his mouth, he was not attacking it with anything like his customary relish.

Alexander wished he could be free of his mother. But there was no one else. No one else he could trust. He had trusted the first wife they had given him. Yes, he had trusted Memmia Sulpicia with all his heart. But then her father Sulpicius Macrinus had plotted against him. The evidence produced by the imperial spies had left no doubt. The *frumen-tarii* of Volo, the Spymaster, had been thorough. Even before Sulpicius was tortured, there had been no doubt. His mother had wanted Memmia Sulpicia executed as well. Alexander had been firm. They had not let him see his wife, but he had commuted her sentence to exile. As far as he knew, she was still alive somewhere in Africa.

The omnivore spluttered, and reached for a pitcher.

Much the same had happened with his second wife, Barbia Orbiana. He had not been fortunate with his fathers-in-law.

The *polyfagus* took a huge draught of wine.

It might have been very different if his father had lived. But he had died before Alexander was really old enough to remember him. Then, when he was nine, they had told him Gessius Marcianus, the half-recalled equestrian officer from Arca in Syria, had not been his father at all. Instead he was the natural son of the Emperor Caracalla. But by then Caracalla too had been dead for a year or more. This unexpected turn in Alexander's paternity had revealed that the newly reigning Emperor Elagabalus was not only his first cousin but his half-brother as well. It had been given out that their mothers, the sisters Soaemis and Mamaea, had committed adultery with Caracalla. And then Elagabalus had been prevailed upon to adopt Alexander. Not many a boy had three fathers publicly acknowledged before he turned thirteen, with two of them worshipped as gods, and the last just five years his senior.

Five years his senior, and perverse beyond measure. Mamaea had tried to shield Alexander from Elagabalus and his courtiers, both from their malice and their influence. Alexander's food and drink was tasted before it was brought to the table. The servants around him were individually chosen by his mother, not drawn from the common pool in the palace. It was the same with the guards. Droves of experts in Greek and Latin literature and oratory had been hired at vast expense, along with men skilled in music, wrestling, geometry and every other activity considered suitable to aid the cultural and moral development of a *princeps*. None had been selected for his light-heartedness. After his accession, many of the intellectuals had remained at court, like Granianus moving to positions in the imperial secretariat. Their augmented status had not instilled any increase in levity.

While his cousin-brother reigned, Mamaea had kept Alexander safe. Yet despite all her efforts, dark stories of depravity and vice seeped from the intimates of Elagabalus. Alexander remembered how, all at once, these whispered stories had appalled and excited him. Elagabalus had cast off any decency, cast off the restraint of his mother. A life of dinners, women, roses and boys, of futile pleasure on more pleasure; a hedonistic Pelion heaped upon Ossa; a life which put the imaginations of Epicureans and Cyrenaeans to shame. Think of the freedom, the power. Like a diligent warder, Mamaea had shielded Alexander from the chance to experience such temptations. But she had not shielded him from the end of it all.

A dark night, torchlight reflected in the puddles. Two days before the *ides* of March. Alexander was thirteen, standing in the Forum with his mother. Shadows shifting on the tall columns of the temple of Concordiae Augustae. The Praetorians handed their victims over to the mob. Both were naked, much bloodied. Elagabalus, they dragged with a hook. It entered his stomach, curled up into his chest. Soaemis, they hauled by her ankles, legs obscenely apart. Her head banged on the roadway. Most likely they were already dead. Mamaea watched the final progress of her sister, a journey she had in part orchestrated. Alexander had wanted to go back up to the palace and hide. No, at a signal from his mother the Praetorians had hailed him Emperor, and formed around him to take him to their camp.

Alexander cast around to get rid of the image. All types of

cold food were presented to his gaze: watermelons, sardines, bread, biscuits. There was a mound of snowy-white imperial napkins. Alexander tossed one across. 'Eat this.'

The *polyfagus* caught it, but did not begin to eat.

'Eat!'

The man did not move.

Alexander drew his sword. 'Eat!'

Mouth hanging open, the *polyfagus* was panting.

Alexander flourished the blade at his face. 'Eat!'

A change in the light. A waft of air in the perfumed stillness. Alexander swung round.

A barbarian warrior stood in the opening. He was young, clad in leather and fur, lank long hair to his shoulders. His sudden appearance defied all explanation. In his hand he carried a naked blade. Alexander became aware of the sword in his own hand. Then he remembered. He had long known this would happen. The astrologer Thrasybulus had told him. Somehow he found the courage to raise his blade. He knew it was hopeless. No one can fight what is ordained.

When his eyes adjusted, the barbarian was visibly surprised. Somehow it was evident he had expected the chamber to be empty. He hesitated, then turned and left.

Alexander laughed, the sound high and grating to his ears. He laughed and laughed. Thrasybulus was wrong. He was a fool. He had misread the stars. Alexander was not fated to die at the hands of a barbarian. Not now, not ever. Thrasybulus was no more than a charlatan. If he had been anything else, he would have seen his own fate, would have known what the next day now held for him. The stake and the faggots; let him burn slowly or suffocate in the smoke.

This would all end well. The Emperor knew it. Alexander had faced death, and he had not been found wanting. He was no coward, no mean little girl. Their words could no longer hurt him. He was a man.

Along with the barbarian, the last of the servants seemed to have vanished. Even the dwarf was gone. The pavilion was empty except for his mother on her throne, Granianus beside her, and Alexander himself with the *polyfagus*. Alexander did not care. Elated, he rounded again on the latter. 'Eat!'

There was a sheen of sweat on the man's face. He did not eat, merely pointed.

Three Roman officers now stood in the doorway, helmeted, cuirassed. The leading one was holding something in one hand. Like the barbarian, they waited until they could see in the gloom.

'Felicianus has returned.' The speaker threw the thing he carried. It landed heavily, half rolled.

Alexander did not have to look to know it was the head of the senior Prefect.

The officers drew their weapons as they moved into the tent.

'You too, Anullinus?' Mamaea's voice was controlled.

'Me too,' Anullinus said.

'You can have money, the Prefecture of the Guard.'

'It is over,' Anullinus said.

'Alexander will adopt you, make you Caesar, make you his heir.'

'It is over.'

Alexander moved to his mother's side. The sword was still in his hand. He was no coward. There were only three of them. He had been trained by the best swordsmen in the empire.

The officers stopped a few paces from the thrones. They looked around, as if taking in the enormity of the actions they were about to commit. The raking sunlight glanced off the swords they carried. The steel seemed to shimmer and hum with menace.

Alexander went to heft his own weapon. His palm was slick with sweat. He knew then his purchase on courage had been temporary. He let go of the hilt. The sword clattered to the ground.

One of the officers snorted in derision.

Sobbing, Alexander crumpled to his knees. He took hold of his mother's skirts. 'This is all your fault! Your fault!'

'Silence!' she snapped. 'An Emperor should die on his feet. At least die like a man.'

Alexander buried his head in the folds of material. How could she say such things? It was all her fault. He had never wanted to be Emperor; thirteen years of self-negation, boredom and fear. He had never wanted to harm anyone. *What you do not wish that a man should do to you . . .*

The officers were moving forward.

'Anullinus, if you do this, you break the oath you took before the standards.'

At his mother's voice they stopped again. Alexander peeped out.

'In the *sacramentum* did you not swear to put the safety of the Emperor above everything? Did you not swear the same for his family?'

His mother looked magnificent. Eyes flashing, face set, hair like a ridged helmet, she resembled an icon of an implacable deity, the sort that punished breakers of oaths.

The officers stood, seeming uncertain.

Could she stop them? Somewhere Alexander had read of the like.

'Murderers are paid in just measure by the sorrows the gods will upon their houses.'

Alexander felt a surge of hope. It was Marius in Plutarch; the fire in his eyes driving back the assassins.

'It is over.' Anullinus said. 'Go! Depart!'

The spell was broken, the thing now irrevocable. Yet they

did nothing precipitous. It was as if they were waiting for her last words, knowing they would receive no benediction, instead nothing but harm.

'Zeus, protector of oaths, witness this abomination. Shame! Shame! Anullinus, Prefect of the Armenians, I curse you. And you, Quintus Valerius, Tribune of the Numeri Brittonum. And you, Ammonius of the Cataphracts. Dark Hades release the Erinyes, the terrible daughters of night, the furies who blind the reason of men and turn their future to ashes and suffering.'

As her words ended, they moved. She stilled them with an imperious gesture.

'And I curse the peasant you will place upon the throne, and I curse those who will follow him. Let not one of them know happiness, prosperity or ease. Let all of them sit in the shadow of the sword. Let them not gaze long upon the sun and earth. The throne of the Caesars is polluted. Those who ascend it will discover for themselves that they cannot evade punishment.'

Anullinus raised his sword. 'Go! Depart!'

Mamaea did not flinch.

'*Exi! Recede!*' he repeated.

Anullinus stepped forward. The blade fell. Mamaea moved then. She could not help raise her hand. But it was too late. Alexander looked at the severed stumps of her fingers, the unnatural suddenness of the wide red gash at his mother's throat, the jetting blood.

Someone was screaming, high and gasping, like a child. Anullinus was standing over him.

'*Exi! Recede!*'

CHAPTER 2

The Northern Frontier
A Camp outside Mogontiacum,

Eight Days before the Ides of March, AD235

A blustery spring day, as was to be expected in Germania Superior eight days before the *ides* of March. It had still been dark, spitting with rain, when they rode out of Mogontiacum. It was mid-morning and the sun was out when they reached the camp near the village of Sicilia. Soldiers moved through the lines with no pretence of discipline. Some saluted, some did not. Most were drunk, a number to the point of insensibility.

The cavalcade dismounted. Maximinus Thrax stretched his large frame and handed his reins to a trooper. The Rhine rolled past, wide and glittering in the sun. The outer walls of the great complex of purple pavilions shifted and snapped in the wind.

'This way.'

Maximinus followed the Senators Flavius Vopiscus and Honoratus. There were naked corpses in the corridors. They were grey-white, waxy, with a sheen as if rubbed in oil.

13

'Not all the *familia Caesaris* fled in time,' Honoratus said.

'Servants and some of the secretaries, easy to replace,' Vopiscus said. 'The Praetorian Prefects were the only men of any account to die.'

A rack of bodies blocked their path. The heads of the dead lay close together in some final conclave.

Maximinus thought of the squalor of blood and death. It did not upset him. He had seen many massacres. He had let none trouble him since the first.

They stepped carefully over the splayed limbs. Maximinus knew his face would be set in what Paulina called his half-barbarian scowl. He thought of his wife and smiled. There could still be beauty, trust and love, even in a debased age.

It was gloomy in the throne chamber. The atmosphere was close, smelling of incense and blood, of urine and fear. Anullinus and the other two equestrian officers were waiting.

'The mean little girl is dead.' Anullinus held the head by its short hair.

Maximinus took the severed head in both hands. As was always the case, it was surprisingly heavy. He brought it close, scrutinized the long face, the long nose, the weak and petulant mouth and chin.

Was it true that this weakling had been Caracalla's son? The mother had claimed so; the grandmother too. Both had boasted of the adultery. Morality had yielded to political advantage, as could be anticipated with easterners.

Maximinus carried the object back to the opening. In the better light, he turned it this way and that. Of course, he had seen Alexander many times before, but now he could really study him. He needed to be sure. The nose was not dissimilar. The hair and beard were cut in the same style. But, although he had begun to go bald, there had been more curl in Caracalla's hair. Certainly his beard had been fuller than this wispy affair. Maximinus was no physiognomist, but the

14

shape of the head was wrong. Caracalla's had been squarer, like a bull's or a block of stone. And his face had been strong, even harsh. Nothing like this delicate, inadequate youth.

Maximinus felt in some measure reassured. Little could have been worse than being party to the killing of the son of his old commander, the grandson of his great patron. Maximinus acknowledged he owed everything to Caracalla's father, Septimius Severus. That Emperor had picked him out of backwoods obscurity, placed his trust in him. In return, Maximinus had given his devotion. Without thought, Maximinus put a hand to his throat and touched the gold torque his Emperor had awarded him.

'Bury it,' Maximinus said, 'with the rest of him.'

Anullinus took the repulsive thing. He turned towards the opening. The other two bloodstained equestrians moved deeper into the dark chamber, presumably to collect the cadaver. They all stopped at a sign from Vopiscus.

'Emperor, your magnanimity to your enemy does you credit, but it might be better to exhibit the head to the army, let the soldiery be sure that he is dead.'

Maximinus considered the Senator's words. Except in battle, it was not his habit to act on the spur of the moment. At length, he addressed Anullinus. 'Do as the Senator Vopiscus suggests, then bury it.'

Before anyone moved, Honoratus spoke. 'Emperor, possibly it would be good to send the head to Rome afterwards, have it burnt in the Forum or cast in the sewers. Such is usually the way with a usurper.'

For an instant Maximinus thought the usurper referred to was himself. His anger flared, then he realized. He could still be astounded at the creative ways in which Senators and the rest of the traditional elite habitually rewrote history, both their own and that of the *Res Publica*. Soon it would be almost as if they had never hailed Alexander Emperor, never sworn oaths for his safety or held office under him. Thirteen years of rule would be reduced to a fleeting revolt, a momentary aberration when Rome was dominated by an ineffectual Syrian boy and his scheming, avaricious mother. Their own part in that ephemeral regime would be buried in deepest obscurity. Perhaps they had spent the time quietly, out of public affairs, on their estates. An expensive education could smooth away the rough edges of inconvenient truths.

'No,' Maximinus said.

'Whatever pleases you, Emperor,' answered Honoratus.

'He was no Nero. The plebs did not love him. There will be no false Alexanders. No runaway slave will gather a following, masquerading as him miraculously saved and come again; not in Rome, not even in the East. As for the Senate . . .' Maximinus paused, scowling as he sought the right words. '. . . the Senate are men of culture. They do not need the thing flourished in their faces to believe. There is no need to paint them a picture.'

'*Quantum libet, Imperator,*' Honoratus repeated.

'Anullinus, when you have shown the head to the troops, bury him. All of him. Come back for the rest.'

The officer shifted his loathsome burden into his left hand and saluted. 'We will do what is ordered, and at every command we will be ready.' The other two equestrians followed him out.

'To deny a man Hades is to deny your own *humanitas.*' Maximinus spoke out loud, yet to no one but himself. He moved deeper into the chamber. Something turned under his boot. It was a finger, cleanly severed, the nail perfect. The place was a slaughterhouse. There was blood everywhere, livid across the white carpets, darker on the purple hangings. The remains of the young Emperor lay, mutilated and decapitated, by his throne. His mother, also naked and hacked about, next to hers. There was blood on the ivory thrones.

16

How had it come to this? Maximinus had not wanted it. He had known Alexander was unpopular. Everyone in the army had known that. Perhaps in his cups he had voiced unguarded criticisms. But he had no idea the recruits he was training would mutiny. Once they had thrown a purple cloak over his shoulders in Mogontiacum, there had been no way back. If he had tried to step down, either the recruits would have killed him there and then or Mamaea would have done so later.

Almost certainly the revolt would have been crushed, and crushed swiftly – Maximinus' head would have been on a pike by the end of the day – if Vopiscus and Honoratus had not ridden into the camp of the recruits. Vopiscus was governor of Pannonia Superior. He commanded the legionary detachments to the field army from both his own province and that of neighbouring Pannonia Inferior. Honoratus was legate of 11th Legion Claudia Pia Fidelis. He had led the detachments from the two provinces of Moesia up the Ister. Between them they had pledged the swords of some eight thousand legionaries, the majority veterans.

Even so, it had been up in the air until Iotapianus had brought them the head of the Praetorian Prefect Cornelianus. Iotapianus was a kinsman of Alexander and Mamaea. The archers he commanded were from their hometown of Emesa. With their desertion, there had been no hope for the Emperor and his mother.

Once you have taken a wolf by the ears, you can never let go. No, Maximinus had not desired the throne, but now there was no going back. At least his son would revel in their new station. Which might be far from a good thing. Maximus was eighteen, more than pampered and spoilt enough already. And Paulina, what would she think? She had always wanted her husband to better himself, to rise in society. But to the highest eminence of mankind? From her senatorial background, she knew all too well how others despised his low origins.

The red gashes on Mamaea's body were painful to look at. Something about the old woman reminded Maximinus of the day long ago when he had walked into a hut and for the first time been confronted with the remains of a family who had been put to the sword: the old woman, the old man, the children.

He turned away. There was a table spread with food, a vast, fat man dead at its foot. Inexplicably, tiny birds hopped through the plates. The food was cold anyway. Maximinus had never cared for cold food. In the corner of the tent, a dog sat with a human head between its paws, contentedly gnawing.

'*Imperator*.'

Vopiscus and Honoratus were at Maximinus' elbow.

'It is time to address the troops, Emperor.'

Maximinus drew a deep breath. He was just a soldier. Either of the two Senators would make a better speech. Either of them would make a better Emperor. But once you have taken a wolf by the ears . . .

Maximinus was just a soldier. The men out there were just soldiers. They demanded nothing elaborate. He would speak to them as their fellow-soldier, as one *comilitio* to another. It would take only simple words. He would march with them, share their rations, fight alongside them, share their danger. Together they must conquer the Germans as far as the Ocean. It was that or Rome would die. He would quote the last words of his old commander Septimius Severus: '*Enrich the soldiers, ignore everyone else.*'

CHAPTER 3

Rome

The Senate House,

Four Days after the Ides of March, AD235

It was still dark when Pupienus walked down from his house on the Caelian Hill. Not a star showed, not even the Kite or the Lycaonian Bear. The torches of his link-boys sawed in the gusting breeze. The pavements were dry, but the air smelt of rain.

Pupienus was in the habit of leaving his home at this hour. Normally, unless it was the day of some festival and piety demanded leisure, he would bear off to the right towards the Temple of Peace and the well-appointed offices of his high magistracy. Today was far from a normal day.

He walked under the Arch of Augustus and out into the Roman Forum. Off to the right, above the great façade of the Basilica Aemilia, the sky was beginning to lighten. Tattered black clouds could be distinguished, pressing down from the north. To most they would bring no more cheer than had the news from that direction the previous afternoon.

Down in the gloom, torches guttered across the Forum,

each followed by an indistinct figure in shimmering white. All were converging on one point, like moths to a flame or ghosts to blood. The Senators of Rome were meeting in extraordinary session.

Pupienus was one of their number. Even after all this time, nearly thirty years now, it both thrilled him and seemed somehow unlikely. He had attained membership of the same order that had included Cato the Censor, Marius and Cicero. And he was not just anyone, not just a foot-soldier. Marcus Clodius Pupienus Maximus, *Vir Clarissimus*, twice Consul, was Prefect of the City of Rome, responsible for law and order in the eternal city, and up to one hundred miles beyond. To enforce his will, he commanded the six thousand men of the Urban Cohorts. He had come a long way since his youth in Tibur, let alone his childhood in Volaterrae. Pupienus stamped down the unwelcome thought of Volaterrae. The gods knew all too soon he would have to make another clandestine trip there and face the past he had taken so much trouble to hide.

The Curia stood four-square in the corner of the Forum, as if it had always stood there and always would. Postumus knew this building was not the original, but in some way that made no difference to the impression of permanence. He climbed the steps and passed under the portico. Pausing, he touched the statue of *Libertas* on the toe for luck, then went in through the bronze doors. He walked the length of the floor. He looked neither left nor right, not at friend or foe, not even at the presiding Consuls. He walked slowly, hands decorously hidden in his toga, eyes fixed upon the statue and altar of Victory. *Dignitas* was everything to a Senator. Without that potent mixture of gravity, propriety and nobility he would be no better than anyone else.

Pupienus ascended the tribunal. He made a libation of wine and offered a pinch of incense at the altar. The fumes curled up intoxicatingly from the little fire. The gilded face of Victory gazed down without emotion. He placed his right hand flat on his chest, bowed his head and prayed to the traditional gods. His prayers were for the health of the *Res Publica*, the safety of the *imperium* and the good fortune of his own family. They were all heartfelt.

His obligations to the divine met, Pupienus turned to the mundane. He greeted the Consuls and went down to his accustomed seat on the front bench. His two sons, Maximus and Africanus, were there. He let them wait, first hailing his wife's brother Sextius Cethegillus, Maximus' father-in-law Tineius Sacerdos and his own long-term ally and confidant Cuspidius Flamininus. Age and rank should come before familial affection. Finally, he embraced his sons. 'Health and great joy,' they repeated to each other. 'Health and great joy.'

The house was very crowded, all the seats taken. Senators of less account stood packed together at the back. This would be a day to tell your grandchildren about. A new reign was beginning, the first for thirteen years. Anyone might seize the throne, but only the Senate could make him legitimate, vote him the powers necessary to rule. Without the Senate a new Emperor was no more than a usurper.

Pupienus let his eyes wander over the ranks on the other side of the Curia. The smooth, open face of Flavius Latronianus smiled at him. Pupienus smiled back. Some of the others he acknowledged more formally; none was his particular friend but, like Latronianus, all were Consulars, and all were men who had done the *Res Publica* good service and whose opinion carried weight. They returned his gesture.

The sight of those on the front bench immediately opposite gave him far less pleasure. Caelius Balbinus had the heavy jowls and florid face of the hardened drinker. He raised a hand to Pupienus with an ironic courtliness. As rich as Croesus, and as decadent as any oriental ruler, the aged Balbinus claimed descent from, among many other families and individuals of antique fame, the great clan of the Coelli. He revelled in the kinship this gave him with the deified Emperors Trajan and Hadrian.

Balbinus sat surrounded by other patricians cut from much the same cloth. Caesonius Rufinianus, Acilius Aviola and the grossly obese Valerii brothers, Priscillianus and Messala – all professed at least one ancestor who had sat in the very first meeting of the free Senate more than half a millennium ago. In recent times Emperors might have granted patrician status to the families of certain favourites, but Balbinus and his ilk looked down on the recipients. For them, no man was a true patrician unless his ancestor had been in the Curia on that day of liberty after Brutus had driven out Tarquinius Superbus and ended the rule of the legendary kings. Some, of course, boasted much more. According to Aviola, his line went back all the way to Aeneas himself and thus to the gods. Neither divine descent nor centuries of privilege tended to breed humility.

The young relatives of these patricians were still worse. Aviola's cousin Acilius Glabrio and Valerius Priscillianus' son Poplicola were two of the three-man board of junior magistrates who ran the mint. They were not even Senators yet. But they stood on the floor of the house, hair artfully curled, drenched in perfume, as if it was their entitlement. They knew as well as anyone that their birth, the smoke-blackened busts of their ancestors displayed in their palatial homes, would bring them office and advancement, irrespective of effort or merit, as it had for generations of their families.

Pupienus considered that he had nothing against the patriciate or the wider circle of the inherited nobility in general. The men on either side of him, Cethegillus and Sacerdos, came from the ranks of the latter. They each had several Consuls in their lineage, but remained men of sound mind and hard toil. They were men who could put public duty before their own self-regard and pleasures.

22

Pupienus himself had ennobled his family when he had held his first Consulship. Cuspidius had done the same, as had his other closest friends. Rutilius Crispinus and Serenianus were absent in the East, governing the provinces of Syria Phoenice and Cappadocia respectively. Part of Pupienus wished they were here now. He would have valued their advice and support.

Across the way, Balbinus was telling a joke, laughing at his own wit, his face porcine. Pupienus detested him. The higher Pupienus and his friends had climbed the *cursus honorum*, the ladder of offices, the more the likes of Balbinus had sneered at their origins. Their families were immigrants. Rome no more to them than a stepmother. Not one of their ancestors had been worthy of admittance to the Senate. What did that say of their heredity? What could a *new man* know of the age-old traditions of Rome?

The snide comments infuriated Pupienus. A *novus homo* had the harder path. He had to rise by his own services to the *Res Publica*, by his own virtue, not by the deeds of his distant ancestors. There was no comparison between the two. True nobility was to be found in the soul, not in a pedigree.

Balbinus finished his joke with a flourish. The patricians laughed, the corpulent Valerius Messala immoderately. Perhaps he was nervous. Perhaps it had penetrated even his obtuse understanding that in this changed landscape his splendid marriage to the sister of the murdered Emperor Alexander might leave him in a dangerous eminence.

One of the Consuls, Claudius Severus, rose to his feet.

'Let all who are not Conscript Fathers depart. Let no one remain except the Senators.'

Some moments after the ritual sanction, the young patricians Acilius Glabrio and Poplicola sauntered towards the rear of the house. They did pass the tribunal, but stopped before the doors, still well inside the Curia itself. Pupienus was not alone in eyeing them balefully. There was always a majority of new men in the Senate.

The other Consul, the polyonymous Lucius Tiberius Claudius Aurelius Quintianus Pompeianus stood.

'Let good auspices and joyful fortune attend the people of Rome.'

As he recited the injunction which always proceeded a proposal there was something of a disturbance behind him in the crowd of onlookers wedged in one of the rear doors.

'We present to you, Conscript Fathers—'

Acilius Glabrio and Poplicola turned. Abruptly, the two arrogant young patricians were thrust aside, Poplicola so hard that he stumbled. A pair of Senators pushed past and got on to the tribunal to make their offerings.

The Consul exhibited the admirable self-control to be expected of a descendant of the divine Marcus Aurelius, and continued speaking.

Having paid their respects to the deities, the two latecomers descended and walked to the floor of the house. They stood there, glaring about them defiantly.

Pupienus regarded them with what he hoped was well-hidden disfavour.

Domitius Gallicanus and Maecenas were inseparable. The former was the elder and the instigator. He was an ugly man with a shock of brown hair and a straggly beard. His toga was conspicuously home-spun. Everything about his un-groomed appearance chimed with his self-proclaimed love of antique virtue and old-style Republican freedom. He was in his mid-forties. He had been Praetor some years before, but his ostentatious free speech and continual truculence towards the imperial authorities had stalled his career and so far prevented him becoming Consul.

Pupienus had never had much time for Gallicanus – a noble spirit should seek the reward of virtue in his consciousness of

24

it, rather than in the vulgar opinion of others; he had even less since last night.

'And that it be lawful for him to veto the act of any magistrate.' The Consul had no need of the notes in his hand. 'And that it be lawful for him to convene the Senate, to report business, and to propose decrees, just as it was lawful for the divine Augustus, and for the divine Claudius . . . '

Claudius Aurelius was proposing Maximinus be voted the powers of a tribune of the plebs, which gave an Emperor legal authority in the civil sphere. Distracted by the theatrical entry of Gallicanus and Maecenas, Pupienus must have missed the other of the twin bases of an Emperor's rule: the clauses about the Emperor's overriding military command.

Events had moved fast since noon the previous day when Senator Honoratus and his escort had arrived from the North, pushing their foundering horses down the rain-swept Via Aurelia and into Rome. It had been three days after the *ides* of March. It was the day of the *Liberalia*, when boys are awarded the *toga virilis* of manhood. Attending family ceremonies, the Senators had been scattered throughout Rome and beyond. It had been late in the afternoon before enough had been gathered in the Curia.

Honoratus was another *novus homo*. His hometown was Cuicul in Africa. Pupienus did not hold that against him. Honoratus had worked his way up the *cursus honorum*. After he had held a Praetorship, he had been given command of the 11th Legion up in Moesia Inferior, and from there appointed to a special command with the field army in Germania. Honoratus knew the ways of the Senate House as well as the camp. There had always been much to admire about him. Now there was something to fear as well.

Still in his mud-splattered travelling clothes, Honoratus had told the tale simply, without affectation. The Emperor Alexander had been murdered in a spontaneous and unsuspected uprising of the troops. The senior officers and the army had proclaimed Gaius Iulius Verus Maximinus Emperor. With mutiny in the ranks and a barbarian war on hand, there had been no leisure to consult the Conscript Fathers. Maximinus hoped the Senate would understand the need for alacrity. The new Emperor intended to take advice from the Conscript Fathers, and to continue the senatorial policies of his predecessor. Maximinus was a man of proven courage and experience. He had governed Mauretania Tingitana, and Egypt, and held high command on both the eastern and the northern expeditions. Honoratus commended him to the house.

It was a fine speech, Honoratus' slight African accent – where the occasional 's' was lisped into 'sh' – notwithstanding. The Senate would have voted Maximinus the imperial powers immediately – some had even begun to chant acclamations – had it not been for Gallicanus.

Like a hirsute revenant from the old Republic, Gallicanus had risen up and thundered against the vitiation of senatorial procedure. It was well past the tenth hour of the day. After the tenth hour no new proposal could be put to the house. It was almost dark. Were the Conscript Fathers ashamed of their deeds? Did they seek to hide in obscurity like foul conspirators, or depraved Christians? Had they forgotten that a decree passed after sunset had no legality?

The Consuls had been left with no choice but to end the session and call for the Senate to reconvene the following morning at dawn.

Custom demanded the Senators escort home the presiding magistrates. Pupienus was one of those who accompanied Claudius Severus through the rain to his house. At least it had not been at all out of the way. The Consul was his neighbour on the Caelian Hill.

Returned to his own home, Pupienus had time only for a quick bath and to put on dry clothes before his secretary,

Curius Fortunatianus, had announced the presence at the door of none other than Gallicanus. For once, his shadow, Maecenas, had not been with the arbiter of traditional senatorial mores. Indeed, Gallicanus had made a request to speak to the Prefect of the City in complete privacy. The circumspect Fortunatianus had suggested Pupienus receive his visitor in the garden dining room. The hidden back door would allow the secretary, and for certainty perhaps another trustworthy witness, to listen unobserved. Although tempted, as it would ensure his own safety, Pupienus dismissed the idea as unworthy. Gallicanus might be unsavoury, a seeker of notoriety, and his conversation might move towards the treasonous – under the circumstances, Pupienus would have been amazed if it did not – but Senators should not inform against each other, and most certainly they should not set underhand traps.

Fortunatianus had shown Gallicanus into the small room where Pupienus had dressed and then left them alone. Gallicanus had never been known for subtlety. Peering into every corner, only just stopping himself from tapping the panelling, he had demanded Pupienus swear that no one could overhear them and that nothing said would be repeated. The oaths taken, Gallicanus had launched directly into business. This new Emperor was but an equestrian. Only one man from the second order in society had ever taken the throne. Pupienus would recall the weakness and brevity of the reign of Moorish bureaucrat Macrinus. This Maximinus was worse still. At best, he was a peasant from the remote hills of Thrace. Some said one of his parents was from beyond the frontiers, a Goth or one of the Alani. Others said both had been barbarians. He was a man of no education, no culture.

Pupienus knew the law of treason was ill-defined, but its malleability tended towards inclusion and condemnation. Gallicanus had already said more than enough to lose his estates and find himself heading towards either an exile-island or the executioner. Still, Pupienus had given his word. 'What would you do about it?' he asked.

Gallicanus had not answered directly. The principate of Alexander had been good for the Senate. Gallicanus' tone was earnest. Both the Emperor and his mother had shown respect to the Curia. They had given the Senators the chance to regain their *dignitas*. More than that, with the creation of the permanent council of sixteen Senators always in attendance on the Emperor, they could be thought to have admitted the Senate into a real sharing of power. You might call it a dyarchy.

Although he had done very well under the regime, a dyarchy would have been far from what Pupienus would have called almost a decade and a half of ineffective and corrupt rule by a weak youth and an avaricious woman who had attached various ambitious and often venal Senators to themselves in an unavailing attempt to gain a reputation for statesmanship. He said nothing in response.

The Senate had been reawakened, Gallicanus had ploughed on. Not since the first Augustus had cloaked his autocracy in fine-sounding words and smothered the last of true freedom – maybe not since long before that – had the Senate been stronger. This Thracian barbarian had not yet squatted securely on the throne. Maximinus had few backers. Most of the Senators with the army would welcome his fall. Maximinus had no legal authority. The Emperor had never been weaker. It was time to bring back *libertas*. It was time to restore the free Republic.

It had been a measure of Pupienus' many years of public service that he neither snorted in derision nor laughed out loud. Apart from the court fools and a man in Africa who had been driven out of his wits by the sun, he had never heard anyone say anything more insane.

Gallicanus must have taken the continued silence of his interlocutor as a sign of something else. 'The Urban Cohorts under your command number six thousand men. Almost all the Praetorians are with the field army on the northern frontier. There are no more than a thousand left in Rome. Many of your men are quartered in their camp. It would be easy to win them over or crush them.'

'Herennius Modestinus?' Pupienus had said, speaking at last.

Gallicanus had smiled like a not over-bright student asked a question he had been expecting. The Prefect of the Watch was an equestrian of the traditional type, imbued with a respect for the Senate. Anyway, if he proved contumacious, the *vigiles* he commanded were just seven thousand armed firemen. There were almost as many in the Urban Cohorts, and they were real soldiers. Modestinus himself was only a jurist, while Pupienus had commanded troops in the field.

'The detachments from the fleets of Ravenna and Misenum?'

At this question Gallicanus had shrugged with a certain irritation. 'A few sailors in Rome to put up the awnings at the spectacles.' It was evident they had not previously crossed his mind.

'One thousand from each fleet, all trained and under military discipline.' Pupienus had always tried to know such details: the numbers of troops, their billeting and mood, the disposition of their officers, the family connections of the latter. He had always talked to all sorts of people. Since his rise, especially since he had become Prefect of the City, he had also paid good money to know such things.

Gallicanus had waved the sailors away as of no consequence. There was something vaguely simian in the motion.

'If I threw my lot in with you—' Pupienus spoke slowly and carefully; even in the security of his own house he felt a vertiginous fear at saying these things '—and if I gathered under one standard all the armed forces in Rome, I would command some sixteen thousand. Of which, as you say, almost half are merely firemen. The imperial field army numbers some forty thousand, before reckoning what further forces could join it from the armies on the Rhine and Danube.'

Gripping him by the arm, Gallicanus thrust his ill-favoured face close to that of Pupienus. 'My dear friend.' Gallicanus squeezed the arm. His gaze and voice were fervent in their sincerity. 'My dear Pupienus, no one doubts your commitment to *libertas*, your devotion to the Senate, or your courage. But in a free Republic it will not be for us to assign ourselves commands. As it was when Rome grew great, the Senate will vote who leads its armies.'

Gallicanus released Pupienus' arm and began to pace the room. He was babbling about electing a board of twenty from the Senate, all ex-Consuls, to defend Italy. Others would be sent to win over the troops and the provincials. In his eagerness he was bobbing about the confined space and swinging his arms like an agitated primate in a cage.

Pupienus was seldom flabbergasted, and he had not been so angry for a long time. What sort of fool was Gallicanus? He had come into Pupienus' home and endangered everyone in it with his talk of treason. And he had done so not to offer Pupienus the throne, not even to offer him a leading role in a new regime. Instead the ape had wanted Pupienus to seize the city for his insane cause, and then, rather than reap the rewards, simply give up his legitimate authority and step down to the level of a private citizen.

'This must stop.' Pupienus had recovered quickly.

Gallicanus had rounded on him, suspicion and anger in his eyes.

Pupienus had smiled. He had hoped it looked reassuring.

'All we Senators wish we had lived in the free Republic. But you know as well as me that the principate is a harsh necessity. The *imperium* was tearing itself apart in civil wars until Augustus took the throne.'

Gallicanus had shaken his head. 'We can learn from history.'

'No—' Pupienus had been adamant '—the same would happen again. The leading men would fight for power until one of them won or the empire fell. You have read your Tacitus. Now we must pray for good Emperors, but serve the ones we get.'

'Tacitus served under the tyrant Domitian. He was nothing but a quietist, a time-server. He was a man of no courage, a coward.' Gallicanus had shouted the last words.

'You and I, we both held office under Caracalla.' Pupienus had pitched his voice at its most reasonable. 'Give up this scheme before you bring disaster on your family and your friends.'

Gallicanus stood wringing his hands and pressing them together as if he could physically crush this opposition. 'I thought you were a man of honour.'

You ape, Pupienus thought, you stupid, arrogant Stoic ape. 'I hope you will think so again, because I will never mention this conversation to anyone.'

Gallicanus had left.

The mellifluous tones of the Consul brought Pupienus back to the Senate House:

'. . . And that whatsoever he shall deem to be according to the custom of the *Res Publica* and the greatness of divine and human, public and private matters, there be right and power for him to undertake and to do, just as there was for the divine Augustus . . . '

The Consul had reached clauses that were surely otiose. As Maximinus had already had been vested with the tribunician power, which brought the ability to make and unmake all laws, of course he could do whatsoever he should deem according to the custom of the *Res Publica*, and any other thing as well. Pupienus was only half listening. He was still watching Gallicanus posturing in his near-rags on the floor of the Senate House. The previous evening he had forgotten that Gallicanus had moved from following the doctrines of the Stoa to those of Diogenes. Not a Stoic ape then. A Cynic dog instead. It made little difference. The ragged Senator was still a dangerous fool, made all the more dangerous by a conviction that profoundest philosophy underpinned all his beliefs and actions.

Gallicanus had not been the only visitor to the house on the Caelian that night. Pupienus and his wife were starting their belated dinner when Fortunatianus had announced another caller. This time the secretary had suggested no ingenious espionage. He was plainly terrified. Honoratus was outside. The street was full of soldiers.

Pupienus had dreaded such a moment since first he acquired wealth and position. The knock on the door in the night. The imperial official standing in the torchlight, the armed men at his back. The muted terror sliding through the corridors of the house. In the reign of Caracalla, it had happened to several men close to Pupienus. Neither those vicarious experiences nor the years of expectation had made the sudden reality any easier.

Surely there had been no time for Gallicanus to have approached someone else. Even that hairy fool must have realized that he could never seize Rome without the Urban Cohorts. Pupienus had felt a hollow deep in his stomach. Could he have so misread Gallicanus? Was all that conspicuous virtue no more than a mask? Was all his talk of the *Res Publica* no more than a trap?

The new arrival could be unconnected. But still lethal. A new regime often began with a purge. But it could be nothing. With all the courage and *dignitas* he could muster, Pupienus had told Fortunatianus to bring Honoratus to him. While waiting, he had managed not to touch the ring on his right middle finger which contained the poison. Instead, he had put his hand on that of his wife, squeezed, and forced himself to smile into her eyes.

Honoratus was still wearing the same clothes muddied from the road in which he had addressed the Senate. He entered alone. Pupienus fought down a surge of hope. If it was premature, it would be all the more devastating.

'Forgive the intrusion, Prefect.' Honoratus had spread his arms wide, showing his empty palms. 'I should have sent a messenger ahead. I have been somewhat occupied.'

'Think nothing of it, Senator.'

Honoratus had bowed to Sextia. 'My Lady, I need the advice of your husband.'

Like a true Roman matron, she had spoken some graceful words and withdrawn. Only the slightest catch in her voice betrayed the relief that her husband would be neither hauled off to the torturers in the palace cellars nor butchered in front of her.

'Have you eaten?'

'No.'

'Please, do.'

Honoratus stopped his host calling for a slave to remove his boots. 'I will do it myself. Discretion might be best.' He pronounced it 'dis*h*cretion'.

Pupienus had watched the younger man wash his hands, tip a libation and start to eat. He sprinkled some salt on a hard-boiled egg, dipped it in some fish sauce. He ate it delicately. He reached for another. The speed of his feeding increased. He was hungry. Pupienus had forced himself to keep quiet. Behind the dirt and fatigue, Honoratus was still ridiculously good-looking: dark hair, dark eyes, the cheekbones of a statue. Pupienus had thought it would be almost unseemly to be killed by someone so beautiful.

Honoratus drained his glass.

'Shall I call for more?'

Honoratus smiled. 'You were never one for much wine, Pupienus. No, leave it until they bring in the next course.'

Pupienus had passed him more bread.

'Alexander had to go,' Honoratus had said. 'He was trying to pay off the Germans. He was too scared to fight. The soldiers despised him. It would have been a disaster, much worse than the East. His mother's greed was getting worse. The troops' pay was late. If we had not acted, someone else would have.'

Pupienus had made an understanding noise.

'Maximinus is a good soldier, a good administrator. He has courage. He will fight the German tribes, and he will win.'

Pupienus had repeated the noise, with just a hint of a question.

'As an equestrian, Maximinus has no experience of the Senate. Although he has governed provinces, his whole attention must be on the northern war. Often he will be beyond the frontier, deep in *barbaricum*. In civil matters he will delegate and listen to advice.'

'Whose advice?'

'I rather hope mine, among others.' Honoratus had laughed. He had very straight white teeth. 'The new Emperor also puts particular faith in the governor of Pannonia Superior, Flavius Vopiscus, and the commander of 8th Legion, Catius Clemens.'

Pupienus considered his words. 'I have known Flavius Vopiscus for many years. Catius Clemens I do not know so well, but if he is like his brother Celer, who is one of the Praetors this year in Rome, then the new Emperor has chosen his confidants well. All three are men of judgement.'

Honoratus had raised his empty glass to acknowledge the

compliment. 'Loyal friends are always the pillars of the throne. Maximinus would embrace you in his friendship. Your excellence as Prefect of Rome argues for its continuation.'

Now Pupienus toasted the kind words.

'You have two sons. When the two Consuls who have given their name to this year step down in a couple of months, Maximinus is minded to appoint your elder son, Pupienus Maximus, as one of the Suffect Consuls. I will be the other. A still greater honour is being considered for your family. Next year the Emperor will take office on the *kalends* of January. Maximinus is thinking of taking your younger son, Africanus, as his colleague as *Consul Ordinarius*. For eternity, it would be the year of the Emperor Gaius Iulius Maximinus and Marcus Pupienus Africanus. So that the Emperor can get to know your son, form a true estimate of his virtues, Africanus will accompany me back to the field army.'

It was neatly done, Pupienus had thought, the blend of high honours binding the family to a potentially unpopular regime and the taking of a hostage. He spoke. 'It will be difficult to live up to the benefactions shown, but we will try.'

'Excellent,' Honoratus had said. 'Who was it who said, "Scratch the surface of any government and you find an oligarchy"?'

'I cannot remember.'

'No, nor me. Of course, you must keep Rome quiet: no rioting from the plebs, no conspiracies among the nobility.'

'Of course.'

'Excellent,' Honoratus had said, again. 'Now perhaps your servants could stop listening at the doors and bring in the main course. I am *sh*tarving.'

Pupienus had rung a little bell.

'One thing,' Honoratus said. 'I brought a new equestrian down to take command of the *vigiles*. I think you will like the new Prefect of the Watch. He is called Potens.'

'Herennius Modestinus?'

'Oh no – gods, no! Nothing like that.'

Inwardly, Pupienus had cursed. His voice must have betrayed him.

'What do you take our new Emperor for? A barbarian?' Honoratus had showed his teeth as he laughed. They really were perfect.

Pupienus had kept a very straight face.

'Not half an hour ago, I thanked Modestinus for his noble efforts patrolling the streets night after night for fires and malefactors. I told him how much the Emperor appreciated his labours, but Maximinus had decided that a skilled jurist might be more sensibly employed handling all the legal entreaties addressed to the throne. When your son and I set off to the frontier, Modestinus will accompany us. At the imperial court the position of Secretary for Petitions awaits the man of law. Modestinus will make a fine *a Libellis*. He has always been dutiful, but somehow it was not right he remain in Rome while the Emperor was elsewhere. It was just that some said he was a little too fond of the old free Republic.' And Honoratus had gazed hard at Pupienus.

The rest of the meal had passed without anything of significance, the conversation harmless.

Up on the tribunal, the Consul finally reached the end of the lengthy list of overlapping powers, privileges and honours proposed for the new Emperor. 'And we recommend that these things be approved by you, Conscript Fathers.' Claudius Aurelius sat down with the air of a task well done.

Laboriously, the Father of the House, Cuspidius Celerinus, used his walking stick to pull himself to his feet. An octogenarian, Celerinus was frail, but his reason remained acute. He knew what was wanted: something of moderate length, traditional in tone and panegyric in nature. His reedy old man's voice still carried all through the Curia.

Like Cincinnatus summoned from the plough, Maximinus had answered the call of the *Res Publica*. The time for vacillation was past. Mars had come down from the heights. Grim-visaged, the god stalked the fields and villas, howled around the walls of towns. The dangers had never been greater. In the time of Cincinnatus, the lone tribe of the Italian Aequi besieged one legion on Mount Algidus. Now, all the barbaric tribes of the frozen North raged against the Romans, held the entire empire under siege, threatened *humanitas* itself. Come the hour, come the man. Hardened by war on every continent, only Maximinus, spurring the flanks of his foaming warhorse, could bring defeat to the savage Germans. As far as the Ocean, they would bow their heads to the majesty of Rome.

With his victory won, great Caesar would return to Rome. In the metropolis the antique virtues bred in his rustic home – piety, frugality, self-control – would cleanse away the stains of recent luxury and wickedness. A second Romulus, he would scour away the filth of corruption to bring forth another golden age. Justice would return to earth. All would salute him: the lands, the stretching leagues of the sea, the unplumbed sky. Let us salute him. Let Gaius Iulius Verus Maximinus become Emperor!

A roar of approval went up to the high ceiling, startling a pair of sparrows and sending them racing out over the heads of the spectators at the open doors. Old Celerinus sat down. His neighbours congratulated him. Pupienus walked over to join them. It had been a good speech, with echoes of Livy and Virgil, the patriotism of both suitable to the occasion.

In order of precedence, the Consuls asked the opinion of the assembled Senators: I agree. I agree. One after another, the four hundred or more assented. The Consuls put it to the vote.

With much shuffling and even a little barging, the vast majority of the Conscript Fathers rushed to arraign themselves on the indicated side of the Curia. They packed themselves together like herd animals threatened by a predator. Some were slower, through age or infirmity, or overtly paraded independence. Gallicanus and Maecenas moved tardily and but a little. Gallicanus barely crossed the middle of the floor.

Perhaps, Pupienus thought, I should have given you to Honoratus. The handsome friend of the new Emperor knew Gallicanus had visited, and must surmise that he talked treason, although possibly not the fanatic scope of it. The free Republic had been dead nearly three centuries. To revive it was a fool's dream. But Gallicanus was a fool. A yapping Cynic dog of a fool. Like an undermined bastion, his arrogance could bring ruin on those around him at any moment. Perhaps indeed he should yet be handed over to Honoratus. But no, an oath was an oath. The gods were not to be mocked. Yet, if a way could be found, it might not stand to the discredit of Maximinus and those around him if an example were to be made of Gallicanus.

'This side seems to be in the majority.' The formal words of the Consul were an understatement. No one, not even Gallicanus, was fool enough to vote openly against the accession.

The Senators began to chant their thanks to the gods for their new Emperor: '*Iupiter optime, tibi gratias. Apollo venerabilis, tibi gratias.*' It echoed around the marbled walls of the Curia like plainsong.

'*Iupiter optime, tibi gratias. Apollo venerabilis, tibi gratias.*'

Singing with the rest, Pupienus wondered how long the gratitude to Jupiter the best, to venerable Apollo, to the other gods not yet thanked, would last. Could Honoratus, Flavius Vopiscus and Catius Clemens control the creature they had elevated? Could they mould Maximinus into something acceptable to more than the soldiery? Perhaps they could. They were men of ability as well as ambition. And there was

Paulina, the wife of Maximinus. She was from the nobility. The Thracian was said to love her. She was reckoned a good influence.

Yet, no matter how he behaved, would the Senators ever truly accept Maximinus? They had fixed views on the person and role of an Emperor. He should be chosen from the Senators. He should respect the Senate and share the lifestyle of its members. Above all, he must be a first among equals, a *civilis princeps*. A shepherd boy from the North risen to equestrian rank via the army could not be such a *primus inter pares*.

Pupienus debated the wisdom of his actions the previous night. There was nothing else he could have done, nothing reasonable. But it might not pay to be too close to this new regime. Circumspection was the order of the day. Information should be gathered, a keen ear kept open for hints and whispers. He should be prepared, but nothing precipitous should be ventured. *Ignorance breeds confidence, reflection leads to hesitation*, as the saying went.

Iupiter optime, tibi gratias. Apollo venerabilis, tibi gratias.

CHAPTER 4

Rome
The Carinae,

Five Days after the Ides of March, AD235

Iunia Fadilla knew herself blessed. A descendant of the divine Marcus Aurelius, she was made aware on many occasions and by all sorts of men that she possessed both beauty and an intellect that they claimed was rare in her sex. Before his untimely death, her father had found her an agreeable and generous husband. Now, two years or so after the marriage, her elderly spouse more predictably had gone the way of her parent. As was proper, the eighteen-year-old-widow wore no jewels and her *stola* was of the plainest grey. Yet, as she left the recital, her demeanour was more than a little at odds with her costume of bereavement.

Her friend, Perpetua, evidently was happy as well. They walked, arm in arm, across the great courtyard of the Baths of Trajan. The rain of the day before had gone, and the sky was a clear, washed-out blue. Gaggles of schoolchildren darted here and there, shrieking, sandals slapping on paving slabs, unconfined by their teachers. Also freed from their labours,

doctors, artisans and worse drifted in and out of the colonnaded doorways. A group of fullers and dyers laughed as
they went to wash away the foulness of their trades. It was
five days after the *ides* of March, the *Quinquatrus*, the day of
the birth of Minerva. Tomorrow, the festival demanded they
spread the sand, and men would die, but today all fighting
was unlawful.

They left via the north-western gates which gave on to
the Oppian hill and turned left. Perpetua's black hair, her
bright gown and gems, formed an attractive counterpoint to
Iunia's head of tumbling blonde curls and sombre attire. They
affected not to notice the many looks of frank admiration.
Each woman was trailed by her *custos* and a maid. Almost
alone, these followers did not obviously share in the general
contentment. The day had nothing of the holiday for them,
and the two guards at least had taken little pleasure in the
modern poetry.

Perpetua was talking politics. 'My brother Gaius says this
new Emperor may be good for our family.'

Iunia thought Gaius immature and ugly. She had no interest in his views on politics, or on anything else. Politics bored
her. But she let her friend talk. She was very fond of Perpetua.

'Now he is one of the *Tresviri Capitales* he was allowed to
listen to the debate from one of the doors of the Senate House
yesterday.'

'Given their own addictions to self-advancement and
sycophancy,' Iunia said, 'it is touching that the Senators think
the junior magistrates will benefit from their example in the
Curia.'

'That,' said Perpetua, 'is your late husband talking.'

'He had a point.'

'Quite a big one, you always said.'

'Well, average at least.'

They had walked down the alley between the Baths of

Titus and the Temple of Tellus, and now took the quiet path to the right across the front of the latter and along the brow of the hill.

'Anyway, Gaius says that, ages ago, this Maximinus served under Grandfather on the northern frontier, somewhere like Dacia or Moesia. Father was a tribune there and met him. Apparently, although a complete peasant, Maximinus is known for his loyalty. Gaius thinks it might mean that father will get to be Consul at last, maybe even as an *Ordinarius*. Imagine a year named after Father.'

'Did he mention the prospects of your husband? Or of Toxotius?' Iunia could never resist teasing her.

Perpetua laughed. 'I am not going to rise to it.'

They went along the front of the Carinae. No one knew why this district of noble houses was so named. Nothing in sight even vaguely resembled the keel of a ship. Off to the left, at the foot of the incline was the Street of the Sandal-makers. Ahead, running around the hill and out of sight to the north, was the valley of the Subura. Down there all was bustle and crowds. On the Carinae a stately spaciousness held sway.

Approaching the *Domus Rostrata*, the grandest house of all, the women were somewhat surprised to find their path blocked by four men. Their rough attire proclaimed their membership of the urban poor. Iunia could think of no good reason why they should have ascended from the slums below and were now standing outside the home of the Gordiani, where once Pompey the Great had lived. Even Perpetua had gone quiet. Iunia sensed her guard move up closer behind.

Three of the men stepped to the side, bowed their heads, and muttered 'My Lady' as the women came near. The fourth loitered. He was little more than a boy, younger than them. He was short, with a thin, angular face like some malevolent creature from a story told to frighten children. He openly wore a dagger as long as a short sword at his belt.

43

At the last moment, he stepped aside. As he bowed, he made no attempt to disguise the way his gaze travelled over Iunia's body.

'Health and great joy.' He spoke in well-accented Greek, as if greeting his social equals.

The women swept past. Neither acknowledged the existence of the plebeian interlopers. They had not gone far when they heard a burst of laughter, at once lascivious and mocking.

'Imagine if they had overpowered our guards.' Perpetua's eyes were shining. 'They could have dragged us down the hill. Once in their robbers' lair, who knows what they might not want to do to two young senatorial matrons.'

Iunia laughed. 'You have read too many of those Greek novels where the heroine is always being abducted and sold into a brothel, from which the hero rescues her at the last moment.'

'Perhaps in my story the saviour might be delayed a little?'

'You are incorrigible.'

'Me?' Perpetua said. 'I was not the one making eyes at Ticida as he recited poems about my breasts.'

'About some girl's breasts. He has never seen mine.'

'But he would like to, just like that young knife-boy.'

'Then his poetry had better improve.' Iunia flung out her arm portentously and declaimed:

> *'Could I but become a crimson rose,*
> *I might then hope you would pluck me*
> *And acquaint me with your snowy breasts.'*

Both women laughed, the more immoderately for their slight scare.

'Ticida is good-looking,' said Perpetua.

'He is,' Iunia agreed.

'You have not taken a lover since Gordian left for Africa.

44

Even male physicians argue that abstinence is a bad for a woman's health.'

'Although your husband is far away governing Cappadocia, it is a relief to know your health is in little danger.'

'Toxotius is wonderful,' Perpetua sighed.

'You should be more discreet,' Iunia said. 'You know you should. If Serenianus finds out when he returns . . . '

'He will not.'

'But if he did. You know the penalties for adultery: banishment to an island, the loss of half your dowry, no prospect of a decent remarriage.'

Perpetua laughed. 'I have often wondered about those exile-islands, full of traitors, adulterers and the incestuous. Think of the parties. Anyway, Nummius did not divorce you, and he knew all about you and Gordian.'

'Nummius was a very different man from Serenianus.'

'They say—' Perpetua leant close, whispered in Iunia's ear '—he liked to watch you and Gordian.'

'Although they were of different generations, Nummius and Gordian were close friends,' Iunia continued in a serious tone. 'They held the same rank in society, both ex-Consuls. After achieving that rank, Nummius devoted himself to pleasure – some would say, to vice.'

'They also say—' Perpetua's breath was hot in Iunia's ear '—your physical demands hastened his death.'

Iunia ignored her. 'Your husband disapproves of hedonistic excess. Serenianus sees himself as a senior statesman: pillar of the *Res Publica*, embodiment of old-style virtue. And, pretty though he is, Toxotius is just a youth. He is not even a Senator yet, just one of the Magistrates of the Mint. The humiliation of being cuckolded by a mere boy will infuriate Serenianus.'

Perpetua was quiet. They were walking past the mansion of the Consular Balbinus, another dedicated voluptuary.

Usually, Perpetua would mention the time he had propositioned her. Today when she spoke, it was of something else. 'Perhaps Serenianus will not come back from Cappadocia.'

Iunia squeezed her poor friend's arm. It was good to be widow. She had no desire to remarry.

CHAPTER 5

Africa Proconsularis
The Oasis of Ad Palmam,

Four Days before the Kalends of April, AD235

A hard ride, and time was against them. Two days after they left the coast of the Middle Sea at Taparura, the country changed. The olive trees pulled back and thinned out. Between their shade the earth was bare and yellowed. The four-square towered villas gave way to isolated mud-brick huts, the comfortable abodes of the elite replaced by the hovels of their more distant dependants. Ahead, south-west over the plain, a line of tan hills showed.

Gordian did not push his men or their mounts too hard, but neither did he spare them. They were in the saddle well before dawn. All morning they rode at a mile-eating canter. A rest in the shade for the heat of the day, then they rode on through the late afternoon and into the darkness. They went in a pall of their own making, the horses' hooves kicking up a fine yellow dust. It got into their eyes, ears, noses; gritted in their teeth. Gordian knew it was worst for those at the rear. At every halt, he reordered the small column. He thought of Alexander in the Gedrosian desert. The army had been short of water. A soldier stumbled across a tiny puddle. He filled a helmet with the muddy water and brought it to his King. Alexander had thanked him and poured the water into the sand. A noble gesture. Gordian would have done the same. But Alexander had not ridden in the rear. A general had to lead. Each time they mounted up, Gordian took his place at the front, flanked by his father's legates Valerian and Sabinianus, and the local landowner Mauricius.

On the fourth day, they reached the hills. Close up, the rocks were not tan but pink. At the foot of the slopes was a small stone tower. Following the unmade road west, up into the high country, they passed three more watchtowers. Gordian said the same to the half-dozen or so garrison of each. Should the enemy return this way, make sure you send word to me at Ad Palmam; after that, exercise your initiative. They were reliable men, legionaries on detachment from the 3rd Augustan based at Lambaesis in the neighbouring province of Numidia. There was no discussion of what forms the initiative of those left behind might take after one or two had ridden off to raise the alarm, taking the only horses or mules with them.

Guided by Mauricius, they turned and took a track that snaked over the crests to the south. Near the top of the pass, Gordian left two men at a place with a good view back over the way they had come.

Having descended, they turned right and rode due west. After a day, another pass came down from the hills. Gordian sent four men up it: two to form a picket on the heights, and two to convey the usual instructions to the watchtowers on the other side and to scout beyond.

Six days' riding since Taparura, four before that. Both men and horses were very worn. Nine horses had gone lame already before the hills. They had been left behind. Their riders had been mounted on baggage horses. The loads had been redistributed. Five men had fallen back out of sight. These stragglers had never caught up. Perhaps they had deserted. It would have been understandable, under the circumstances. Now the going was worse. A horse foundered. It was killed without ceremony. Its rider took the last baggage animal. The burden of the latter was tossed aside and abandoned.

Not far now, Mauricius assured them. Soon – today; tomorrow morning at the latest – we will reach the oasis of Ad Palmam. All will be good there.

They pressed on, the dust working its way into them as if every particle were animate with malice.

The landscape was like nothing Gordian had seen. The cliffs to the right were steep and jumbled, their stratifications tipped and fanned. In the main they were bare slopes. Some of the heights were ringed with darker, vertical rocks like cyclopean crenellations. A harsh place, but not that out of the ordinary. There were pockets of green in the dips and hollows. Now and then a flash of white or black movement betrayed the presence of a flock of goats.

To the left, there was no remission to the harshness. A great flatness stretched as far as the eye could see. Its surface was banded like agate; brown, tan and white. There were pools of standing water and dusky lines coiled between them. There was no telling if they were tracks, animal or human, or now dry channels carved by last winter's rain. In the high sun mirages shifted; water, trees, buildings. Once, Gordian thought he saw a boat. Nothing else moved in all that vastness. Nothing real.

This was the Lake of Triton, the dreadful, great salt lake. Once it had been a real lake, if not an inlet of the sea. The *Argo* had sailed its waters. But even then it had been an evil place. Two of the Argonauts had been killed here; Mopsus by a snake, and Canthus by a local herdsman. For the rest to escape had needed an appearance by Triton himself.

Mauricius had told Gordian the local legends. At night men saw torches moving far out in the desert. They heard the music of pipes and cymbals. Some said they had seen the satyrs and nymphs gambolling. There were stories of buried treasure: a huge tripod from Delphi, solid gold. Those who searched never found it, and many never came back. Once, a caravan of a thousand animals had ventured off one of the two safe paths. Nothing was seen of them again. There had been no epiphany for them.

Looking hard, Gordian saw there were patches where the crust was broken, and a dark sludge exposed.

'Ad Palmam.'

There – two or three miles ahead – was a line of green, utterly incongruous in the waste.

They rode on without speaking, every man trying to hide his trepidation.

Two hundred yards short, Gordian called a halt. Time was against them, but he did not know by how much.

Gordian dismounted, to ease his horse. Most of the others did the same. They watched the oasis. Nothing much moved. A couple of chickens scratched in the shade of some outlying trees. Once, further in, a flight of doves clattered into the air.

'Well, we can not stay here for ever,' the legate Sabinianus said. 'I had better go and take a look.'

Gordian felt a rush of affection at the calm courage of the man.

'Of course,' Sabinianus continued, 'if Arrian were here, I would recommend you send him. He is far more expendable, and I would sacrifice him happily to ensure my safety.'

Men smiled. Sabinianus and Arrian were the closest of friends, always laughing at each other, and at everything else.

'Actually,' Sabinianus said, 'I would sacrifice anyone at all. I want you all to remember that.'

Gordian gave Sabinianus a leg up into the saddle. He wanted to say something, but the words would not come. The wry look on Sabinianus' face, the turned-down mouth, was more pronounced than usual. With his knees, the legate moved his horse into a walk down to the settlement.

It had all happened with a dislocating suddenness. Just fourteen days before, all had been normal. As far as Gordian and his father, the Proconsul, had known, the province had slumbered under the North African sun in a state of profound peace. They had passed February in Thysdrus for the olive season; a round of local festivals and outdoor meals in the shade of the evening. As ever, the presence of the Proconsul had drawn intellectuals from all over the province, and abroad. There had been literary recitals and plays. The old man had formed a strong fondness for the town. He had bought two estates nearby, and had commissioned a new amphitheatre at vast, possibly ruinous personal expense. Gordian Senior had lingered there until the *nones* of March, when he had felt compelled to give orders to begin to prepare the journey north to the town of Hadrumetum, where he had to fulfil his duty as a judge on his assize circuit. There was much to organize in the entourage of a Proconsul. The representative of the majesty of Rome could not arrive like a beggar. When, finally, they took to the road, the gubernatorial carriage and its cavalcade went by easy stages. Gordian's father was a septuagenarian; things should not be rushed. Ten miles a day was enough. Hadrumetum was in sight, but still some miles distant, on the *ides*, when the messenger drove his sweat-lathered horse up to them. The beast stood, head down, trembling, as he told them the bad news. Gordian found it difficult to accept. His mind kept shifting to the horse; the way it was standing, it might be permanently broken down.

The nomads had come up out of the desert to the west of the Lake of Triton. There had been no warning. They had rampaged through the oases – Castellum Neptitana, Thusuros, Ad Palmam, Thiges; each was left a scene of desolation. Not yet sated, the barbarians were riding north. Soon they would reach Capsa. Their numbers were immense; like nothing seen before. Their leader was Nuffuzi, a chief of the Cinithii. His prestige was such that warriors from other tribes of the Gaetuli had joined him, some from as far south as Phazania.

Gordian's father might be nearing his eightieth year, but he had a long career behind him. He had governed many provinces, armed and unarmed. He had not survived, and usually prospered, by giving way to panic. 'If you left the barbarians on the road to Capsa, and we are outside Hadrumetum, we have time to finish our journey, go to the baths, and then take counsel over dinner.'

The defence of Africa Proconsularis was overseen by Capelianus, the governor of Numidia, the province adjacent to the west. Between Gordian Senior and Capelianus there was a personal disagreement of very long standing. It was a delicate subject, best not mentioned in front of either man. The governing elite of the empire had long memories for any slight, let alone anything worse. Duty, or at least fear of imperial displeasure, would make Capelianus act eventually, but habitual animosity would not encourage the governor to rush to the aid of his neighbour.

The governor of Africa had few troops at his disposal. There was an Urban Cohort in Carthage and two auxiliary cohorts in the west, one at Utica and the other at Ammaedara. They were there to prevent riots in the towns, and the latter to suppress banditry in the countryside. Strung out along the borders to the south-west was a cohort of legionaries from 3rd Augustan and an irregular unit of mounted scouts, and to the east three cohorts of auxiliaries in Tripolitana. Although within the province of Africa, all the troops along the borders were notionally under the command of the governor of Numidia. For his father's security, and greater dignity, Gordian had sought volunteers throughout the province from the regular units and from the various small groups of soldiers on detached duties. With these, and some veterans who found life outside the army less than they had expected, he had raised a mounted bodyguard one-hundred-strong for the Proconsul. This unit of Equites Singulares Consularis had been the sole military force with them in Hadrumetum.

The plan which the younger Gordian advanced over dinner was bold and did not meet with universal approval. Menophilus, the Quaestor in the province, and Mauricius, the local landowner, saw its merits. One of the Proconsul's legates, Valerian, had been talked around, but the other two, the inseparable Arrian and Sabinianus, remained deeply sceptical. 'Putting your hand in a rat's nest,' said Arrian. 'You are not Alexander, and I am not Parmenion,' said Sabinianus. You should abandon this desire for military glory. It does not fit the type of philosophical life you profess. You should take the sort of cautious advice the Macedonian King rejected from the old general.

Nevertheless, Gordian had persevered.

The nomads had come to pillage, not to conquer. It was too late to head them off – the worst damage was done – so they should be caught as they returned. Whether they took Capsa or not, it was unlikely they would venture deeper into Roman territory. They would know troops from Numidia would be mobilized to chase them. Almost certainly, the raiders would seek to leave the province by the same route they had entered. Ad Palmam was the key. At that oasis the land narrowed between the Lake of Triton and the smaller salt lake to the west. One of the two safe paths through the great waste ran off south-east from there. It intersected the other somewhere out in the wilderness. A force at Ad Palmam dominated both escape routes.

Gordian, guided by Mauricius and accompanied by Sabinianus and Valerian, would lead eighty men of the mounted bodyguard as a flying column. They would go via Thysdrus and Taparura. When they reached the hills, Mauricius could take them south by unfrequented ways to avoid running into the nomads.

Arrian was by far the best horseman among them. He would ride ahead, take spare horses on a lead rein. At the high country he would bear west for Thiges. He could take a couple of troopers with him, but, if he came across the nomads, he would have to rely on his mount and his skill.

'I might try praying as well,' Arrian had said, 'although I know some think it useless.'

After Arrian reached the frontier wall, it was not far to the Mirror Fort. At their headquarters, he would take command of the five hundred scouts and then force march them back to join Gordian and the others at Ad Palmam.

Meanwhile, Menophilus would have ridden west from Hadrumetum, through the Sufes Pass, and collected 15th Cohort Emesenorum from Ammaedara. He would bring them down from the north through Capsa.

The raiders would be burdened with their plunder. They were barbarians, and had no discipline. They would straggle all over the country. Their retreat would be slow. Gordian and Arrian, if they acted with alacrity, could be waiting at the oasis long before the nomads appeared. Between them, the Romans would dispose some six hundred cavalry. More than enough to delay the enemy until Menophilus appeared with five hundred infantry in their rear – like a hammer on to an anvil.

'You are proposing to surround a much greater number with about a thousand men,' Sabinianus had said.

Gordian had agreed. 'But we are not trying to massacre or capture them all. Merely retake their loot, kill some of them and teach the rest a lesson. Make them think twice before crossing the border again. Show weakness, and they will be back before the end of the year. There will be more of them. Garamantes, Nasamones, Baquates . . . tribesmen from far away will flock to the banners of this Nuffuzi. You all know the nature of barbarians: success breeds arrogance.'

No one at the dinner had an answer to that, not even Arrian or Sabinianus. He was self-evidently right: that was how barbarians were. Gordian Senior was predisposed to be won over. He had no desire to be rescued by Capelianus. The thing had been clinched by Mauricius. Could he join the expedition? The local magnate had twenty-five mounted, armed retainers with him. He was sure other nearby estate owners would contribute more. If there had been time, he himself could have produced perhaps nearly a hundred from his own lands.

The Proconsul had approved the plan. He told his son to take all the *equites*. The younger Gordian would not hear of it; nor would the others. Together they urged the governor to have a ship prepared in the harbour to take him and his household to safety, if things should go very badly wrong and the nomads threatened Hadrumetum. Gordian Senior had replied that he had never run from his enemies, and he was too old to start now.

Menophilus and Arrian had ridden their separate ways the next morning. Three days had passed getting ready the men, weapons, supplies, and animals of the flying column. When finally Gordian led them out, he was at the head of eighty troopers and a similar number of armed locals. He had waved to his father, blown kisses to Parthenope and Chione, his two mistresses, and wondered if he was doing the right thing.

When they had ridden through Thysdrus, they had got the news that Capsa had fallen. The barbarians appeared to be taking their time over their looting. The estimates of their numbers remained unreliable, hopefully vastly inflated. They had received no further word on the journey.

Gordian shaded his eyes, and watched. Another flock of doves got up as Sabinianus disappeared into the oasis. Perhaps his friend was right – perhaps he was doing this for the wrong motives. Still, it was all too late to worry now.

The doves circled and swooped back into the treetops. The chickens had vanished. It was quiet – dreadfully quiet – and very still. Now and then Gordian thought he half saw movement deep in the shade. If something happened to Sabinianus . . . Odysseus must have felt this apprehension when he sent Eurylochus to scout the smoke drifting up over the Aeaean island. Eurylochus had returned from the halls of Circe. It would be all right. *We won't go down to the House of Death, not yet, not until our day arrives.* But Eurylochus had not come back from Sicily. *All ways of dying are hateful to us poor mortals.* If he had sent Sabinianus to his death . . . Gordian pushed the verses from his mind. No point in entertaining such thoughts; not until necessary.

'There!'

Sabinianus had emerged from the tree line. He was still mounted. His horse was ringed by children. He beckoned.

'Mount up.'

It was dark under the high fronds. Sabinianus led them through the oasis towards the settlement. There were conduits everywhere. Of all sizes, they crossed and recrossed each other, elaborately regulated by dams and aqueducts of palm-stems. Where the sun penetrated, the water was jade; elsewhere, a cool brown. The hooves of their mounts rattled over narrow wooden bridges. Sheltered by the date palms, there were fig trees and a profusion of shorter fruit trees: lemon, pomegranate, plum and peach. Below, almost every inch was set out in gardens for grain or vegetables. With the arrival of the other riders, the children had withdrawn to a distance.

Gordian caught glimpses of them, and of adults through the trunks of the trees.

'They have had a bad time,' Sabinianus said. 'I talked to the headman. Only a few killed, but the nomads seized everything portable – all the food stocks, everything of value. The women and girls were much raped; many of the boys too. The nomads took some with them. The headman seemed most concerned about the animals.'

'The animals?' Valerian sounded appalled.

'No,' Sabinianus said. 'Not that. The nomads took all the animals, and, while they were doing it, trampled some of the irrigation.'

Pale mud-brick walls showed through the foliage ahead. Gordian signalled the column to wait while he rode around the settlement with his officers. It was laid out in an oval. There was no defensive wall as such. But the houses abutted each other, their windowless rear walls forming a continuous circuit, only occasionally pierced by a narrow, easy-to-block passage. Flat roofs with low parapets could form a fighting platform. A watchtower and some higher walls at the south end must be what passed for a citadel. The whole was not big – maybe seven, eight hundred inhabitants, certainly not more than a thousand; difficult to tell when the houses were packed that close. Gordian might be able defend the place when Arrian arrived with the *speculatores*, but the perimeter was much too long to be held by the fewer than one hundred and sixty men with him now. If only Arrian had got here first with the Frontier Wolves.

'I had hoped—' Gordian stopped himself, wished he had not spoken. He did not want to lower the spirits of the others. There was no point in unsettling himself. Disquiet was to be avoided, no matter the external circumstances. Unhappiness, even misery, was nothing but the product of ignorance or faulty judgement. Knowledge and correct thinking would dispel any suffering. But, somehow, the thing was too obvious. He had hoped; they had all hoped – expected, even – that Arrian would be here before them.

Three men, leading spare mounts, cover much more ground than the fastest of cavalry columns. The Mirror Fort was much nearer than Hadrumetum. The *speculatores* were famous rough riders. Something must have happened to Arrian: an accident, an encounter with the nomads. *All ways of dying are hateful to us poor mortals.*

Gordian took charge of himself. He would send another rider to bring the scouts. At least the nomads had neither left a rearguard at this oasis nor already returned. Gordian felt better, thinking and acting correctly. A philosophical education paid dividends. Mental disturbance was to be avoided like the plague.

'We could impress the able-bodied inhabitants, arm them somehow.' In the face of the silence of the others, Valerian stopped.

Sabinianus answered, in tones of mock-sympathy. 'My poor, dear innocent friend, these people will not fight for us. They do not want us here. If we had not arrived, on the way back the raiders would have passed them by; just a bit more raping, perhaps a final bit of torture to try to prise out the hiding place of some probably imaginary treasure. But there would have been no killing, no wholesale destruction. Valerian, my dear, you are far too trusting. One day it will be the death of you.'

The citadel was built around a courtyard, with thirty stables opening off it. The other lean-to sheds were empty. Another forty horses were stalled in them. The remaining mounts were tethered in the open. It was not ideal, but most were in the shade. As the riders rubbed them down, Gordian was given a formal, if guarded speech of welcome in heavily accented Latin by the headman.

'Riders!'

The shout stopped everything.

'Coming down from the north!' The man in the lookout tower was leaning far out, pointing, as if those below might have forgotten the track of the sun.

'Riders, lots of them.'

'Fuck.' Sabinianus was eating some dates. His servant was grooming his horse. 'Just when I was thinking of a nap.'

Holding his scabbard well away from his legs, Gordian took the stairs two at a time. No sooner had they arrived, and this had to happen. Exhausted men and horses. No Arrian or scouts. Probably untrustworthy inhabitants . . . The great Epicurus himself might have had trouble keeping his equanimity through all this shit.

At the top, Gordian doubled up, blowing hard. Too much soft living, rich food and drink, too many nights with Parthenope and Chione, never enough sleep.

A pillar of dust: tall, straight, definitely made by cavalry. There were a lot of them, coming this way, travelling fast. Under two miles away.

Gordian looked around. Mud-brick battlements, five paces square, above the top fronds. Excellent vision in all directions. Odd he had not noticed the tower when looking in at the oasis. Valerian was next to him. Gordian drew a deep breath. 'Send a rider . . . No, go yourself. Get to the Mirror Fort. Bring the scouts.'

Valerian saluted. 'We will do what is ordered—'

'Too late,' Mauricius interupted. 'They have passed the turning. He would have to go south, through the desert, around the western salt flats. He would need a camel. It would take days.'

'How many?'

'Hard to say, but everything here will be long finished before he gets to the Mirror Fort.' Mauricius shrugged. 'I will send a couple of my men. Maybe—'

'I would not bother.' Sabinianus was shading his eyes with his hat. His bald forehead shone with sweat. He started laughing.

Gordian wondered about the effects of the ride, the desert.

'Time for a nap, after all.' Sabinianus said. 'Unless I am much mistaken, here comes Arrian, and my little white-bottomed friend has brought the famous tough Frontier Wolves.'

Gordian held his war council in the room at the foot of the tower. It was the largest in the citadel. It had a high ceiling and, with the shutters closed and boys wielding fans, it was cool. There were six of them: Gordian himself, Valerian, the reunited Sabinianus and Arrian, Mauricius, and another local, Aemilius Severinus, the commander of the *speculatores*. They drank fermented palm wine and ate pistachios. From outside came the smell of chicken on a grill. Perhaps, Gordian thought, the nomads had not been entirely wrong: peasants always have something hidden.

'Yes,' Arrian said, 'I could have got here quicker. But the scouts were dispersed all along the wall. Aemilius Severinus here agreed that it would be best to gather as many as possible. There are four hundred camped in the oasis.'

'No one is criticizing you,' Gordian said.

Sabinianus snorted.

'No one apart from your twin, the other of the Cercopes.' Gordian smiled.

'The day I give a fuck about his views, I will—'

'Sell your arse at the crossroads,' Sabinianus said.

'Possibly, although I was thinking of something else.'

'If we could postpone the discussion of your descent into male prostitution,' Gordian said, 'it might be useful if you gave us some estimate of how many bloodthirsty savages were chasing you, and how soon they might be here.'

Arrian scratched his short, stubbly beard. He pulled the end of his upturned nose.

'Hercules' hairy black arse; it is as if he is auditioning to be in a comedy without a mask. What would a physiognomist read in his soul?'

Gordian gestured amiably for Sabinianus to be quiet. 'If it helps him think.'

Arrian looked up, hands and face still. 'I saw about two thousand, all mounted. But there was a lot of dust to the north of them. Although the majority of that would have been raised by baggage animals and captives.'

'How long?'

Arrian spread his hands in a sign of hopelessness. 'At first, the two thousand chased us hard. They gave up when they realized they would not catch us.'

'Where was that?'

Arrian gestured to Aemilius Severinus.

'Ten miles south of Thiges, fifteen north of here.' The officer answered immediately and with confidence. Although most appointments were decided by patronage, probably the commander of the Frontier Wolves would not last long without certain qualities.

'The afternoon wears on; most likely we can expect them at some point tomorrow.'

No one contradicted Gordian's estimate.

'How shall we greet them?'

Silence, until Gordian carried on. 'I was thinking of a barrier – palm trunks, thorn bushes, whatever – across the neck of land.'

'But it is near two miles across, and we are too few, with too little time,' Sabinianus said.

'A mounted charge, in a wedge,' Valerian said. 'No irregular troops will stand up to it, let alone a horde of nomads from the desert.'

'True,' Aemilius Severinus said. 'But they would not need to. With their numbers, they would give way, flow all around us. Quite likely we could charge clean through them. But what good would it do? We would be charging at nothing, and all the time their arrows and javelins would be whittling down our numbers. Getting back might prove difficult, and if we ended up out there surrounded, on spent horses—'

'What do these nomads value above everything?' Gordian went straight on to answer his own rhetorical question. 'They would do anything rather than leave behind the plunder they have amassed.'

'They do claim to have a sense of honour.' Aemilius Severinus spoke somewhat hesitantly. 'Of course, they seldom live up to it. Things are not the same among them as with us.'

'They are barbarians.' Gordian waved aside the concept. 'They saw several hundred *speculatores* riding here—'

'And,' Sabinianus cut in, 'the gap between the salt lakes is narrow, and they will realize that it will be difficult to drive their stolen beasts and prisoners away under our noses.'

'Exactly.' Gordian grinned, feeling like one of those street magicians who haunt the *agora* when they produce something from up their sleeves. 'Either they have to defend the herds, and we have something to charge, or they must come and root us out of the oasis. Either way, we get to fight hand-to-hand. And that is our strength, and their weakness.'

A breeze got up in the night, some time before dawn. It hissed and rattled through the palm fronds. Gordian leant on the parapet of the watchtower, waiting. He had been unable to sleep. There was little to see as yet. The shifting canopy of foliage just below him was black. It hid the settlement. Beyond the oasis, the desert was flat, laid out in tones of blue and grey. There was no moon. The thousands of stars were as distant and uncaring as gods.

The previous evening, not long after the war council ended, the first of the enemy had arrived. The *speculatores* that Aemilianus Severinus had put on picket had been driven back into the village. In the night, off to the north, the campfires of the nomads had parodied the stars. At last, the fires had burnt out, leaving just the real firmament and the blackness.

All ways of dying are hateful to us poor mortals. No, Gordian thought. There was nothing to fear, he told himself. If, in the end, everything returns to rest and sleep, why worry? Death is nothing to us. When we exist, death does not, and when death is, we are not. Anyway, it would not come to that, not today. Menophilus would be here in the morning; and with him would be the five hundred men of the 15th Cohort Emesenorum. There was nothing to worry about.

Even thinking of Menophilus somewhat calmed Gordian. As Quaestor, Menophilus had been appointed by the Senate, unlike the legates, who were family friends chosen personally by the governor. Gordian had not known Menophilus before they came to Africa, but had warmed to him. On first meeting, Menophilus had seemed reserved, even gloomy. The Italian was young – still only in his twenties. He had sad eyes and wore an ornament in the form of a skeleton on his belt. He talked readily of the transience of life and was known to collect memento mori. And, to cap it all, he was a Stoic. Yet he little inclined towards the boorish asceticism many of that school so often paraded. No sooner had the governor's entourage established itself in Carthage than Menophilus had begun an affair with the wife of a member of the city council. Her name was Lycaenion; she was dark, full-bodied, very beddable, Gordian thought. Menophilus liked to drink as well. While these traits showed an agreeable capacity for pleasure, it was the calm competence of the Quaestor on which Gordian was relying now. Menophilus would be here. There was nothing to worry about.

Swiftly, but by imperceptible stages, the sky lightened, turning a delicate lilac. Behind a haze, the white disc of the sun topped the horizon. For a moment, the Lake of Triton once again filled with water. Waves rolled across its dark surface. You could almost hear them. And then the sun rose higher and the illusion was dispelled. And again there was nothing but salt and mud and desolation.

Gordian looked off to the north. The leading edge of the barbarian encampment was about a mile distant. Dust and smoke were already shifting up from it. In the low, raking light of dawn, everything was blurred and indistinct.

If Gordian could make out little of the enemy, he could see even less of his own forces. There were four men – one for each cardinal point – with him on the watchtower, and below there were the sentinels on the walls of the citadel and the horse handlers in the courtyard. All the rest, and the whole of the settlement, were hidden by the thick, interlaced fronds of thousands upon thousands of palms. Gordian knew the men were in position. In the dead of night, when sleep had refused him, he had walked the lines. He was convinced that he had made the best dispositions he could, but he was far from content.

The narrow ends of the oval of the oasis were north and south. The tree line was about two thirds of a mile long and at its widest just under half a mile across. There were no defences – no ditch, wall or rampart – around this perimeter, and, anyway, Gordian simply did not have enough men to defend such a length. The village was set in the southern end of the cultivated land. As every inch of irrigated soil was used, the crops, shrubs and trees grew right up to the walls of the houses. There was no killing zone. Attackers could remain in cover until almost the moment they tried to scale the walls or storm the openings.

It was not a strong position, but Gordian had done what he could to remedy its deficiencies. Traps – sharpened wooden stakes concealed in shallow pits; the ones the soldiers called 'lilies' – had been dug in the more obvious trails through the gardens. Half the *speculatores*, a full two hundred men under a young centurion of local birth called Faraxen, were lurking among the undergrowth. In small groups they were to harass the nomads, falling back before them into the village.

The remainder of the scouts, under their commander Aemilius Severinus, waited in the settlement. All the entrances were blocked, except the two by which Faraxen's men would retreat. Moveable barricades had been prepared to put across the latter. Gordian would have liked to make the place a more difficult proposition, but it had been impossible. There had been no time to cut back a space in front of the defences. There was no blacksmith, and no metal, to make caltrops to scatter where their sharp spikes would pierce the soles of the enemies' feet. Normally, he would have ordered the collection of firewood and metal cauldrons in which to heat oil or sand. He had not done so, because the roofs of the mud-brick houses whose rear walls formed the defences did not look capable of withstanding the heat of a fire. Most were held up by palm trunks, and not a few were thatched.

If, as was likely, the nomads broke into the village, all the *speculatores* were to retreat into the citadel by its main gate. The labyrinthine alleys, and the nomads' inextinguishable desire to pillage, should somewhat slow down their pursuit. Gordian did not allow himself to think what would happen to the inhabitants cowering in their homes.

The citadel was situated at the extreme southern tip of Ad Palmam. Mud brick, like every other construction, at least its walls were a bit higher and appeared a little more solid. Except on the north, it was ringed by only a shallow belt of trees. Two of its gates opened out west and south on to the plain; the third, the biggest one, north into the village. The seventy-seven remaining Africans raised by Mauricius and the other estate owners were distributed along the parapets. Mauricius was to act as second in command to Valerian. The *equites* of the Proconsular guard also were stationed in the citadel. Thirty-seven of them were on the walls to stiffen the resolve of the irregulars. The other forty were down in the yard with their horses, acting as a reserve. Arrian and Sabinianus were reunited as their leaders. The former in charge of those on the parapets, the latter the reserve.

Looking down, in the gathering light Gordian saw the two legates inspecting the close-packed lines of horses tethered in the courtyard. Every mount was saddled and bridled. All was ready in case the entire force had to try to cut its way out. Gordian had no intention that this should be remembered as the site of a desperate and ultimately doomed last stand.

Arrian and Sabinianus were checking the girth of each animal, and peering into the mouth to check the bit. Yet somehow they still managed to convey an air of patrician disinterest, even indolence. They never appeared to take anything seriously, and the appellation as the mythical Cercopes suited them. The originals had been brothers from Ephesus. They had roamed the world practising deceptions, until captured by Hercules. The hero had tied them up and slung them upside down from a pole over his shoulder. The skin of the Nemean lion did not cover Hercules' arse, which was blackened by the sun. Luckily for the Cercopes, when they told Hercules why they were laughing, he saw the humour.

'Riders coming!'

Maybe a dozen men on horses and camels had left the nomad camp. They were dark shapes under a dark flag. Now and then light saddlecloths, tunics or head coverings caught the early-morning sun. They rode at a canter, twisting between isolated clumps of vegetation and thorn bushes. A semi-opaque smear of dust marked their route.

They skirted the western edge of the oasis and reined in some hundred paces from the thin belt of trees which fronted the west gate of the citadel. There they sat, under their gloomy banner.

'They are carrying a palm branch.' Sabinianus had appeared at the top of the watchtower. 'If they were civilized, you would assume they wanted a truce to talk.'

'We had better make that assumption anyway,' Gordian said.

'Perhaps we should send Arrian, in case we are mistaken.' Sabinianus shuddered. 'The village headman told me the unspeakable things they do to their captives.'

'No, you can come with me,' Gordian said.

'Is it too late to renounce your friendship?' Sabinianus' tone was one of polite enquiry.

Gordian grinned. 'We will take twenty of the *equites* with us; to calm your girlish apprehensions. While we are gone, Arrian can take command.'

'How reassuring.' Sabinianus turned and started to climb down the ladder. 'At least I have a good horse.'

The nomads neither came to meet them nor moved in any way when the party trotted out from the oasis.

As they got close, Gordian's mount put back its ears and began to baulk. Behind him, one or two were sidestepping. Camels, he thought: their smell upsets horses. He had forgotten. It was in many histories. He drove his horse forward on a tight rein. You would have thought a horse from Africa would be used to the malodorous brutes. Perhaps some camels smelt worse than others.

Gordian pulled up a couple of lengths away. His horse stamped and shifted in agitation. He calmed it, while taking in the barbarian deputation. They all wore tunics and sheepskin cloaks, carried three or four light javelins, a small shield and a knife each. Several had swords on their hips, all of Roman manufacture. Some had a scarf wrapped around their heads, veiling everything except their eyes. Most were bare-headed, with thick, braided ropes of dirty hair. One or two of the latter had shaved parts of their skulls to create strange, intricate patterns.

The camels were very tall beside the horses. They regarded him with disdain, jaws slack, slobber hanging down. They did smell. No wonder his horse did not want to be near them.

Nuffuzi sat on a chestnut horse, just off centre of the group. Gordian could tell him not by his costume but by the way the heads of his followers turned inward towards their leader.

The chief was dark, his face thin, with high cheekbones. His greying hair was in elaborate braids, bright with beads, and he wore a small beard only on his chin. The rider next to him was a younger version of Nuffuzi.

No one seemed inclined to speak.

Gods below, Gordian thought, perhaps none of them even speaks Latin. There was no likelihood of them knowing Greek. Unless he took control, this could soon turn into a debacle.

'You are Nuffuzi of the Cinithii?'

Inexplicably, the nomads hissed and glowered annoyance at Gordian's question. Nuffuzi himself remained calm. The chief spoke in the Latin of the camps. 'Where have you come from?'

Unable to see its relevance, Gordian ignored the question. 'Without provocation you have raided into the *imperium*. You have pillaged from many innocent people.'

'Where are you going?'

Again, to Gordian, it seemed a non-sequitur. 'I cannot let you pass.'

Nuffuzi nodded, as if weighing these words. 'You do not know how things are here. There was no innocence. Every summer when my people come north they are abused and cheated, their goods are stolen, their animals taken, their women and boys raped. This—' he jabbed a finger towards the camp '—is not plunder, it is retribution.'

'You know I cannot let you pass.'

'I know this.' Nuffuzi smiled like a sage close to enlightenment. 'I wanted to see who I was fighting, before the killing and the evil began.'

With a gesture almost of benediction, the desert war-leader turned and rode away.

There was all the time in the world to study the nomad encampment. It was big, sprawling and betrayed no discernible order. From a distance, all seemed intermixed: men and animals, warriors and captives. Different-coloured flags fluttered over it at what appeared random intervals. Certainly, the nomads were in no hurry to attack. A good breakfast, Sabinianus suggested, perhaps a last rape or two. You know how none of them can resist a good-looking camel.

Gordian stood down his own men in sections to take their breakfast. He tried to eat himself – some flat bread and cheese, a few olives and dates. It did not go down well. When men visited the barracks to watch the gladiators eating the night before they fought, most would bet on those who ate with a good appetite. They often lost. Gordian would be fine when the fighting started. He would be hungry afterwards. Now, he found it hard to eat. It signified nothing, nothing at all. He drank a little well-watered wine. He wanted his head clear.

The encampment began to stir. The flags moved, first this way then that. Dark shapes eddied at their bases. High yelps and cries drifted across the plain. The music of strange instruments.

'We have some time; they need to work themselves up,' Gordian said to no one in particular. He was surprised to find he was chewing a piece of bread.

Warriors were streaming out from among the tents. The riders at the front could be distinguished as individuals, but those behind were a dark mass. Low down, light flickered between the legs of their animals as they raced across the parched earth.

'Here they come.'

They came like a herd of beasts migrating. Thick white dust obscured all but the forerunners. Some horses were bolting. Their riders could be seen hauling on the reins. Their mounts ran on, heads held sideways. Some ran across the line, baulking others. Those on camels bobbed, seemingly precarious above the mass.

The nomads lapped all around the oasis. With no regular standards or set formations, numbers were hard to judge. They were not close-packed, and they were kicking up great clouds of dust. Such things could deceive. That and the terrible noise. There were fewer of them than an untutored eye might judge. Three thousand at most, perhaps considerably fewer. It could be there were no more than the two thousand that had chased Aemilius Severinus the previous day. Odds of about four to one against the Romans.

In which case – Gordian looked at the camp – how many were still guarding the captives? Among the tents and shelters, the beasts of burden and squatting, dejected humanity, it was impossible to tell. Gordian looked north, beyond the camp. Still nothing: no tell-tale smudge of dust in the sky.

From the watchtower Gordian had a view as good as watching the games from the imperial box in the amphitheatre. Nearby, around the southern end of the oasis, the barbarians had halted just out of effective bowshot. They remained mounted, brandishing their weapons, and chanting a strange, ululating song. Now they were stationary, it was easier to assess numbers. There were no more than five hundred of them, spread in a wide semicircle but clustering thickest under a big black banner. Most likely, Nuffuzi was there. They were there to block any attempt at escape.

Further north, the nomads rode right up to the line of trees. Those on horseback leapt out of the saddle. The process was more laborious for the camel-mounted. First, the beasts were forced down on their front knees, then – the rider rocking violently – on their rear ones as well. Finally dismounted, the warriors could follow the example of the horsemen and toss their reins to their less courageous companions who had remained mounted.

A camel rider was plucked backwards by an unseen arrow. Faraxen's *speculatores* were about their business. The nomads surged out of sight under the palms.

Gordian peered closely through the rising murk. Those still in the saddle were cantering away; each with two, at most three animals on a lead rein. He made rapid calculations. Say two thousand five hundred of the enemy, five hundred of them so far were unengaged here in the south. That left two thousand in the north. But, of those, one in three were holding animals. There could be only about one thousand five hundred rushing into the attack. Odds of three to one; the bare minimum needed to assault a defended position. And the nomads were unarmoured. All the defenders, even the retainers of the landowners, had some form of body armour, hardened leather or padded linen, if not mail. Before he let his hopes rise, Gordian reminded himself that Ad Palmam was not in truth a properly fortified village. Without Menophilus, the odds were still heavy that this could only end one way.

The noise of the unseen battle issued up. Gordian stared, as if an exercise of will would penetrate the blanket of fronds. Frightened birds clattered away, out over the salt flats: doves, the blue flash of a kingfisher. The din was getting closer. The most dedicated follower of Epicureanism would struggle to remain free from mental disturbance. Very few Epicureans were military men. The enforced inactivity of command would try anyone's philosophical principals.

Looking down, Gordian saw a sudden surge of people pouring through the open gate into the courtyard of the citadel. They were a mix of civilians and *speculatores*. The nomads must be inside the settlement already. So many were fleeing, they were pushing and fighting in the confined space. Figures were falling. A child went down. As its mother went to scoop it up, she was trampled. Soon the mob would block the entrance. The enemy would enter on their heels, cut their way through them.

'Legate!' Gordian bellowed for Arrian. 'Get up here and assume command!'

Gordian quickly took stock. Out on the plain the big war standard of Nuffuzi had not moved. Some of the warriors were caracoling their horses, racing along the line, but the majority sat motionless. A fair few had dismounted and were squatting, talking and drinking. If Gordian charged at the head of his father's guard, quite probably they could punch through the nomads and ride to safety. He suppressed the ignoble thought.

'Sabinianus, with me!'

Before going to the ladder, Gordian look a last look to the north. The pall raised by thousands of hooves had screened the camp of the raiders almost completely. Beyond it, nothing at all could be seen.

Down in the yard was chaos. The horses were stamping and squealing, rearing against their tethers. Wild-eyed, they lashed out at each other. The forty troopers were struggling to control them. Gordian shouted for them to leave the horses and form on him.

In a compact wedge Gordian and his men forced their way into the press in the gateway. With fists, boots and the flats of their swords, they cleared a passage. Men swore at them.

Women screamed and small children howled. Once, Gordian nearly went down when his boot turned on a body.

Outside, in the main avenue of the settlement, they scrummed together into a rough wall of shields about a dozen wide and three or four deep. Panicked inhabitants swirled around them like a river in spate around a boulder. In twos and threes, *speculatores* emerged from under the palms screening the innumerable side-alleys. Aemilius Severinus was leading one group.

'They outflanked us. They were here before, and know this maze better than us. They were all around us, too many of them . . . ' The report trailed off. Aemilius stood, panting; shamefaced. There was a gash on his forearm, blood on his face.

Gordian gripped his shoulder. 'Not your fault. Get your survivors together inside. When the enemy gets here, close the gate. Never mind about the civilians. Never mind if we are still outside.'

Aemilius Severinus nodded. 'We will do what is ordered, and at every command we will be ready.'

Gordian waited in the front rank, shoulder to shoulder with his men. The civilians stumbled and jostled past, wailing like mourners. Behind, the horses trumpeted and screamed. Agonized yells and alien shouts echoed out from the alleyways in front. There was something unnerving in waiting silent and motionless at the centre of so much noise and movement. Here in the shade of the palms which lined the street it was cooler. The light was green, subaqueous.

Death is nothing to us. Gordian repeated it to himself. *Death is nothing to us.*

The press of refugees bumped and bored past. The guards waited. The din seemed to recede, as if it came from a great distance.

If at last all returns to rest and sleep . . .

A nomad ran out from a lane. The locals shrank away. He skidded to a halt, dumbstruck by the presence of the soldiers. Someone shot him. The arrow spun him around and dropped him in the dirt. The men around Gordian laughed.

'And things were going so well for him,' Sabinianus said.

From somewhere out of sight came a high call and response, the rhythmic stamping of feet, the beat of weapons on shields. The villagers hurled themselves past, sandals slapping on the compacted dirt. The street in front of Gordian emptied. He glanced back. A seething mass of bodies was stuck fast in the gateway. All sense gone, they clawed and struggled.

'Steady!' Sabinianus shouted.

A roar, and the barbarians came around the corner. A volley of arrows hissed over Gordian's head. The foremost warriors twisted and fell. Those following leapt over them. More arrows, like spattering rain. Not enough to stop the charge. The nomads' right arms went back, snapped forward. The air was full of barbed javelins. Gordian jerked his shield up. A jarring impact ran up his left arm. A splinter of wood narrowly missed his eye. The head of the javelin had penetrated the shield. He dropped the useless thing, got his sword up.

Braids flying, a nomad was on him, jabbing wicked steel down at his face. Gordian crouched, stepped forward. The javelin went over his left shoulder. He drove the tip of his blade into the guts. For a moment, they were together, face to face, in the hideous intimacy of an embrace. The stench of urine and blood. The breath of the warrior feral and hot on his face.

Gordian stepped back, pushing the dying man away. Another took his place, swinging a sword. Gordian blocked; once, twice, three times. The ringing of steel was loud in his ears. He gave ground. The soldiers around him likewise. Men were falling on both sides, but numbers were telling. Emboldened by his opponent's passivity, the nomad lifted

74

his arms high to deliver a mighty overhead chop. Gordian waited until the weapon was at its apex and neatly drove three inches of steel into his throat.

Again the line retreated and contracted. In the momentary respite, Gordian tried to take stock. Only three soldiers to his right now, Sabinianus and no more to his left. Nomads working around both flanks. The rear ranks of the guardsmen had turned to make a circle. The gateway was still full of massed humanity.

Like an ebbing tide, the enemy receded. Arrows from the wall plucked at their cloaks, thumped into their shields. One or two crumpled, hands clutching at the shafts. Before hope could rise, they charged again. The young chieftain at their head angled straight for Gordian. A flurry of blows, and Gordian's back collided with that of the soldier behind. Hampered in his movements, he emptied his mind of everything except his opponent's steel. Long training and the memory in his muscles guided him.

The briefest of pauses, and Gordian recognized him. With a curious precision and delicacy of footwork, Nuffuzi's son feinted and lunged. Gordian took the strike high up near the pommel. This youth could fight. The sound of shouting from behind. No time for that. Gordian parried and riposted.

Sweat stinging in his eyes. Pain in his chest. Gordian was tiring, his movements slowing, growing clumsy. He had to finish this soon. He forced his feet to move, thrust to the face, and pulled back to buy himself some time. The shouting was louder. Some of the nomads were looking up over the knot of soldiers, others glancing over their shoulders. Nuffuzi's son struck again. Gordian's slight distraction almost killed him. A late, desperate block forced the blade down. It sliced open his left thigh. He staggered, fighting for balance. The youth readied the killing blow. Gordian brought his sword into a shaky guard. On either side the nomads were stepping back.

Nuffuzi's son shouted, glared at his warriors. Gordian stepped off his right foot, on to his left – a sickening surge of pain – and brought the edge of his blade down into his opponent's right wrist. The youth screamed and dropped his sword. Before he could double up, Gordian got the point of his weapon up under his chin.

'Surrender.'

Clutching his wounded arm, eyes wide, the young chief said nothing.

All the nomads were running. A drift wrack of bodies and abandoned weapons left behind across the shaded street. The shouting from the citadel redoubled.

'Surrender.'

Despite the pain and the imminence of death, Nuffuzi's son kept his dignity. 'I surrender.'

Now Gordian could make sense of the shouting.

'Menophilus! Menophilus!'

CHAPTER 6

The Northern Frontier
A Camp outside Mogontiacum,

The Kalends of April, AD235

Outside the imperial pavilions, Timesitheus stood with the governor of Germania Superior, Catius Priscillianus. Behind them, the others were growing restive. They were all waiting for admittance into the presence of the Emperor, and they had all been there some time. The morning was wearing on. The chill wind from across the river was plucking at the folds of carefully arranged togas, teasing neatly arranged hair into disorder. It was getting cold. Men were beginning to talk at more than a respectful murmur, and to shift about. Sanctus, the Master of Admissions of the court, darted here and there. The *ab Admissionibus* was relentless in his attempts at chivvying men back into the correct precedence and demeanour.

Timesitheus nodded in the direction of the busy imperial functionary. 'If he had been this diligent in controlling who was let in during the last reign, Alexander would still be alive today.'

Catius Priscillianus laughed, not very loud, and not very

long. That was perfunctory, Timesitheus thought. Far too perfunctory for a joke made by the acting governor of the neighbouring province of Germania Inferior, the man who was overseeing the finances in both their provinces and that of Belgica as well. Nowhere near enough for a joke by the man charged with the logistics of the whole northern campaign. And, questions of the elevation and propinquity of offices aside, Timesitheus was acknowledged to be one of the closest intimates of Priscillianus' brother Catius Celer. Some greater show of hilarity would have been appropriate.

Still, it might have been just the weather. Priscillianus had not been back up on the frontier all that long. No time to get used to its ghastliness all over again. Timesitheus' thoughts ran to his own initial venture into this gods-forsaken region years before. Nothing in his previous travels had prepared him. Leaving Greece for the very first time, he had passed through Italy on his way to his inaugural military command in Spain. A year later, he had retraced his route and beyond to Arabia. Another year – his career had flourished from the beginning – and he was sent to the North. Now it was more than a decade ago, but he remembered his arrival clearly. It had been autumn, the sky grey, the air sharp like a knife. He had not thought it could get colder. He had been wrong. That winter the Rhine had frozen, not only the shallow, winding side-channels but the main stream itself. You could walk across, drive a carriage over. The locals and soldiers, muffled and indistinguishable, had cut holes in the ice to fish. It was said that the frozen waters had trapped terrible man-murdering monsters so huge that teams of oxen had to be used to pull them out. Apparently, they looked like enormous catfish, only blacker and stronger, although Timesitheus had not seen them himself.

Priscillianus produced a handkerchief. A fine, purple one, maybe from Sarepta in Phoenicia by the look of it. Very expensive, Timesitheus thought. Priscillianus dabbed his nose. Hypochondria also might have curtailed his appreciation of humour. All three of the Catii brothers spent a great deal of time judging their health, and usually they found it wanting. Twenty-four-hour-fevers and two-day chills, black humours and common colds, each brought on by exposure to the elements or being cooped up inside, their lives were measured by many, much deliberated ailments. Even writing from Rome, exulting at his appointment as one of the Praetors for this year, Timesitheus' dearest Catius Celer – the youngest of the brood – had complained of a headache, a sprained wrist and finding a snake in his bed.

Trepidation might have to be included in a consideration of Priscillianus' state of mind. A level of apprehension came with any invitation to the council of an Emperor. This could only be heightened when it was the first *consilium* of the reign. Rewards would be handed out: magistracies, commands, proximity to the throne and influence. But, to clear the way for supporters and other favoured recipients, existing men must fall. They were all bound to chance, like Ixion to the wheel.

So far, only the permanent board of sixteen Senators had been allowed beyond the purple hangings. Some time ago, the Master of Admissions had said the provincial governors would enter next. There were five governors with the field army. Yet just Timesitheus and Priscillianus stood waiting in the wind. Given the turn of events, Flavius Vopiscus of Panonnia Superior would no longer need to mark time with the rest of the gubernatorial herd. But what had happened to Faltonius Nicomachus of Noricum and Tacitus of Raetia? One possibility was promotion. They might be inside already, ushered in by a secret door. Now snug and close to the Emperor, they were whispering into his ear with Flavius Vopiscus. Or perhaps they were riding hard to some new and prestigious post, to Rome or one of the great and wealthy provinces of Africa or the East, their anticipation and exertions warming their blood. None of the other possibilities was so good. Forced retirement was the best; a life of dissembling, pretending to be grateful for an existence free of the heat and dust of politics. Beyond that lay only some terrible combination of arrest, torture, condemnation and confiscation, exile and execution.

Yes, Priscillianus might be feeling a certain trepidation. Yet he was a *nobilis*, an aristocrat with two influential brothers and many ancestral connections. Timesitheus lacked those possible sureties. He had risen high – some would say too high. He was an equestrian from a Greek backwater. His main patron was elderly, and his sole relative was his own dependant. Timesitheus had no protection except his intelligence and an acquired fortune, and both attracted envy. He was more than anxious.

It would not have been so bad if his wife has been with him. On his decision, Tranquillina had remained behind in Colonia Agrippinensis. She was to keep an eye on Axius, the Procurator he had placed in charge of the province. It had been a mistake. Axius really did not need watching, and Timesitheus needed his wife by his side. She had ways of calming him, of putting things in a better perspective. And she had foresight; better than his own, he now had to admit. If she had been here, the coup would not have caught him by surprise and left him unprepared. He hated being unprepared. He was frightened.

Fear feeds on inactivity, like a sleek rat in an unfrequented feed shed. Timesitheus knew all about fear, although so far, somehow, he had never given way. The trick was to occupy your thoughts with something else. Now, he summoned up the outlines of the great commission laid upon him. But would it still be his task by the end of the day? He stowed the doubt deep down in the hold of his mind, battened the hatches. The image came naturally to a Greek from his island. Over the years it had served him well.

The logistics of a full-scale imperial campaign into free Germania were daunting. Vast numbers of soldiers and animals, huge amounts of food and fodder, mountains of ancillary items – tents, replacement weapons, boots and uniforms, prefabricated defences, dismantled siege weapons and bridging equipment, miscellaneous ropes and straps, ink and papyrus, sutlers, servants and whores – had to be assembled here at Mogontiacum and then moved into what remained largely terra incognita. Despite nearly three centuries of intermittent campaigning, the Romans were still remarkably ignorant about the geography of northern *barbaricum*. Before setting out from Rome he and some of the other advisers of the previous Emperor had used detailed itineraries to plan the stages of each day's march to the frontier. All had been published in advance: which roads which units would use, where the supplies were to be gathered, when the Emperor would arrive in each town. Beyond the Rhine there were no maps, and all was vague.

In the East, the Euphrates and the Tigris helped. The great rivers ran away from Roman territory into that of the Persians. They made it harder to get lost. Supplies could accompany your forces downriver on boats. Movement of bulk goods was always infinitely easier and cheaper by water. The rivers of the North were not so amenable. Somewhere beyond the Rhine was the Ems, beyond that the Weser, and beyond them the Elbe. Timesitheus was diligent and had learnt of the yet more distant Oder and Vistula. All these rivers ran across the line of advance. If anything, they were likely to prove barriers.

And in the East there were roads and cities; proper roads which had been used for millennia, some of them paved, and Hellenic cities founded by Alexander and his successors. Both were lacking in the North. Nothing to march down, and no tempting target at which to aim. Nothing but tracks and woods, wilderness and marsh.

The absence of roads exercised Timesitheus. Almost all Roman units moved at least a part of their equipment by wagon and cart. These would all have to be replaced by pack animals. It would be expensive and resented. But it had to be done. What Timesitheus needed were accurate figures for existing transport animals and the numbers of men serving with the standards. The latter would prove particularly hard to get at, given the prevailing corruption of the previous regime. Under-strength units still drew the pay due their numbers on papyrus; the differences found their way into various private coffers.

'Come,' Sanctus said.

Timesitheus had not noticed the approach, but now followed the *ab Admissionibus.*

They passed through the heavy hangings into the purple-tinted labyrinth. At least it was good to be out of the wind. Sanctus led them left and right, this way and that, along silent corridors and through empty halls where unseen voices whispered. They went through shade and deeper darkness, seemingly turning back on themselves. At last, like initiates at Eleusis or some other mystery cult, they emerged into the throne room.

A shaft of light was arranged to fall from directly above on to the seated Emperor. The ivory of the throne gleamed. Maximinus sat robed and immobile, like a gigantic statue of porphyry and white marble.

On the right hand of the Emperor stood Anullinus. No surprise there, Timesitheus thought. Everyone knew there had been three of them, but Anullinus was the only one whose identity was certain. It was the Prefect of the Armenians who had beheaded the young Emperor and his mother. Camp gossip held he had stripped the old woman naked, outraged her headless corpse. Anullinus was wearing armour and a sword on his hip. Was it the one with which he had killed them? Had it been in this room? Motionless in the half-light, Anullinus' eyes exuded brutality and menace.

Two togate figures on Maximinus' left. Nearest to Maximinus was Flavius Vopiscus. It was common knowledge that the Senator from Syracuse, together with Honoratus, had orchestrated the change of regime. The latter was not yet returned from Rome. So Flavius Vopiscus stood closest to the Emperor they had created. The consummation of his designs did not seem to have lightened the demeanour of the Sicilian. As ever, he looked haunted. Pious to a fault or just riddled with superstition, it was said he dared not embark on the simplest endeavour – getting dressed or going to the baths – until he had consulted the *sortes Virgilianae*. How many times had he had to unroll the *Aeneid* and stab his finger on a random line before he considered the gods had guided him to one that read propitiously for the breaking of sacred oaths, for treason and murder?

The other toga-clad figure was less expected. Caius Catius Clemens – the middle of the three brothers – commander of the 8th Augustan legion and legate to his eldest sibling, the governor of Germania Superior. So Priscillianus had been more cold than apprehensive when they were waiting. A terrible thought caught Timesitheus. He could feel the teeth of the rat gnawing, hear the scrabble of its paws. His brother would have told Priscillianus everything that was about to happen. Perhaps, outside the pavilion, in front of dozens of witnesses, Priscillianus had not wished to be too closely associated with a man bound to the wheel on its downward turn. Again, Timesitheus hurriedly forced his fear down deep.

As was proper, the ex-Consul Priscillianus approached the Emperor first. Priscillianus came close and waited for a hand to be extended so that he could kiss the ring bearing the imperial seal. Instead Maximinus raised one of his great hands palm out.

'While I reign, no man will bow his head to me.' Maximinus' voice was deep, grating like a mill wheel.

Timesitheus gave a manly, Roman salute; nothing of the Hellene about it at all. He could have been an officer of the old, free Republic before Cannae. That was an ill-omened thought. He altered the image to before the gates of Carthage or Corinth, or some other wealthy city through whose streets the Romans had killed and raped in their heyday.

Behind Anullinus there were two men: Domitius, the Prefect of the Camp, and Volo, the head of the *frumentarii*. The latter commanded the imperial spies and assassins and was feared throughout the empire. The former dealt with latrines, horse lines and bundles of hay. Yet it was the presence of Domitius that worried Timesitheus more. He had heard that Domitius had survived the coup, but he had not known that he had remained in his post. Timesitheus very much hoped Domitius had not been a part of the plot.

It had started some years earlier in the East. Three men – all equestrians – had been charged with securing the supplies for the Persian war of Alexander Severus. One had been Timesitheus, another Domitius. Timesitheus had taken no more than was customary; if anything, rather less: just the usual presents, certainly no more than one part in ten. His wife had chided him with his restraint; but then Tranquillina was ever boldness itself. The spouse of Domitius would have had no grounds for complaint. His peculation had been egregious. Units had marched hungry and with no boots, the money having vanished into the ledgers of Domitius. Each man had threatened to denounce the other. No charge had been lodged, but by the time the campaign limped to an inglorious close, the enmity was deeply rooted.

The third man who had dealt with the logistics now sat on the throne of the Caesars. In the East, Timesitheus had met

Maximinus only once, and they had exchanged no words in a crowded council. But what he had learnt of the Thracian's actions spoke of reasonable efficiency and complete, even priggish probity. Yet when, back in Rome, this campaign against the Germans became an inevitability, Alexander's mother and senatorial councillors had decided that Timesitheus alone would handle all issues of supply. The role of Domitius had been cut back to digging ditches and mucking out stables. Maximinus had been assigned the role of training recruits. Timesitheus had interpreted that as a demotion. Now, he hoped the big Thracian had not seen it the same way.

The Senators of the standing inner council were grouped to the left of the throne. Seeing them in a group was never pleasing. They appeared to have been selected on grounds of advanced age and evident venality. Also, Timesitheus thought, they shared ill-favoured looks as a common possession. Petronius Magnus had the bulging eyes of some crustacean adapted to dim light. With his long, artful hair, Catilius Severus resembled an eastern priest, one of the scum who dance along the roads begging for coppers, clashing their cymbals and shaking their arses. The enormously fat Claudius Venacus seemed to have been dipped in something viscous. The other thirteen were hardly more aesthetic.

'Let in the rest,' Maximinus said.

Timesitheus followed Priscillianus to the opposite side from the sixteen Senators. This was too near Domitius for his liking. Timesitheus could feel the eyes of the Prefect of the Camp on him.

The others entered. Most, especially the Senators, tried not to push and shove, tried to preserve their *dignitas*. It was not easy. Too many men were trying to get in at once. Senators and equestrians, those holding commands and magistracies and those without, jumbled together. All wanted to get to the front, catch the eye of the new Emperor.

It had to be deliberate. Sanctus had been *ab Admissionibus* for years. Not a bad ploy, Timesitheus thought. Let them in at once, and have them demonstrate their own inferiority by scrabbling to get near you. Much more likely the hand of Flavius Vopiscus was at work than that of his putative ruler.

Sabinus Modestus struggled through the throng, grinning in a slack-jawed way. Timesitheus thought that, while his cousin might not be over-intelligent, at least he was good with his elbows and commendably loyal. Although, on second thoughts, it might be that Modestus had failed to realize the precarious nature of Timesitheus' position.

Maximinus had sat serene apart from the scrum. Now, he got to his feet. His vast, powerful bulk dominated the space. There was a scabbard in his hand. With a practised, fluid motion, he drew his blade. While one or two of the other eminent Senators flinched a little, the bovine Claudius Venacus almost stumbled backwards.

Reversing the weapon, Maximinus held the hilt to Anullinus. 'As my Praetorian Prefect, take this sword. If I reign well, use it on my behalf. If I reign badly, turn it against me.'

Anullinus took it, and the council applauded.

That either was brave or very foolish, Timesitheus thought. Had Maximinus not considered the fate of Alexander? Timesitheus was certain he would be in no such hurry to entrust his own survival to a judgement of his virtues carried out without advice by an ignorant, treacherous murderer like Anullinus.

Maximinus sat down, and indicated for Flavius Vopiscus to speak.

Timesitheus arranged his face. No trace of amusement, as he watched Vopiscus' hand come up without volition and, through the folds of his toga, finger the amulet hidden at his breast.

'A dispatch has arrived from Rome.' The voice of Vopiscus was melodious, trained. 'The Conscript Fathers have passed a decree awarding Gaius Iulius Verus Maximinus all the powers held by previous Emperors. Their joy was unconfined. Their acclamations lasted for three and a half hours.'

More applause.

Was it a *bulla*? Did Vopiscus still wear the little model of a phallus designed to keep him safe as a child? Or was it something else – an Egyptian scarab, a piece of amber, a sculpted vulva?

'Rome is secure and quiet. The incumbent Consuls Ordinarius have been told that their tenure will not be shortened. Of course, the virtues of certain men demand reward. Space must be found among the Suffect Consuls for Caius Catius Clemens, Marcus Clodius Pupienus Maximus and Lucius Flavius Honoratus, most likely others. But Honoratus himself has assured those already designated that their time in office will be little curtailed, and future preferment will be shown them.'

Vopiscus' hand still toyed with the hidden object. The Emperor Augustus had worn a seal-skin amulet. This could be something altogether different: a fingernail or some small, desiccated body part of a drowned man.

'Our most gentle and unassuming Emperor Maximinus has no desire to deprive other men of their honours. In his magnanimity and modesty, he has decided not to hold a Consulship until next year. Then he will enter into office on the *kalends* of January with Marcus Pupienus Africanus as his colleague.'

Maximinus himself interrupted. 'I do not want to forget the sons of the commanders of my youth here in the North. The following year, Lucius Marius Perpetuus will be one of the Consuls Ordinarius. And Pontius Proculus Pontianus the year after that.'

Now that was ill-advised, Timesitheus thought. Although,

these days, the role was almost entirely ceremonial, to be Consul, especially to be one of the two after which the year was named, was still the life ambition of many Senators. The *nobiles* regarded the office as a birthright, and others wanted to join them. To begin to allocate the position years in advance was sure to alienate a large number in the Curia.

'Your piety does you credit, Caesar.'

Was there something else in Vopiscus' tone, something implying that the words of Maximinus said less commendable things about other aspects of the new Emperor's character? Vopiscus was not to be under-rated. There was an asperity beneath the daemon-ridden exterior of the Senator.

'Since the death of Ulpian, no one can claim greater eminence in the field of law than his pupil Herennius Modestinus. The greatest jurist of his generation must stand by the Emperor advising him as his *a Libellis*. The new Secretary for Petitions is on his way north. His previous post as Prefect of the Watch has been granted to Quintus Potens.'

Like the tumblers and levers of a well-made lock, the pieces shifted together in Timesitheus' mind. It had been neatly done. A Consulship for each of his sons, the younger as colleague of the new Emperor next year, had bought Pupienus, the Prefect of the City, and with him had come the six thousand men of the Urban Cohorts. The offer of the most important legal post in the empire had eased Herennius Modestinus out of Rome. His command of the seven thousand *vigiles* had been given to a man well linked to the new regime. Potens had been Prefect of the Parthian cavalry here with the field army. His brother-in-law was Decius, the governor of Hispania Tarraconensis. Decius was from a family which, time out of mind, had held wide estates across the Danubian lands. These stretched into Maximinus' native Thrace, and Decius himself had been an early patron of the Thracian trooper's career. With the vast majority of the Praetorians here on the Rhine, all the soldiers that mattered in the eternal city were in the hands of Maximinus' men. Vopiscus might be riddled with superstition, but he and the urbane Honoratus had seized control of Rome with admirable skill.

'Here in the North, we face a terrible war,' Vopiscus continued. 'Everything must be done to ensure victory.'

This was the moment. Timesitheus smelt the fetid breath of the rodent, felt its wet muzzle seeking his throat.

'The governors of Moesia Superior and Pannonia Inferior, Titus Quartinus and Autronius Justus, have served dutifully. It is time they had a certain relaxation from their arduous labours. They have been summoned here to join the imperial court.'

Timesitheus forced himself to breathe normally. Quartinus was tall, scholarly, ineffectual. The cultured Senator might have escaped lightly.

'Their former provinces will be governed by Tacitus and Faltonius Nicomachus.'

So that was where the two had gone. Advancement, not condemnation; the wheel was turning up for them. Tacitus, of course, was another northerner.

'Quintus Valerius will be the acting governor of Raetia, and Ammonius of Noricum.'

Two equestrians, one the commander of the Cataphract heavy cavalry, the other of an irregular unit of Britons. Both promoted above all expectation or likelihood. That answered the question of who the other two armed men in Alexander's tent had been. Gods below, what would come next? Timesitheus had to keep a brave face, keep his wits about him.

'Our Emperor is minded to make no other changes for now among the governors of the North.'

Hollow with relief – Zeus Protector, he still had his offices – Timesitheus was not going to let it show.

'Commanders will be assigned to vacant units at the next meeting of the council.'

The Armenian and Parthian mounted bowmen, the British infantry and the Cataphract horsemen; cousin Modestus might not make too bad a mess as Prefect of one of them. Timesitheus began wondering how he might bring it about. He had always recovered fast.

Vopiscus waved for a Senator with his hand up to speak.

'While we fight on the Rhine, the province of Dacia holds the key to the Danube.'

The intervention came from one of the standing council, but was unexpected. Smooth and oiled, Vulcatius Terentianus had made a career out of quietism. He had never been known to strike out against the current, never to utter his real opinions, certainly never to stake anything on the truth. Who had put him up to this?

'With the armies of the provinces of the Pannonias and the Moesias stripped to provide detachments to the field army, Dacia becomes the bulwark which must hold the barbarians north of the river. The Sarmatians and the Goths will press hard. Other tribes will join them. It will demand much of the man who opposes them. Julius Licinianus is a man of proven ability and loyalty. But he was Consul many years ago. Dacia needs a younger man at the helm.'

Vulcatius' eyes flicked to Domitius. The Prefect of the Camp already had his hand up for permission to speak. It was given.

'The wisdom of years of debating imperial counsel and of profound learning from the records of history inform the words of the noble Consular Vulcatius Terentianus. If I may endorse his proposal from my much lower but practical perspective.'

Gods below, Domitius was an oily, repulsive little reptile. As if anyone could mistake the precious verbosity of this jumped-up member of the vile hoi polloi for the words of a man of culture.

'And if you allow me the further temerity to proffer the names of two men: Licinius Valerian and Saturninus Fidus. Both combine long military experience with civil governance, the decisiveness of youth with the prudence of maturity.'

And both are close with the Gordiani, father and son, who are governing Africa. Timesitheus wondered where the initiative lay; with the senatorial family, or this equestrian's desire to ingratiate? This had to be stopped before it gathered momentum. Hand up, Timesitheus was stepping forward before he knew what he was going to say.

Vopiscus was pointing at him. They were all looking at him. The great, white face and great, grey eyes of the Emperor Maximinus were turned on him.

'The defence of Dacia demands experience. Neither Valerian nor Fidus has commanded an army in the field. Licinianus has fought the Carpi, the Sarmatian Iazyges, and the free Dacians. He is too modest to boast it himself, but the noble Consular Licinianus has yet to be defeated.'

'And the Peukini.' Everyone looked at Maximinus when he spoke. 'The Greek is right. Licinianus is a good leader of men.'

Timesitheus dipped his head, not enough to be a bow. 'Yet your Prefect of the Camp is not altogether mistaken, my Lord. Combining the duties of peaceful administration with leading an army taxes any one man.' Domitius had not said anything of the sort, but that did not matter.

Maximinus grunted assent. 'Civilians always get in the way when you need to fight.'

'To free Licinianus to concentrate on the defence of the frontier, you might appoint a deputy to whom he could delegate the more time-consuming civil affairs, finances especially.' Timesitheus pressed his advantage. 'Quintus Axius

Aelianus has served as Procurator of the imperial treasury in Africa, in Spain and here in the North. He has shown his worth governing Germania Inferior in my absence.'

'Let him be appointed,' Maximinus said.

Behind the Emperor's back, Vopiscus and Catius Clemens exchanged a glance. The latter shrugged almost imperceptibly.

Furious, Domitius did not wait for permission to speak. 'With you and your deputy absent, who will govern your province – your wife?'

Timesitheus counted to five before replying. 'She might not do badly.' He made a little gesture towards Domitius. 'Probably better than some.'

Maximinus looked over his shoulder. A slow grin spread across his face. And everyone laughed, even Vulcatius Terentianus. No one could ever fail to share imperial mirth. After a few seconds, Domitius forced his expression into something like a smile.

Resuming his survey of the empire, Vopiscus turned to the West. The governors of Aquitania in western Gaul and Baetica in southern Spain needed to be replaced. One was ill, and had asked to retire; the other had died. There was nothing suspicious in either case. The provinces were unarmed – just a few auxiliaries – both militarily overlooked by the 7th Legion in Decius' Hispania Tarraconensis, so the new regime could allow debate on the appointments.

One councillor after another urged the merits of a friend or relative. Timesitheus was quiet. He had no one in particular to advance. Anything was possible, but you had to pick your battles. Demurely, he kept his gaze lowered, just glancing up to register each new speaker. Below the modulated voices of the council of imperial friends, from somewhere beyond the hangings, he heard rougher men calling orders. The *silentarii* had been more in control in Alexander's reign. But perhaps their numbers or morale had suffered when their last imperial master was cut down. Insignificance had not saved all the household. Even the glutton had been killed.

Domitius was not talking either. Timesitheus became very aware of the Prefect of the Camp staring at him. His hands hidden in his toga, Timesitheus averted the evil eye; thumb between first and middle finger. He was not superstitious. If they existed, the gods were far away and had no interest in mankind. He did not believe in daemons, ghosts, werewolves or bloodsucking *lamia*. But it was as well to take precautions. Back on Corcyra, his old nurse had told him of certain evil men and women who could focus their envy and malice through their eyes and send out a stream of invisible dust which surrounded and slipped into their victims. Illness, madness – even death – might result. Out beyond the frontiers there were tribes who could kill with a glance. Since then, in his reading and at *symposia* across the empire, he had found grown men of high culture who largely shared the views of the peasant woman who had nursed him.

'Africa, nothing much new out of there.' Vopiscus was into his flow. He no longer needed the amulet, but was making sweeping oratorical gestures. 'Gordian and Capelianus will keep a close eye on each other.' Vopiscus winked, like an actor in a mime.

Timesitheus was already laughing, joining in with everyone else, before his memory supplied the reason for the mirth. Back in the reign of Caracalla – half a lifetime age, long before he entered public life – there had been a scandal. The elder Gordian had been charged with adultery with the wife of Capelianus. Gordian had been guilty, yet he had been acquitted. Gordian's career had been retarded, and Capelianus had divorced his wife. As she had been declared innocent, Capelianus had been cheated of his hopes of hanging on to her dowry and other property. The men had blamed each other for their misfortunes. Now they had ended up as the governors of the neighbouring provinces of Africa Proconsularis and Numidia, and still they detested each other.

Lechery must run in the blood, Timesitheus thought. All the Gordiani were like sparrows, avid for intercourse, and always with women. The son had been servicing the young wife of old Nummius – what was her name? – until he went to be his father's legate in Africa. Old Nummius had been complacent. It was said he had liked to watch, then join them. It was also said her demands had brought about his demise. There were worse ways to go. She was blonde, attractive. What *was* her name?

'Mauretania Caesariensis is another matter.' All humour was gone from the manner of Vopiscus. He had his serious, tragic-actor mask on. 'Orders have been sent for the arrest of the governor. He will be brought here to face charges of treason.'

Simple chronology ruled out sedition. Alexander had been killed eight days before the *ides* of March. Today was the *kalends* of April. Twenty-five days, counting inclusively, as almost everyone did. Not enough time for news of Maximinus' accession to reach Africa, the governor to say or do something seditious, a report to travel to the Rhine and *frumentarii* to be sent to arrest him. Timesitheus knew little about the fallen governor of Mauretania Caesareniensis, but now he knew the man had an enemy among the inner circle around the new Emperor. But who? And why? It could be one of the Senators Flavius Vopiscus or Honoratus, the new Praetorian Prefect Anullinus, one of the other equestrian assassins Quintus Valerius or Ammonius. And, Timesitheus thought, he should not overlook Catius Clemens; being the brother of his friend did not preclude a murderous vindictiveness. There again, it could be another who had not yet shown his hand. It could be Maximinus himself.

Domitius was speaking. 'Vitalianus has served the

traditional equestrian career with distinction. He commanded an auxiliary cohort in Britain, was a legionary tribune with the 3rd Augustan in Africa, the Prefect of a cavalry unit here on the Rhine, and a Procurator of imperial finances in Cyrenaica. For the last four years he has commanded the Moorish cavalry, leading them through the difficult fighting of the Persian campaign. Twice in Africa, a proven military man, accustomed to the ways of the Moors; there could be no better candidate for the governorship of Mauretania Caesariensis.'

Several hands went up. Maximinus nodded towards Timesitheus.

'There is no doubt Vitalianus is a fine soldier, and there are always brigands to catch and a few barbarian raiders to chase. But Mauretania Caesariensis is not the scene of a war. The wider protection of the African frontier is in the hands of Capelianus and his 3rd Legion in Numidia. Peaceful provinces, like Mauretania Caesariensis, call for different expertise and experience.'

The eyes of Maximinus were as blank and as watchful as those of a big cat. Timesitheus ploughed on.

'Gaius Attius Alcimus Felicianus has commanded troops, but most of his life has been devoted to serving the *Res Publica* in civil capacities. He has been an advocate of the imperial treasury, run the Transpadane poor-relief and been a Procurator in all the four Gallic provinces. For the last two years he has been in charge of the inheritance tax. As you know, he cleaned out an Augean stable of corruption, and again monies flow unimpeded into the military treasury. Without his work, this field army would be an impossibility. Loyal and industrious, the next step for him must be a province.'

As he stopped, Timesitheus felt a coolness emanating from the throne. Certainly, a bureaucrat like Alcimus Felicianus

95

was not obviously going to appeal to an Emperor risen from the barracks.

'You have never been in either of the provinces of Mauretania?' Maximinus did not pause for an answer. 'Before I was Prefect of Egypt, I governed Mauretania Tingitana. The high country runs for hundreds of miles through Caesariensis; good for sheep and bandits, and beyond are the Atlas Mountains and the nomads. Endless tribes of nomads: the Baquates, the Macenites, the Melanogaitouloi, the Quinquegentiani – long, uncouth names; violent, uncouth men. Their chiefs come to the negotiating table at the point of a sword. Peace comes after the stench and horror of massacre.'

Maximinus' voice had thickened. He stopped talking, his gaze far away, as if on old, unhappy sights. No one spoke. On its low altar, the sacred fire ticked.

A metallic crash. Somewhere beyond the hangings someone had dropped something. Maximinus came back from wherever he had been. He rallied, spoke almost conversationally. 'So you are wrong, little Greek, there is much marching and fighting and talking to barbarians to be done in the Mauretanias. Legal advocacy, knowledge of the laws concerning wills or poor children; they are less use there than a good seat on a horse and a strong right arm. Let the soldier, Vitalianus, be appointed.'

Timesitheus nodded; it could be taken for nothing but a bow. Fuck! How had he forgotten? Of course Maximinus had campaigned in Mauretania; the stupid, bloodthirsty barbarian would have started a war in the Elysian Fields. Fuck.

Domitius was smirking at him. A space seemed to have opened around him, around the object of imperial rebuke. Even his brainless cousin was giving him a strange look. Probably, Modestus was trying to remember where he had heard the phrase 'Augean stable'.

Vopiscus had now moved on to the East. The Prefect of

Egypt was a creature of the late tyrant's mother. No one should profit from vice. Another equestrian officer was en route to arrest him, and take control of Egypt.

Timesitheus was so angry, he could scarcely listen. *Little Greek*. It was bad enough when Romans called a Hellene a *Greek*, let alone a *Graeculus*. And here was this hulking, ugly Thracian barbarian calling him *little Greek*; calling him *Graeculus*, in front of the entire imperial counsel. *Graeculus* – one step up from *Boy*. And a Thracian saying it! Maximinus probably had ancestral tattoos hidden under that toga. It was a wonder he did not file his teeth into points.

Like any upper-class Hellene, Timesitheus saw all Thracians through the smoke of the sack of Mycalessus in Thucydides. Once read at school, the passage could never be forgotten. It was just after dawn, the citizens of the small Boeotian town innocently stirring, when the Thracians burst in through the open gates. There was confusion on all sides, and death in every shape and form. They cut down everyone; the women and the old alike, the farm animals, every living thing. The children had taken refuge in a school building. The Thracians broke in and killed every one of them.

Domitius was still smirking at him. You little fucker, Timesitheus thought. One day I will lead you out for execution. Not the clean blow of a sword for you. I will have you nailed up on a cross like a slave, or killed the ancient way, stripped and hooded, bound to a barren tree and scourged until your backbone shows through the flesh, or thrown down on the floor of the arena, mauled by the beasts amid your own filth and fear.

The tramp of many feet could be heard behind the curtains, like a herd of clumsy servants. Vopiscus had stopped talking. Timesitheus had half heard him announce that Crispinus would move to Achaea, and Pomponius Julianus replace him in Syria Phoenice; all other eastern governors were to remain in place. It took him a moment to realize the import: his friend Priscus still held Mesopotamia.

Maximinus rose from the throne. Anullinus closed up beside him. Anullinus drew his sword. Everyone else looked at each other.

'Now!' Maximinus called.

On all sides hangings were pulled back. The heads of the counsellors swung in all directions. Everywhere the gleam of armour, the nod of plumes, as the Praetorians filed in and surrounded the *consilium*.

Annealed in the fires of imperial politics, none of the counsellors cracked. Timesitheus saw the hands of one or two go to the special rings many Senators wore; the rings which contained poison. Vopiscus was clutching his amulet. He and Catius Celer looked at each other, each probing the other for betrayal. Timesitheus arranged his face.

'War is a hard master,' Maximinus said. 'We must advance to the Ocean, or the Germans will take Rome. It is a war to the death. On one side civilization, on the other darkness. Everything must be sacrificed to bring victory. There is no time for the luxuries of peace, no time for endless talk. Everything in the empire must be subject to military discipline.'

Maximinus turned to the standing board of sixteen. 'The *Res Publica* is grateful to you. Conscript Fathers, we detain you no longer.'

Timesitheus watched the good and the great, the possessors of famous names and the designers of beautiful careers. Some could not hide their shock and anger; the eyes of Petronius Magnus bulged with fury, and the effeminate Claudius Severus was almost spitting. Others, like the unctuous Vulcatius Terentianus, appeared relieved still to be alive. The rotund Claudius Venacus blinked as if unsure what was happening.

With unconscious cruelty, the Praetorians gave the

dismissed councillors time – one by one – to gabble their thanks, before driving them from the imperial presence.

Now, that was interesting. Timesitheus watched them leave. Sixteen rich, influential men, all thoroughly alienated and full of resentment; now, that could be useful to someone.

Flavius Vopiscus and Catius Celer were still staring at each other.

Well, well, Timesitheus thought, neither of you saw that coming. Your little Thracian is not as tame as you thought.

CHAPTER 7

Rome

The Subura,

Seven Days after the Ides of April, AD235

It was not yet dawn. The meeting was over. The owner of the house quietly unbolted the door, looked up and down the narrow street and gestured for the die-cutter to leave first. No further farewell passed between any of them.

Outside, it was still near dark. The die-cutter did not carry a torch. His vision was not good, anyway, beyond a few paces. As far as he could tell, the street was deserted. Hefting the bag with his tools, and his staff, he set off south. His footsteps came back loud from the blank walls. He tried to walk normally; not too fast, not too slow. The bag banged against his leg. The staff clicked on the pavement. The walls were tall, close around him. He had done this before, many times. It did not get any easier. He fought down the urge to run.

Now and then he looked over his shoulder. He did not expect to be able to see anyone, but alone at night in this district not to look around would have been suspicious. He had no particular fear of robbers. He had been born here in the Subura, knew its ways. It was too late for all but the most desperate of the prostitutes and their clients, and thus for the men who preyed on them. Although he himself had renounced violence, more than a year ago, he knew that conversion had yet to impress itself on his looks or demeanour. And he carried a big stick and had a long knife at his belt. It was not the threat of local knife-men that was making his heart pound and his palms slick with sweat.

It had been over a year. He had been lucky. They had all been lucky. They had been careful, taken every precaution, and they had prayed. Yet somehow he knew it could not last. Someone – most likely someone close to them, a neighbour, a friend – perhaps worse still a relative or one of their own – would denounce them. There would be no warning. One morning the men who the die-cutter feared would be waiting in the dark. He would not see them until it was too late, and then no weapon, no resource of character or body would save him.

The sky was lightening. There was woodsmoke in the air. He heard the first homely noises of the new day: voices muffled behind shutters, boots clumping on stairs, a child crying. Doors were thrown open, and the life of the Subura again spilled out on to the streets. Blacksmiths, cobblers, workers in wool or linen, rag-pickers, fullers and barmen; all sorts of men called back to their women, and, almost rubbing shoulders in the narrow confines, greeted each other. Once again the die-cutter was one among many, just another of the *plebs urbana* jostling his way through the slums of the Subura. He had survived another dawn. He was safe for another day.

The great featureless wall at the rear of the Forum of Augustus reared up in front of him, and he turned left into the street of the sandal-makers. As his fears receded, they were replaced by the mundane matters of the coming day. At the third hour he had to report to the magistrates who ran the mint. Acilius Glabrio, Valerius Poplicola and Toxotius were like all the boards of the *Tresviri Monetales* under which he had served – rich, arrogant, thoughtless young men blinded by their own wealth and position. Perhaps the first two were even worse than most; the style of their hair and their perfume hinted at unnatural vices. The writing was on the wall for their sort. Until the day of reckoning, the die-cutter would obey their commands, remain beneath their notice and stomach their disdain.

He glimpsed the shaded flower beds and hedges of the Temple of Peace through the gate on his right. High on the brow of the hill to his left the sun struck the roofs of the beautiful mansions of the Carinae. Swallows swooped and banked up there in the clear light. His mood lifted. He liked this street. It was broad and clean. The bookshops were opening. There had not been a sandal-maker here in living memory. The first bearded intellectuals were nosing about. Roughly barbered philosophers glowered disapproval at elegantly clad sophists. The latter moved languidly, trailed by wealthy students and an air of urbane success. The lone young men with dark circles under their eyes were probably poets. Almost everyone clutched a papyrus roll, the universal badge of culture.

The die-cutter yawned. It was early. There was plenty of time. He would treat himself to breakfast. It would be another long day. The food and drink would sustain him. By the statue of Apollo Sandaliarius he went into an eating-house called The Lyre. The owner, clad in the high-belted leather tunic of his profession, greeted him and took his order. There were only two other customers; draymen talking sleepily in a corner. The die-cutter took a seat at a table on his own.

Waiting, he ran his hand over his bag, felt the reassuring shapes of the carefully wrapped tools: the three different drills, his cutters, the burin and the graver, the tongs and pincers, the files, the compass and the pouch of powdered corundum. He knew he was good at his work. It was the one place where, far from being a handicap, his myopia became an advantage. Not for him the cunningly angled lenses, the peering through glass bowls filled with water. It was as if his eyes were designed for nothing but the closest, finest work.

The owner brought him bread and cheese, and warm watered wine. The die-cutter thanked him and began to eat.

It was not just technical virtuosity. Pride might be a sin, but he knew he was blessed with talent. For years he had interpreted the vaguest of instructions. Often, they were so vague he suspected they were meaningless to the aspiring young politicians who issued them. All those ignorant youths wanted was to offer up to the Emperor an image of his own majesty which might appeal should the man on the throne ever chance to view it. In their dreams such exalted approval translated into their own rapid elevation: a Quaestorship as one of Caesar's candidates: then a Praetorship before the minimum age; a rich province to follow; at the summit a Consulship and its spurious immortality, all gold and purple, the tawdry glories of this world. From such pedestrian and self-serving concepts, and with recalcitrant physical materials, the die-cutter created art.

With this initial issue of coins, it had quickly become apparent that Acilius Glabrio, Valerius Poplicola and Toxotius had no more idea than the die-cutter himself what might be the virtues, aims, interests or religious sympathies of this new Emperor. He was an equestrian army officer from Thrace. From the way they spoke, neither of these things recommended him in the eyes of the young noblemen. Beyond that, Maximinus Augustus was a complete mystery. None of them could remember meeting him, and not one of them had the faintest clue what he looked like.

Given all of which, the die-cutter considered that he had made a fine portrait. Maximinus in profile gazed off to the viewer's right. Neither too old, nor too young, the Emperor was in vigorous maturity. His hair was short, and he wore a wreath. The latter was a safer choice than the radiate crown, which some saw as the Emperor placing himself too close to God, possibly demanding worship, and thus was indicative of *hubris*. The jaw line was strong and clean-shaven. A beard could be good, hinting at the manly virtues of the old Republic, but if too elaborate it might evoke thoughts of soft, ineffectual Greeks, and if too short of brutish soldiers. The die-cutter had given Maximinus an aquiline nose and had tried to get something of the keen intelligence of Julius Caesar about the eyes. Surely no ruler could object to any of that.

He had made just the one obverse for the other die-cutters to follow. Given the greater stresses put on them in the minting process, already he had created no fewer than five different reverse dies. The guidance of the *Tresviri Monetales* had been less than useless here. 'The usual sorts of things,' Acilius Glabrio had said, as if the subject bored him. The die-cutter had given it some thought. The first one he did had the Emperor between two military standards; after all, he had come from the army. After that, two imperial virtues, *Victoria* and *Pax Augusti*; in the Roman view the latter was always dependent on the former. Then *Liberalitas*; a safe bet, as a hand-out followed an accession as night follows day. Finally, *Votis Decennalibus*; everyone, including the die-cutter himself, had already taken vows for the safety of the new Emperor over the next ten years.

These initial reverse types were well chosen. There was nothing innovative. They played to traditional tastes. Yet the die-cutter knew they would win no praise from those set over him. Either the *Monetales* would appropriate them as their own, or they would quibble and claim others would have been better. The day of reckoning could not come too fast.

The die-cutter jumped as a hand descended on his shoulder.

'Guilty conscience?' Castricius sat down next to him.

'You young fool, I nearly shat myself.'

'Incontinent as well as blind and deaf – things are almost all over for you.' When Castricius smiled, odd, angular lines ran across his thin, pointed face.

The die-cutter could not stop himself smiling back.

Castricius called for unwatered wine.

There was no doubt that Castricius was a bad person. He claimed to be from a good family in Gaul and to have had sound reasons to run away from the tutor who had brought him to Rome. His accent and manners seemed to support the story but, true or not, he had settled with alarming ease into the life of a cut-purse in the Subura. Yet, despite it all, the die-cutter could not help but like his young neighbour.

'You are up early.'

'No, up late.' Castricius took a drink. 'This will help me sleep. Not that it should be a problem. Yesterday I went up to the Carinae to look at the women. Gods, what I would do to one of those rich bitches. Anyway, having made myself horribly priapic, I went down to visit Caenis. She wore me out; said it was good to have a young man between her legs instead of your old, shrivelled carcass.'

The die-cutter felt his affection for the young Gaul turn to anger. It was irrational. Castricius was not to blame. It was his own weakness. Caenis was a whore who lived in the same tenement block as them. The die-cutter had been her client for years. He had changed much in his life, but he had been unable to change that. Even now he felt his prick stir as he thought of her body. He lacked self-control. Now she was in his mind, he knew he would be unable to stop himself going to her tonight. He was a weak man.

The die-cutter got up. He gripped his bag of tools, like a man seeking certainty.

'Sleep well. I am going to the mint.'

His fears had receded, but, as the die-cutter stepped out into the sunshine, he could not help glancing up and down the street, checking every man loitering in a doorway. You could trust no one. Certainly not Castricius.

CHAPTER 8

Africa
The City of Hadrumetum,

Eight Days after the Ides of April, AD235

The curtains were drawn back to catch the breeze in the room designated for the court. Gordian looked at the others on the tribunal. His father, presiding as judge, was beginning to look his age. He still had a full head of hair, unlike Gordian himself. It had been silver for years, but now the face below was drawn, the cheeks sunken, the eyes rheumy yet somehow staring. There was a tremor in the elder's voice and hand. It saddened Gordian, both for itself and for what it implied about his own mortality. He regarded the other assessors. Serenus Sammonicus, his old tutor, was elderly like his father. Valerian, Sabinianus, Arrian and the local Mauricius were of an age with himself; men in their forties, either in the prime of life or halfway towards death, depending on your view-point. Only Menophilus, the Quaestor, was younger, still in his late twenties. Not one of them, not even the two patrician Cercopes, looked as bored as Gordian felt.

The villa commanded a fine view of the harbour of

Hadrumetum. Inside the jetties the water rippled gently, flashing in the sun. A gang of men were loading amphorae on to a big cargo vessel. They wore loincloths and their bodies glistened with sweat. An overseer dabbed at his face with a handkerchief. The olive oil was destined for the tables, lamps and perfume bottles of Rome. It had been centuries since the eternal city had been able to feed herself from her Italian hinterlands. All the staples – grain and wine as well as oil – had to be imported. Every year, vast quantities were shipped from Egypt, but the majority was sent from Africa. Long ago, in the reign of Claudius, a governor of Africa had cut off the supply when he made his bid for the throne. In those days, the Proconsul had still commanded the 3rd Legion, and he had raised another legion. None of it had done him any good.

A line of moored fishing boats formed a contrast to the relentless activity around the merchantman. They would have been out the previous night, but now, with their weath-ered paint, rough tarpaulins and piles of sand-coloured nets, they looked abandoned. Beyond them, at the end of one of the moles, a group of young boys sprawled on the rocks of the breakwater. When the mood took them, they would stand and dive into the water. Laughing, they would climb out, shake themselves and lie down again to let the sun dry their brown, naked bodies. They were poor, but they were free. Gordian wished he was back in Ad Palmam.

His plan had worked. The nomads guarding the camp had been so engrossed in the assault on the oasis that they had failed to notice the approach of Menophilus with the 15th Cohort. They had broken at the first contact. Their panic had spread to the animal holders, and from them had infected those fighting in the trees and at the gate of the citadel. Pell-mell, they had fled south. Most had got away. Apart from Nuffuzi's son, there had been only about twenty captured, almost all of them wounded. No more than thirty bodies were found. There had been no pursuit. The 15th Cohort was on foot, and the horsemen with Gordian in the settlement had been handled too hard to be sent out. It would have made little difference. Nuffuzi had managed to keep a grip on many of those around him, and had screened the rout.

Gordian had remained at the oasis for five days. To win back self-respect for himself and his men, Aemilius Severinus had sent his Wolves patrolling south. They had ridden far beyond Thusuros and Castellum Nepitana, far out into the desert, but had encountered nothing except the carcasses of horses and camels. The other troops had buried the dead and tended the wounded. Despite the intensity of the fighting, there were not many of either, no more than forty all told, the majority *speculatores*, and at least twenty would return to the ranks. A caravan had been organized to take the freed captives back north to their homes. The plunder had been divided among the men. The complications of restoring it to its original owners were prohibitive, and soldiers need an incentive to fight. On the fourth day, those nomad prisoners able to march had set off under the guard of the 15th Cohort to its base at Ammaedara. Along with Nuffuzi's son, who Gordian had kept in his entourage, they should make useful bargaining counters in the diplomacy which inevitably would follow. The remainder – seven of them – were killed.

With the governor's horse guards and the African irregulars, Gordian had returned via Capsa, Thelepte and Cillium. He had halted for two days at Vicus Augusti, just short of Hadrumetum. Men and horses had needed a rest. He had paid a courtesy visit to the villa of Sulpicia Memmia just outside the little town. The Emperor Alexander had divorced her, but it was not unknown for the fortunes of such eminent exiles to revive. The short sojourn had given time for news of the victors' arrival to proceed them to Hadrumetum, and for a suitable reception to be arranged. While he set little store on such things, the men appreciated them. As it transpired, the attention was not disagreeable.

'Name? Race? Free or slave?'

The principals in the next case had been ushered in. The court had heard one already; a tedious dispute between two smallholders about an inheritance. The younger Gordian judged the position of the sun. Only mid-morning – at least three hours until the recess for lunch – and after that they would be confined in legal wrangling again until dusk. Thank the gods it was April. They had reached Hadrumetum in the middle of the Cerialia. There were just eight days between it ending and the beginning of the *Ludi Florales*, and three of those were given over to briefer festivals. This was the first of only five days when the governor could give justice until well into May.

The plaintiffs were a bunch of tenants from an estate owned by the Emperor. Gordian watched them make their offerings of a pinch of incense to the Emperor and the traditional gods. Their tunics were patched, but they were clean, and their hands and faces scrubbed.

The man they were accusing was an unctuous-looking Procurator who ran the estate. Clad in a toga with the narrow purple stripe of an equestrian, he was doing his best to appear unconcerned, as if their accusations were beneath him, barely worth answering.

The tenants seemed overawed, their spokesman as much as any. Nevertheless, when the water-clock was turned, he managed to get underway.

'We are simple men, workers in the fields. We were born and raised on the Emperor's estate, and we ask, in the name of the most sacred Emperor, that you succour us.'

As he realized that he would be given a hearing, he gained in confidence.

'In accordance with the laws of the divine Hadrian, we

owe the home farm not more than six days of work each year, two ploughing, two cultivating and two harvesting. This we have always done, with joy in our hearts, as our fathers did before us, and their fathers before them.'

The Procurator gave up inspecting his nails and, delicately, with one finger, adjusted his hair.

'In the past more has been demanded of us by false reckoning. But last year the Procurator dragged us off so often that our own fields went untended. Our crops went unharvested and rotted ungathered. When I complained, he had soldiers seize me. On his command, they stripped and beat me, as if I were a slave and not a Roman citizen. Marcus and Titus here suffered the same shameful treatment.'

The others in the deputation murmured their agreement.

The Procurator shot them a look of contempt, tinged with menace.

The speaker, his blood up now, ignored him and moved on to detail many more instances of ill treatment and brutality.

Gordian's thoughts drifted off to the festivals. The *Cerialia*, with its meagre offerings of spelt and salt, its priggish emphasis on purity and its fasting until a sparse meal at star rise, had never held much appeal. And the strange ritual on the final day was thoroughly uncongenial. He was always saddened watching the fox run and twist in its doomed attempt to escape the burning torch tied to its tail. On the other hand, he was looking forward to the *Ludi Florales*. Six days and nights of fine clothes and lights, drinking and love. The prostitutes slowly, teasingly, revealing their charms for all to see in the theatre. He remembered how Parthenope and Chione had welcomed him back from the victory at the oasis; their dark hair and dark eyes, their olive skin sliding against him, against each other, their fingers and tongues pleasuring each other, stroking and opening, pulling him into them.

Epicurus had said that if you take away the chance to see

and talk and spend time with the object of your passion, the desire for sex is dissolved. But he also held that no pleasure is a bad thing in itself. Some desires are natural and necessary. Gordian could not imagine anything more natural and necessary than the pleasures of the bed, especially if you owned two girls like Parthenope and Chione.

The Procurator took the floor.

Gordian had no desire to listen to the string of denials that would follow. No doubt, respectable-seeming witnesses would be produced to appear in support. The side with better connections and greater money always produced more of them. Gordian was already reasonably sure the Procurator was guilty.

What was he doing here? *Live out of the public eye*, the sage had said. An Epicurean should not engage in public business, unless something intervened. All his life, something had intervened. Gordian looked at his father. The elder Gordian's ambitions for his son, his love for his father: both had been constants. Now his father was old and was governing a major province. If Gordian did not take some of the burden, he would be tormented with guilt. To help his father was also to help himself. It was the right thing to do. Gordian bent his mind to the proceedings.

The Procurator opened his defence with a flourish. All men of education were brought up knowing bucolic poetry.

That was a conceit, Gordian thought, which neatly excluded the rustic plaintiffs and was intended to forge some link between the defendant and those on the tribunal. He looked at his father and the other assessors. Their faces gave away no more than did his own.

The *Eclogues* and *Georgics* of Virgil showed a world of innocence and honesty, the Procurator said. Old men of antique virtue were bent and gnarled by their life-long labours. Young shepherds played the pipes as they chastely wooed virginal shepherdesses. The visitor found homespun hospitality and wisdom on offer at every humble hearth.

So far, so good – the Procurator appeared to be enjoying his own performance – but men who combined an active life with that of culture, men who accepted their duties towards their estates and towards the *Res Publica*, men who actually ventured into the countryside, knew different. There they found rough, uncouth accents and manners. Worse, they found squalid indolence and base superstition. Unguided by philosophy or any higher culture, the hairy locals learnt to lie as they took their mother's milk. Untrammelled by compassion, they regarded violence and force as the ultimate argument. Who had not heard the saying *Make your will before you venture down a country lane*?

After the Procurator's litany of rustic iniquity ended, three witnesses swore to his innocence. Finally, the elder Gordian ordered the principals to withdraw and asked the advice of his assessors.

Mauricius launched into an extempore oration of his own. His family was as old as any in Africa, descended both from local landowners and Roman colonists. For generations they had bred too many children. Equal inheritance had reduced them to poverty. He himself had been left just one small field by his father. At first he had worked it with his own hands. He had rented other fields, hired men. Gradually, by backbreaking labour, and the favour of the gods, he had rebuilt his family fortunes. Now he owned wide estates and sat on the city councils at Thysdrus and here at Hadrumetum. He offered his own life as evidence that poverty did not have to drive out honesty and virtue.

More relevant to the case in hand, Menophilus pointed out that the tenants had much to lose by bringing the case. If they lost, they had laid themselves open to the reprisals of the Procurator and his friends. All they were asking for was what the law should already give them.

One by one, Gordian included, the assessors agreed this was true.

Those involved were brought back into the court.

'In the name of our sacred Emperor Gaius Iulius Verus Maximinus, and by the powers vested in me as Proconsul of Africa, I find the complaint upheld. Let the plaintiffs erect an inscription on stone setting out this judgement and the laws of the divine Hadrian. Let no one in future demand more of them than the laws allow, and let no one offer them violence or oppression.'

The Procurator bridled. 'These rustics are liars. Avoiding the duties they owe to the Emperor is tantamount to treason. Supporting them runs the risk of the same charge. As part of my duties, I am in regular correspondence with the sacred court.'

There was a silence in the courtroom.

'You think the Emperor would value your word above mine?' There was no tremor in the elder Gordian's voice.

On an instant, the Procurator capitulated. No, no, nothing of the sort. Indeed he was sure the noble Proconsul was right. Some of his own agents may have been over-zealous in the interests of the sacred Maximinus. He would see it never happened again.

In the interests of the sacred Maximinus. The irony of the phrase struck Gordian. They had fought the battle of Ad Palmam in the name of Alexander, not knowing that the Emperor was already dead and mutilated. One Emperor died; another took the throne. The governance of the empire continued. It was unlikely this Maximinus would affect them much out here in Africa.

CHAPTER 9

The Northern Frontier
A Camp outside Mogontiacum,

Eleven Days before the Kalends of May, AD235

When they had spread the food and blankets, Timesitheus sent the servants away. No one's loyalty was infinite.

They reclined in the shade of an apple tree: Timesitheus, his wife, Tranquillina, and the two disaffected Senators. Eleven days before the *kalends* of May, and even here, at long last, spring had arrived. The sun shone, and the first blossom was on the boughs above their heads. They ate and talked, ostensibly at their ease. Of course, there was no ignoring the activity down at the river. And, Timesitheus thought, the Senators must have been wondering why they had been invited to this outdoor midday meal. His own wheel was very much in the ascendant; theirs on a downward turn.

The noise rolled up the slope: shouts of encouragement, jeers and catcalls, the squeal of wood on wood, the rhythmic ring of hammer on anvil, the deeper thump of a pile-driver and, intermittently over it all, stentorian voices of authority. Down there, all was movement and bustle. Teams of horses dragged big baulks of timber down to the riverbank. Mobile sawmills cut and trimmed them. Gangs of men unloaded huge cables from wagons. Smoke curled up from the forges. Out on the water, the sixth boat was being manoeuvred towards the pontoon bridge. It was guided from a rowing skiff upstream; the men let it drift down. When it reached the right place, a big pyramid-shaped bag of stones was heaved over its prow to act as an anchor. At the same instant ropes snaked out, and in moments the new addition was lashed in place at just the correct interval. Timbers already connected the next one into the rest of the bridge. On those closer to the land, these beams had been decked over, and screens erected on either side.

About twenty yards upstream from the bridge the first breakwater showed above the surface. It consisted of three stout stakes. Iron clamps held it together, making an arrowhead facing into the flow of the water. The raft bearing the pile-driver was moored where the second breakwater would stand. Timesitheus let his gaze linger on the men working the pulleys. Inch by inch, the massive plug of iron was pulled up its curved wooden runner. The order to halt carried clearly to his ears. Another command, a lever thrown, and – oddly noiseless at that distance – the weight fell. The sound of the impact lagged behind its viewing. As the men bent to their task and the lump of shaped metal began another ascent, the great stake it had hit could be seen to have been driven at least three feet further down into the muddy bed of the Rhine.

'Your bridge is most impressive.' Marcus Claudius Venacus was of middle height, corpulent. If he was intelligent, his face did him a disservice. However, Maximinus' abolition of the standing committee, among whose sixteen Senators Venacus had served, appeared to have done nothing to diminish his self-regard.

'Your energy puts all of us to shame.' Although somewhat protruding, Caius Petronius Magnus' eyes promised rather more intelligence than those of Venacus. Yet that did not pledge much, and Magnus had been unable to conceal how badly he had taken the end of their official position. 'I do not know how you have found time to add the many duties of Prefect of Works to those involved in collecting all the supplies for the expedition. You seem overburdened, while others remain in enforced inactivity.'

Timesitheus smiled. 'The labour is long and hard, but that makes intervals of leisure like this, snatched moments with such pleasant company, all the more enjoyable.'

Both Senators murmured politely.

Timesitheus gave Venacus his most winning smile. 'But you are over-appreciative of my efforts.' Timesitheus pointed off upriver, where a line of unconnected piles of masonry crossed the stream. 'If we had been making something to last, something worthy of Rome, we should have rebuilt the super-structure of the old bridge of Trajan. Or, at least, we could have copied Julius Caesar and made a proper, well-fixed wooden bridge. But Maximinus Augustus said time and money were against such plans. My bridge is not built to last.'

And Maximinus had called him *Graeculus*. And, once again, it had been in public. How dare the big Thracian barbarian call him *little Greek*. Timesitheus felt the tightness in his chest. No point shying away now. If he did, Tranquillina would hold him in contempt.

'Yet perhaps its ephemeral nature might prove its greatest virtue. Should circumstances demand, I could dismantle it in a matter of hours. It reminds me of the bridge of Darius in Herodotus. The one the Scythians tried to persuade the Ionian guards to demolish, leaving Darius and his army trapped on the other side. How did their argument go? *Men of Ionia, the gift we have to bring you is freedom from slavery, if you follow our advice.* Something on those lines.'

No one spoke. The eyes of both Senators were fixed on

him. In those of Venacus was a look which might be growing comprehension. Magnus' were bulging out like those of a lobster.

'Men, you are always the same,' Tranquillina said. 'You never think of the things done by women. If Agrippina had not stood on the bridge over this very river and stopped the soldiers from dismantling it, her husband Germanicus would have been left at the mercy of the barbarians.'

Timesitheus looked at his wife. Approaching twenty-four, she was short, but slender. Her skin as white as marble, her eyes and hair so very black. He knew she had not married him because she loved him or found him attractive in any way. But he loved her, and he hoped – he would have prayed, had there been gods to hear – that over the eight years of their marriage he had inspired more than an iota of affection. Certainly, this daughter of a decayed senatorial family had invested much in the career of her equestrian husband. Nothing was going to stop her raising him to the heights, perhaps to the Palatine, or to Olympus itself.

'You think it could come to that?' Magnus put the question to Timesitheus, but his eyes flicked back to Tranquillina.

Timesitheus paused, and arranged his face. Gravity, serious consideration and a certain reluctance, perhaps even sadness, were the intended evocations.

'The expedition proposes to go further than any for centuries, into the far North, to the ocean. Varus did not come back from there. If the bridge had been cut, nor would have Germanicus. There is nothing but forest and marsh up there. It is the worst terrain for our armies. The German warriors are at their most dangerous in that environment. There are many of them. With their backs to the ocean they will have nothing to lose. They will fight to the death.'

Timesitheus could feel his fear rising, could feel the wet breath of the rodent in his ears.

'It is my duty to Rome to be ready to sever the bridge. If that means stranding some Romans north of the river . . . '

The scrabbling of the rat's claws were loud in his head. He wanted to scream. He spoke slowly, with normality.

'That is my duty as an equestrian. Those of a higher rank should be ready for a more onerous duty. Rome cannot abide without an Emperor.'

'"Ready"?' Magnus said.

'The regalia must be ready,' Tranquillina said. 'Remember, under Alexander, how those pretenders in the East made fools of themselves, undermined their already slim chances, by having to steal purple cloaks off the backs of the statues of the gods, cobble together sceptres and scrabble around to find things that looked like a throne. What were their names?'

'One was Taurinus, I am sure of it,' Venacus said.

'Coins,' Timesitheus said. 'A smooth transmission of power demands a plentiful supply of coins.'

'Or was it Raurinus?' There was a sheen of sweat on Venacus' upper lip. The others continued to ignore him.

'The man in charge of the finances of three provinces and of the supplies to the field army has access to vast sums of money,' Magnus said.

Timesitheus nodded in agreement. 'The coins must bear the head of the new Emperor.'

'No – Taurinus; one was definitely called Taurinus.' The moon face of Venacus turned from one to the other, as if willing them to talk about anything else.

Timesitheus smiled urbanely at the frightened Senator but paid no attention to his words. 'Coins of the previous regime can be over-struck with new images easily. A competent blacksmith could produce thousands in a day. What takes time is cutting the new dies – although any competent forger could do the work. In the course of raising contributions for the war effort, one was denounced to me recently.

121

His neighbour informed against him; people can be very heartless. I have not had the forger arrested yet. He lives here in Mogontiacum.'

Tranquillina smiled. 'Perhaps that is enough for now. We do not want to arouse suspicion; have anyone inform against us. We should talk of other things.' She waved for the servants.

'Do you want to see me?'

'Yes,' Timesitheus said.

'Perhaps you deserve a reward.'

She was wearing just a tunic. Slowly, Tranquillina pulled it off her shoulders, and down. She bared her breasts. Then, laughing, suddenly pulled the flimsy garment back up.

'More.'

'That was enough for Helen to stop her cuckolded husband killing her.'

'Is that a novel way of breaking the news of some infidelity?'

Tranquillina pulled a face. Her hands went to the hem of the tunic. Teasingly, like a whore at the *Floralia*, she lifted it, up over her white thighs, until it was above her waist.

'Come here,' he said.

Instead of moving, she let go of the hem and her hands went to the neck of the tunic. She shrugged and wriggled it off, until it lay puddled around her feet.

The lamp was lit in the bedchamber. She was naked. No respectable wife, no woman with any claim to virtue, let her husband see her naked. Not after the wedding night. He felt a surge of lust, tinged with what might have been fear, or even repulsion.

She came over to him, pressed herself against him.

'What would I do without you?' he said.

'Probably herd goats.' She reached down between them, feeling his stiff prick through his breeches.

'My family have never been goatherds.'

'Then you would be an unheard-of equestrian officer commanding some obscure unit in the middle of nowhere.'

She disengaged herself and climbed on the bed, leaning back on her elbows.

He went to join her. She stopped him, told him exactly what she wanted him to do.

Knowing he looked a fool, he hopped around the bedroom, tangled in his breeches in his hurry to get out of his clothes. Gods below, what if someone found out? What if a servant was spying? No doubt they would talk. The shame of it – all self-respect, all dignity gone – he would be ridiculed, a laughing stock for the rest of his life.

From between her thighs, his face near her cunt, he looked up. 'I might die without you.'

'I am sure of it,' she said. 'Now, do what I told you.'

CHAPTER 10

The Northern Frontier
The Town of Mogontiacum,

Four Days before the Kalends of May, AD235

About the tenth hour of the night, a raft of black cloud came up from the west. As the first drops pattered down, Maximinus wondered what it would be like to be a fish looking up at the hull of a great ship, at something huge, alien and inexplicable. The rain increased, falling hard on the roofs of Mogontiacum. It sluiced through gutters, and gushed out from spouts down into the street, where it shifted then floated away the rubbish lying in the central drain. Although sheltered under a porch, Maximinus pulled the hood of his canvas cloak further over his face. He was tired. His mind wandered to the fable of the frogs who asked Zeus for a new king. When he sent them a water snake, they regretted their disloyalty to the log that had previously ruled them.

More suddenly than it had started, the rain stopped. Maximinus peered out from his place of concealment. No light or sound escaped from the blank wall of the house across the street. But he knew the conspirators were in there.

Maximinus stepped back into the darkness where the four of them sheltered. His bodyguard, Micca, and Volo, the head of the *frumentarii*, flanked him. The fourth man stood at the rear. Water dripped down in front of them from the eaves. They did not speak.

The treachery galled him. Long ago, the senators of Rome had been men of virtue. They had lived simple lives, summoned from the plough to fight great wars. But once the terrible enemy Carthage had been burnt, centuries of peace had unmanned them. Their riches and luxury, their fishponds and libraries, their painted whores and simpering catamites – all the revolting eastern practices they had rushed to embrace – had combined to corrupt them. Now, a new enemy threatened. The tribes of the North were marching south, bringing with them fire and sword, untold misery and slaughter, and the senators were found wanting. Worse, they conspired against those men who saw the danger and had the courage to fight. Most high equestrians were little better. Praetorian Prefect after Prefect had proved false. The plot of Plautianus against the divine Severus had failed, but Macrinus the Moor had betrayed that Emperor's son, the brave and doomed Caracalla. There was no faith to be found in the rich of the empire. New blood was needed. Only men untainted by wealth or supposed sophistication could save Rome. Only rough men from the countryside – men who honoured the gods and kept their word – could lead Rome out of the mire of its imported filth and back to the old-fashioned ways of decency and honour.

Maximinus moved forward again. He looked up and down the dark street. Under every portico and in every doorway slumped figures huddled in cloaks against the night and the rain. If their numbers were not noted, a casual observer would take them for beggars. The house was surrounded. Macedo and his men watched every exit. As a tribune and three centurions of the Praetorians were implicated, Maximinus had summoned the Osrhoene auxiliaries. It had come to a sad pass when an Emperor of Rome could put more trust in a Greek officer and a unit of archers hired from Mesopotamia than in his own household guard. Still, a man must use what is to hand. All was well, if it worked. How he prayed the three ringleaders were together in there.

The storm cloud had passed and the stars were beginning to pale. Over the way, a bedraggled wreath, relic of some forgotten debauch, could be made out in the mud by the closed doors of the house. Maximinus thought of all the times he had waited outside the houses of Senators in Rome. A junior officer, recently promoted to the equestrian order, he had sought patronage and advancement. He had seldom been admitted. On occasions beyond number some oiled and perfumed servant who most likely had come to Rome in a slave chain from Cappadocia or some such part of the East had sent him away with contempt. At least, now he wore the purple, his son would never know such humiliation.

The thought of Verus Maximus brought its own worries. Maximinus and Paulina had always employed the best tutors they could afford and, since his elevation, the best that money could buy. Certainly, the boy could recite reams of Homer and Virgil. He could translate them from one language to the other with ease and fluency. Those whose fees suggested that they should know, said the love poetry that he composed in the style of Catullus showed sensitivity. He had a fine singing voice. But the more manly accomplishments were lacking. Despite the very best instruction, Verus Maximus remained awkward and reluctant at arms drill. When persuaded to go hunting, he was often found sitting under a tree reading yet more books, often filthy stuff, Milesian tales and the like. And there was his lack of self-control: the frequent outbursts of puerile temper, the drinking, the endless affairs with married women. The very day after he had come to the throne

Maximinus had had to pay off a centurion whose wife had been outraged. The woman was old enough to be the boy's mother. Maximinus was sure the corruption was caused by the affluence of his upbringing. The fawning of leading Senators and equestrians would only make things worse. What Paulina thought, he was less certain.

While seldom sure of his wife's views – women were largely unaccountable, worse than civilians – Maximinus had been left in no doubt of her horror at his elevation to the throne of the Caesars. The highest eminence was too lofty for an equestrian, even more so one of his background. The senators would despise and hate him. He had entered a world where nothing was as it seemed, where words said one thing but meant another. The open language of the barracks and parade ground would no longer serve. He must practise reticence, weigh out his words like a miser his gold, reveal his true thoughts to no one. Maximinus thanked the gods for Paulina. At least with her he could be unguarded, speak what was on his mind – although he knew this did not stretch to the behaviour or character of their son.

Yet something had to be done. Perhaps the new imperial *a Studiis* summoned by Vopiscus might be the answer. Aspines of Gadara did not seem a bad man, for a Syrian. Everyone spoke highly of his culture and his probity. Among all those tomes in the imperial libraries there must be some that might instil martial virtues in the young. Maximinus smiled. Always turn the weapons of your enemies against themselves. Anyway, talking to his son would give Aspines something to do. The sophist's titular duties of guiding the cultural studies of the Emperor were unlikely to occupy much of his time.

The distant rumbling of a wagon brought Maximinus back to his surroundings. The gates must have been opened, the first supplies brought into the town. In the east, the sky was marbled with purple. It was nearly dawn, the best time to attack.

'Good faith.' Maximinus gave the watchword and set off, knowing the other three would follow.

In the street, dim figures emerged and fell in behind. By the time he reached the door there were thirty men at his back.

'My Lord.' It was Macedo. 'Let my men go in first.'

Maximinus pushed back his hood. 'I will never order men to do what I will not.'

Two of the Osrhoenes carried axes. Maximinus waved them aside. He shrugged off his cloak. It fell in the mud before anyone could catch it.

'Leave it. We have work to do.'

He steadied his breathing, touched the gold torque around his neck, then the silver ring on his left thumb. The first was a gift from his Emperor Septimius Severus, the second from his wife. It was not so much for luck – the gods would see to that – but to remind himself of what mattered: trust and good faith. They had moulded him, and he would never let them down.

He measured the door, then gave it a mighty kick. The wood splintered; the boards reverberated, bounced on their hinges, but did not give way. His strength was legendary. His soldiers talked of how he could punch the teeth from the jaw of a horse, drive a finger through an apple or the skull of a child. Men talked much nonsense.

A deep breath, and he lashed out again. His enormous boot landed by the lock. The leaves of the door crashed open. He drew his sword and hurled himself into the house.

A dark corridor opening on to a colonnaded atrium. A face popped out of the porter's lodge and ducked back. Shouts from deeper in the house. Maximinus ran down the passage. Behind him, rather too late, someone shouted to open in the name of the Emperor.

It was lighter in the atrium. There was a pool with a fountain in the middle, lamps burning in a room off the far side.

Two men – soldiers by their belts and the swords in their hands – ran towards him from the right. Another was coming around the pool from the left. Micca and Volo brushed past to take the first two, Macedo and an Osrhoene went for the other. More archers jostled in the confined space behind Maximinus.

The clash of steel echoed back from the walls. A misjudged blow sparked against the stone. Both narrow colonnades were blocked. Shapes flickered against the lamps in the room beyond.

The traitors must not escape.

A foot on the rim, and Maximinus jumped down into the blackness of the pool. He skidded as he landed, regained his balance. The water was very cold. But, thank the gods, not deeper than his knees. It sloshed into his boots as he waded past the fountain.

A young man with a sword appeared at the edge. The elaborately curled hair and finely worked sword-belt proclaimed him the treacherous Praetorian tribune.

'Tyrant!'

The blade shimmered as the officer thrust. Maximinus' left foot went from under him. Somehow, falling, he blocked. He landed hard on his arse, in a great spray of water. The impact jarred up his spine. His sword was knocked from his grip. Almost gracefully, the tribune stepped down into the pool. Feverishly, Maximinus ran his hands across the floor of the pool. The tribune came on carefully. Maximinus' hand closed on the hilt. He floundered backwards to his feet. His opponent closed, feinted high and cut low to the left thigh. Maximinus caught it near the hilt of his weapon, gave ground.

They shifted, seeking an opening. The dark water sucked and pulled at their legs as they moved. Distant, irrelevant sounds of fighting. Of more pressing concern were the noises of men jumping into the pool, moving towards them. The tribune flicked a glance beyond Maximinus. It was enough. With brute strength, Maximinus forced his adversary's sword wide. Stepping inside, he smashed the pommel of his weapon into the man's face. Reeling, off balance, the young officer could do nothing to prevent Maximinus bringing the edge of sharp steel down into his sword arm. It was over. The tribune screamed. He dropped his sword. Clutching his wounded wrist with his good hand, he doubled up.

'Do not kill him.' Maximinus moved past, and clambered out.

There were two men in the dining room. Maximinus scanned all four corners. There was no other exit; nowhere to hide. Perhaps the fat Senator Claudius Venacus was not as stupid as he looked. Either that, or cowardice had kept him away. Whatever the motive behind his absence, it would do him no good. Volo's *frumentarii* would catch him before midday.

'Wh—what is happening?'

Maximinus looked at the Senator who spoke.

'We have done nothing.' Catilius Severus was very pale. His hands, soft and feminine, were spread in a mime show of incomprehension. 'We were making offerings . . . offerings to the gods.'

Maximinus was aware of armed men filling the doorway behind him. 'The traditional gods do not hide from the sun. Any deity that demands his worshippers meet in secret, lurk in the dark, is an enemy of Rome.'

The other Senator spoke. 'It is time for the truth. We were talking treason.'

With his protruding eyes, Caius Petronius Magnus looked like some creature which scuttled along the seabed, but Maximinus felt a flicker of admiration.

'We were approached to join a conspiracy.' Magnus' voice was steady. 'We needed to know how wide it went, needed conclusive evidence, before we denounced it.'

'Who approached you?'

Magnus looked straight into the face of Maximinus. 'One you trusted, the governor of Germania Inferior.'

Maximinus gestured over his shoulder. A man walked forward. Maximinus put an arm around his shoulder. 'What do you think of that, my little Greek?'

'I told you they would say that,' said Timesitheus.

CHAPTER 11

The East
Northern Mesopotamia,

Three Days before the Kalends of May, AD235

A new Emperor sat on the throne of the Caesars. As his horse plodded, head down under the hot sun, Gaius Julius Priscus turned the news over in his mind. The governor of Mesopotamia and Osrhoene had plenty of time to think. The messenger had reached him, at long last, as he rode north on the desert road back to his province from the client kingdom of Hatra. The mountains beyond the town were in sight, but the small column was still some hours from the outpost town of Singara.

What would the accession mean for the provincials between the upper reaches of the Euphrates and Tigris? Ceremonies would be enacted, with many sacrifices and a new name in the oaths. In time there would be a new portrait on the coins they handled; that same face would stare down from statues in the marketplaces and from portrait busts and paintings in official buildings and the homes of the conspicuously loyal. The most immediate impact would be the additional expense. Every community in the territory would have to *voluntarily* send their new Augustus a crown of gold. There would be a lather of activity. No town, no matter how insignificant, would want to risk imperial displeasure by being late or niggardly with its contribution. The Emperor might be as distant as a god but, like a deity, at any moment, completely unforeseen, he could reach down into their lives. The local elite would pledge ostentatiously large sums and then squeeze what they had promised out of their tenants and clients. And then the provincials would get on with their mundane existence: the poor herding goats and scratching a living from the soil; the rich borrowing money they never intended to repay, committing adultery with each other's wives and launching malicious litigation aimed at their neighbour's property; and everyone, high and low, would still worry that a Persian raid would end it all, would see them and their loved ones driven off into slavery or left dead among the ruins of everything they had known.

Some, his brother Philip among them, would consider his views jaundiced, but Priscus had never had any time for sentimentality. And he knew these people. He had been born in a dusty village in the province of Arabia, had grown up speaking a dialect of the Aramaic they spoke here in Mesopotamia. It was a hard world – nowhere harsher than the arid frontier lands of the East – and you had to be hard to rise up out of such an environment.

There was a dry wadi about a mile ahead. It curled around from the east and ran across their way. The landscape was not quite as desolate as it had been. For two days after leaving Hatra there had been nothing but a vast expanse of ochre-grey sand, occasionally punctuated by scatters of rocks and the derelict-looking huts of shepherds which clustered around the few sulphurous wells. Since they broke camp this morning, there had been isolated patches of green, a few yellow and blue flowers in the odd hollow. Even the flies did not seem to cluster quite so maddeningly around their eyes and those of their horses. The country might be a little less bleak, but the road was still an unmade track, and they would have to negotiate the steep sides of the dry watercourse, for there was no bridge.

Priscus had met the new Emperor a few times three years before during the eastern campaign of Alexander. A huge man, strikingly ugly, Maximinus had been one of the officers charged with gathering supplies. Taciturn and grim, he had carried out his duties with honesty and efficiency, if without charm. An equestrian like Priscus, he had risen through the army. Now, as Emperor, he had inherited a full-scale war on the northern frontier. No doubt Maximinus would wage it with the utmost vigour. And that, for Priscus, was an alarming proposition.

There was no declared war in the East, but Persian incursions were increasing in number and range. Only an imbecile could fail to realize that they heralded a major attack. The Sassanid Ardashir had fought the field army of Alexander to a standstill, and the King of Kings had shown no sign of renouncing his claim to all the lands once held, centuries before, by the Persian dynasty of the Achaemenids. If the threat could be made reality, it would take Persian horsemen to the Aegean and beyond.

The Romans could hardly be worse prepared. When the northern tribes had crossed the Rhine, Alexander's advisers had stripped the East of troops. Mesopotamia had suffered as badly as anywhere. Notionally, Priscus still had two legions; the 1st and 3rd Parthica, based at Singara and Nisibis respectively. But the detachments that were marched west, combined with desertion and sickness, had reduced them to fewer than three thousand men each. The situation with the auxiliaries was worse. Unfortunately, the Osrhoene archers had distinguished

135

themselves in Alexander's war. As a result, the foolish councillors of that weak Emperor had ordered almost all of them hundreds upon hundreds of miles from their homes to fight the Germans. Neither the feelings of the soldiers nor the weakness created by their absence had been considered. There were just eight auxiliary units left. The pair of thousand-strong cavalry *alae* would be lucky to put that many in the saddle between them. The remaining six formations, cavalry and infantry alike, were all below their roster strength of five hundred. On the most optimistic estimate, Priscus had fewer than ten thousand regulars, and whatever levies he could raise, to defend his province. And now the new Emperor might demand yet more reinforcements for his expedition into the forests of Germania.

If any consolation were to be found, outside the specious posturing of the schools of philosophy or the messianic ravings of depraved sects, Priscus sought it in the calibre of his higher command. The Prefects of his legions, Julianus and Porcius Aelianus, were equestrian officers from Italy. Each had a long record of service and had fought well in the Persian war at the head of local auxiliaries. Priscus had promoted them. Both were competent and loyal – as far as any man could be judged the latter in this debased age. To the west, the garrison at the strategically important Castellum Arabum was commanded by the youngest son of the King of Hatra. It was not just a political appointment. Although still in his twenties, Prince Ma'na was a veteran of Alexander's expedition and the Sassanid attack on his father's city a few years before.

Priscus turned in his saddle. He rode a few lengths in front of the others. Nothing could stop the flies, but he saw no reason to be choked with dust as well. At the head of the column was a large, flamboyant figure with flowing embroidered silks, elaborately curled and arranged hair, a moustache teased into points and kohl-lined eyes. Prince Manu of Edessa had been raised as the heir to the throne, until the Emperor Caracalla had abolished that small kingdom. Now a corpulent man in middle age, Manu had adapted to his changed circumstances. He retained his title as a courtesy and remained an immensely rich landowner, influential throughout the area. More to the point, like his younger near-namesake from Hatra, he was a natural leader of men in battle.

Priscus felt a twinge of unease. Surrounding himself with scions of eastern royalty could be easily misrepresented at the court of the new Emperor. He put the thought aside. What else could he do except call on local potentates, now that his province had been denuded of Roman forces?

Riding next to Manu, Priscus' brother Philip looked incongruously Roman. Immaculate despite the heat, his muscled cuirass gleaming beneath the nodding plume of his helmet, the legate might have just come down from the Palatine or off the Campus Martius. Philip had always loved to display his *romanitas*. Priscus smiled as he ran his eyes across the thirty scruffy troopers who followed. He had recruited his guard from volunteers from all the units in the province. The criteria for selection had been horsemanship and skill with both bow and sword. Philip had argued that they should be outfitted in uniform fitting the dignity of a Roman governor. Priscus did not care what they looked like, as long as they could fight.

Using the horns of the saddle, Priscus hauled himself back around. He was tired, dirty and hot. His harness and mailcoat pulled at his shoulders, and sweat ran down under its heavy embrace. He was forty-five, and regretted he was beginning to lose the stamina of his youth. Still, not far to go now. He looked ahead, past the rider on point duty, past the wadi, above which a brace of doves circled. Singara was not in sight yet, hidden by the haze. Beyond, the clouds piled up over the mountain wall. His thoughts ran to a bath, a meal, bed. Before setting off to Hatra, he had bought a new slave: soft white thighs, blonde, fifteen years old.

His horse stumbled slightly and jolted him from the anticipation of sensuous pleasures. Unbidden, his mind again took up the duties of office. All the forces in the East, Roman and allied, were threadbare, worn down by war and enforced contributions to the imperial field army. Much would depend on the men who led them. Tiridates of Armenia and Sanatruq of Hatra were bred to war, and had every reason to fight the Persians. Tiridates descended from the Arsacid dynasty, which Ardashir the Sassanid had overthrown not ten years before. The Armenian had a better claim to Ctesiphon and the throne of the King of Kings than the upstart from the house of Sasan. It was something neither monarch would forget. Sanatruq had lost his eldest son to a Persian arrow when Ardashir had descended on Hatra.

The governors of the Roman provinces were of more mixed quality. In the course of long careers, both Rutilius Crispinus of Syria Phoenice and Licinius Serenianus had commanded troops in the field and led them with distinction, first as equestrians then as Senators. They would do their duty like the Romans of old. Priscus smiled. The antique virtue of his friend Serenianus had stretched to leaving his beautiful new wife, Perpetua, behind in Rome. Men like these could be relied upon. With the best will in the world, Priscus could not say the same of his own brother-in-law, Otacilius Severianus, who held Syria Palestina, or Sollemnius Pacatianus in Arabia. Yet the weakest link in the chain had to be Junius Balbus in Syria Coele. A wealthy Senator of infinite torpid complacency, it was said he had only been awarded the governorship because he was son-in-law to old Gordian, who held Africa. At least, when trouble came, natural indolence should encourage Balbus to lean on Domitius Pompeianus, the capable *Dux Ripae* who oversaw the frontier forces from the fortified city of Arete. Of course – the insidious thought could not be denied – none of them, Priscus himself included, might be in office that long. When a new Emperor took the throne, powerful men fell. It was the natural way of things.

A shout from ahead. The outrider was wheeling his mount. The ends of his cloak gathered in his right hand, he waved them above his head: *Enemy in sight.*

'Close up. Battle order.' As he gave the orders, Priscus scanned the terrain. They had to be in the wadi. There was no other cover, just the wadi across their front and running off around their right.

Behind him, the stamp of hooves and the jingle and rattle of men hurriedly arming. Priscus waved in the two scouts from the flanks, passed the word for the last men in the column to summon the one from the rear.

He remembered that the wadi was steep-sided, but not that deep or wide. How many mounted men could it conceal?

The question was answered. Behind the galloping scout, over the lip of the watercourse, about two hundred paces away, scrambled some three dozen widely spaced horse archers.

'To the right!' Manu said.

More of the enemy, many more; at least a hundred. They were further away – a good half-mile – and they were also light horse, but far too many to fight.

As the first war cries rang out, the scout skidded to a halt. Priscus fastened his helmet and weighed his few options. There was open ground to the west and south, but no refuge. They would be hunted down.

'Form a wedge on me!'

The colourful bulk of Manu of Edessa moved up on his right knee; his brother on his left. Sporakes, the governor's personal bodyguard, and the scout tucked in close behind. An arrow fell in front of his horse, skidded up the dust.

'We are armoured, they are not. We ride through them. No bows, just swords. Across the wadi, and north to Singara. No matter who goes down, no one stops.'

There was no time for anything more.

'Charge!' Priscus drew his blade and kicked on without looking round.

The Persians were almost on them. Loose tunics and wide trousers billowing, at full gallop, they put away their bows and drew their long, straight swords. They were natural horsemen. The first came at him from the right, long black hair flying. The easterner's blade described a great arc of steel, cutting at his neck. Dropping the reins, Priscus gripped his hilt in both hands, took the blow just in front of his face, deflected it over his head. The impact knocked him backwards. A sharp pain at the base of his spine. His horse ran on. Only the high rear of his saddle stopped him being thrown over the rump of his mount. Dismounted, you were finished. His left hand found one of the saddle-horns. As he hauled himself upright, struggling for balance, another swung at him from the left. Somehow, he got his blade across. Steel scraped on steel. A fierce dark face, close to his, shouting. Then their horses pulled them away from each other.

Clear ground in front. Nothing between them and the wadi. Manu on one shoulder, Philip the other. They were through. Priscus felt contempt for whoever led these Persians. He gathered the reins, looked back. Sporakes was there, the rest following, not too dispersed. Further back, Sassanids like wild dogs circled a couple of troopers who had been separated from the rest. One was on foot, the other still mounted. It made no odds: it was over for them.

'Ahead!' Philip shouted.

More Persians were emerging from the gully, four or five dozen of them. They were on the far side, milling and wheeling, bright like exotic birds. A big young Sassanid with reddish hair was getting them into line. Not such a fool, after all, Priscus thought. The first group was intended to delay us. He means these to hold us until the main body from the East comes up in our rear.

'Close up.' Priscus got his horse in hand, eased its pace a little to let the others get in order.

They were nearly at the wadi. There was nothing else for it. They had to cross. Alexander the Great had crossed the Granicus in the face of an entire Persian army.

'They are only Persians. They will not stand.' Priscus did not believe his own words. 'Thrust at their faces. Remember the Granicus! Alexander!'

Above the thunder of hooves, one or two troopers yelled: *'Alexander! Alexander!'*

From ahead, louder, a roar came back. *'Garshasp! Garshasp!'* The Persians brandished their weapons. The big red-haired leader was in the front rank, laughing.

As the drop loomed, Priscus gave his mount its head, urging it with his thighs to make the leap. The ground fell away. Priscus leant back. He was lifted from the saddle, then, as they landed, slammed back hard down into it. An awful numbness arched up his back. The horse stumbled. Almost on its knees, it gathered itself.

A couple of strides, and they were going up the far side. Priscus stretched forward over the horse's neck, clutching its mane. Loose stones and sand shot out from under its slipping hooves. It gathered its quarters; two titanic thrusts and they ran into a Persian horse at the top. A blade thrust at him from the right. He parried, rolled his wrist and thrust back. The resistance jarred up his arm. The reek of blood, hot horse, and fear. Men and beasts screaming, indistinguishable. A flash of light to his left. A blow clanged off his helmet. Head ringing, he struck out blindly, left and right.

They had been stopped. Only a few were with him. Most of

the troopers were still down in the wadi. He had to clear the way. If they did not get moving, they were dead. He fended off a cut from his left. His right was exposed. The easterner there drew back his blade, and stopped, staring stupidly at the severed stump of his sword arm. Manu shaped to finish the man. Another horse crashed into the melee. Manu's mount was thrown backwards; its hooves fought for purchase on the edge of the gully. Manu had lost his seat, was almost over its neck, his kohl-lined eyes wide. They toppled backwards.

Only one Sassanid ahead. Priscus called to his horse, kicked his heels into its flanks. The easterner's animal turned across their path. They were flank to flank. The Persian raised his sword for a mighty overhand stroke. Priscus thrust the tip of his blade into the man's armpit. The way was open again.

'Forward! Get moving!'

Priscus looked over his shoulder. Philip was there, and Sporakes. Troopers were urging their mounts up the incline. Down in the wadi, Manu was on his feet, ringed by Persians.

'Forward! On to Singara!'

CHAPTER 12

Rome
The Carinae,

Seven Days before the Ides of May, AD235

Iunia Fadilla always smiled when she walked over the mosaic of the bath attendant with the enormous, jutting penis, its glans picked out in purple. It was the right response. All sorts of malign daemons sought out bathhouses, even those in private houses such as hers. They congregated especially in doorways. Nothing dispelled them like laughter. So everyone said.

In the *tepidarium*, she kicked off the clogs which had protected her feet from the floor of the hot room, a maid took her robe and she climbed naked on to a couch. A slight intake of breath told her masseuse the oil had not been warmed quite enough. The girl murmured an apology. You got a better massage in the Baths of Trajan. Since the ruling of the last Emperor, they remained open after dark. But, from midday, the best rooms were reserved for men; too many things were in life. And there were the complications of bothering to organize a return in the dark; the need for a litter, linkmen, guards. Perpetua was joining her, and she would have been especially silly, as tonight was the first night of the *Lemuria*, when the gates of Hades stood open. Maybe she should just sell the girl and buy a new masseuse.

The girl smoothed the scented oil up her back. Iunia Fadilla gazed at the wall decoration. Compared with those her late husband had commissioned for the bedrooms, Jupiter abducting Europa was very tame. In the form of a bull, the deity shouldered aside the waves. On his back, Europa lightly steadied herself with one hand; from the other dangled a basket of flowers. Given the turn of events – one moment innocently gathering flowers on the shore with her friends, the next crashing through the sea on the back of the lust-crazed King of the gods in bestial form – she appeared oddly unconcerned, even complacent. Perhaps Jupiter had reassured her: he would transform himself into an eagle before he raped her; and the man she would then be forced to marry was, after all, a King among men: worse things could happen to a girl a long way from home.

As the slave got to work on her shoulders, Iunia Fadilla's breath came in little gasps, almost as if in the act of love. But her thoughts had moved to very different matters. She had decided which of the two villas on the Bay of Naples she would buy. There was a crack in one of the external walls, but the engineer had assured her it did not affect the integrity of the structure, while the other property had a problem with its supply of water and an ongoing boundary dispute. Also, the one she had chosen had more extensive vineyards. The rent they would bring should not only cover the costs of the repairs to the house, but eventually begin to offset the price of the purchase.

At midnight tonight, the first of the festival, Iunia Fadilla would perform the age-old ritual to appease the departed. She had reason to remember old Nummius fondly. Although she had inherited less than half his estate – the majority of the rest had gone to the Emperor Alexander, which ensured her huband's distant relatives had been unable to contest their own more meagre legacies – he had left her an extremely wealthy widow. He had ensured her dowry was returned intact and, in a final act of kindness, his will had specified that she could choose her own *tutor*. Although legally in sole charge of her finances, her cousin Lucius would never dream of countermanding her wishes.

The quick *clack clack* of shoes announced the arrival of her friend. At a glance it was obvious that Perpetua had some news that she was bursting to tell. She fidgeted as two of the maids busily pulled out pins, untied laces and removed her clothes. For once, she paused only briefly, turning slightly, inviting admiration of her naked body; engrained habits were not easily held in abeyance.

Another friend had once told Iunia Fadilla that all girls had a Sapphic side. She wondered about Perpetua. Now and then her own thoughts moved to such things. Not, of course, to the crude, grunting fantasies of men. There was nothing appealing about a mannish woman wielding a dildo. It was a sign of the arrogance of men that they could not imagine a woman finding pleasure except in a penis or its simulacrum.

'You will never guess what has happened.' Perpetua had not waited to settle on her couch.

You have a new lover, Iunia Fadilla thought. Or a good-looking stranger paid you a compliment when you were shopping.

'Theoclia has been arrested. The Praetorians came for her this afternoon.'

'Who?'

Perpetua tutted with exasperation. 'Theoclia, the late Emperor's sister. The one married to fat Valerius Messala. They took him too. The Praetorians kicked in their door, dragged them out into the street. They say she was half naked.

They beat them in full view of everyone. The last that was seen of them, they were being thrown into a closed carriage. Apparently, they are being taken to the North, to Maximinus himself.'

'Why?'

Perpetua rolled her eyes. 'Treason, of course. They were involved in the conspiracy of Magnus.'

'Have any others fallen?'

'My brother does not think so, but his friend Poplicola is terrified. Messala is his uncle.'

Iunia Fadilla felt a shiver of vicarious fear. This was horribly near. Messala and his brother, Priscillianus, were the closest of friends with her neighbour Balbinus. The Valerii brothers were always in and out of his house.

'What do you think will happen to them?'

They will be tortured and executed, you foolish girl, Iunia Fadilla thought. Their estates will be confiscated. Before they die, in their agony, they might implicate others, guilty and innocent alike.

'There is no telling,' Iunia Fadilla said.

Her heart went out to Theoclia. She remembered her now: a pretty girl, dark, and delicate-looking, in an eastern way. She had seen her several times when Alexander was on the throne. Whatever her husband might have said or done, she was unlikely to have been a part of it. Iunia Fadilla muttered a prayer. A few generations back, or a turn of the stars, and it could have been her. She was the great-granddaughter of the divine Marcus Aurelius. Thank the gods her father had been without political ambition and her husband had retired into private life after his Consulship.

'They say—' Perpetua lowered her voice, oblivious to the two slaves massaging them '—Maximinus is a monster. He went with the guards to arrest Magnus and the others, because he wanted to see the fear in their faces.'

Iunia Fadilla said nothing.

'And when Alexander was killed, he took his head, carried it about for hours, gloating, peering into its eyes, and talking to it. They even say—' Perpetua shuddered '—he outraged the corpse of the old Empress.'

Iunia Fadilla signed to her girl to stop the massage. 'You said Maximinus had named your father as *Consul Ordinarius* for the year after next.'

'Yes, it is wonderful,' Perpetua said. 'Maximinus will take up the Consulship on the *kalends* of January next year, with Pupienus Africanus, the son of the Prefect of the City, as his colleague. The following year my father will share that honour with Mummius Felix Cornelianus.' She frowned, thinking hard. 'Gaius said that Father has been dining with Catius Celer, the brother of the Catius Clemens who helped the gorgeous Honoratus and the other one put Maximinus on the throne. Father is to go north to serve on the imperial staff.'

Iunia Fadilla turned over on to her back. The slave girl started to massage her thighs. 'Holding office under a monster?'

Perpetua raised herself on one elbow. 'They are just rumours, probably all made up. Gaius said that Father said that, all things considered, the reign had not started too badly. Maximinus has taken an oath that he will not kill any Senator. Honoratus, Clemens and Vopiscus – that is the other one, Vopiscus – are all men of honour. A conspiracy has been uncovered, and there has been no persecution. Only the guilty have suffered.'

'All Emperors take that oath,' Iunia Fadilla said. 'Elagabalus took that oath, and he killed them if he did not like the look of them.'

'Father always says we should pray for good Emperors, but serve what we get.'

Iunia Fadilla actually snorted. 'Every Senator has said that, especially when they were serving a tyrant they hated. Nummius was convinced that all reigns get worse. He was so old he remembered when Commodus came to the purple; a young man of incredible promise, before the conspiracies made him afraid and his profligacy made him avaricious. Nummius said fear and poverty were the true secrets of the empire. After a time, all Emperors kill men for their money. Accusations are no longer investigated, but believed.'

Perpetua lay face down again. 'Perhaps someone will inform against Serenianus,' she said quietly, 'and then there will be no danger of my husband coming home.'

CHAPTER 13

Africa
The Town of Theveste,

Two Days before the Ides of May, AD235

Thank the gods for the baths at Theveste. Gordian had spent most of the morning in the *laconicum*. Lying in the dry heat, the sweat and alcohol had poured out of him. Now, although weak as a lamb, he felt somewhat better. Standing with the others on the top step of the temple, clad in his best parade armour, only a little queasy, he now thought he could get through the rest of the day.

It had been a good night, Bacchic in its frenzy. Alexander and his Companions had never drunk deeper. Menophilus had been less congenial than sometimes. Reverting to Stoic type, he had claimed duty called him and had left early. A shame: if you cannot rely on a man at a *symposium*, can you trust him on a battlefield? Of the others Valerian had been preoccupied throughout, but Mauricius good company and Sabinianus on sparkling form. Gordian looked along the line of waiting dignitaries and caught Sabinianus' eye. The latter smiled back. Perhaps he had gone too far. After the others had departed, when his head was reeling from the wine, he had told Parthenope and Chione to disrobe. After they had pleasured each other, he had shared them with Sabinianus. Doubtless, many would disapprove, but he had no intention of being bound by provincial morality. Only what you share with your friends is yours for ever.

'I do not see why we should pander to these barbarians,' Valerian was saying. 'Rather than negotiate with them, we should burn them out of their lairs.'

No one answered. Menophilus had his nose deep in some gilded official document.

'If they are too remote, then we should extend the frontier defences, keep them out.'

Gordian thought the view of Valerian had much in its favour.

'You know we cannot do that. We have to admit them.' Mauricius spoke patiently.

Valerian grunted, not seeming mollified. At times, he had quite a capacity to be a bore. Last night, amid the food and wine and levity, he had inveighed at some length against the appointment of some new imperial Procurator. The man was a savage, a new Verres. He would not shear the provincials but flay them. They did not call him 'the Chain' for nothing. As the gods were Valerian's witnesses, there would be trouble. The Africans were not the Sicilians Verres had tyrannized in the days of Cicero. Mark his words, there would be blood.

When Valerian had exhausted that topic, he had complained at length that, although his name had been put forward in the Emperor's *consilium*, he had not replaced Julius Licinianus as governor of Dacia. After that, he had explored the causes and negative implications of the removal of one of his kinsmen by marriage from the governorship of Achaea. Egnatius Proculus had been appointed curator of roads and overseer of poor relief in a district of Italy: not quite an insult – but it had to be considered a step down. At best, Egnatius had lost his province only so that Rutilius Crispinus could take his place. But, even in that case, it indicated that the Egnatii were not high in imperial favour. And the reasons could be far worse.

Gordian studied Valerian's disgruntled face. Valerian should count his kinsman lucky. That morning, news had arrived that Memmia Sulpicia, the mousey ex-wife of Alexander Severus whom Gordian had visited on his way back from Ad Palmam, had been executed. Neither her sex nor living quietly on her estate outside the backwater settlement of Vicus Augusti had spared her. The given reason was that she had been in correspondence with the traitor Magnus on the northern frontier. The killing had been the first action of this new Procurator. Perhaps Valerian had a point about Paul the Chain after all.

A trumpet call hurt Gordian's head. He arranged his military cloak over his left arm, squared his shoulders, put on his stern Roman face. Someone had once said he looked like Pompey the Great. Alongside, the others straightened up too. The soldiers around the Forum came to attention. It had been Gordian's idea to bring the deputation this far into the province, and to have a sizeable contingent of 15th Cohort Emesenes on hand. The *speculatores* had guided Nuffuzi past Ad Palmam, the scene of his defeat. Hopefully, the chief of the Cinithii might reflect on the extent and power of the *imperium*.

The arch at Theveste was typical of a small provincial town. Only two men could ride side by side through its gates. Aemilius Severinus escorted Nuffuzi into the Forum. Two nomads followed, then, in column of twos, the detachment of the scouts.

As the cavalcade crossed the open space, the auxiliaries shouted the password: '*Fides!*' Ideally, at this point, the barbarians would be surprised, give evidence of their fear, perhaps cower or weep. That was what they did in stories. Nuffuzi did none of those things. Calmly, he rode up to a couple of lengths from the steps of the temple, and dismounted. A groom ran out to hold his horse. The two tribesmen jumped down and fell in behind their leader. Aemilius Severinus and his Frontier Wolves remained on horseback.

As Quaestor of the province, Menophilus descended to meet the embassy. He stopped two steps from the bottom. Gordian wondered if the nomads would find it strange that the youngest of those meeting them should take the lead. Presumably, they had nothing like magistracies in their ever-shifting encampments.

'May the gods give you many greetings.' Nuffuzi looked unchanged; the greying, long braids strung with colourful beads, the small beard on his chin, the air of unhurried assurance.

'May you and yours be safe,' Menophilus said.

'No evil, thank the gods.' Nuffuzi nodded. 'On you only light burdens.'

'No evil, thank the gods. May only good happen to you.' Menophilus had gone to the trouble of learning the rituals of the desert. Apparently, it was bad form ever to ask who anyone was. That accounted for the reaction to Gordian's words outside Ad Palmam.

The final *'no evil'* having been said, Nuffuzi turned to business. 'Your soldiers have turned back our people at the frontier. Since the time of the first men the tribes have crossed from the desert to the sown in the early summer.'

'You crossed not long ago,' Menophilus said. 'You brought fire and sword.'

'Those evils lie in the past.' Nuffuzi might have learnt the language in army camps, but there was still an archaic stateliness to the chief's Latin diction. 'You need us. Your rich need our young men to help gather their harvest. Later, when the children and the women bring the herds, the animals will manure your fields. Your rich hire our warriors to oversee their workers in the fields. Unlike their own slaves and tenants, we do not steal.'

'And you need us,' Menophilus said. 'Your animals would die without our grazing. Without our markets, your tents would contain no fine things. We will need assurances.'

Nuffuzi nodded. 'My eldest son, Mirzi, is the joy of my heart. Although his absence pains me, let him remain among you as a hostage.'

Gordian had forgotten the youth, who stood off to one side of the temple podium, flanked by two auxiliaries chosen for their physique and fierce demeanour.

'That is a noble gesture.' Menophilus paused, evidently weighing his words. 'The governor, the noble Gordian Senior, desires amity with the Cinithii. Sometimes the majesty of Rome grants honours to the leader of a friendly people from beyond the frontier. The citizenship of Rome, the title of friend and ally of the Roman people, these are things of consequence. Those especially trusted, once in a lifetime, might be granted Roman office over those peoples among which he lives. To be *Praefectus Nationes* brings a man honour, within the empire and outside.'

Nuffuzi remained impassive, but the two tribesmen murmured. So, Gordian thought, they know Latin as well. But had his father really decided to give office to this barbarian? His memory of the governor's council back in Hadrumetum was clouded.

Menophilus produced the gold- and ivory-bound document he had been reading earlier. So that was the duty that had summoned him away from the revels of last night.

'Friendship is sealed not just by words, but by actions,' Nuffuzi said. 'The eastern marches of your province have been plagued by bandits. Their village is in the hills southeast of Tisavar. It is not easy to find. My son will lead you there. The village is well fortified. There will be hard fighting. Mirzi is a warrior. He will fight in the front rank.'

Gordian glanced over at the Cinithian youth, at the bandaged right wrist where he had near severed Mirzi's sword arm. How well would the boy fare now close to the steel? The thigh wound Gordian had taken in return still troubled him.

'The leader of the robbers is a brigand called Canartha. He has plundered many caravans, many villages and villas. There is much wealth there. It would be a fine thing to take it from him. Should any be offered to Mirzi or his father, it would be well received.'

Gordian could not help but smile. Old Nuffuzi wanted to use the Romans to rid himself of a rival, and to get rich from their efforts. Still, Gordian felt the lure of action. He was better at leading men in the field than listening to lawsuits. That sort of drudgery was best left to dutiful young Stoics like Menophilus. Like Mark Antony, Gordian could revel in peacetime, then shrug off his pleasures and rise to the stern demands of war. If only his father would give him the command.

'Friendship is sealed with oaths as well,' Menophilus said. 'Bring forth the standards.'

The silver images of Maximinus Augustus gazed down from on high. Handsome, his strong jaw clean-shaven, there was a look of the divine Julius Caesar about him.

The desert chieftain kissed the tips of his fingers, touched the palm of his hand to his forehead. 'By the immortal Macurtam, Macurgum, Vihinam, Bonchor, Varissima, Matilam, and Iunam, the august, the holy, the saviours, I, Nufuzzi of the Cinthii, swear to be true to the Romans.'

As the uncouth names were recited, the pointlessness of it all struck Gordian. Why should these outlandish deities – or any other – care? The gods were immortal, perfect in their happiness, contained in themselves. If they could be pleased by

154

offerings, or angered by inadequate rituals, they would not be content in themselves, and thus they would not be divine. The gods had no interest in the doings of men. But now, perhaps, Nuffuzi would think twice before he broke his word.

CHAPTER 14

The Far North
The Harzhorn Mountains,

Four Days before the Ides of July, AD235

Caius Petronius Magnus rose from the swamp, blood-bedraggled. His eyes bulged, his hands beckoned. Timesitheus went to move back. The mud sucked at his boots. He put up his hands to push back the dead Senator.

Another bad dream. Timesitheus opened his eyes. By the light of the single lamp, he saw the low ridge pole, his travelling chest and his armour on a stand, a folding stool. Outside the tent he heard a horse whicker, men talking and moving: the sounds of the camp stirring.

Just a bad dream. No daemon: they did not exist. Not a message from the gods: they did not exist either. And not guilt, definitely not guilt. He had tested Magnus and the others. If they had been loyal, they would not have been so ready to conspire, would not have had the forger make coin-dies with a portrait of Magnus as Emperor. If they had been loyal, they would have denounced him, and they would have been rewarded. Tranquillina was right. If he had not exposed their latent treachery, another would have done. They had possessed ambition without intelligence. They deserved their fate.

Timesitheus yawned. His eyes were watering. He rubbed them with the back of his hand. At least neither that fat fool Venacus nor the mincing Catilius Severus had yet taken to haunting his sleep. No wonder he had bad dreams. He was exhausted in mind and body, and now everyone in the army had good reason to be afraid.

The campaign had started well enough. They had crossed the Rhine, paraded under the ancient Arch of Germanicus on the far bank and trudged off into the vast forests of the North. The Germans had melted away before them. The native settlements were deserted. Maximinus had let the soldiers loot what little they contained and then ordered them burnt. From time to time, they captured untended herds. These too the Emperor handed to the soldiers. The few barbarians they took – the slow and unlucky – were also given to the soldiery.

After some days things began to change. The campfires they came across were still warm, some smouldering. Strange figures were half glimpsed through the trees. First stragglers, then scouts began to disappear. The initial attacks fell on parties out foraging. They were beaten off easily enough, but each left a few men dead or wounded. Together, they added to the rising apprehension.

Finally, they emerged from the mountains on to a broad plain. Several days further march and the hostile tribes – the Alamanni, Cherusci and Angrivarii – offered battle. They were drawn up in front of a marsh. No sooner had the legions closed than the Germans fled into the swamp. Disregarding all caution, Maximinus had pursued them, spurring his mount into the morass. The water had risen above its belly. The Emperor was mired. Tribesmen swarmed all around him. Only the courage and prompt action of the men of 2nd Legion Parthica had saved him.

It had been a victory of a sort. Laurelled dispatches had been sent back to Rome. Great paintings of the success were to be set up in front of the Senate House. The gods alone knew if the messengers had reached the frontier. After the battle, embassies from the barbarians had come to the camp. Those from the friendly tribes of the far North had been led by Froda the Angle, the son of King Isangrim, who ruled the shores of the Suebian Sea. When the barbarian prince departed, weighed down with gold, he had left one thousand warriors to serve with the army for the next two years. Deputations had also come from the Alamanni and their allies. They asked for peace. Timesitheus had not been alone in doubting their sincerity. Maximinus had demanded hostages. They had been promised, but never arrived.

The dead were buried, a victory monument erected, and the army turned south for home. They had not gone five miles before the attacks began again The Germans had driven in the pickets. For some desperate moments it had seemed they would cut the long column in two. Again, Maximinus had fought hand to hand. This time it could not be denied that his prowess and his example had turned the tide. The next day they had resumed the march in a square, the baggage in the middle. It had slowed their progress and brought only a certain amount of security. Continuously, bands of warriors rushed from thickets, hurled javelins and retreated. Those ill-disciplined enough to give chase were surrounded. Few made it back to the army. Obstacles – felled trees and diverted streams – further hindered the army. Timesitheus had thought of the story in Thucydides of the Athenians harassed in the wilds of Aetolia. It had not ended well for them. All order lost, they had been chased into dried-up watercourses and trackless woods and hunted down. The talk around the campfires was of Varus and his lost legions.

Fighting almost every step of the way, the expedition had crawled south. The ambushes increased in intensity. The warriors made the horses and mules their particular targets. The army left a trail of abandoned material, rich pickings for their tormentors. Any who had thought the mountains would bring relief had been sadly disillusioned.

The pass was about three hundred paces wide. A ditch and rampart had been dug across. Behind, waited innumerable Germans. On either side were steep slopes. More barbarians were stationed at the crests. There was no way around. The army had encamped. Now supplies were running short. If the military council this morning did not produce an answer, they may as well all resign themselves to death.

Timesitheus called for his slave, swung his legs off the camp bed. He did not want to die. He thought of Tranquillina, and he thought of their daughter. She would be eight in the autumn. What would life hold for the child without him? What would Tranquillina do? The thought brought him no comfort. Tranquillina would marry again. Some other man would enjoy the pleasures of her bed, would be inspired by the goad of her ambition.

The boy brought in a chamber pot and a bowl of clean water. Timesitheus told him to bring food.

Groaning slightly, Timesitheus got up. He pissed in the pot, then washed his hands and face in cold water. What was he doing here? Back in Mogontiacum, the day after the conspirators had been arrested, Maximinus had summoned him. Never effusive, the Emperor had praised him briefly. His loyalty would be rewarded. As he had petitioned, his cousin Sabinus Modestus could have command of the cataphracts. For him, there was a more difficult task. There was trouble in Bithynia-Pontus: the finances of its cities were in disarray, the province overrun by Christians. The senatorial governor was not up to the task. With a special commission, Timesitheus would end these problems. But not yet. Maximinus was not ready to part with his little Greek. Who but his *Graeculus* could keep the army supplied? The atheists and the corrupt councillors of Bithynia-Pontus could wait. So Timesitheus had found himself in charge of the baggage train, weighed under with work, shouting himself hoarse. Needless to say, the carts, which he had been unable to proscribe, had caused the worst problems: forever shedding wheels, breaking axles, getting bogged down. He had found a grim satisfaction in every one they had left broken in their wake.

The boy brought in some biscuit and cold bacon. Timesitheus ate it as he was helped into his equipment. Here he was, hundreds of miles of gloomy forest from safety, a victim of his own efficiency. Gods below, he did not want to die. He told himself to be a man. He was just tired. It had been hard to get any sleep with the low-lying valley and the surrounding woods echoing with the sounds of barbarian exultations. Once again he looked into the flat, black eyes of his fear and forced the rodent to scrabble back into some dark recess.

It was near dawn. A breeze was stirring the black trees. The low fires smoked with damp wood as Timesitheus walked through the encampment. There were high clouds, but it might not rain.

Maximinus could not stand any ostentation. The imperial pavilion was much smaller than in Alexander's day, although still huge. Officers were waiting outside in the gloom. They stood in small groups or on their own. Few were talking. Sanctus, the *ab Admissionibus*, blocked the door.

'Health and great joy.' Timesitheus greeted Macedo in their native language. The Greek commander was standing on his own.

'Health and great joy.' Macedo's tone belied his words.

'Is the Emperor awake?'

'Yes.'

'Has anyone been admitted?'

'The triumvirate.' Since they had put the Thracian on the throne, the three Senators Vopiscus, Honoratus and Catius Clemens were seldom apart, and almost always close to their Emperor. Their collective nickname was fitting. 'And the favoured equestrians.' There was no need to name them.

'Anullinus is Praetorian Prefect, and Volo the head of his *frumentarii*.' Timesitheus lowered his voice. 'But in Mogontiacum it was we who saved Maximinus as certainly as Julius Capitolinus' 2nd Legion in that swamp. And Domitius has done nothing.'

Macedo grunted.

'Yet they are in there, and we are out here.'

'You will get your reward in Bithynia-Pontus.' Macedo did not try to hide his bitterness. 'And I will get nothing.'

Timesitheus smiled. 'If we live through this, I will get my reward.'

Macedo glowered. 'If we live through this, I will get nothing.'

The courtly voice of the *ab Admissionibus* announced that His Sacred Majesty would see his loyal officers.

Maximinus sat on the ivory throne. On his right was the triumvirate, on his left the four equestrians. Behind him stood his son Maximus and another youth, some second cousin from the Thracian hill country called Rutilus. The other figure, towards the rear of the room, was far more disconcerting. Everyone knew that Ababa, the druid woman, had travelled with the expedition. It was rumoured she went to Maximinus in the dead of the night, to satisfy his lusts or to practise unholy sacrifices, perhaps to do both. Yet so far she had never appeared in public with the Emperor.

Timesitheus studied Ababa. Neither old, nor young, she was very tall, her face not unattractive, unmarked by the torture she had suffered in the previous reign, her figure hidden by her cloak. Having a woman at a council of war was always a mistake. Cleopatra had done Antony no good. Having a northern barbarian woman, one tainted with proximity to alien gods, would disturb all the high command. Worse, this was the German bitch that had prophesied the death of Alexander.

Almost every decision Maximinus had made in his short reign had been bad. Before they left Mogontiacum, buoyed up by the influx of wealth from the crown gold offered on his accession and the confiscated estates of those condemned with Magnus, Maximinus had decreed that the pay of all soldiers would be doubled. The triumvirate had been unable to dissuade him. Once announced, there could be no going back. The thing was irrevocable – and completely unsustainable.

'Fellow-soldiers.' Maximinus got to his feet. His bulk dominated the room. 'By their treachery the Germans believe they have put us in a bad position. They are wrong. Since we set out, we have sought battle, and they have avoided it. Now they have delivered themselves into our hands.' The grey eyes of Maximinus shone in his great white face. 'They have the short-lived ferocity of beasts. We have courage and discipline. They have blind savagery. We have torsion artillery, and we have a plan.'

Despite his misgivings, the harsh, grating voice lifted Timesitheus. Led by a Titan like this, an elemental force from a bygone age, a new Prometheus, who or what could stand against them? They could storm the heavens.

CHAPTER 15

The Far North
The Harzhorn Mountains,

the Ides of July, AD235

On the third morning Maximinus climbed the tall tribunal in front of the camp, and the trumpets rang out as they had on the previous two days. He ran his eyes over the close-packed ranks of his soldiers. Practice had made the manoeuvre quicker. All the units were in place, the last few wagons with the bolt-throwers being manhandled into line. Only an hour after sunrise. It had taken twice as long on the first day.

The Emperor looked out at the enemy position a little under four hundred paces distant. The pass was perfectly flat. The Germans had dug a shallow ditch across its entire frontage of some three hundred paces. Behind was an earth bank, four or five feet high and topped with a wooden palisade. In front of these defences were two bands of obstacles. First, an attacker would have to clamber over a tangle of felled trees, their branches cut into jagged points. Then he would have to avoid putting a boot into the numerous half-concealed pits containing sharpened stakes. The soldiers called them stags and lilies. They would have to get through them under a murderous hail of missiles before even attempting to storm the wall. The Germans had created a fine killing ground.

The bluffs thrust up on either side. The eastern crest, off to the left, was higher, and further away. On the right the climb was shorter, but steeper, although landslips had left three natural ramps. There was timber on the heights, but no defences. Only isolated stands of trees here and there on the approaches. Most likely, every winter the run-off from torrential rains carried away topsoil and saplings.

The enemy camp was on a line of hills several hundred paces beyond the palisade. In that blue distance wagons, tents and shelters, hazed by the smoke of cooking fires, sprawled without discernible order. The barbarian numbers were unknowable, but without doubt huge. The chiefs of the Alamanni, Cherusci and their allies had ordered, cajoled or forced every warrior they could to gather in this remote place. Their summons had emptied the forests of Germania. They had brought their women and children to mark their valour, and to witness the destruction of the Roman army. If the gods were kind, Maximinus thought, they would regret that decision.

Now, in the raking light of early morning, there were few tribesmen to be seen along the palisade or up on the hills. They knew what was coming. And perhaps Maximinus' ploy was working. Aspines, the *a Studiis*, had likened it to Alexander before the Hydaspes. The Macedonian had repeatedly led his army out, but not committed it to battle until the vigilance of his enemy had been worn down. Maximinus did not know about Indians, but these Germans lacked discipline. The gods willing, many would be back in their camp, lolling in indolence or drunken slumber.

Maximinus would have liked to continue for several more days, but Timesitheus had warned that supplies were dangerously low. The army had food for just five further days, and, although the *Graeculus* had had all the blacksmiths working day and night, there were only enough ballista bolts for one final extended barrage. When the battle was won, Maximinus would order the men to scour the ground to recover all the missiles they could find. *When the battle was won.* The thought tempted fate. Maximinus spat on his chest to avert bad luck.

The spittle ran down the chased steel of his breastplate. Maximinus noticed several of his staff looking. He had had more than enough of most of the imperial *amici*. They were friends in name only. Their sidelong glances and disparaging airs infuriated him. The march had been long and hard, rations short and comfort a thing of memory. While they had burnt a satisfactory number of villages and captured many head of cattle, it was true they had not killed nearly enough barbarians. But what these effeminate fools in gilded armour failed to grasp, no matter how often they were told, was that the whole campaign had been designed for just this end, to bring the Germans to offer battle in some desolate location of their choosing.

'All in position, Lord.'

Maximinus did not respond. He needed to review his dispositions one last time before he cast the die.

The army was arrayed in three columns. In the centre Honoratus would lead the first wave, a twenty-deep phalanx of six thousand men drawn from the legions of Moesia Inferior and the two German provinces. Shooting over their heads as they went in would be fifteen hundred Emesene and Parthian archers commanded by Iotapianus. Another six thousand legionaries, from Moesia Superior and the Panonnias, comprised the second assault. Flavius Vopiscus had charge of them. The reserve was stationed around the tribunal: eight thousand Praetorians and, to their right, three thousand cavalry made up of Equites Singulares, Osrhoene horse archers and cataphracts, in roughly equal numbers.

The vanguard of the right wing was fifteen hundred irregular infantry from Britain and from the tribes ruled by the Angles around the distant shores of the Suebian Sea. The former were led by the equestrian Florianus, the latter by one of their own tribal chiefs, Eadwine. Hard on their heels, Julius Capitolinus would charge the slope with four thousand legionaries of 2nd Legion Parthica. A thousand Osrhoene bowmen on foot would provide covering shooting.

The left wing under Catius Clemens was smaller. The initial attack would be the five hundred auxiliaries of 5th Cohort Dalmatarum, the second the two thousand legionaries of 3rd Legion Italica from Raetia. They would be backed by a thousand Armenian and Persian archers.

So many of these men would be dead by sunset. Aspines had told Maximinus a story about a Persian King looking at his army and crying because soon they would all be dead. Maximinus was no Persian. He mastered himself, touched the cold metal of the torque at his throat and the ring on his left thumb. He would let down neither his old Emperor nor his wife. Trust and good faith, they were worth the fight.

Maximinus turned slowly to take in the rear echelons. The camp was entrenched in old-fashioned Roman style. It was guarded by the 1st Cohort of Thracians and the Ostensionales, the dead Emperor Alexander's favourite parade unit. The latter were good for pomp and little else, and Maximinus was half minded to disband them when they returned to the empire.

The woods ringed the encampment at a distance varying between fifty and a couple of hundred paces. It was all too easy to imagine a horde of screaming barbarians emerging from their gloom. Next to no army will stand if taken by surprise from the flanks or rear. Maximinus had detailed a light armed force to move out through the trees on either side. He could spare only one auxiliary cohort and a troop of five hundred Moorish horsemen for each. It was against all tactical doctrine to commit cavalry into woodlands, but the Moors fought in no set formation. If the Germans were waiting, the Roman numbers would be inadequate, but those who survived would give a warning. If the woods were empty, Maximinus had told the commanders to try to find a way around the enemy positions. He wondered if he had chosen the right men for the task. Marius Perpetuus and Pontius Pontianus were the sons of two commanders from his youth on the northern frontier. Yet neither was the man his father had been. They were soft, pampered Senators, no better than all the others. Still, if these two wanted the Consulship that he had held out to them, they would have to earn it on the battlefield like their ancestors.

'Lord, it is time.' It was unlikely any other but Anullinus would interrupt, let alone dare to sound as if he might be chiding Maximinus. Perhaps the Praetorian Prefect was getting above himself. Rapid promotion after having killed an Emperor might encourage dangerous notions of self-worth in anyone. And there was something feral in Anullinus' eyes.

'Load the artillery!'

Maximinus' order was relayed through the ranks. The metallic *click, click* of the engines winding sounded sharp over the low rattle of men and the shifting of horses. Fifty light bolt-shooters mounted on carts were spread across the front of the army. Most were in the centre, but there were more on the right wing than the left. Maximinus hoped that if the enemy had noticed, they would not have drawn the correct conclusion.

'Loose.'

Back from all along the line came the distinctive *click-slide-thump* of torsion weapons. Fifty steel-tipped projectiles sped away with inhuman force. Some punched into the palisade; others vanished over its top. The latter should spread terror among those sheltering behind the defences from this man-made storm. A few, with inexcusable bad aim on this third morning, embedded themselves in the earth bank. Even before they hit, the air was again filled with the clicking of the ratchets as the machines were wound back.

From behind the tribunal came a deeper noise, a resounding impact. Maximinus forced himself neither to duck nor look over his shoulder. Several of the imperial staff lacked his self-possession.

'Baby on the way!' The traditional shout went up, and after a moment Maximinus saw the stone, its great size reduced to next to nothing by the distance, hurtling down beyond the defences. The big stone-thrower was shooting over their heads from the camp, operating at the very limit of its range. Transporting the thing all the way from the Rhine had caused grave difficulties. Even disassembled, it had needed three large wagons. From the start, Timesitheus had argued it should be rendered unserviceable and left behind. Of course, he had wanted to get rid of the smaller carts as well. Maximinus wondered if the *Graeculus* was watching from the camp and admitting to himself that he had been wrong. Most probably not. More likely he was fuming because the Camp Prefect Domitius had been entrusted with holding the base. The two equestrians had hated each other for years, at least since the days when, in company with Maximinus himself, they had organized the supplies for Alexander's Persian expedition.

'Sound the advance!'

Trumpets blared, centurions shouted, and the standards inclined towards the enemy. With a measured tramp, the three phalanxes began to edge forward.

Maximinus checked the columns detailed to go into the woods. Both were slow off the mark. What were Marius

Perpetuus and Pontianus doing? Probably having their legs depilated or listening to revolting poetry about interfering with small boys. Typically irresponsible, completely hopeless – you could not rely on a Senator for anything.

Trumpets rang out from the front. The attack columns shuffled and barged to a halt. The central one was about a hundred paces short of the fortifications. The ones on the wings had stopped at the foot of the slopes. The men had their shields up, locked together. Barbarian arrows were arcing down. Were there fewer than on the other days? Considerable numbers of warriors could be seen up there now. It was impossible to tell. The trumpets sounded a different order. After a moment, volleys of Roman arrows hissed away, filling the air like a host of bats. So far everything was the same as on the previous days.

Maximinus turned. Two of his entourage were talking, young Pupienus Africanus and another Senator. They fell silent under his gaze. He turned back. He knew he was scowling. Paulina was right: these Senators despised him. But in return he had nothing but contempt for them. During the long march, the soldiers had complained. Soldiers always did; it had no significance. The real defeatism, bordering on cowardice, had come from the upper-class officers. They had lurked in their tents, quoting gloomy lines of verse, which Aspines told him were from Virgil. How they wished they were back safe in Rome or their villas in Campania. The ramifications of Magnus' conspiracy had shown the disloyalty of the Senators. In its aftermath they had rushed to denounce each other. Many equestrians also had turned informer. Only the soldiers could be trusted. The sons of peasants, the sons of soldier fathers – only among these did any spark of antique virtue remain. The words of his mentor, Septimius Severus, were often in his mind: *Enrich the soldiers, ignore everyone else.*

'Sound the attack!'

The trumpeter on the tribunal blew and the call was picked up by every musician in the army. The legionaries from the Rhine and Danube surged forward. Honoratus had them well in hand. On the left the auxiliaries of 5th Cohort Dalmatarum raced up the incline. There were far fewer of them, operating in greater space, and they spread out. Maximinus checked the right. No movement there. That was good. No movement in the woods beyond. That was good too.

Honoratus' men in the centre were clambering over the stags, hacking at the projecting branches. Arrows were slicing through their ranks. Men were falling but, slow and steady, they were advancing. A loud cheer made Maximinus look to the left. A great boulder was rolling down the slope, gathering pace. At the crest the barbarians roared again as they pushed another off. The first one was moving fast, bouncing up, crashing back down, raising clouds of dust and debris. The Dalmatian auxiliaries scattered in front of it. One was too slow. In a blink of an eye he was gone, just some flattened rags and a smear of blood.

The attack on the left had stalled. The auxiliaries were huddled together in small groups, some in the few stands of trees, more out in the open. At the top the barbarians were about to release another great rock. The Dalmatians could advance no further, but it was not time to recall them. They would have to take the punishment.

The legionaries of Honoratus had now cleared the stags and were picking their way through the lilies. Only a few were going down, but the pits had broken their cohesion. The leading men reached the ditch and palisade in scattered groups, not a close formation. A solid mass of barbarians was waiting for them. This was not going to be an easy victory. But Maximinus had never thought it would be. Nothing in life was easy. It never had been.

Not many arrows were being exchanged on the right. It was as if both sides were watching the play of events in the centre. With luck, the barbarians might think the Romans lacked the will to brave that slope. Maximinus prayed that would not turn out to be true.

'Sound the recall!' Honoratus and his men had done enough. Thousands of men shuffled backwards, faces to the enemy, shields out. They had lost all order, but they were not running. Things were different on the left, where the auxiliaries hurled themselves pell-mell down the hill, every man for himself.

When the legionaries of Honoratus reached the eastern bowmen, there was much pushing and shoving as they passed through their ranks. The confusion was much worse as they forced their way through the serried formation of the other body of legionaries waiting with Flavius Vopiscus.

A counter-attack now would cause havoc, perhaps sweep the entire Roman army away. Of course, it was unlikely that a barbarian leader could exercise that degree of control over his warriors. They would be unwilling to leave their fortifications. They would have to cross their own traps, perhaps twice, if they met solid resistance. The odds were against it, but Maximinus thought this moment worth remembering. All too many barbarian chiefs were serving as officers in the Roman army and then returning to their tribes. The gap between the armed might of Rome and *barbaricum* was narrowing. If Roman discipline was allowed to slide, the gap might close to nothing.

'Send in the second wave.'

The Panonnian and Moesian legionaries under Vopiscus knew their trade. They had re-formed their ranks and passed through the archers without trouble. Again, the sky darkened as squalls of arrows fell in both directions.

On the left, Maximinus saw Catius Clemens. Mounted on

a huge black warhorse, he rode out in front of his two thousand Raetian legionaries. The Senator might always complain of colds and fevers but, unlike the majority of his order, he remembered his ancestral courage. Catius Clemens led them up at a steady walk. No boulders tumbled down to impede their slow, silent progress. The suffering of the Dalmatian auxiliaries had not been for nothing.

Maximinus gazed off to the right, where 2nd Legion Parthica and the Britons and warriors from the Suebian Sea were hunkered down at the foot of the bluff. The Osrhoene archers with them exchanged desultory arrows with the barbarians on the crest. How events went from now on, Maximinus thought, was all about timing.

Vopiscus' legionaries had cleared the stags, were pushing on through the pits with their vicious spikes. Not yet, the Emperor said to himself. Have the courage to wait.

The Raetians were within javelin cast of the eastern crest. A storm of steel greeted them. Maximinus saw Catius Clemens' horse go down. The legionaries kept moving. A wedge of barbarians rushed down to meet them. The two sides crashed together. Maximinus ground his teeth. It was still too soon. Just a little longer.

A great noise, like a storm in the mountains, reverberated back across the field. The legionaries of Vopiscus were at the fortification. Steel flashed in the sunlight. A glimpse of red as a legionary was hoisted on to the palisade. He fell back. Another took his place. Further along, a legionary jumped down the other side. Men were fighting the entire length of the barricade. Now. It had to be now.

'Hoist the black standard!'

Maximinus peered to the right, willing the answering signal to appear. If it did, he missed it. The Britons and Angles were charging up the incline. The 2nd Legion Parthica was following, slower, but more compact. The Osrhoenes were shooting as fast as they could over their heads. *Jupiter Optimus Maximus, give us victory.* Silently, Maximinus mouthed a brief prayer to the Rider God of his ancestral hills. Had the barbarians taken the bait? Lulled by the inactivity below the western bluff, had they or their chiefs drifted off to face the obvious threat to the centre?

A huge tree trunk, lopped of its branches, rolled down. The Britons in its path leapt aside; some vaulted clean over. It smashed into the legionaries. Their line buckled, until, at the cost of buckled shields and broken bodies, they stopped its momentum. The troops flowed around and over it, re-forming their line.

The northerners were now at the summit. The legionaries piled in behind them. The line moved forward to the edge of the trees. Its progress faltered. It stopped. In one place it bulged backwards. Maximinus caught sight of Julius Capitolinus, riding his horse behind the melee, urging his men on. The fight hung in the balance.

Maximinus unbuckled his cloak. He stepped back and draped the heavy purple cloth around the shoulders of his cousin Rutilus. He put his helmet on the youth's head. 'Be Emperor for an hour.'

Rutilus said nothing, his fingers tying the laces beneath his chin.

'Father, why—'

'He has my build. You do not.'

'But—'

Maximinus silenced his son with a fierce glare. The imperial entourage was twittering like a flock of disturbed birds.

'Anullinus, take command. If Vopiscus' men fall back, throw in the Praetorians.'

The Prefect saluted.

'Silence, the rest of you! Stay here. Micca with me.'

Maximinus clattered down the steps of the tribunal, his

bodyguard at his back. At the bottom he took the reins of a messenger's horse. Micca gave him a leg up, then vaulted on to his own animal.

The Praetorians opened ranks to let them pass. They rode along the front of the cavalry, past the Equites Singulares, until they reached where Macedo had his station at the head of the Osrhoene horse archers.

'Take your men to the left flank. Support Catius Clemens, if he is still alive. If not, take command there. Do not let the barbarians disengage, give them no time to think.'

'We will do what is ordered . . . '

Maximinus kicked on across to the right of the lines, to find the commander of the heavy horse.

'Modestus, follow me. Draw your men up in three groups at the bottom of the ramps. When you see a signal, lead your cataphracts to the top.'

'What signal?'

Maximinus thought the promotion of Modestus might have been a mistake. 'Give me your cloak.'

The officer handed it over. It was a showy thing, saffron with fringes and embroidery. Maximinus put it on. 'When you see me on the crest holding this above my head, bring your troopers.'

'Lord.' Modestus grinned, embarrassed, but eager to please. 'What do we do when we get to the top?'

By the Rider, this Modestus was slow. It was hard to believe he was related to Timesitheus. 'When you see the signal, the infantry will have forced a gap in the enemy line. You go through it, down the reverse slope, turn to the east – that is your left – and take the barbarian centre in the rear.'

'We will do what is ordered, and at every command we will be ready.'

'Repeat your orders.'

'Follow you, wait at the ramps, see the signal, ride up the

slope, through the gap, down the other side, turn left, and charge the enemy.'

'The enemy centre.'

'We will do—'

'Get your men ready. Follow in good order.'

Without waiting, Maximinus gestured to Micca and pushed his horse straight into a gallop. Two streams lay across their path. They jumped the first and splashed through the other in a maelstrom of spray.

By all the gods, let this work. The barbarians would see equal numbers of cavalry going to each flank. With luck, they would still see a big figure wearing the purple on the tribunal, and not realize the Emperor was joining the assault in the west. If they did not send reinforcements, he would turn this right flank, even if he had to cut his way through on his own.

Maximinus ignored the nearest landslip and put his mount at the second, towards the heart of the fight. The ascent was steep, and then he felt the horse go lame. It might have shed one of its hipposandals, but he did not spare it. Leaning forward, right over its neck, he drove it up the slope. The Osrhoene bowmen scattered out of their way. Obscene curses turned to cheers as they recognized him.

Coming up on the rear ranks of legionaries, Maximinus jumped to the ground. Micca was next to him. The horses stood, heads down, blowing hard.

'With me! With your Emperor!' Maximinus unsheathed his sword.

'*Io, Imperator!*' The men beamed. Even the wounded pulled themselves up straighter. The news of his arrival rippled through the ranks. '*Io, Imperator!*'

Maximinus picked up a discarded shield and pushed into the tree line towards the front. Micca and others pressed after him. The combatants had pulled a few paces apart, both sides getting their breath, trying to raise the courage to cross that small space of beaten ground, back into mortal danger.

Maximinus took his place in the front rank. He towered over the men around him.

The barbarians were perhaps ten paces away, shaded by the foliage. Round shields, brightly painted, some in the insignia of Roman units. Pale eyes above, blond hair, not many helmets, the glitter of spearheads, a few swords. Maximinus could see only two warriors wearing mail; standing together, a little off to his right. They were chieftains, the leaders, but this was not a hearth troop around them. This was a levy: herdsmen brought from their animals, farmers dragged from the plough. There would be bands of better warriors on this ridge, men used to swordplay, sworn to die if their lord fell. But not here. Jupiter and the Rider God had led him to a weak point in their array. Kill the two leaders, and the rest here would run.

Raising his sword to the heavens, Maximinus bellowed a war cry. The time for subterfuge was past. Let them all know he was here. Let those two chiefs and their peasants from the forests feel fear.

'Are you ready for war?' Maximinus' voice boomed over everything.

'Ready!' The legionaries roared back.

Three times, the call and response. The 2nd Legion was in good heart.

At the last shout, Maximinus hurled himself forward, angling towards the men in mail. He did not reach them. A spear jutting down over a shield at him. Not breaking stride, bringing his sword up, he deflected it past his shoulder. Full tilt, turning his shoulder into the impact, he rammed his shield into that of the spearman. The German staggered back. Maximinus stepped into his space in their line. A backhanded cut bit into the skull of the man on his right. Twisting the other way, he sheered away half the jaw of a warrior in the second rank. A sickening pain in his ribs. A spear point gouging through the armour on his exposed right. Doubling over, Maximinus felt a blow to the back of his head. No helmet, blood hot down his neck. If he went down, he was dead.

Maximinus bent his knees, covered himself with his shield. Thrust blind from beneath it. His blade meeting resistance. Someone howling. Steel on steel. Steel on wood, sickeningly into flesh. Men grunting with effort and terror. All momentum gone.

Gathering all his strength, Maximinus drove forwards up behind his shield. Two Germans knocked off balance, floundering. He cut one down. Micca took the other.

A blur of motion, and from nowhere a spear embedded itself in Micca's back. The bodyguard fell, his armour clattering.

No time to mourn.

'Kill the men in mail!' Half aware he was shouting, Maximinus cut the legs out from behind a barbarian warrior all unsuspecting on his right.

The nearer of the enemy chiefs started to turn. Too late; he could not get his shield around to face the unexpected attack from the side. With his weight behind the thrust, the point of Maximinus' sword snapped through the cunningly wrought rings of metal, through the leather underneath and deep into the flesh they had failed to protect.

'Kill the other chief!' Maximinus pushed the corpse away. 'The other chief!'

'Emperor.' A legionary held a severed head by its long hair.

'Your name?'

'Javolenus, 2nd Century, 1st Cohort, *Imperator.*'

'If we are not in Hades by tonight, I will remember.'

'Thank you, Emperor.'

The press of men had thinned. Their leaders dead, the enemy were running. Maximinus hunted for an officer. 'You,

Centurion, lead your men to the left. Drive the barbarians from the ridge.'

The man saluted, and was gone. A horse picked its way through the dead and dying. 'Julius Capitolinus, take men to the right. Keep the gap in their line open.'

The commander wheeled his mount, shouting for soldiers to follow him.

All that remained was to send the cavalry through. Maximinus ran back the way he had come. Emerging from the trees, he sheathed his sword and yanked off the gaudy cloak. Modestus and his men were dismounted at the foot of the slope. The yellow cloak was ripped, stained with blood. He waved it above his head. Down below, troopers pointed. Modestus gazed up, scanning along the ridgeline. Gods below, surely the fool could see his own cloak? A little blood had not changed it out of all recognition. Maximinus watched a trooper take Modestus by the arm, point in the right direction. The officer started shouting, gesturing for the groups at the bottom of the other two ramps of fallen earth to join him. A soldier helped him into the saddle. The men scrambled to horse.

After the cataphracts had thundered past, Maximinus felt the wound on the back of his head. It was nothing too bad. He wiped the blood from his hands on to his breeches. Stepping carefully, to avoid the arrowheads and spears strewn across the ground, he walked through the belt of trees and looked down the other side. Modestus and his men were riding hard to the east. The valley was filled with fleeing Germans. Those in the path of the Roman heavy cavalry were ridden down. Soon the routed warriors would reach the encampment. Amidst the wagons and terrified non-combatants, chaos would reign. The path to safety would be choked, impassable. When the Roman soldiers reached them, all would be slaughtered: the old, women and children. None would be spared, not even babes in arms. Maximinus felt no pity. He had waited all his adult life for revenge on this scale. These were different tribes, but all northern barbarians were the same. Born to deceit and cruelty, they were human only in form.

CHAPTER 16

Rome

The Forum Romanum,

Three Days before the Kalends of October, AD235

It was an auspicious day. Pupienus followed the newly inaugurated Consul out of the Senate house. To avert envy, he touched the toe of the statue of *Libertas*. He could not have been prouder, more happy. Marcus Clodius Pupienus Maximus, his elder son, was Consul of Rome. His small grandson would grow up the son of a Consul, the grandson of a Consul and, from next year – if the gods allowed – the nephew of a Consul. The child's place among the nobility was secure. It no longer rested only on the personal favour of Septimius Severus, and that long-dead Emperor's grant of patrician status to an ambitious young officer who had served him well against the barbarians, and even better in two vicious civil wars. It was the hard-earned culmination of a lifetime of endeavour. His grandson would never have to resort to the evasions and subterfuge that had marked his own life.

They processed down the steps and out into the Forum. It was true that his son was only a Suffect Consul, and that his term as one of the replacement chief magistrates had come later in the year than Honoratus had implied it would. But there had been many leading families that the regime had needed to conciliate. That Maximus' colleague had had to enter into his Consulship *in absentia* concentrated all the honour in the eternal city on his son. As soon as it was framed, Pupienus regretted the selfish thought. He was delighted that his son had Crispinus as his colleague. He had written his friend a fulsome letter of congratulation. Crispinus was Consul and governor of Achaea. He may no longer command armies, as he had in Syria Phoenice, but a true Roman possessed the virtues of peace as well as war. Crispinus must not forget that he ruled over the birthplace of civilization, over the descendants of Pericles and Demosthenes. The Greeks may have fallen from the lofty heights of the past, but they deserved respect for the character and achievements of their ancestors.

Under the stern gaze of an equestrian statue of Septimius Severus, they made their stately way past the black stone where Romulus had ascended to the heavens. The plebs, out in reasonable numbers despite the chill autumn winds, cheered and moved back to open a passage.

The paintings were set up on enormous panels which stretched from the sanctuary of the Lake of Curtius to the Rostra. The figures on them were brightly coloured, larger than life. The action moved from left to right, drawing the eye straight to Maximinus. The Emperor rode a magnificent charger into a marsh. Barbarians floundered in the water around him: some fell mortally wounded or cowered in despair; others still resisted wildly. None of it did them any good. Roman soldiers followed their *Imperator*, hacking and stabbing, staining the mere with enemy blood. Above the chaos, Maximinus, clean-cut and handsome, seemed oddly indifferent to the slaughter.

In a break from tradition, Marcus Clodius Pupienus

Maximus was to give the speech of thanks for his Consulship not in the Curia but here, before the freshly unveiled depiction of the triumph of his benefactor. As he started to speak, no one could doubt the panegyric nature of the ensuing words.

'Our ancestors, in their wisdom, Conscript Fathers, laid down the excellent rule that a speech no less than course of action should commence with prayers.'

Pupienus had helped his son with the oration, and knew it off by heart. Half listening to the elegant phrases, he looked off to his left. On the pediment of the sanctuary another armoured horseman galloped into a watery place. The erection of the paintings of Maximinus had been in the charge of the ex-Consul Sabinus. The Consular was an intimate friend of Vopiscus, and so closely bound to the new regime. Sabinus was a man of culture. He would have given thought to their location, to their juxtaposition with the ancient monuments here in the sacred heart of Rome.

Pupienus looked from one rider to the other. In the statue, the horse of Curtius was head down, sinking. That of Maximinus was rearing, as if about to leap clear of the mud and reeds, to break free of the painting altogether and land on the Rostra. Some thought Curtius had been a Sabine warrior who had escaped death in battle at the hands of Romulus by putting his horse through the marsh that had once been in the Forum. Thoughts of defeat and enmity to Rome were unpromising. However, the Sabines had long become Roman, had formed the backbone of ancient legions. Perhaps the message was that Rome should embrace the Thracian Maximinus, who would bring his native courage to the battlefield.

Others considered Curtius a Roman equestrian who had sacrificed himself to the infernal gods for the good of Rome. Perhaps they might read Maximinus as another who had offered his life for Roman victory but, such were his virtues, the gods had spared him.

By coincidence, the Consul had moved to a passage mellifluously praising the Emperor as a new Aeneas, a Trojan saved by the provident deities to refound Rome.

Pupienus' gaze tracked back over the paintings: Maximinus and the army crossed a bridge; under the eye of the commander the soldiers burnt a village, butchering the men, manhandling women and children; the surviving barbarians lurked in woods, before Maximinus led the charge into the marsh. The story had no ending. Victory looked inevitable, but the fighting was not done. At the time the messenger had arrived with the laurelled dispatch and the instructions for Sabinus, the war had continued. A second messenger had brought news of another great victory in a remote pass. Maximinus and his army were nearly back at the frontier. The Alamanni, Cherusci and countless other tribes had offered their surrender. But, given their perfidy, the Emperor was not minded to accept. He would winter at Castra Regina, repair the nearby forts, rest and refit the army, raise new levies, and in the spring he would again march into the North. There could be no peace with the Germans until their eradication. The lands as far as the ocean would be turned into a province. All who resisted would be killed.

Nothing good would come of this, Pupienus thought. As a young officer, he had seen action on the Rhine; as a senior commander, he had led men in Caledonia; and he had governed provinces on the Danube. There was nothing but hard marching and savage fighting with the northern barbarians. You could win battles, but none would prove decisive. The divine Augustus had attempted to conquer Germania. He had failed. The young prince Germanicus and the divine Emperor Marcus Aurelius had conceived the same bold intention and they had failed as well. Always the cry went up: Just one more campaign! Just another year! The elderly Emperor Tiberius may have been a tyrant, steeped in vice, but he had known how to deal with the tribes of the North. Send favoured chiefs sacks of coins, crates of fine tableware, amphorae of wine for them to pass on to their followers. When they failed to heed the commands of Rome, cut off the gifts and watch their men desert them. If one became over-mighty, set the surrounding tribes to pull him down. Should all else fail, send in the legions to burn a swathe through the forest, install a new chieftain and then return to the boundaries of the *imperium*. The Greeks were right: the Romans held all the world that was worth holding.

No province would result from this war of Maximinus'. It would consume men and materials. It would devour money. Maximinus had got his hands on the wealth hoarded by Alexander's grasping mother. Now that he had doubled the pay of the troops, it would soon run out. Refitting the army would be expensive; conducting new levies even more so. Perhaps the treasury was empty already. Pupienus had loathed Valerius Messala, but was unconvinced that he had conspired with Magnus. The sybaritic patrician had been too indolent. More likely, his crime was marriage to Alexander's sister Theoclia. Of course, she had died too. The accusation of treason against the dead Emperor's ex-wife, inoffensive Memmia Sulpicia, strained all credulity. The victims had been chosen because of their links to Alexander, but they had been killed for their estates. They would not be the last. When an Emperor runs short of money, informers thrive and the rich live in fear.

It was good that one of his sons was Consul now, and better that the younger was with the army and would take up office with Maximinus in January. Pupienus remained Prefect of the City. All of this proclaimed the loyalty of the family to the regime. Yet, in a climate of suspicion, more active proofs might be required.

Pupienus ran his eyes over the assembled Senators, like a stockman surveying his pens. He had given Gallicanus his word, but the Cynic was a traitor. Besides, Gallicanus posed a threat. If his posturing led him to the cellars of the Palatine, how long would his much-vaunted philosophy sustain him when his body was racked on the horse and men skilled in their task got to work with the claws? What account might he give of the conversation in Pupienus' house? Of course, the accusations he mouthed in his agony would win no credence if Pupienus himself had denounced him.

And there, standing by Balbinus, was Valerius Priscillianus, brother of the freshly condemned traitor Messala. He was rich as Croesus. There was a family history of treachery. His grandfather had been sent to the block in the reign of Caracalla. Priscillianus' father, Apollinaris, was governing Asia, a wealthy province far out of sight of the court; an old man embittered by the execution of both father and one son; the remaining child whispering vengeance . . . the accusation almost framed itself.

And what of Balbinus himself? Venal, porcine, debauched – who could consider the world would not be a better place without his heavy, shambling tread?

Pupienus reined in his thoughts. Senators should not denounce Senators. Since Actium, they had had two and a half centuries living under one Emperor after another Emperor. Tacitus showed how it was to be done with integrity and dignity. Walk the middle path between, on the one side, outspoken independence, with its dangers and futility, and, on the other, grovelling servility, which debases and corrupts. Pray for good Emperors, but serve who you get. It should be possible to live under the principate and not be too deeply tainted.

'I call on the gods, the guardians and defenders of our empire, speaking as Consul on behalf of all humanity, to look to the safety of our Emperor. As he rules the *Res Publica* well and in the interests of all, preserve him for our grandsons and great-grandsons.'

Noble sentiments and fine phrases on which to end. There was scattered applause. For many of the plebs the inclement weather had overcome their curiosity or interest in elite rhetoric. Most of the Senators accompanied the new Consul back to his home on the Esquiline. Pupienus found himself walking next to Balbinus. His thoughts held in like a horse on a cruel snaffle bit, he made polite conversation with the corpulent patrician. A Senator should strive to avoid public rivalry and bickering with his colleagues. It was undignified to win such battles and ignominious to be beaten. When they reached the Carinae, Balbinus turned aside to his own house. Although his departure showed less than perfect respect for the new Consul and his family, nevertheless, it was not disagreeable to Pupienus.

Pupienus Maximus' house was crowded. It was not a large property. This was an expensive area. The dowry that had come with Tineia had been large, but not ostentatious. Pescennia Marcellina was prominent among those waiting in the atrium. Pupienus had known she would be there. She looked frail, but Pupienus was nearing sixty himself. He had been very young, just arrived in Rome, when he had caught her eye. She had taken him in, clothed and fed him, taught him the ways of the world. She had launched him into public life, paid all his expenses until his Praetorship. It was not until the profits of his governorship of Bithynia-Pontus that he had acquired any money of his own.

Pupienus watched his son greet Pescennia with unfeigned pleasure. The scandalous reasons that rumour supplied for an unmarried woman having showered her wealth on a younger man merely served to make both Pescennia and Pupienus more dashing in the eyes of his son. Youthful indiscretions gain glamour when they are safely in the past. Pupienus knew his wife did not share such a view.

Sextia Cethegilla was seated at the far side of the atrium. After a few words with Pescennia, affectionate but formal,

Pupienus made his way to the side of his wife. Sextia was talking to two younger women. One was a neighbour, Iunia Fadilla. There was no denying the beauty of this great-granddaughter of the Emperor Marcus Aurelius, but her life was thought to be disreputable. Old Nummius had left her wealthy, and scandal attached to her widowhood. Even before the death of her husband, she was said to have been the mistress of the younger Gordian, and recently there had been stories concerning her and a worthless young poet called Ticida. The other young woman – dark where Iunia Fadilla was blonde – was Perpetua, wife to his friend Serenianus. Greeting them affably, Pupienus considered that if he were overseas governing Cappadocia, he might wish his young wife left in Rome had some companion other than Iunia Fadilla.

The women talked and Pupienus took in the crowd. He had expected to see another from his youth, from before the days of Pescennia, from the years at Tibur. Among this affluence, Pinarius would have stood out, but there was no sign of him.

Over by the shrine of the household gods, his brother-in-law Sextius Cethegillus was cloistered with Cuspidius Flaminius. With them was Flavius Latronianus. It was an honour that the eminent ex-Consul had attended. Making polite excuses, Pupienus moved to join them.

'Let me through.' There was no mistaking the arrival of Pinarius. Large, clad in rustic homespun, the old man barged towards Maximus. The new Consul looked less than delighted.

'Come here, boy.' Pinarius enfolded Maximus in a bear hug. The latter stood very rigid. It was one thing to be presented with a reminder of his father's raffish past as a young politician in Rome, quite another to be confronted with living evidence that your progenitor was raised in the apartment of the head gardener of the Emperor's villa at Tibur. If only you knew what came before that, Pupienus thought.

'What is it?' Pinarius had released Maximus. The latter had stepped back. 'The smell of onions?' The old man laughed. 'My cart shed a wheel, near the fourth milestone. I had to get a ride in a farm wagon.'

Pupienus felt a surge of affection so strong it almost brought tears to his eyes. In an uncertain world where friendship so often was tempered by advantage, it was good to have one man you could trust without reserve. Pinarius had brought him up without complaint, with rough fondness, as if an old-fashioned father. In almost half a century Pinarius had not spoken of Voleterrae, of the things that had gone before and what Pupienus had done there since.

CHAPTER 17

The Northern Frontier
The Town of Castra Regina,

Eight Days after the Ides of December, AD235

It was lucky for the messenger that Caecilia Paulina had been there. Her husband had had him by the throat. Maximinus had been about to smash the soldier's head against the wall. She had not had to raise her voice. She had always been able to ameliorate his outbursts. Maximinus attributed his ferocity to the tragedy in his youth. Paulina thought its origins lay more in a lifetime among the brutal soldiery. But she had never voiced her opinion. Maximinus would never hear a word against the army.

The summons to join the imperial court in winter quarters at Castra Regina in Raetia was expected and delightful to Paulina. The journey from Mogontiacum was neither difficult nor long, and the autumn weather had been kind. While the legionary fortress might lack some of the amenities of the provincial capital, Augusta Vindelicorum, it was comfortable enough. Of course, imperial responsibilities would demand the attention of Maximinus. The succession of petitioners would bore him, but he would be conscientiousness itself in inspecting the repairs to the frontier forts and drilling the army in preparation for the following year's expedition. Yet, despite his diligence to duty, she had fondly hoped he would have time to spend with his family. She had missed him, and she had not seen her son for months. Rumour claimed that Maximus was not getting on well with his father. When winter closed in and they were closeted together, she had been convinced she could effect a reconciliation. The news brought by the messenger had dashed her tender imaginings.

The Sarmatians had descended on Dacia. They had been joined by the free Dacian tribes from the mountains and Goths from the shores of the Black Sea. The barbarians were there in numbers. Julius Licinianus, the governor, was blockaded in Ulpia Traiana Sarmizegetusa. It had taken all Paulina's influence to calm Maximinus. For a time it had looked as if he were going to break several pieces of elaborate furniture as he roared. His campaign into the North would have to be deferred. After his victories, one more season and Germania would have been transformed into a province. The glory that had eluded Augustus and Marcus Aurelius had been within his grasp. Now, when the spring came, instead, he would have to march east.

As the snow had fallen and the Danube froze, the headquarters became a hive of activity. There was seldom time for intimate dinners, and the mood was not right for furthering familial harmony. Day after day, the Emperor summoned his *consilium*. Worse still, Paulina had to attend. Maximinus said she reminded him of his duty. Certainly, her presence helped him keep his temper. But she knew no one else wanted her there. Mamaea had sat in all the previous Emperor's councils, and Alexander had been derided for his weakness. It had been the same with Elagabalus and his mother. It had always been the same. Before Actium, men of otherwise unimpeachable loyalty had deserted Mark Antony when he insisted Cleopatra accompany them on campaign. No Roman expected a general to include a woman in his deliberations. The place of a woman was in the home. Paulina prided herself on the virtues appropriate to a matron: modesty, thrift, chastity, a sensible and agreeable disposition. She was good at running a household. She had no knowledge of warfare, and did not want any. She sat very still, and said nothing.

At least, she consoled herself, there was one thing with which she had helped her husband. The night after her first meeting, in the intimacy of their bed, she had done everything she could – perhaps more than a matron should – until finally she had convinced Maximinus of the dreadful impropriety of continuing to summon the druid woman Ababa to his council. Men might object to his wife, but a *barbarian* woman . . .

Flavius Vopiscus was holding forth. 'More funds are needed. Much equipment was lost or damaged in Germany. Supplies have to be stockpiled for the new campaign. The levies are costing a great deal.'

Paulina had listened to them go over this many times. Solutions had to be found.

'Raise taxes,' Maximinus said. 'Demand a one-off contribution from the provinces, from the rich. They live in luxury, sleep safely, because we march and fight on the frontiers.'

Vopiscus fingered the amulet he thought no one knew he wore under his clothes. 'I have suggested before that such measures would cause widespread unrest, my Lord.'

Maximinus shrugged his broad shoulders. 'What can a few civilians achieve?'

'In the long run, nothing,' Vopiscus agreed. 'But, *Imperator*, a revolt – even the most doomed and ephemeral – has to be crushed. As you have wisely stressed, we must clear the barbarians out of Dacia this summer, and return to Germania the next campaigning season. A revolt might demand your presence.'

Maximinus frowned. He looked fearsome, but Paulina knew he was merely thinking deeply. 'All the cities throughout the empire raise their own local taxes. What the town councillors do not steal, they fritter away building new baths or giving oil to the undeserving. We take the proceeds of these existing taxes for the military treasury.'

This was new. The idea was so radical, it made Vopiscus pause. Paulina wanted to smile. Her husband might lack a formal education and polish, but only a fool would deny his intelligence.

'Again, my Lord, it would cause untold trouble. There would be endless riots. All the cities in the empire would follow any pretender who promised to rescind that ruling.'

'What, then?' Now Maximinus looked genuinely angry. He did not care for what he saw as obstruction, any more than he did for civilians or the rich. Paulina moved slightly, enough to catch her husband's attention. His face relaxed a little; not as far as a smile, but into his – utterly adorable – half-barbarian scowl.

Paulina resumed her look of benign distance from the proceedings. Maximinus was too straightforward to be Emperor, too honourable to be surrounded by imperial councillors. Since the German campaign, the senatorial triumvirate, Vopiscus, Honoratus and Catius Clemens, and the equestrians Anullinus, Volo and Domitius had been joined by two more aspiring members of the latter order. As commander of 2nd Legion Parthica, Julius Capitolinus had done well in the final battle, and the Greek Timesitheus had made sure that the men had boots and no one starved. Despite his performance, the duties of Timesitheus had been handed to Domitius. Timesitheus would soon depart for the East to govern Bithynia-Pontus. Paulina was unsure if it was an advancement or a demotion. Whatever the opaque intricacies of court politics, however, there was no disguising the ambitions of the men in the room.

'The regime of Alexander was weak and corrupt,' Vopiscus said.

You did well enough out of it, Paulina thought. So did every other man in this room.

'Mamaea was insatiable for money. On payment of a bribe, many who deserved death or at least confinement on an island of exile were merely relegated from Italy and their home province. Some escaped any penalty. Either way, the guilty retained their estates. Justice demands their cases be reopened.'

The whole *consilium* voiced its approval.

Maximinus nodded. 'Volo, have your *frumentarii* round them up.'

Vopiscus hesitated. He massaged the concealed charm. 'There are vast treasures gathering dust in the temples.'

'No,' Maximinus said. 'If we take from the gods, they will turn against us, bring defeat on Rome.'

'Not the gods.' In his alacrity to deny any impiety, Vopiscus interrupted the Emperor. 'Nothing of the sort, my Lord. There are many treasures which have not been dedicated to the deities but have been deposited in their temples for safekeeping. Many of these have remained unclaimed for generations. The families of those who placed them there have died out. The Taker of Petitions, Herennius Modestinus, confirmed to me that the estates of those who die intestate belong to the Emperor. The legal term is *bona vacantia*. You will be reclaiming what is your own.'

Paulina was far from sure the devout would see it in quite those terms.

Maximinus leant forward, hands on his knees. 'To a soldier, that sounds the typical fiction of a jurist. I am reluctant to risk offending the traditional gods. We are not desperate yet. Crown gold is still coming in from cities after the German victories. They will have to send more when we have beaten the Sarmatians. We will keep the temple treasures in mind. Should it become necessary, who will take on this duty?'

'My Lord, I would be happy to carry out your wishes,' Anullinus said. Even without the rumours about his actions in the coup – surely not, not after Mamaea was *dead* – there was a sinister, even frightening air about the Praetorian Prefect. Perhaps, Paulina thought, it was his eyes. At first they seemed dull, but when you looked more closely they appeared to burn with an energy that had no moral purpose or restraint.

'Make it so.' Maximinus sat back, resting his forearms on the arms of the curule throne. There was something Paulina found attractive about a man's forearms; that smooth curve of muscle a woman's lacked. One thought began to lead to another.

'Is there anything else that we need to discuss before we turn again to the question of remounts?'

Paulina's spirit sank at her husband's evident enthusiasm.

'Emperor.' With his high cheekbones and dark eyes, Honoratus was far too handsome. Paulina had never trusted men with such good looks. 'May I talk about the future?'

Maximinus grunted an assent that sounded as if he hoped the discussion of military horseflesh would not be delayed for any great length of time.

'My Lord, you and the Empress are blessed with a son.' Honoratus gave Paulina a dazzling smile. He was beautiful and suave: Paulina would not be the only one to distrust him on sight. 'Maximus took the toga of manhood some years ago; he is now eighteen. Last summer, he served with distinction under the standards.'

'Well,' Maximinus said, 'he travelled with us.' Paulina shot him a look which stopped him saying any more.

'There is nothing your subjects desire more than security, and nothing gives them more security than living under an established dynasty. No matter how they love their Emperor, if he lacks an heir, the future worries them. *Imperator*, your courage and your virtue impel you to risk your life on behalf of Rome. Should anything happen to you, there is the terrible fear of civil war. Nothing harms the *Res Publica* more than when ambitious men lead her soldiers in fratricidal strife. My Lord, I speak for all your loyal friends when I urge you to name your son Caesar.'

Paulina had known it would happen, but not now, not like this, with her present in the *consilium*. People would talk. They would say she had connived to get into the council, that she had exerted her influence to have her son elevated. Was Maximus ready to be Caesar, let alone Emperor? His father was right: the boy was immature. There had been that terrible incident with the serving girl. Thank the gods, Paulina had managed to cover it all up. What Maximinus would have done had he found out did not bear thinking about.

Wrapped in her concerns, Paulina missed what Honoratus had said next.

'. . . no imperial dynasty has ever been more loved than that of Marcus Aurelius. To join the two families would bring their many influential connections renewed influence. It would conciliate the nobility and link your regime to the age of silver. The girl is beautiful and amiable. As a widow, she is trained in the duties of a wife. Again, I speak for all when I urge you to betroth your son Maximus Caesar to the great-granddaughter of the divine Marcus, Iunia Fadilla.'

CHAPTER 18

As the last outpost of civilization, Tisavar was unimpressive. Sited on a low rise, the irregular stones of its walls were the same colour as the surrounding sand dunes. It was more a blockhouse than a fortress. As Gordian rode up, he judged it not bigger than forty paces by thirty. Nevertheless, the column would find the rest welcome.

Gordian had ridden down from Carthage with the Quaestor Menophilus and the legates Sabinianus and Arrian. Each had brought just the one servant. The hostage prince Mirzi was accompanied by six of his father's warriors. At Tacape on the coast, Aemilius Severinus had been waiting with two hundred troopers of the *speculatores*. A day's march south, they had rendezvoused with a hundred men of 3rd Legion Augusta under a centurion called Verittus at the small town of Martae. From there, for three days, they had followed a white track winding through the ochre mountains to the west. Descending, they had turned south-east across a flat, stony plain. Two days later, at Cententarium Tibubuci, a small outpost in the middle of nowhere, they had met two hundred auxiliaries from 2nd Cohort Flavia Afrorum. As instructed, their Prefect, Lydus, had brought provisions, grappling hooks and ropes, materials to make scaling ladders and light baggage carts to carry them. Two more days, bearing south then west, had brought them to Tisavar.

It had been a hard march over unmade roads, but possibly nothing compared with what lay ahead. There were no roads where they were going. Gordian liaised with the centurion in charge of Tisavar. He wanted to make the men as comfortable as possible. There were twenty-eight small rooms backing on to the walls of the fort. These were crammed with soldiers, as was the diminutive headquarters building in the courtyard. The officers would bed down together in the shrine. The stables that stood outside the defences were emptied of animals, mucked out, and more men billeted there. Even so, more than half the expedition would have to camp in the open.

They brought out food, wine and firewood. Gordian made sure the troops had a hot meal and ordered a double ration of wine. Of course, the men would drink more than the official allowance – they always had their own supplies – but they would sweat out any ill-effects the following day.

To get some privacy, Gordian and his officers walked out into the desert night. It was very cold, the stars very bright.

'The men of 2nd Cohort are grumbling.' Menophilus' breath plumed in the frigid air. 'They do not like turning out of their winter quarters, not to march nine days in a huge circle. They say the village is only two days, three at most, from their base at Tillibari.'

'I explained it would have alerted the enemy,' Lydus said. 'The brigands would never expect an attack from out of the desert from the west. And winter is when we will catch all of them in their lair with their plunder.'

'Soldiers grumble,' Gordian said. 'It means nothing. It is their way.'

They were silent for a time. A fox barked somewhere in the desert.

'A Persian army once went into the desert,' Menophilus said. 'The sands covered them while they slept. Not one of them was seen again.'

Gordian smiled. 'Words of ill omen, if ever I heard them.'

'An Epicurean such as yourself should not care,' Sabinianus said.

'We make allowances for those still mired in superstition, especially gloomy Stoics like Menophilus.'

They laughed, passing a flask of wine around.

'Mind you—' Sabinianus spoke to Gordian, '—we have more than drifting sand to worry about. We are going into the desert led by a young tribesman you maimed. If it were me, I would bear a grudge. This youth's father recently murdered his way across the province. You are far too trusting. It is asking to be betrayed. A small force, lost in the unknown, surrounded by barbarians . . . when the water runs out, we will have to do each other the final kindness.'

'That,' Gordian said, 'was almost poetry.'

'You may well laugh,' Sabinianus said, 'but I have a lot to live for. It would be a tragedy if talents such as mine were cut off before their time. I want to live. Do not expect me to sacrifice myself in a doomed cause.'

'Young Mirzi will not betray us,' Gordian said. 'He has been treated well as a hostage. His father has sworn friendship.'

'Your philosophy claims the gods do not listen to such oaths,' Menophilus said.

'On the whole, I find it unlikely that Nuffuzi chief of the Cinithii is a follower of Epicurus. Besides, we have promised him a share of the plunder.'

They moved out before first light. When the sun came up it

revealed the great rocky plain they traversed. Off to the right were the first sands of the true desert; to the left the foothills of the grey uplands. The day grew warmer. Even in this wilderness there were signs of life. Lizards scuttled out of their way with surprising speed. Gordian saw larks, wheatears and shrikes in the sky.

Mirzi told them about the men they had come to kill. 'Canartha is a man of much evil. No stranger who has entered his lair at Esuba has ever left. The fortunate he asks to join him; the rest die. When he raids, he tortures his captives not to discover their hidden wealth but for his own enjoyment. He ruins the looks of attractive women and boys. Afterwards, they are no good for pleasure, and are worth little.' The young tribesman shook his head at such profligacy. 'Those who follow him are little better. Most are from the Augilae tribe. They worship only the infernal gods. Like the Garamantes, they hold their women in common. They are very dirty, the women foully soiled.'

'In the West,' Sabinianus said, 'the Atlantes curse the rising and setting sun. Alone among men, they have no names, no dreams.'

Mirzi looked at him, puzzled.

'Take no notice,' Gordian said. 'It is from a book. For us, the desert is a mysterious place.'

Gordian was tracking a flight of sandgrouse when Aemelius Severinus motioned him to pull his horse aside.

'We are being watched.'

'Where?'

'My men have seen movement in the hills to the left.'

'Not goatherds?'

'They are following us.'

'How many?'

'Not many.'

'Your men should not tell the others.'

Aemilius Severinus wheeled his horse and cantered away.

Gordian rejoined the head of the column.

'What was that?' Arrian asked.

'Nothing.'

Gordian had faith in the report of the *speculatores*. Aemilius Severus' Frontier Wolves knew the desert. He would tell Arrian and the other officers in camp that night, when they could not be overheard. He had trusted Mirzi. Now, he was not so sure. Perhaps the cynicism of Sabinianus was not misplaced.

It rained that night. A cold, hard rain. Mirzi was delighted. It showed their expedition was blessed by one of his seven gods. Neither the Roman officers nor the men were convinced. They ate cold rations. Gordian had ordered no fires – although, by now, everyone knew they were observed.

In the morning, they turned east and entered the hills by what should have been the dry bed of a watercourse. The rain had turned its surface to mud. Men and horses sunk to their knees. The going was particularly bad for those towards the rear. The carts got stuck. Soldiers cursed as they laboured to free them. After an hour, progress was so slow Gordian decided to leave the carts. The water and food were strapped on to the baggage animals. The infantry would have to carry the timber to make the siege ladders.

By midday, those following them had abandoned all pretence of secrecy. Small groups of horsemen sat on the heights and regarded the column's laboured advance.

Gordian moved up and down the line, assuring the men that it made no difference. 'They know we are coming. They will be all the more afraid. A rabble of barbarians cannot stand against us.'

They sighted the village late in the afternoon. It was built on a spur of rock jutting out from the hills like the ram of a warship. Mirzi led them around up into the hills behind, where they camped. As the bare rock prevented entrenching, they made the best perimeter they could with thorn bushes.

The men gathering and arranging these took many nicks and cuts. It did nothing to improve their mood.

The only blessing was that the natives did not intervene. In fact, their scouts had disappeared.

The sun was arcing down towards the horizon when Gordian and his officers rode forward with Mirzi to inspect the enemy position. Not tempting fate, they were screened by a party of *speculatores*.

There was only one approach, along the causeway from the hills. It was flat and wide enough for twenty men abreast in close order. Some time long ago much effort had been expended to dig a ditch in front of the village. Although its banks did not look too sheer, it was about six feet deep. A pace or two behind it was a wall of unmortared stones, perhaps twelve feet high, with rough battlements. There was one solid-looking gate. There were no other fortifications. On all other sides the slopes were as precipitous as if they had been deliberately cut to make them so. The settlement itself consisted of close-packed, flat-roofed stone huts. There was no citadel, but if the dwellings were defended, it would be hard to fight through the narrow alleys between them.

The Romans had no siege engines. Artillery would have been useful, playing on the wall and the village from the higher slopes of the range. But the trouble of getting them to this place would be prohibitive. As for rams and towers, even if you hauled them all the way here, a sally by the defenders might easily topple them over the edge of the causeway. Mining was out of the question. It would have to be the ladders and a frontal assault, with all the heavy casualties that entailed. Send in the auxiliaries first. If they did not take the place, their attack would kill some barbarians, tire the others, and then the legionaries would have to storm the wall. The Frontier Wolves could provide some support by shooting over their heads. This was going to be a bloody business.

'There is another way,' Mirzi said.

'You have waited until now to tell us.' Gordian tried to keep the suspicion out of his voice.

'The cliff at the far end can be climbed. It is dangerous, but possible.'

'How do you know?'

'I saw a child climb down to collect snails.'

Sabinianus rounded on the youth. 'You said no one left Canartha's village unless they joined him.'

'My father talked to Canartha before he knew the evil of his nature. I came with my father.'

Gordian intervened. 'Could armed men climb this cliff?'

Mirzi fiddled with the bandage on his right wrist as he thought. 'Not with shields and spears. Not with helmets or in armour. It would be best if they were barefoot.'

'If they were seen from the top, they would not stand a chance,' Menophilus said.

'They would have to climb at night,' Mirzi agreed.

'If I took fifty of the Frontier Wolves,' Menophilus said, 'we could make the ascent tonight. When you attack the wall just before dawn, we could take them in the rear.'

'Why you?' Arrian asked.

'I am a great deal younger than the rest of you,' Menophilus said with a straight face.

'This is madness!' Sabinianus exclaimed. 'We are miles from anywhere, deep in tribal territory. To divide our forces, send some off almost unarmed into the night, is the final idiocy. The barbarians knew we were coming. We have been led into a trap.'

The damaged hand of Mirzi automatically went to his hilt. 'You doubt my word?'

Gordian stepped between them. 'Sabinianus doubts everything.' He turned to Menophilus. 'What do you think?'

The Quaestor toyed with the ornament in the form of a

skeleton on his belt, considering slowly. 'Rather than assign men from the *speculatores*, we should ask for volunteers. Offer good money for those who get to the top, and the same for the dependents of those who fall. No armour, helmets, shields or spears. But we must have boots. Our men are not used to marching without them. The rocks would cut their feet to shreds. Also, we will take iron tent pegs and ropes, as many as we can carry.' Menophilus paused. 'If we have some of the light shields the Frontier Wolves use and some javelins, we may be able to haul them up when we have made the climb.'

'Have you done much climbing?' Sabinianus asked.

'It is not one of my favourite pastimes.' Menophilus' line was funnier for being delivered with his customary Stoic earnestness.

After nightfall, no campfires were lit until Menophilus and his volunteers had left. Gordian found that sleep eluded him. In the middle watch, he got up and walked the perimeter. Snatches of music and songs drifted from the village. Lights flickered as the barbarians came and went from their huts.

All ways of dying are hateful to us poor mortals. Gordian had grown fond of Menophilus. He did not want to be responsible for his death, did not want his friend to die. With a horrible clarity, he knew that he did not want to die himself. No, that was not how it should be. As so often, he summoned up the tenets of his philosophy. There was no pleasure or pain after death, just as there was none before birth. There was nothing to be scared of. *Death is nothing to us.* But there was a tightness in him that his words did nothing to loosen. After a time, he went back and rolled himself in his blanket, watched the stars wheel, and settled to wait for the night to end.

A hand shook his shoulder, and Gordian surfaced from the deepest of sleeps.

'Two hours before dawn,' Sabinianus said quietly.

Somewhere in the back of Gordian's mind, wisps of a dream twisted out of his grasp; his father . . . Parthenope and Chione weeping . . . some lines of Homer: 'There will come a day when sacred Ilion shall perish'.

In the darkness, Lydus drew up the auxiliaries of the 2nd Cohort with as little noise as possible. Even so, the rattle of their arms and the scrape of the hobnails seemed loud enough to wake the dead. Gordian moved among them, a word here, a pat on the shoulder there. It was never easy to send men into combat.

No sounds or lights could be detected in the village.

The sky lightened in the east, enough to reveal the dark bulk of the phalanx of men, twenty wide and ten deep. No trumpets rang out. A murmur ran through the ranks and they began to edge forward.

Still no shouts of alarm from the barbarians.

Gordian and his officers mounted up and rode back through the lines of the *speculatores* and the men from the 3rd Legion. They went a little uphill, far enough to hope to view the fighting.

Half-glimpsed movements along the wall. The unmistakable twang of bows.

'*Testudo!*' Lydus' shout echoed among the rocks. A crash as the shields of the auxiliaries swung up and locked together over their heads. Moments later, the *thunk* of arrows into leather and wood. Wild barbarian yells, but as yet no screams of pain from the Romans.

'Loose!' The voice of Aemilius Severinus carried well. The first volley of Roman arrows vanished into the gloom. The archers, shooting blind, had been ordered to aim long. Most likely, the majority of the arrowheads would embed themselves harmlessly in the flat roofs of the village, but their passage overhead would remind the men making the assault that they were not alone.

There was a fast rattling, like the tambourines of the followers of Cybele greatly amplified. The defenders were throwing stones. They were bouncing off the shields. Gordian noticed that the light had strengthened enough to let him take in the whole scene.

Descending the ditch broke the cohesion of the *testudo*. Arrows and stones were finding their mark. Men were falling. The ladders were adding to the confusion. As the auxiliaries went up the far side, the first casualties were being helped to the rear. Gordian sent Arrian to usher the unwounded back into the fight.

The 2nd Cohort had reached the foot of the wall. Ladders reared up. The barbarians were well prepared. The battlements were thick with warriors. Poles and pitchforks levered the ladders sideways, sent them crashing down. The barrage of missiles intensified. At the extreme left a soldier got on to the wall, then another. Both were surrounded, cut down. The ladder was pushed away. At two other places a few attackers achieved the wall walk. Both inroads were swamped by sheer numbers.

Gordian gazed beyond the fighting. All was quiet in the village. There was no sign of Menophilus and his volunteers.

The retreat began with a few men at the rear. Soon, all the auxiliaries were backing away. They did not break and run but edged backwards, dragging their injured and the ladders.

'Aim for the wall!'

Aemilius Severinus acknowledged Gordian's shouted order. The defenders ducked down behind the parapet. For the first time, they had to cower beneath their shields. It allowed the 2nd Cohort to withdraw and re-form behind the other two units virtually unmolested.

'Third Legion, advance!'

The legionaries took up the scaling ladders. Again twenty men wide, this column was only five deep. They roofed themselves with their shields and trudged forward. Centurion Verittus had them in good order.

The barbarians showed restraint. Only the occasional individual popped up and wasted an arrow on the *testudo*. Gordian thought this Canartha had a remarkable grip on his men.

When the legionaries reached the ditch, the *speculatores* had to switch back to aiming for the village for risk of hitting their own men. The defenders reappeared. The storm of arrows and stones resumed; if anything, more intense than before. Perhaps the natives were encouraged by the repulse of the previous attack. With luck, they might soon run short of missiles.

Beyond the noise, still nothing moved in the village.

Legionaries clambered up the ladders. Some went sprawling back to the ground. Others, in the face of sharp steel, hauled themselves over the parapet. Fighting became general along the wall. The day hung in the balance. Again, numbers began to tell. One by one, the legionaries on the wall were cut down. Below, the first men began to retreat.

Gordian dug in his spurs, calling for Sabinianus. They rode through the lines of the 2nd Cohort, through the *speculatores*. At the ditch, Gordian jumped down, turned his horse free. It clattered away.

Gordian snatched up a discarded auxiliary shield. The grip was wet with blood. He slipped as he went down into the ditch. A jagged rock skinned the back of his legs. By the time Gordian had cleared the obstacle, all the ladders were down. No attackers were left on the wall. The legionaries were pulling back. Gordian shouldered his way to the standard-bearer, ordered him forward. The man looked blankly at him. Gordian seized him by the shoulder, pushed him towards the wall.

'With me!' Gordian grabbed one end of a ladder. Sabinianus helped him swing it up. The men hung back.

Covered by his shield, Gordian climbed one-handed. A rock thumped into the shield. Another dinged off his helmet. The wound Mirzi had given him ached. Blades hacked down at him. He thrust the shield over the parapet. A wide sweep of his sword cleared a space. He scrambled off the ladder, one foot on the parapet, and jumped down on to the wall walk.

A barbarian came at him from the right. He blocked the blow with his blade, smashed the edge of his shield into the bearded face. The man staggered, getting in the way of his companions. Gordian checked over his shoulder. Sabinianus had his back.

Seeing their officers alone on the battlements, the legionaries surged towards the wall. Men fought to get on the ladder.

Two more warriors jabbed at Gordian. He took one blow on his shield, parried the other. He shaped to cut left, but thrust right. Both natives gave ground. There was a throng behind them.

A crack of wood, sharp over the sounds of battle, then shouts of pain and fury. The ladder had broken under the weight of men. The barbarians roared, triumphant and mocking. The pair facing Gordian rushed forward. A lifetime of training took over. Gordian stepped inside one blow, took the other on the rim of his shield. Turning, he used his weight to force one off the battlements, then chopped down into the knee of the other, finished him with a neat backhand.

High shouts, obviously orders in some barbaric tongue. The enemy shuffled away. A man down in the village, pointing up at the isolated Romans. A hideous sound as an arrow tore past Gordian's ear. It felt to Gordian as if he had been here before: trapped on the wall, the ladders broken. It was Alexander the Great in some Indian town. The Macedonian had jumped down.

'Sabinianus with me.'

Gordian charged the barbarians to his right. Its very unexpectedness made them shy away. Hacking and cutting, he

212

drove them back past the head of some steps. Without pause, he plunged down.

The steps protected their right. They huddled together, crouching low behind their battered shields. Arrows thudded into the wooden boards, struck splinters out of the stonework. Gordian was gasping. His chest hollow and empty. *Death is nothing to us.* An impact jarred up into his shoulder. Something smashed into the side of his helmet. Blood ran hot down his neck. *Death is nothing.*

The hail of missiles slackened. A confusion of competing noises. The clash of steel behind and above. High-pitched yells of surprise and horror in front. Gordian's head was ringing. He peeked around the rim of his shield. The barbarians were milling, their heads turning in all directions.

'Menophilus!' Sabinianus shouted. 'Rescuing us is becoming a habit.'

A wedge of men was fighting its way down one of the alleys from the village. The enormity of the surprise robbed the barbarians of their senses. Some were fighting back; some stood and let themselves be cut down. The majority were running, this way and that, wildly seeking an illusory safety.

Hobnailed boots clattered down the steps. A knot of legionaries covered Gordian and Sabinianus with their shields.

'Are you hurt?'

Gordian did not reply. He was trying to clear his head, think what needed to be done.

'The gate – we have to get the gate open.'

A legionary helped Gordian to his feet. He was surprised that he was staggering. His thigh ached; his head hurt.

Groups of legionaries were appearing all along the wall. Up there, resistance was sporadic, still fierce in some places. The legionaries with Gordian overran those who stood between them and the gate.

It was the work of moments to lift the bar and open the

gate. Legionaries flooded in, the Frontier Wolves hard on their heels. The auxiliaries of the 2nd Cohort would not be far behind. They had friends to avenge and would have no intention of missing out on the raping and plunder.

Gordian leant on his shield. Doing the same next to him, Sabinianus looked as white as a man who had stepped barefoot on a snake. Gordian thought that someone ought to keep some troops together, in case there was further opposition or other barbarians lurking in the hills. He was too tired. Gingerly, he explored the cut on his scalp. It had largely stopped bleeding, probably was not too serious. The lines of poetry from his dream came to him:

> For I know this thing well in my heart, and my mind knows it:
> There will come a day when sacred Ilion shall perish,
> And Priam, and the people of Priam of the strong ash spear.

CHAPTER 19

The Northern Frontier
Near the Town of Viminacium on the Danube,

the Ides of May, AD236

Timesitheus watched the beaters working down the field. Next to him, Macedo, the Prefect of the Osrhoenes, sat his horse in silence. It was good hunting country: gentle timbered slopes coming down to broad plains dotted with villas and stands of mature trees. The wide channels of the Danube glinted in the spring sunshine off to the north.

The imperial field army had left Castra Regina in Raetia as soon as the worst of the winter had broken. The immense column had taken two months by easy stages to reach Viminacium in Moesia Superior. It was camped in and around the legionary fortress and town, readying itself to cross the river into Dacia. Maximinus was eager to confront the Sarmatians and other barbarians infesting that province.

The campaign was of little interest to Timesitheus. The next day, with Tranquillina and his household, he would continue on south and east. Naissus, Serdica, Hadrianoupolis – they would follow the great military highway to Perinthus, where they would pick up the Via Egnatia, and so on to Byzantium and the crossing of the Bosphorus into his new province of Bithynia-Pontus. There was a long journey still ahead, and demanding work at the far end, unravelling complex civic finances and confronting the intransigence of atheist Christians, in addition to the normal duties of a governor. He was glad to be out hunting, glad to be away from the intrigue of the court.

Macedo owned a dozen well-bred Celtic gaze-hounds. Timesitheus had always enjoyed hunting. This was very different from what he had known in his childhood on Corcyra. There, the mountainous, broken ground had meant going on foot with a few local scent-hounds and nets. It might have been back in the days of Xenophon. If he were honest, the resources of his family would never have stretched to Celtic hounds, Illyrian horses and liveried huntsmen.

The beaters, more than twenty of them in line abreast, were walking a field sown with wheat. One of Macedo's huntsmen had been out before dawn, and reported that there were several hares. It was well known that the braver, more intelligent hares made their seats in such open, worked land. They did so, Arrian of Nicomedia had written in his *Cynegeticus*, to challenge the hounds. Timesitheus thought it more probable they chose such places because they could not be stalked so easily by foxes. Whatever the reason, it promised good sport.

Macedo had not invited anyone else. The two mounted men waited behind a huntsman with two hounds on slip leashes. Other hunt servants, likewise clad in thick, embroidered coats and stout boots, held the rest of the hounds further back. The red and white feathers of their scarers flashed as the beaters drove across the front of those waiting. Timesitheus ran an educated eye over the two bitches in the slips. A brindle and a black, both long in the stand from head to tail, they trembled slightly, necks arched and proud.

A shout came from one of the beaters, taken up along the line. They had put up a hare. It took three or four huge jumps from its seat. Ears pricked, it sat for a moment then bounded away from the noise and the motion.

The huntsman crouched, walked the hounds forward, getting himself down to their horizon. The bitches were well trained. They pulled lightly on their collars but remained completely silent. The huntsman released the top ends of the slip leads. In a blur the hounds were gone. No one, Timesitheus thought, could fail to thrill at the beauty of their acceleration. He put his heels into his horse's flanks.

The hare saw the hounds and angled diagonally away.

Timesitheus and Macedo put their mounts into a fast canter.

The hare ran straight until the brindle bitch in the lead was but a pace or two behind, then jinked to the right. The brindle turned fast, but overshot. The black cut inside. She turned the hare left, then right. The brindle was coming up again, clods flying from her claws. The black turned the hare again – two, three, four times. Her strike was clean. She pulled up in a flurry of mud, shaking her prey. If the snap of her jaws had not killed the hare, its neck was broken now.

Macedo jumped down and took two eggs from a straw-packed bag on his saddle. He handed one to Timesitheus and retrieved the hare. The bitches frisked around, panting, wagging their tails. Dismounting, Timesitheus caught the brindle bitch. He pulled her muzzle up, cracked the egg and tipped it into her mouth. Both men made much of the bitches, rubbing their ears, praising them.

No sooner had they returned, and another two hounds been led out, than another hare was running. The next huntsman made a mess of things. The hare was panic-stricken, almost under them, when he slipped the hounds. Less than ten paces, and the lead dog had killed. Macedo looked furious.

'Fine hares have often perished ingloriously, having had no time to do anything worth remembering.' Timesitheus spoke to avert his companion's anger from the hapless huntsman.

'You are right.' Macedo mastered himself. 'Let us have a drink and something to eat.'

The hunt servants led away horses and hounds and busied themselves spreading blankets in some nearby shade. Timesitheus and Macedo were left alone.

'"Let me at least not die without a struggle, inglorious, but do some big thing first, that men to come shall know of it."' As he recited the lines, Macedo looked down, brushing some dirt off his trousers.

'Hector's words before he fought Achilles,' Timesitheus said.

Macedo did not meet his gaze. 'You may think you will be well out of it in Bithynia-Pontus.'

Timesitheus made a noise of assent, his senses suddenly very alert.

'Vitalianus has been made deputy Praetorian Prefect. You spoke against his previous appointment in Mauretania. He will prove a dangerous enemy.'

'Most likely,' Timesitheus said.

'The Prefect of the Camp hates you. Domitius would like to eat your liver raw.'

'I would rather watch someone else consume his intestines,' Timesitheus said.

Macedo did not smile, but looked at him now, a mature consideration in his eyes. 'Unworthy men are being promoted. Quintus Valerius has been given Mauretania, Lorenius has replaced him in Raetia. My Osrhoenes and the heavy cavalry of your relative Sabinus Modestus gave Maximinus victory against the Germans. We have received nothing. You brought to light the conspiracy of Magnus, and you are put out of the way in Bithynia-Pontus.'

There was something about the way Macedo had said 'brought to light'. Timesitheus arranged his face. 'Not long ago, you envied me that province.'

Macedo shook his head. 'You will not be safe there. The last few months have shown that a governor of a distant province cannot defend himself from informers at court. Perhaps Antigonus was plotting in Moesia Inferior, but more likely he died because Honoratus wanted his command against the Goths. But harmless old Ostorius of Cilicia was condemned for his money. Domitius made the profitable accusation. The Prefect of the Camp took a quarter of the estate, the imperial treasury the rest.'

Timesitheus murmured something non-committal. He heard the scuttle of fear in his mind.

'The Senators will never truly accept an equestrian on the throne, and when he starts to kill members of their order . . .' Macedo left that sentence hanging.

Timesitheus said nothing.

Macedo continued. 'Volo reopening the cases of those acquitted of treason under Alexander, his *frumentarii* dragging back those who were merely relegated from Italy – these things have terrified them all. When innocence is no defence against wealth . . .'

The fetid, rodent breath was hot in Timesitheus' ear. 'My province is unarmed.'

'I have always admired the alacrity of your mind,' Macedo said.

'Thank you.'

Now Macedo smiled. 'The province of your friend Priscus is not lacking in troops. Nor is that of his friend Serenianus. Between them they have four legions, many auxiliaries. Together, Bithynia-Pontus, Mesopotamia and Cappadocia could sway the East.'

Timesitheus battened his fear deep down. He had to keep

219

his head. 'You just said the Senate will never accept an equestrian on the throne.'

Macedo actually laughed. 'No goddess has dazzled *me*. Another.'

'Who?'

Macedo shook his head. 'Someone better qualified than me.'

Timesitheus said nothing.

'We ask nothing from you. But, after the event, when a messenger reaches the East, an early declaration by several provinces would be both good for Rome and well rewarded.' Macedo turned towards the trees. 'No more now. Let us go and eat.'

Following, Timesitheus felt as if he were walking on the edge of a precipice. Who were the *we* who asked nothing of him? *Was* there a conspiracy? Was Macedo trying to do to him what he had done to Magnus? Was he already implicated? Would only decisive action save him? Or could he ride away tomorrow, leave it behind him as if the words had never been spoken? Tranquillina would know the answer.

Let me at least not die without a struggle. Hector had fought, but it had not saved him from Achilles.

CHAPTER 20

Rome
The Valley between the Esquiline and Caelian Hills,

the Nones of June, AD236

The high, blank wall prevented the die-cutter having any view of the Temple of Venus and Rome until he passed its northern entrance. He peered in, as he did every morning on his walk to work. His long-distance vision was getting worse. All he could make out was a blur of grey columns and the glare of the gilt roof. Although out of his sight, he knew the seated statues of the two goddesses were so big that their heads nearly touched the ceiling. It said something about human stupidity that the deities had no room to stand. It said worse that anyone might believe such idols could become animate.

He came out into the open space by the colossal statue of the Sun. Wreaths from some festival lay about its base, wind-bedraggled, their leaves dry and faded in the early-summer heat. The Flavian Amphitheatre beyond was a building site. It had been struck by lightning in the reign of Caracalla. Almost twenty years later, the repairs had not been finished. As was his habit, the die-cutter squinted up between the scaffolding at the arches on the top two levels. All were meant to contain statues. Most were empty. Like the Tower of Babel, this monument to mortal pride and cruelty would forever remain unfinished.

To his left, he passed the steps up to the Baths of Titus. He had a vague impression of greenery at their summit. That was what Rome should stand for: gardens, bathing, lectures in shaded porticos, cultured leisure after hard labour, peace after war, civilization. It was worth fighting for those things. The thought stayed with him as he went down the Via Labicana. On his right hand were the shops and their greed which fronted the brutality of the gladiatorial school behind; on his left – albeit little more than a haze to him – the elegant roofs of the Baths of Trajan. Two sides of a coin. It must be possible to have one without the other, to purge the sins of mankind. He had to be brave for the things that mattered.

After another block, he turned right into an alley. Halfway down were the doors of the mint. He crossed the courtyard and opened the shutters of his workroom. He carried his bench and stool to the open air. It was always better to work in natural light. For a moment, he stood irresolute, as the apprehension of what lay ahead that evening threatened to overwhelm him. Work, that was the answer. It would clear his mind.

Amid the clatter and bustle, he studied the new obverse die. It was very different from those he had made before. Maximinus' chin was thrust out, rounded, solid like a battering ram. His nose hooked down as if to meet it. The Emperor now wore a short beard. An indentation on his cheek suggested muscles, powerful jaws that would not let go. The eyes, if not conveying quite the same intellectuality, remained wide and clear, fixed on an objective.

The huge pictures set up in front of the Senate House had been a revelation. The die-cutter did not know if they were close to reality or represented the conscious projection of the image of a rough soldier. Either way, Maximinus must have approved of them. The die-cutter's portrait was very similar. The new issue of coins should please the Emperor. It was a good piece of work.

He set it down and picked up the four new reverse dies. After the German campaign the previous summer, and with Maximinus fighting the Sarmatians, another Victory had been an obvious choice. A tiny, naked captive sat at the feet of the goddess, hands bound behind his back. The conspiracy of Magnus had raised more difficulties. Not to allude to its suppression might be interpreted as disloyalty, but any direct reference was out of the question. For the other three reverses the Die-cutter had chosen the Safety of the Emperor, the Foresight of Augustus and the Fidelity of the Army. There was nothing original, but they seemed fitting.

Those who had fallen with Magnus had been only the beginning. It was the talk of the bars and tenements of the Subura, brought back by maids and cooks, that their betters were growing to loathe and fear Maximinus. The *frumentarii* were scouring the empire for those Senators who had been either acquitted of treason or merely relegated for that offence under Alexander. Holding office seemed to offer no protection. The governor of Thrace had joined Ostorius of Cilicia and Antigonus of Moesia. Bundled into a closed carriage, they had been driven night and day to the North. There were dark rumours of abuse, even tortures fit only for slaves. The sole certainties were that their estates had been confiscated, and they had not been seen or heard of again. No trials; they were just gone. In their fine houses the Senators were said to murmur among themselves of another Domitian, a new reign of terror.

In their blind arrogance, the magistrates in charge of the mint had talked in the hearing of the die-cutter. When his uncle Messala had been arrested, young Valerius Poplicola had burst into tears. He was sure he would be next. No one was safe. The other two agreed. Acilius Glabrio had whispered – as if the die-cutter were of no more account than a piece of furniture – that Maximinus was a monster.

The die-cutter did not see it in that light. The Emperor campaigned on behalf of Rome and, for that, he needed money. Far from fighting, these pampered youths and their senatorial families wallowed in indolence and depravity, and they had wealth beyond imagining. Not to contribute any of their riches to the defence of the *Res Publica* was close enough to treason. The Emperor took what should have been offered. He did not oppress the plebs. Nor, thankfully, did it appear that his agents pried into their lives. Every morning, in the dark, with his brothers and sisters, the die-cutter prayed for the success of the Emperor.

Taking a blank disc of hard bronze, the die-cutter fixed it tight in a vice. He unpacked the tools from his bag and spread them on his bench. The new Caesar presented a challenge. Maximus had not been depicted in the paintings. Taking a drill bit of soft bronze, the die-cutter dipped it oil then rubbed it in a bowl of powdered corundum. Having fitted it into a bow, he began to bore holes to mark the mouth, eyes, ears and nose. When satisfied, he used a steel graver to cut the flowing lines freehand. With long practice, the burr thrown up before the tool was lost in the cavity it created.

When, a long time later, he straightened to view his work, the face of a young man had begun to emerge. Maximus was short-haired, clean-shaven; his classical good looks contained just a hint of his father's chin. With civilian dress peeking at his neck, he looked a model of familial propriety. This youth could have been a scion of the Severan dynasty, or any other. Of course, soon he would be married into that of Marcus Aurelius. The die-cutter had seen Iunia Fadilla once. Castricius had pointed her out as she walked down from the

Carinae to the Forum. Blonde, good-looking, there was one member of a Senatorial family who had no reason to fear this new regime.

The creative work accomplished, as he cleaned up the image, the die-cutter's thoughts returned to the coming evening. A man called Fabianus was coming in from the country. The die-cutter had been told to meet him at the Porta Querquetulana and take him to meet Pontianus. This Fabianus was a rustic. He would gawp and stare. What if he drew attention to them? What if he betrayed them by gesture or word? The die-cutter imagined the cellars on the Palatine. He could not help it. He was no hero. Shackled in the dark, in the fetid air, how long could he stand the rack, the terrible claws? Once they knew who you were, they hung you from beams, unequal weights tied to your legs. When their arms tired from whipping you, they threw you in cells whose floors were covered deep with thousands of pot shards, their edges razor sharp. Their cruelty knew no end. Once they knew who you were, they treated you worse than a murderer.

CHAPTER 21

Italy

The Julian Alps,

the Ides of June, AD236

The mountains were more desolate than any Iunia Fadilla had ever seen. On the climb up, she had caught occasional glimpses of the great empty ridges and valleys of Mons Ocra off to the right. Most of the time the pine-clad slopes through which the road ran cut off the view. They had left the small fortified resthouse of Ad Pirium that morning to follow the road as it twisted and turned down to a place called Longaticum. After an hour or so they had passed an unmanned blockhouse. Apart from that, there had been no sign of human habitation. The close, gloomy forest oppressed her spirits. Even the air seemed dark.

At least she travelled in relative comfort. The big four-wheeled carriage jolted and bumped over every stone and rut, but it was furnished with a surfeit of cushions. The hangings could be drawn to take in the passing scenery or, as often since they had entered the mountains, to block it out. It was reasonably quiet. She was not bothered by conversation.

All her attendants, apart from one maid and her old nurse, Eunomia, had been sent ahead with the baggage. The maid would not speak unless addressed, and Eunomia had never been one to chatter. The axles and brakes of the carriage were well greased with olive oil. There was just the rumble of its iron wheel-rims, the creak of wood and harness and the clop of the draft horses and the mounts of the eight-man escort.

Outside Rome, Iunia Fadilla had been amazed by the size of the baggage train. Innumerable large wagons were loaded with tents, bedding, clothes, food, wine, cooking utensils, tableware, toiletries, commodes. There was fodder for the animals, spare wheels, ropes, timber and nails to effect repairs, even a portable forge. Dozens of slaves carried the more fragile and precious household goods on their backs. Those handling the animals were joined by droves of maids, valets, chefs, scullions and stable boys. There were ten Numidians in colourful embroidered livery to run ahead and clear the traffic from the road. The vast assemblage was shepherded by a detachment of thirty troopers from the Equites Singulares Augusti under the command of a tribune.

Their route had taken them up the Via Flaminia to Narnia, over the Apennines – their bright, open slopes now so friendly in hindsight – and along the shores of the Adriatic. The Via Popilia had led to the plains of northern Italy and the way to Aquileia. From that civilized city they had set out for the mountains.

Every morning the baggage had left several hours before Iunia Fadilla had risen. It spared her the noise and dust, and ensured that her lodgings – a sumptuous pavilion where no imperial post house was convenient – were suitably prepared for the night. Her own progress had been slow. As well as the driver, a man walked in front leading the horses. Although not garrulous, Eunomia adhered to one traditional trait of her calling. At every wayside shrine, the old woman insisted on being helped down. Between Rome and the Alps, there was not a humble altar at which she had not offered a libation and mumbled a prayer, not one of Mercury's cairns to which she had not added a stone.

Late one afternoon, somewhere in the damp marshlands at the head of the Adriatic, the carriage had broken a wheel. A trooper had been sent galloping off to bring aid. It had not arrived by nightfall. There was a small inn about a mile back up the road. The Hind was not reserved for those on official business, and did not have to adhere to the standards of the *cursus publicus*. The tribune and his men had summarily evicted its guests. Suitably roused, the patron, his wife, two slatternly-looking girls and a potboy busied themselves with brushes and dusters. They had prepared a meal of mutton, bread and olives. It was disgusting. The meat was tough, and there was grit in the bread. The wine was sour. Iunia Fadilla exhibited all the graciousness of good breeding. She insisted the other wayfarers have her leftovers and be allowed to sleep in the stables. She had studied them as they were ushered in to thank her: a family on the edge of destitution, a soldier on his way back from leave, two rough-looking travellers in riding clothes. All the men were hard-eyed, the mother and her young daughter wary, if not frightened. Iunia Fadilla had thought how hard it must be to travel alone, near impossible for a woman.

The carriage ground to a near-standstill. Pulling back the curtain, she looked out. Another sharp corner, more trees, another dismal slope. The sun was out. It barely penetrated the timber. It was the *ides* of June, the festival of Minerva. If she had still been in Rome, she would have been watching the flute players wandering through the whole city in their masks and long gowns. Men with rods would rush after them, playfully threatening them if they did not fill the streets with music.

229

Four of the cavalrymen dismounted to help brake the carriage as it descended a steep incline. Iunia Fadilla let the hangings fall shut.

The third day after the *ides* of June, the Virgins would sweep out the temple of Vesta and throw the dirt in the Tiber. For the first time in the year, the wife of the *Flamen Dialis* would comb her hair, cut her nails and let her husband touch her. And as the river carried the filth to the sea, and the high priest of Jupiter enjoyed his conjugal rights, men and women might marry without fear of ill luck.

She had feared something worse when Vitalianus, the new deputy Praetorian Prefect, had come to her door. She had thought of the poor Syrian girl Theoclia. When she had not expressed joy at the news, he had smiled patronizingly, and said it was no wonder: any girl would be overwhelmed by the magnitude of her good fortune.

The next day, she had signed the agreement before witnesses. As custom required, her guardian was there. Poor Lucius had appeared as uncertain as she had felt. Her cousin had looked a great deal worse a few days later when he had to set off before her to the North. Like her father, and in later life her first husband, he had no taste for politics.

After the signing, Vitalianus had placed the circle of iron set in gold on the third finger of her left hand. The one connected to the heart, he had said unctuously. With some incongruity, his Praetorians had brought in the betrothal gifts. A necklace of nine pearls, a net-work cap with eleven emeralds, a bracelet with a row of four sapphires, gowns with gold thread – one after another the costly but unwanted items had accrued. The party that evening had been a strained affair. Perpetua had snivelled throughout, and Ticida had recited bad poetry and looked as if he wanted to kill himself. All sorts of other people had thronged to the Carinae to invade her house. The pompous Prefect of the City, Pupienus, both

Consuls and her repellent neighbour Balbinus were among those offering congratulations. Another neighbour, Gordian's sanctimonious old bitch of a sister, Maecia Faustina, had the temerity to give her a lecture on how she should behave now she was betrothed to Maximus Caesar.

She was going to marry the heir to the throne. One day, she would be Empress. She did not want to be Empress. Mamaea had wanted to be Empress, and Mamaea had been hacked to pieces. Sulpicia Memmia had been Empress, and divorce had not saved her. Iunia Fadilla did not want to become a living icon, weighed down with brocade and gems, in endless court ceremonials. She did not want to become an imperial brood-mare, the timing of her menses the subject of speculation: Was she pregnant? Would it be a boy, an heir born in the purple? Above all, she did not want men with swords coming for her in some revolt against her father-in-law or husband.

The carriage lurched. It jarred her back and neck. Europa, carried off on the broad back of a bull, had travelled in greater comfort, and her abductor had been a god, not a mortal. Iunia Fadilla wanted to be in her house in the Carinae. Would she ever see her new house on the Bay of Naples again?

She controlled herself. There was no point in railing against fortune. What was it Gordian used to say? The sole aim of life is pleasure, and the first step on the road is the avoidance of pain. Right actions and right thoughts bring pleasure.

Maximus was young. He was said to be good-looking and cultured. The famous sophist Aspines of Gadara constantly attended him. Maximus wrote verse. It could not be worse than that of Ticida. There were many rumours of affairs with women and girls; matrons and virgins from respectable families. At least her husband would not desert her for the beds of his pages, as Hadrian had Sabina. There was something disgusting about the young boys kept by men of that sort, men like Balbinus. Running about the house naked except

231

for some jewels, when they had to venture outside they went veiled, not for modesty like Greek women, but to protect their delicate complexions.

She did not want to marry anyone – not now. When Nummius had died, if he had asked, she would have married young Gordian. If he had asked, she would have been spared this journey, this marriage, a life of restrictions at court. She checked herself. It was neither her beauty nor her wit that had caused this betrothal. She was the great-granddaughter of Marcus Aurelius. It was a dynastic arrangement. An Emperor could do as he pleased. Nero had wanted to marry Poppaea, so he had told Otho to divorce her. She was the great-granddaughter of Marcus Aurelius. She would never be safe.

The carriage was wrenched to a sudden halt. Those troopers still mounted clattered up alongside. Iunia Fadilla opened the curtain.

There was a hairpin bend a few paces ahead at the bottom of the slope. A dozen or more horsemen sat waiting there. They wore hooded cloaks and carried weapons.

The soldiers closed up around her carriage.

'Clear the road in the name of the Emperor.' The voice of the tribune betrayed his anxiety. The mountains were full of men denied fire and water.

Iunia Fadilla thought of Perpetua's fantasies of bandits and rape. These men might be worse. All Emperors have enemies.

One of the horsemen rode forward. From under his hood, he took in the soldiers.

'Stand aside!'

Ignoring the tribune, the horseman pushed his cloak off his head. He looked straight at her.

The rider was neither old nor young. His face was weather-beaten, but groomed. He leant forward, put his fingers to his lips and blew her a kiss.

'We were hunting.' His tone was educated. There was a

gold ring on his left hand. 'But it seems my heart has become the prey.' He unpinned a brooch, let his cloak fall on his horse's crupper. 'My Lady, accept this as an offering.'

She took the gift. It was heavy, with garnets set in gold.

'Show respect.' The tribune moved close. 'The Lady Iunia Fadilla is on her way to marry the Caesar Maximus.'

The rider did not take her eyes off her. 'The Caesar is blessed.' He backed his horse to the side of the road, motioned his companions to do the same. 'Should you come this way again, my Lady, accept my hospitality. My name is Marcus Julius Corvinus, and these wild mountains are mine.'

CHAPTER 22

*The Northern Frontie
The Town of Viminacium,*

Seven Days before the Kalends of July, AD236

The light was excellent by the big window at the top of the house. Flanked by her women, Caecilia Paulina sat and bent to her work. The tapestry was nearly finished. Cincinnatus was summoned from his ploughing, defeated the Aequi, rode in triumph through Rome and returned to his tiny farm by the Tiber, where his oxen still waited in their harness. Maximinus approved of Cincinnatus, took him as an *exemplum*. The tapestry was not large. It could travel in his baggage.

Paulina always worried when her husband was on campaign. It was Maximinus' firm conviction that a general should lead from the front. There had been skirmishes, but so far the barbarians had retreated before the imperial army. The town of Ulpia Traiana Sarmizegetusa had been relieved. In his last letter, Maximinus had said that he was marching north. He believed the Sarmatians and their confederates intended to make a stand somewhere in the further recesses of the province of Dacia.

In many ways, Maximinus was better off in the field. He was in his element surrounded by his soldiers, like a tyrant in his citadel. The image was ill-omened. Paulina paused in her weaving and put her thumb between her fingers to ward off harm. Maximinus was no tyrant. Her husband was many things – a fine general, a loyal husband, a man of antique honour – but he was no politician. He was well away from the intricacies of civilian government. Hordes of embassies and petitioners from all over the empire thronged the town of Viminacium. Macedo, and his Osrhoene archers who held the bridge, had detained them here. Apart from the military, the only travellers allowed to cross the Danube were those arrested for treason and their guards in shuttered carriages. Paulina was uncertain of the wisdom of re-examining those who had been acquitted or given a light sentence under Alexander. It could only increase the hostility of the Senators to the regime. But it was not Maximinus' fault. The idea had come from Vopiscus. The rest of the *consilium* had supported the proposal. Certainly, the war demanded money. When the Gauls sacked Rome the rich, women as well as men, volunteered the ransom. When Hannibal was at the gates, the wealthy volunteered their precious things, even handed over their slaves, for the safety of the *Res Publica*. Such patriotism belonged to a different age. A time of iron and rust called for harsher measures.

Paulina resumed her task, leaning into the loom, beating down the weft with a wooden comb. She prayed for the health of her son. Maximus was too delicate for an army camp – although, it had to be said, it would remove him from temptation. His last outburst had pained her more than any before. The girl had been one of her attendants, from an equestrian family. Paulina had sent her away, veiled, in a closed carriage, to the farm of one of her own freedmen in the backwoods of Apulia. The girl could stay there until she was fit to be seen again in public.

Perhaps Maximinus was right. She had mollycoddled Maximus. He was her only son. The birth had been terrible. Afterwards, the doctors had told her that she would bear no more children. She had offered Maximinus a divorce. She owed him the chance of further heirs. He had dismissed the idea out of hand.

There were Consuls in her ancestry, but her family had been short of money. Maximinus had been a favourite of the Emperor Caracalla, and of his father before him. Her mother had been unwilling for Paulina to marry him and, although her father had proposed the match, his doubts were evident. They had left the decision to her. She had never regretted her choice. Now and then she wondered how different her life would have been if she had been blessed with beauty. She might have married into one of the great families of Rome. Her husband might have worn the elaborate boots of a patrician, might have possessed conventional good looks. They might have passed their days in echoing marble halls, the busts of his stern antecedents glowering down. Yet she doubted she would have been happier with her husband. Maximinus was a good man. He had a quick temper but, with her help, he could bring it under control. Above all, he had a noble simplicity and a greatness of soul. Their son could learn from his father.

There was much Maximus had to learn. Marriage often calmed the hot passions of a high-spirited youth. Paulina knew that would not be the case with Iunia Fadilla. The letter from her friend Maecia Faustina had told Paulina all she needed to know about this great-granddaughter of Marcus Aurelius. If Iunia Fadilla had inherited any of the goodness of her imperial ancestor, it had been irredeemably tainted by her first husband. Priapic despite his senility, Nummius had initiated her into vices which would have been abhorrent to a Corinthian whore. He had prostituted her, in his ancestral

237

home, not for money but for his own perverse pleasure. Dribbling, the old goat had watched her debauched by other men before joining them in foul threesomes, *spintriae* such as even Tiberius had hidden away on Capri. Nummius had left her without any shame in her wanton immorality. Meeting her, respectable men and women recoiled from her kiss, from the impurity of her mouth. What Maecia Faustina could never forgive was the corruption of her brother. If a grown man like the Younger Gordian had succumbed, Paulina thought, what hope was there for a youth like Maximus? If only Maecia Faustina had written sooner, Paulina was sure she could have dissuaded Maximinus from consenting to this appalling betrothal.

The door was thrown open. A dishevelled girl rushed in like a maenad.

'The soldiers . . . they have acclaimed Quartinus. The Senator struggled, begged them, but they put the purple on him.'

Poor fool, Paulina thought. Resisting will do him no good. Maximinus will have to kill him.

'My Lady, they have torn the images of the Emperor from their standards. Those of the Caesar too. The Osrhoenes are coming here.'

There was pandemonium. The women wailed as if at a funeral. One fainted clean away.

Paulina forced herself to sit very still. If only Maximinus were not a hundred miles away.

Two of her attendants were pawing at her. 'Come with us, my Lady, we will get you away, hide you.'

Paulina felt an urge to laugh at their stupidity. There was no place of safety except with her husband, and he was beyond reach.

They were tugging at her clothes.

'Leave me,' she said. 'Hide yourselves. All of you, leave. It is the Empress they want.'

One or two scuttled through the door. Most remained, keening, rooted to the spot.

'Go! All of you!' If she had to die, she would do so with dignity, not surrounded by this display of womanish weakness.

A stampede of terrified women threatened to block the door. The one who had fainted revived enough to rush after them. Then they were gone. All but two: Pythias and Fortunata. Her high-born women had fled, but these two slaves remained.

'Save yourselves,' Paulina said.

'We will not leave you alone.' Fortunata bravely nodded at Pythias's words.

'Then rearrange my *stola* into respectability.'

Now the room was quiet, they could hear the gathering uproar through the open window.

A man barrelled through the half-shut door.

Paulina could not stop her sharp intake of breath, a slight start.

'My Lady.' It was Maximinus' old body servant, Tynchanius. He had been with her husband all his life. Although promoted to Groom of the Bedchamber, Maximinus had said he was too old now for the rigours of campaigning. It was a kindness that looked to be about to cost Tynchanius his life.

The door swung almost shut.

Down in the street, men were shouting, all the more frightening for being in some eastern language. Then, from inside the house, came the sounds of things breaking, heavy boots on the stairs.

Tynchanius faced the doorway. He had a sword. His shoulders were shaking. Fortunata and Pythias stood in front of Paulina.

Two archers pushed the door wide. They had drawn blades. Tynchanius lunged. They avoided him easily, slipped past. Two more archers crowded in. The Osrhoenes ringed the old man. He slashed this way and that. The easterners stepped back, laughing. As his back was turned, one jumped forward, sliced the old man's thigh. Tynchanius wheeled. Another cut him from behind. The old man staggered, flailing like a bear baited in the arena.

'Leave him!' Paulina shouted.

An Osrhoene grinned, perfect white teeth in his dark face. 'As my Lady wishes.'

The soldier thrust. Tynchanius blocked. Another soldier drove his blade into Tynchanius' back. The old man's weapon clattered to the floor. His hands groped behind, vainly reaching for the wound. He collapsed.

The Osrhoenes moved forward. Fortunata and Pythias shrank back against Paulina's knees.

Tynchanius was not dead. Through his own blood, the old man was trying to crawl to his sword.

'Where is your commander?' Paulina was surprised by the control in her voice.

The soldiers stopped.

'Take me to Titus Quartinus.'

One of the soldiers said something in their incomprehensible tongue. The others laughed.

'Stand aside!'

The ranks of the archers parted at the command from behind them.

Macedo Macedonius was in parade armour, his sword in its scabbard. The Greek took in the scene.

Tynchanius, trembling, slipping in the gore, was using his blade to lever himself up.

'Kill him,' Macedo said.

An Osrhoene brought his blade down into the back of the old man's head, like a man chopping wood.

'Take the girls, and leave. Amuse yourselves with them.'

Fortunata and Pythias wailed as they were dragged from

240

Paulina's knees. Their clothes were nearly all torn off before they were manhandled out.

Paulina remained seated. The arms of the chair were digging into her palms. Her breathing was harsh, like something ripped from her.

Macedo went and closed the door. He turned back and walked around the corpse. The pool of blood had spread across the marble floor, had reached a carpet and was darkening its silk.

'What of your military oath?'

Macedo stopped. 'None of this was my doing, my Lady. If I had not gone along with them, I would be dead by now.' He spread his hands wide. 'I will escort you to your husband. Trust me.'

Paulina hesitated. Hope can defy reason.

The door was pushed open. A tall middle-aged man with a purple cloak hanging from his shoulders and a wreath on his head came in. He was followed by six Osrhoene officers.

'*Imperator*, your presence is not necessary here,' Macedo said.

Quartinus ignored him, spoke to Paulina. 'My Lady, you have my assurance you will not be harmed.'

Macedo turned to one of the officers. 'Mokimos, escort the Augustus to the Campus Martius. It is time he made a speech to the men, promised them their donative.'

Quartinus opened his mouth but said nothing. He did not resist as two officers took him by the elbows and walked him out of the room.

'Shut the door. Let no one else in.'

The last man out did as he was told.

'While I have some authority over them, I can get you away.'

Paulina stood now. Although her legs threatened to betray her, she backed past the loom to the window.

'We must be quick, before they shut the gates, set a watch on the bridge.'

'Liar,' Paulina said.

Macedo looked hurt.

'Curse you, and your life.'

Macedo smiled, almost sadly. 'Well, in that case . . .'

CHAPTER 23

The Northern Frontier
Pincus, a Fort on the Danube,

Three Days before the Nones of July, AD236

Maximinus sat on the ivory throne. The imperial travelling companions were ranked behind him, but he was alone.

The news had reached him at Apulum, three days' march north of Ulpia Traiana Sarmizegetusa. It had been in this tent. He had been sitting on a chest off to one side, mending a strap on his armour. Things on which your life depended should not be left to slaves.

The bearer had been a young equestrian military tribune with 2nd Legion Parthica. Returning from leave, he had witnessed the events at Viminacium. He had got away while the men were looting, before they had thought to close the bridge. Riding night and day, two horses had foundered under him.

The story was quickly told. The Osrhoene archers had risen. They had torn the portraits of Maximinus and his son from their standards. The man they had proclaimed was a Senator called Titus Quartinus. He had been governor of Moesia Superior, until dismissed by Maximinus the previous year. The tribune was sorry, but he did not know what had happened to the Empress, and – a look of surprise on his face at the question – he knew nothing about a *cubicularius* named Tynchanius.

Maximinus had burst into action. There was time to save her. By nightfall, he had a flying column ready. Five units, all mounted – the Equites Singulares, the Parthians and Persians, the Moors, and the cataphracts under Sabinus Modestus – four thousand men, more than enough to deal with two thousand rebels. The Osrhoenes were bowmen. They would not stand against the heavy cavalry hand to hand. The next day, they had covered the sixty or more miles back to Ulpia Traiana. Two days later, they had reached the Danube, opposite Pontes. They crossed unopposed. Maximinus knew they had been fortunate. Six days, and the traitors had not yet moved east to block this bridge.

They had caught the man in the camp that night. He had been talking sedition to some of the officers of the cataphracts. Sabinus Modestus had handed him over to the *frumentarii* of Volo. The man had not stood up well to the pincers and claws. Maximinus had watched every probe, every twist and scraping. Leaning close, inhaling the reek of blood, he had listened to every sob, every shuddering word. Yes, the man confessed, he was a centurion of the Osrhoenes. He had been sent to watch the bridge. Quartinus wanted to bring Maximinus' troops over without fighting. *Gods, just ease the pain, just for a moment.* The Empress was dead. Yes, he was certain. He had seen her corpse lying in the street. Quartinus had ordered her cremated. *Please, for pity's sake, just stop the pain.* It had been hours before Maximinus had granted his wish. His mutilated body was thrown out for the dogs.

Maximinus' residual momentum had carried them west for a day. That night, he had drunk himself insensible. The next morning, he had not left his bedchamber. Catius Clemens had come to ask for orders, the watchword of the day. Maximinus had knocked him down, thrown him bodily from the tent. He had called for more wine. He had drunk for three days. Afterwards, he had a blurred memory of having his son by the throat, threatening to tear out Maximus' eyes because they did not weep for his mother.

Paulina had had every virtue a woman should possess. Loyalty, reasonableness, affability, religion without superstition, sobriety of dress, modesty of appearance – the list had no end. She had always dismissed her looks, but they had delighted him: her pale eyes, her delicate, small mouth and chin. Why had she died before him? He was older. He should have proceeded her to the grave. She should have buried him. Had they even placed a coin in her mouth for the ferryman? He would not let her life be lost, not let her go as if she had never existed. From his memories of her words and her actions, somehow he would draw the strength to resist fortune. But, when he thought of her, sorrow wrenched away his self-control. How could he hold steadfast to such a promise? How could such a thing have happened? Were the gods so uncaring?

On the fourth morning, it was Aspines who had coaxed him out from where he lay. Talking all the time of how a man had to endure, quoting lines from Homer, the *a Studiis* had washed him, with inexperienced fingers helped him arm:

> *There is not*
> *any advantage to be won from grim lamentation.*
> *Such is the way the gods spun life for unfortunate mortals.*

When they resumed the march, Maximinus had Aspines ride at his side. He had listened intently as the sophist drew on all his learning to offer consolation. Aspines did not know if the soul survived death; no one did. If it did not, there was just sleep. If it did, then there was a deity and, by definition,

245

a god was good, so the souls of the good would not flit like bats through the dark but find a haven, safe and happy with the immortal gods for eternity. Maximinus was suffering, but others had suffered more. Jason witnessed his bride burn, and saw the broken bodies of his sons. Aeneas rescued his father and son, but lost his wife and had to endure the sight of Troy in flames. And then there was duty. Maximinus owed it to himself, to the memory of his wife, to crush the usurper, to drive the barbarians from Dacia, to restore the Pax Romana.

Words, Maximinus thought, just words. But sometimes words have their place. He shifted slightly as he waited. On a small portable altar, the sacred fire smoked. He had made his decisions, but had told no one.

A guard pulled back the hanging.

Macedo walked in. The *Graeculus* was wearing a gilded and chased corselet. In one hand he carried a sack, in the crook of his other arm he held an alabaster urn.

'Emperor, I have done all I could.'

Maximinus neither spoke nor moved.

The Greek placed the sack on the floor. Bent over, one-handed, he fumbled to open it.

No one went to help him.

Macedo lifted the thing free by its hair. 'The usurper is dead.'

The tent was silent, except for the ticking of the fire.

Macedo dropped the severed head of Quartinus. It landed heavily on the ground.

Everyone in the tent looked at the repulsive object, except Maximinus.

'How?' Maximinus said.

Macedo wiped his hand on his trousers. 'Last night, avoiding his guards, all alone I crept into the usurper's room. As he lay like Polyphemus in swinish drunkenness, I killed him. This morning, the sight of his head brought his rebellious soldiers to their senses. In the light of day, before gods and men, I administered the military oath to their rightful Emperor.'

'The Empress?' Maximinus said.

'Her ashes, gathered in reverence.' Macedo held out the white urn.

Maximinus got up from the throne. His guards tensed. He took the reliquary, held it tenderly in his great, scarred hands. He would not weep. A man has to endure. He turned, and placed the urn on the seat of his throne.

'What happened?'

Macedo shook his head despondently. 'The rebels were looting the house. She fell from a high window. Some think she jumped to her death to preserve her honour. Others say she was pushed.'

Maximinus felt the blood pounding in his temples.

'She has been revenged, my Lord. This morning, I executed all who had invaded her home, all who had offered insult to her sacred person. Their corpses were thrown in the river, given to the fishes. Their souls will wander for ever in torment.' Macedo looked at Maximinus with tears in his eyes.

'All?'

'Every man.' The tears ran down Macedo's cheeks.

'Seize him.'

Macedo struggled, then stopped. Two soldiers pinioned his arms. Another removed his sword and dagger.

'*Imperator*, if I had not pretended to join them, they would have killed me. I would have had no chance to rid you of the traitor.'

Maximinus took Macedo's sword from the guard. 'You did not kill all who went into the house.'

'I swear by the gods below, I killed them all.'

'Not all.' Maximinus balanced the sword on his fingertips. 'I killed the centurion Mokimos five days ago at Pontes. You Greeks overrate your cleverness.'

'*Dominus*—'

Maximinus drove the blade through Macedo's breastplate into his stomach. He released his grip. The hilt was hard against the gilded leather and the point had burst through the armour on Macedo's back.

Going back to the throne, Maximinus picked up the urn, sat. His hands left smears of red on the alabaster. More blood stained the ivory throne.

The guards let Macedo slide to the floor of the tent. He was still breathing.

Maximinus' head throbbed, but his thoughts were clear.

'Send a messenger to the Osrhoenes that I will take their oath in person. Tell them to assemble, without arms, this afternoon outside Viminacium on the Campus Martius. Have the parade ground ringed by our cavalry.'

Maximinus pointed at Macedo. 'Take his head. Send it to Rome, with that of Quartinus. Put them on pikes outside the Senate House. Honoratus, you will go to Rome, and announce that Caecilia Paulina will be worshipped as a goddess.'

'*Imperator*, Flavius Honoratus is in Moesia Inferior, fighting the Goths,' Catius Clemens said.

'Then you will take my command. Caecilia Paulina will have a temple, priestesses, sacrifices. All our resources must go to the northern war. Tell the Prefect of the City, Pupienus, to reduce the expenditure on the cults of the other deities. If that is not enough, cut the corn dole and sell the surplus.'

'We will do what is ordered, and at every command we will be ready.'

Maximinus sat back, gazing at the bloodstained urn. Paulina was dead. It was unthinkable that the world might carry on unaffected. If the idle rich and the feckless plebs of Rome wanted spectacles, let them remember her. If they wanted bread, let them work for it.

His grief threatened to unman him. Aspines had done

his best, but he had been wrong. Neither Aeneas nor Jason had suffered as much. No one had. Maximinus had been fifteen. He had been out in the Thracian high country, hunting with Tychanius. He had known something was wrong long before they reached Ovile. The village was too quiet. He had seen the first dead bodies in the mud, but he had still hoped. He had walked into the hut, and his entire family had been there: father, mother, his little brother and his two sisters. They were all dead; his mother and sisters naked.

The northern barbarians had killed his family, and now these easterners had murdered his wife.

CHAPTER 24

Africa
The Outskirts of Carthage,

Four Days before the Kalends of August, AD236

Zeus Philios, the King of the Gods, was looking old and a little weary. He had laid down his thunderbolt next to his wine cup, but he was nodding happily. Even at his age completely in character, he was admiring the scarcely concealed charms of Aphrodite. Across the room, Hephaistos, a wreath of roses slipping over his eyes, was limping back to the table.

Gordian unbuckled Ares' grim helm. It was hard to relax under its weight. He looked around the table. The dinner of the twelve Olympians had been one of his best ideas. All the male guests were playing their part. Naturally, as governor, his father was Zeus. Valerian had the trident of Poseidon, and Arrian the winged hat of Hermes. It had taken some effort to persuade Sabinianus as Hephaistos to leave his mule outside. Stoic severity put aside, Menophilus was a suitably drunk Dionysos. As guest of honour, the sophist Philostratus, looking only slightly uncomfortable, now and then remembered to pluck Apollo's lyre. All their efforts, however, were as nothing compared with those of the goddesses. Gordian's own mistresses, Chione and Pathenope, wore costumes unlikely to have been chosen for any dinner party by the virgin deities Artemis and Athena. The better to draw a bow, she said, the right breast of the former was bare, the nipple rouged, while the latter had foregone her armour and reclined in nothing but a tiny tasselled cloak as her aegis. Two courtesans from Corinth played Hera and Demeter with less than matronly reserve. But the palm for lubricity had to be awarded to Menophilus' mistress. Thank the gods her husband was overseas. Lycaenion was Aphrodite risen from the sea. The sheer silk of her gown clung as if wet. There was something more arousing about her nearly concealed body than her companions' naked flesh. Gordian felt his cock stiffen whenever he looked at her. Perhaps later, when he had had enough to drink, Menophilus might share her with his friend.

Girls from Gades – no Ganymedes here, his father's tastes had never run in that direction – waited at the table. The main course was not ambrosia but suckling pig, pheasant and partridge, with artichokes, courgette, cucumber and rocket leaves. The latter were a sure aphrodisiac, as were the snails and oysters already consumed. In place of nectar, they drank the finest wines of the empire, Falernian and Mamertine, Chian and Lesbian. In the perfect seclusion of this suburban villa – they were some way outside Carthage – Gordian wondered if it might be a good idea if the serving girls took off their tunics.

'I remembered, also, the discussions we once held about the sophists at Antioch, in the temple of Apollo at Daphne.'

The elder Gordian removed his gaze from Aphrodite and smiled at Philostratus' words. 'That was a very long time ago,' he murmured.

'And, of course, I know that your family has always been known for its love of culture.'

252

Surely, Gordian thought, Philostratus must have seen wilder dinners when he was at the court of Caracalla.

'I was not that old when I governed Syria.' Gordian's father was thinking out loud. 'It seems a lifetime ago.'

'And the great sophist Herodes was among your illustrious ancestors,' Philostratus continued.

'In some way or other.' The mind of Zeus was far away. 'Daphne, there was a place made for enjoyment.'

'So, most illustrious Antonius Gordian, it gave me pleasure to dedicate to you the two volumes of my *Lives of the Sophists*.'

Gordian's father came back from distant, remembered pleasures. 'My dear Philostratus, no literary work has brought me more profit, nor given me such pleasure, since your own *Life of Apollonius of Tyana* many years ago. The conclusion, when you write of yourself and your contemporaries Nicagoras of Athens and Aspines of Gadara, when, in your magnanimity, you include your rival Aspasius of Ravenna, you give an old man hope. When the divine Marcus Aurelius died, as is often said, our world descended to an age of iron and rust. Politics became the haunt of the unworthy, and freedom fled from the *imperium*. Yet your book shows that culture will endure.'

Sabinianus laughed. 'If Maximinus leaves any of the educated alive.' He did not look up from caressing the thighs of Artemis. The goddess gave no appearance of finding his attentions unwelcome.

Gordian wondered if that night in Theveste might have been a mistake.

'Quartinus was a fool,' Arrian said. 'The only results of his misguided coup have been more arrests, more condemnations. Quartinus was a fool, just as Magnus was a fool.'

Sabinianus snorted, his hand still busy. 'Maximinus never needed an excuse. The roads were already choked with closed carriages rushing prisoners to the North.'

'Cutting the grain dole and the spectacles is a sure way

to make the plebs of Rome take to the streets,' Arrian said. 'Bread and circuses are all that has ever stopped them from rioting.'

Menophilus looked up from his cup. 'If other Procurators are anything like Paul here in Africa, the provincials will soon be in uproar. They say the Chain has resorted to the old trick of Verres. When farmers deliver their tax corn to Thysdrus, they are told to take it to Carthage or somewhere further away, unless, of course, they pay a fee for its transportation.'

'Thracians have always been savage.' The younger Gordian could not take his eyes off Sabinianus' hand. 'Remember what they did at the school at Mycalessus. Any hope of restraint was killed with Paulina.'

'Proconsul, is such freedom wise?' The voice of Philostratus was very sober, thick with apprehension.

Gordian's father raised a hand as if in benediction. 'Freedom that need cause no worry tomorrow, and nothing you might wish unsaid. Nothing said here will go any further. As tent-companions, we are bound by loyalty and friendship.'

'Even your son?' Sabinianus said. 'Individual pleasure is the only aim in life for an Epicurean.'

'You have all the understanding of a stevedore,' Gordian said, possibly more sharply than he intended, because of Chione.

'Am I not right?'

'If I did not act correctly to my friends – even to you, Actaeon – it would cause me pain.'

Sabinianus removed his hand from between Artemis's thighs. 'I have no wish to be torn apart by my own hounds.'

All applauded the interplay.

'On my way, I stopped in Athens,' Philostratus said. 'While I was there, Nicagoras delivered an extempore oration on the virtues of friendship. He began with Harmodius and Aristogeiton.'

Not the best way to bring the conversation on to safer topics, Gordian thought. It would be hard to find more famous tyrannicides in all of history. Perhaps the sophist was more drunk than he looked. But soon the table talk revolved around display oratory.

Gordian's mind wandered off to the storming of the village of Esuba. Unlike Sabinianus, his trust in Mirzi had never wavered. It had been a bold stroke, one worthy of the great Alexander, to overrule the doubters and send Menophilus with the native prince to scale the defences from the rear. He looked out through the colonnade at the dark plains before Carthage. It must have been somewhere out there that Scipio had asked Hannibal who was the greatest general of all time. The answer had been Alexander, then Pyrrhus, and third Hannibal himself. The Roman had persisted. And if you had defeated me? In that case, the Carthaginian had said, the greatest would have been Hannibal.

CHAPTER 25

The East

The City of Samosata on the Euphrates,

the Day before the Ides of September, AD236

Timesitheus was lucky to be alive. It tempted fate to put himself at risk again. As he rode towards the Euphrates, the thoughts ran ceaselessly through his mind.

The coup of Macedo could not have been a more abject disaster, mishandled from its beginning to its blood-soaked end. Thank the gods Tranquillina had told him to do nothing, neither denounce the plot, nor join it, just ride away before anything happened. But when news of its failure had reached Bithynia-Pontus, as he joined the provincials to offer sacrifices for the deliverance of the Emperor, Timesitheus could not have been more frightened. It was something near a miracle that he had not fallen in the immediate aftermath. Time had passed, but he remained unconvinced of his safety.

The death of Paulina was said to have maddened Maximinus. The Emperor had raged, attacked Catius Clemens, threatened to blind his own son. The Thracian had tortured Macedo to death with his own hand. Orders had been issued for the arrest of everyone connected to the conspirators. It was common knowledge that Timesitheus had been a friend of Macedo. Volo's *frumentarii* must have told him about them hunting, just the two of them, the day before Timesitheus had left for the East. Volo was inscrutable. Surely Domitius did not know about that outing. The Prefect of the Camp hated Timesitheus with a vengeance. Domitius had access to Maximinus, and would have denounced him straight away.

It was possible both men knew and that, against all probability, the influence of his dull-witted cousin had protected Timesitheus. In a typically repetitive and badly phrased letter, Sabinus Modestus had boasted of his new-found standing with Maximinus. He had won the Emperor's favour by fighting like a Homeric hero in the battle in the German forest. Of course, his dearest relative had seen him smiting the barbarians as Paris or Thersites had smote the Trojans. More recently, during the revolt, he had captured a dangerous officer of Macedo who had been tampering with the loyalty of his troops. How that had come about was not explained, and Timesitheus could not imagine. Had this centurion walked up to Modestus and announced that he was a seditious revolutionary and, like a Christian, that he wanted to die? Maximinus had asked Modestus to name his reward. Untold riches, adlection to the Senate, powerful governorships – anything had been within his grasp. Modestus had said he wanted nothing but to serve the Emperor by continuing to command the cataphracts. From a man of intelligence, it would have been a reply of genius, a public exhibition of old-fashioned loyalty and duty. From Modestus, it merely laid bare his complete lack of ambition and understanding.

The small party crested the final range of stony hills, and there to the south-east were Samosata and the Euphrates. Timesitheus reined in to look. His service in Alexander Severus' Persian campaign had not brought him this far north.

The town was large and sprawling, its outer walls following the lines of natural declivities. Inside, the streets appeared to follow no plan, but he could make out the usual open spaces and temples. The whole was dominated by a citadel cited on a tall, flat-topped hill. The great river ran close beneath the far walls and the wide level plains of Mesopotamia spread out beyond.

Timesitheus pushed down the thought of what might happen in the town and signalled the column to advance. The wheel of fortune never halts; you either rise or fall. He had travelled a long way for this meeting. To Sinope, at the eastern extremity of his province, across high Cappadocia through Comana, Sebasteia and Melitene; too far for a faint heart now. A large part of him wished the summons had never arrived, or that he had set it aside as if unread. Yet Tranquillina had been right. It might have been as dangerous to ignore as to attend.

The gate was open, but a queue of rustic wagons and peasants on foot were waiting to be admitted. Timesitheus sent a rider ahead to clear them out of the way. Even so, there was a delay. The walls of Samosata were faced in a diamond pattern of bricks, unusual for fortifications. There were buttresses every few paces. They would hinder the enfilading shooting of the defenders. In any event, the town walls were too long to be held except by an enormous body of men. The citadel looked more defensible. The legionary base somewhere within the town might make another strongpoint. The town itself, however, would fall to any attacker with reasonable numbers and enough determination.

A young tribune from the 16th Legion riding a glossy chestnut led them inside, and along a street which ran straight to the foot of the citadel. There, Timesitheus took leave of his escort, dismounted and made the ascent on foot. He was puffing by the time they reached the top. He stopped and got his breath before letting the officer conduct him past a basilica and into a south-facing garden. The others were already here, sprawling on couches under the stern marble gaze of a rank of famous philosophers.

As Samosata was in Syria Coele, its governor, Junius Balbus, was playing host. He introduced the others: Licinius Serenianus of Cappadocia, Otacilius Severianus of Syria Palestina, Priscus of Mesopotamia. Timesitheus knew these other three governors. He had not met the young princes Chosroes of Armenia and Ma'na of Hatra, nor Manu, the heir to the abolished kingdom of Edessa. The latter was a surprise. The last Timesitheus had heard, Manu had been a prisoner of the Persians.

Servants spread a table with food and drink, then withdrew out of earshot. For a time, conversation was general and trivial. Timesitheus arranged his face and let it flow over him. The wall of the basilica was finished in the same diamond pattern as the town walls. Once, it must have been the palace of the vanished Kingdom of Commagene. Perhaps it was thoughts of the transience of power that made Timesitheus suddenly feel very afraid.

No governor was allowed to leave his province without imperial authority. No sanction had been given, yet here he was with four other governors, who between them controlled eight of the eleven legions in Rome's eastern territories. Priscus was related to Otacilius Severianus by marriage, Licinius Serenianus was his close friend, and the same was true of Timesitheus himself. Lucretius of Egypt and Pomponius Julianus of Syria Phoenice had been appointed by the regime of Maximinus, and they had not been invited. Then there was the presence of the sons of two client Kings, and a man whose birthright had been taken from him. Priscus had called this conference to discuss a coherent strategy against the Sassanid attack. But an observer from the Emperor's court – a perspicacious man such as Flavius Vopiscus or Catius Clemens, let alone a hostile witness like Domitius – might well doubt that motive. Indeed, they might well reach the same conclusion as Timesitheus had himself.

'Thank you for coming.' Priscus' face was heavily lined, serious. Everyone listened.

'Persian cavalry are less than sixty miles from where we sit. Bypassing Hatra and Singara, a Sassanid army – infantry and cavalry, said to be twenty thousand-strong – is besieging Nisibis. A mounted column is camped before Resaina. Its outriders have been seen as far west as Carrhae. Depleted by drafts for the northern war, the forces at my disposal in Mesopotamia cannot meet this threat in the field. You command six legions and a greater number of auxiliaries between you. Unless we take drastic action, the cities of Mesopotamia will fall one by one.'

'If the lands between the two rivers are lost, the whole ast is in danger,' Licinius Serenianus said. 'I can send four thousand legionaries and the same number of auxiliaries from Cappadocia.'

Otacilius Severianus spoke next, with evident reluctance. 'My men would have much further to march. Palestina is much further away.'

'And so less exposed.' Licinius Serenianus spoke sharply.

'That is true.' Otacilius Severianus looked at his brother-in-law. Priscus nodded almost imperceptibly.

Timesitheus wondered if the nervous Otacilius Severianus had the courage to say whatever it was he had obviously been told to say.

'They would be longer on the road, but I can pledge the same from Palestina.' Otacilius Severianus looked unhappy at the idea.

All eyes turned to Junius Balbus. 'Before assembling a field army, we should seek imperial permission,' the corpulent Senator said.

'There is no time,' Priscus said. 'Mesopotamia will be gone before a messenger returns from the North.'

Balbus squirmed with indecision.

'If we hesitate, it will be too late,' Licinius Serenianus said.

'Yes, I suppose so. I suppose you are right.' Balbus took a deep breath. 'Very well. Although my own province could be invaded at any time, I think I could spare perhaps two thousand legionaries and a matching number of other troops.'

'Ardashir and the bastard line of Sasan can never be secure on their stolen throne until they have murdered the last of the Arsacid house,' Chosroes said. 'My father, Tiridates of Armenia, the rightful King of Kings, promises ten thousand horsemen to fight the pretender.'

The vehemence of the statement, and the scale of the commitment, drew a murmur of appreciation.

'My father Sanatruq lost his first born to the Sassanid,' Ma'na said. 'Although surrounded by the enemy, Hatra will send two thousand riders.'

'Rome will not forget such loyalty,' Priscus said. 'An army of over thirty thousand experienced soldiers and warriors, it would be hard for any foe to resist.' He stopped.

As if on cue, Licinius Serenianus spoke. 'Imagine what it might achieve, if the Persian menace were to recede.'

There it was, almost out in the open.

'When I was a captive of the Persians, I was taken into the presence of Ardashir.' The disinherited Prince of Edessa narrowed his kohl-lined eyes. 'The Sassanid released me to carry a message. Ardashir said he would withdraw his men, if the cities of Singara and Nisibis were handed over to his rule.'

Timesitheus made himself sit very still. So that was how it was to be done. Priscus, ever the pragmatist, would sacrifice two of the cities of his province. But who would put on the purple? Not Priscus himself; not another equestrian. Otacilius Severianus, his senatorial brother-in-law, was weak enough to make a pliable tool. No, it would have to be the capable Licinius Serenianus. It would not be ambition in the mind of the earnest governor of Cappadocia. No doubt he had convinced himself he had been summoned to shoulder a heavy responsibility for the good of the *Res Publica*.

'The Persian reptile is a liar,' Chosroes said. 'He will not be satisfied with two towns.'

'He has said he will take all the lands as far as the Aegean.' Junius Balbus sounded thoroughly alarmed.

Surely, Timesitheus thought, the fat fool had seen this coming when the meeting was proposed. Everything hung in the balance.

'Should the other forces be called away,' Chosroes said, 'the warriors of Armenia will continue the fight against the Sassanids.'

'Hatra is too hard-pressed for her men to leave Mesopotamia,' Ma'na said.

Priscus and Licinius Serenianus should have made sure of them beforehand, Timesitheus thought. The thing was slipping away.

'Perhaps we should discuss where and when our forces should muster against the Persians,' Junius Balbus said.

'The Euphrates crossing at Zeugma would be the obvious place.' Otacilius Severianus joined in eagerly. 'But supplying such a force will pose many difficulties, especially when it leaves the river.'

There was a pause before Priscus spoke. 'Materials can be taken by boat to Zeugma. Beyond that, we will need to establish stockpiles in Edessa and Batnae.'

It was over. Priscus and Licinius Serenianus, with the connivance of the Edessan Manu, had brought them to the brink, but had failed to lead either the irresolute Roman governors or the scions of local dynasties to make the dangerous leap. Now they would all have to hope the approach would not be seen as treason in itself. If anyone present turned informer, he would implicate himself.

The talk turned to the intricacies of logistics. As a man with experience in the field, Timesitheus made several contributions. After a time, he looked away, and found himself staring into the marble eyes of Bion of Borysthenes. Next to that philosopher was Aristotle. The old Kings of Commagene had liked their Hellenic culture organized alphabetically.

Timesitheus was relieved. Tranquillina would be disappointed. But he knew that, without her by his side, he lacked the stomach for open rebellion. His talents lay in other areas, in more indirect paths. One door shuts, and another opens. This coming winter he would travel to the neighbouring province of Asia to discuss city finances with its governor, Valerius Apollinaris. One of the sons of Apollinaris had been married to Alexander's sister. No doubt the old man was still mourning his execution. Over dinner, with plenty of drink, and sympathetic company, it would be surprising if he did not express a certain rancour, say things which, if reported to the throne, he might regret. It was evident that the man was not to be trusted. There was a history of treason in his family.

CHAPTER 26

The Northern Frontier
The Town of Sirmium,

Two Days after the Ides of October, AD236

One of the advantages of a second marriage was the removal of some of the rituals. It would have been farcical for Iunia Fadilla to have feigned the terror of a Sabine girl about to be raped as she was pulled from the arms of her mother, let alone for her to dedicate her toys and child's dress to her household gods. Anyway, her mother was dead, and this house in Sirmium was not her home.

It had struck her as high-handed that the owners of this house, solid citizens of this remote, cold northern town, had been summarily turned out. Not that they had seemed to mind. The opposite, in fact. They had said that they were honoured and hoped the Emperor's daughter-in-law would remember them fondly. Actually, Iunia Fadilla had already forgotten their names.

A maid passed her a mirror. Iunia Fadilla disliked what she saw. A second marriage did not get rid of all the ancient customs. That morning her women had parted her hair with a bent spearhead, rusty with the blood of a slain gladiator. Then they had pulled and scraped her curls into six tight locks. They had bound these with woollen fillets into a tall cone and placed a wreath of marjoram around their creation. She looked like a sacrificial animal, an offering to some outlandish deity.

The rest of her costume was more pleasing: a plain white tunic with a flame-coloured veil and matching shoes. A girdle cinched her waist tight, emphasizing her hips and breasts. The metal collar around her neck almost hinted of servitude. The bridal outfit was meant only to be worn once. Old Nummius had found the combined suggestions of innocence and bondage irresistible. Although she had demurred at the ritual coiffure, and some of his stranger suggestions, her first husband had persuaded her to wear the rest on many less public occasions.

Iunia Fadilla stood in the atrium with her bridesmaids. The girls were the daughters of the inner circle of the imperial court. Chief among them was Flavia Latroniana. Her father was an ex-Consul the regime wished to conciliate. Iunia Fadilla knew her no better than the others. Only two members of her own family were present. Her cousin Lucius was off to one side. Looking awkward, he stood with a distant kinsman called Clodius Pompeianus, another descendent of Marcus Aurelius. Eunomia lurked at the back. As ever, her old nurse had a hand pressed to her chest, mumbling prayers.

Three pages led Maximus into the house. They were followed by his father. The Emperor would fulfil the role of *auspex*. Behind came a horde of men of high standing. Flavius Vopiscus, Catius Clemens, the Praetorian Prefect Anullinus, many others; most were accompanied by their wives. The latter, along with the bridesmaids, had been rushed to the North inauspiciously, in the closed carriages more usually employed conveying prisoners to the same destination.

Since the army had returned from its interrupted campaign

in Dacia, Iunia Fadilla had seen Maximus on several occasions. He was young, no older than her, and he was tall, well proportioned. There was no denying his beauty, and he spoke both Latin and Greek in the tones of an educated man. Beyond that, she could say little about him. Of course, they had never been alone, and her betrothed had given no indication that such a state of affairs irked him.

A pig was brought in, and sacrificed. The attendants slit its belly and drew out its innards. As *auspex*, the Emperor lifted the slippery things and inspected them. He announced them propitious and said a brief prayer.

Maximinus stood, his hands dripping blood, as he waited for a bowl and towels. He was enormous; very ugly. His expression was closed, brutal. Perhaps it was to be expected. His wife had been murdered. By all accounts, Caecilia Paulina had been a gentle woman, kind-hearted. Maximinus would feel her loss, and he lacked the education which might have offered some consolations. Self-control could not be expected from a half-barbarian herdsman.

Iunia Fadilla thanked the gods for the slowness of her journey. If her carriage had not shed a wheel, if Eunomia had not prayed at every wayside shrine, she might have been in Viminacium when the revolt broke out. Her corpse might have joined that of Caecilia Paulina in the street. Perhaps Gordian had been wrong. The gods might not be far away and uncaring. Perhaps piety occasionally was rewarded.

Flavia Latroniana took Iunia Fadilla's hand and placed it in that of Maximus.

'*Ubi tu Gaius, ego Gaia.*' Iunia Fadilla spoke the traditional words. She had no more idea of their meaning than anyone present.

The bride and groom sat on chairs covered with the fleece of a freshly slaughtered sheep and nibbled a morsel of spelt cake. In solemn silence, ten witnesses signed the wedding document. Lucius was the only representative of her family to do so.

The thing was done.

'*Feliciter!*' The assembled party shouted their blessings. 'Good fortune!'

In view of the lateness of the season – in Rome, the October horse would have been slaughtered two days before – and the northerly latitude, the couches of the wedding feast had been spread in the rooms opening on to the atrium. Braziers had been lit to keep the chill at bay.

In the chamber of honour, in the presence of the Emperor, the celebrations were muted. Maximinus ate vast quantities of roast meat, drank unfeasible amounts of wine. It did nothing to lighten his mood. Under his baleful gaze, even the self-assurance of his son seemed to wither. Several times Iunia Fadilla found that the Emperor was staring at Maximus and herself. There was an intensity in his look she found frightening. In his savage grief, did he resent their felicity? Her stirring of compassion gave way to anxiety. An Emperor was above the law. Nummius had told her of a wedding he had attended in the reign of Elagabalus. The bride had been attractive. Elagabalus had led her from the room. Half an hour later, he had brought her back, dishevelled, crying. The Emperor had assured her husband that he would enjoy her.

Abruptly, Maximinus announced that he needed to relieve himself. As soon as he was gone, conversation became more animated. As Catius Clemens regaled the others with an anecdote from the Dacian campaign, Maximus leant close to Iunia Fadilla. He smelt of cinnamon and roses, and he was very attractive.

'I had imagined,' he said, 'my wife would be a virgin, not soiled. They say you have sucked off half the men in Rome. At least you should be good at it.'

CHAPTER 27

The Northern Frontier
The Town of Sirmium,

Two Days after the Ides of October, AD236

'*Talassio!*' the crowd shouted. '*Talassio!*' They did not know
what it meant. It was what you shouted at a wedding
procession.

'*Talassio! Talassio!*'

Maximinus followed the bridal couple. A page walked on
either side of Iunia Fadilla, holding her hands. For a woman
who had been married before, she looked oddly apprehensive. Rather than stay by her side, Maximus went ahead with
the page who carried the nuptial torch. The young Caesar
threw nuts to the crowd, answering their ribald comments,
revelling in their admiration.

How could the boy be so happy, just months after the death
of his mother? Maximinus stopped himself from grinding
his teeth. He could not imagine smiling. Everyone had been
taken from him. He thought of the forest in Germany, of the
spear thrusting into Micca's back. For forty years, Micca had
guarded him. After the massacre at Ovile, he had been one of

the first to join his band. Together, they had hunted the high hills of Thrace, and along the banks of the Danube, bringing wild justice and retribution to brigands and barbarian raiders. When Septimius Severus had enrolled Maximinus in the army, Micca had accompanied him as a servant. Micca had been at his side in Dacia, Caledonia and Africa – wherever he was posted across the *imperium*. Tynchanius had been with him even longer. He had been an older neighbour; his family had died in the hut next to the one in which Maximinus had found his father, mother, brother and sisters. Tynchanius had shared his hatred for the northern tribes. Maximinus could not remember a time before Tynchanius. And now, like Micca, he was gone.

Yet the loss of them paled beside that of Paulina. It was twenty-two years since they had walked, in a far smaller procession, to his rented apartment in Rome. Returned from Caracalla's campaign against the Alamanni, newly raised to the equestrian order, he had been favoured by the Emperor. Yet he had sensed the doubts of Paulina's parents. They had been wrong. The marriage had been happy. Even in the reign of the perverted Elagabalus, when Maximinus had retired to the estate he had bought outside Ovile, Paulina had stood by him.

Now she was dead, and it was his fault. If he had not become Emperor, she would not have died. He had not wanted the purple. It had been forced upon him. She had been brave, but she had seen it would end in tragedy. If he had found a way to avoid the fatal throne, she would be alive. Paulina, Tynchanius, Micca: they were all dead, and it was his fault.

'*Talassio!*' The shouts gave way to a song of the joys of the wedding bed; the groom would conquer his bride in the heated wrestling, the god Hymen would preside.

Maximinus did not pretend to join the merriment. In the guttering torchlight, he considered the throng: the flute players, the couple and their pages, the guests and Iunia's maids. Two of the latter carried a spindle and distaff. They were about all Iunia Fadilla had brought to the wedding.

Maximinus had never wanted to be Emperor, but when you have a wolf by the ears you can never let go. Honoratus and the others in his *consilium* had assured him that this marriage would reconcile the descendants of Marcus Aurelius and the nobility to his rule. It seemed they were wrong. The only relatives of the bride in attendance were one Lucius Iunius Fadillus, an equestrian cousin, and a more distant kinsman, Clodius Pompeianus, an ex-Quaestor of dubious reputation. Apart from them, a second cousin of her first husband had dared to appear, letting ambition triumph over propriety. This Marcus Nummius Tuscus might think himself fortunate merely to have been sent away. The reprieve might not be permanent.

Paulina had been right. The good and the great of Rome would never accept him as their Emperor. No Emperor had ever stepped down from the throne. Maximinus had asked Aspines. The nearest parallel the sophist could find was the Dictator Sulla renouncing his powers. But that was long ago, and the divine Julius Caesar had said it proved Sulla had no understanding of politics. If disease had not carried off Sulla soon afterwards, would the safety of his retirement have been certain?

Self-preservation was joined to duty. Unlike the Senate, Maximinus understood duty. He had served Rome all his life. While he sat the throne, he would continue to serve. The safety of Rome depended on defeating the northern tribes. Everything must give way to the war. Dacia was restored, and Honoratus had held the Goths on the lower Danube. Over the winter, Maximinus would raise more troops, more money. Early in the new year, he would pursue the nomad Sarmatians out on to the great plains. Once he had defeated them, driven off their herds, he could turn again to Germania, and the advance to the Ocean.

They had reached the requisitioned house, which, with its wreaths and guards, served as a palace. The lead page threw the torch. Among the onlookers, men and women scrambled to catch it, risking the flames for its promise of long life.

There was an old wives' tale. If a bride forced into marriage caught and extinguished the torch and put it under the bed, her unwanted husband would soon depart this earth. You could only wonder how she might achieve her aim undetected.

Iunia Fadilla went forward to anoint the door posts with oil and wolf fat. The archaic combination was intended to bring divine favour on the marriage. Maximinus knew it would not succeed. Paulina had done the same. If the gods cared, they would not have let her be killed. Was she pushed, or had she jumped? The centurion had not known and, giving way to rage, Maximinus had killed Macedo too soon to find out. Maximinus had failed to save her, and even after death he had failed her again. What were her last thoughts in the few moments as the pavement rushed up? It was too horrible to contemplate.

If the gods existed, they would not have allowed her to fall. There would have been intervention. Flavius Vopiscus could talk for hours about the intentions of the gods being inscrutable to man. With his amulets, and his finger jabbing at lines of Virgil, he was a superstitious old fool. Yet Vopiscus was the one who had suggested they confiscate the unclaimed treasures deposited in the temples. To Hades with *bona vacantia*, and other legal niceties. They would take everything. The dedications to the gods themselves would be seized. They would take whatever they needed. If the northern tribes won, they would sack the temples. If the gods were real, and they had any understanding, any care for Rome, they would surrender their gold and silver willingly. The civilians would whine, wring their hands, cry sacrilege. Let them. His troops would suppress any trouble. Doubtless, the learning of Aspines could produce suitable precedents.

Inside, the groom offered his new wife fire and water. The wedding song was sung, and the women led the bride away for the bedding. Maximinus felt sorry for the girl. She was still young, pretty. Life had not been kind to her. Apparently, her family had married her off to an aged Senator of vile habits. Freed from him, now she was joined to Maximus. Paulina had thought Maximinus did not know what their son did with the women and girls unfortunate enough to catch his eye. But an Emperor had spies everywhere, especially in his own household.

As far as Maximinus knew, no Emperor had disinherited his son. For all his virtues, the divine Marcus Aurelius had let the weakling Commodus succeed to the throne and bring ruin on the *imperium*. Even his stern patron, the divine Septimius Severus, had given in to parental affection and allowed the traitorous Geta to share the purple and try to murder his brother the glorious Caracalla. Things had been better in earlier days. When the Brutus who had founded the *Res Publica* discovered his sons were plotting its overthrow, he had them flogged in the Forum, bound to a stake and beheaded. The modern age was debased. But it could be reformed. The will of the Emperor was law. An Emperor should put the safety of Rome before the claims of his own blood.

CHAPTER 28

Rome
The Mint, off the Via Labicana,

Five Days before the Kalends of December, AD236

The die-cutter was so accustomed to the striking-room in the mint, he forgot the effect it could have on others. Fabianus stood transfixed by the noise, the relentless movement, the stifling heat. Most likely, he saw it as an image of hell. Since the arrest of Pontianus, the idea might well be in his mind. The die-cutter had chosen the place precisely because it was hard to be overheard. He waited while Fabianus tried to make sense of it all.

By each small furnace, the slaves laboured in four-man teams. With long iron tongs, the first man took a heated blank disc of metal from the furnace. He placed it on the reverse die, which was secured by a tang to the anvil. Holding its iron collar, the second positioned the obverse die just above. The third swung the hammer. While the noise still rang, the fourth removed the struck coin and put it in a tray. The first took another blank from the furnace. They worked without ceasing, their movements instinctive from endless repetition.

'More bad news?' The die-cutter spoke close to Fabianus' ear.

'Hippolytus has been arrested. The *frumentarii* came for him this morning.'

The die-cutter considered this. 'Then he was not the informer.'

'It seems not.'

They watched the slaves.

'Antheros thinks they are just the first,' Fabianus said.

In the die-cutter's thoughts were the claws and the scrapers in the cellars of the palace, hard-eyed men wielding them with refined cruelty.

'Antheros advised me to leave the city. He said to warn you. He thinks they will try to take us all.'

'Perhaps not.'

Fabianus took his arm. 'The flesh is weak. Pontianus is an old man. And Hippolytus is an outcast. He has no reason to protect us.'

'Africanus?' The die-cutter asked.

'I came via the library. He is brave, but his links to Mamaea make him a marked man for the creatures of Maximinus.'

A sudden shout, and the rhythm of the nearest team of slaves faltered and broke down. A struck coin had adhered to the upper die. The speed at which they worked meant it had been hammered down on to the next blank. Cursing, the second slave poked the upper die from its sleeve and used a fine chisel to try to pry it and the ruined coin apart. The other three put down their tools and drank from the water butt by their station. The one with the hammer tipped water over his head. It ran down his bare chest.

An overseer walked across and with a look told the slaves to resume.

The die-cutter waited until the noise of the hammer covered his words. 'The authorities might have more pressing concerns. The plebs have been restless since the money for the shows was cut back. There have been several incidents over the reduced grain dole. Now Maximinus has ordered the temple treasures seized there is talk in the Subura of keeping a vigil at the temples, stopping the soldiers. They say Gallicanus and the other philosopher Senators will lead them.'

Fabianus looked unconvinced. 'Pontianus would want us to take precautions. He is not a fanatic like Hippolytus. You can come to the country with me.'

The die-cutter managed to smile. 'I have never left the city in my life.'

'Antheros told me to take you. I do not command you as though I were someone of authority. I know my limitations. Those who question are doomed. Do not seek notoriety. Come with me.'

'I was there when they took Pontianus,' the die-cutter said.

Fabianus released his arm, looked sharply at him.

'I watched from the other side of the street. The crowd was jeering, baying for blood. Further than my hand, my vision is not good, but my hearing is sharp. Even above the mob, I heard what was said. Pontianus asked the soldiers why they were arresting him. They said they had orders to take all our leaders, all those who were spreading unrest and corrupting the innocent.'

There was suspicion in the face of Fabianus. 'You did nothing?'

'I did nothing.'

'You might not be so fortunate next time.'

'I will stay here.'

Fabianus nodded. He went to make a gesture. The die-cutter caught his hand. 'Do not be a fool.'

Fabianus disengaged himself, and turned to go.

Afterwards, the die-cutter returned to his workroom in

the courtyard. He sat at his bench in the open air. He picked up his latest design. Work always calmed his mind.

Rome's latest goddess, Caecilia Paulina, stared back at him. As with Maximinus at the beginning, he had no idea what she really looked like. A hideous old crone, Acilius Glabrio had said unhelpfully. The other two magistrates had been less offensive, but no more informative. It was a sign of the regime's lack of concern for anything apart from the northern wars that the arrogant young fools had not been replaced when their normal term of office had come to an end.

He had given the late Empress a hairstyle favoured by women of the previous dynasty: clear waves drawn into a bun at the back. On top he had added a modest veil. For her features he had relied on an obviously spurious resemblance to her husband. Throughout the empire, Caecilia Paulina would be remembered for the prominence of her nose and chin.

It was a good piece of work. The peacock, the empty symbol which tradition demanded for the reverse could not occupy his mind. He had stood and watched as Pontianus was arrested. He had lied to Fabianus. He had not done nothing. In his weakness and his fear, he had denied knowing Pontianus. When the mob chanted, the die-cutter had mouthed the words. In the past, other men had done the same. There were names for them. There were names for him.

CHAPTER 29

The East
Northern Mesopotamia,

the Ides of May, AD237

'Chaboras River ahead.'

Gaius Julius Priscus raised himself on the horns of his saddle and peered over the heads of the legionaries and archers.

Julius Julianus, the Prefect of 1st Legion Parthica, pointed.

Through the dust raised by the cantering Persian cavalry, Priscus could make out a line of dark trees across the low horizon, a mile or more ahead. He caught flashes of colour against the foliage. Below what he knew must be Sassanid standards he saw a glint of sunlight on steel. It would be another contested river crossing.

'Here they come again.'

The big shields of the legionaries clattered up and together. Sporakes moved his mount up alongside that of Priscus. The bodyguard covered them both with his shield. With their greater range, the Roman archers on foot and the handful of slingers shot first. Priscus kept his head down. There was no point in watching the effect of the volley. No matter how many easterners went down, there were always more.

With a horrible tearing sound, the Persian arrows rained down. They thumped into wood, dinged off steel. The feathers of one quivered in the shoulder of a horseman near Priscus. He rocked in the saddle. His horse shied, and he crashed to the ground.

'Help him,' Priscus shouted. He pointed to another of his Horse Guards. 'You, get him to the baggage, then rejoin the standard.'

The trooper swung down by his fallen comrade. Another caught the reins of both horses. There had been thirty Equites Singulares when they set out. There were twenty left. Nineteen now.

'Not far to go, boys.' Priscus called over the din. 'One more river, and we will be safe in Resaina. Kill a few more reptiles, then a cool bath, a good meal, a young girl or boy; whatever you want.'

Despite it all, the men gave a shout of mock lust.

'Hold your places. Silence in the ranks. Listen for your orders. We are almost home.'

Nothing had gone right with this campaign. At the meeting in Samosata the previous autumn, knowing the reluctance of Persian armies to remain in the field over winter, the governors had decided the field army would gather in the new year. They had underestimated the determination of the Sassanid King. The outlying columns around Resaina and Carrhae had withdrawn, but the main force remained encamped under the walls of Nisibis.

In March, when the contingents had straggled into Zeugma, several were under strength. Licinius Serenianus had not come himself. An earthquake had devastated several cities in Cappadocia, and the governor had been forced to remain to quell widespread unrest as the locals sought to lynch every suspected Christian in the province as being the cause of the disaster. He had, however, sent the eight thousand men he had promised. Likewise, Ma'na of Hatra had appeared with the two thousand riders he had pledged from his father's city. The others had not fulfilled their obligations. Junius Balbus had sent two thousand, not four, from Syria Coele, and Otacilius Severianus just two thousand, not eight, from Syria Palestina. Priscus had never had much time for his brother-in-law Severianus. The family had thought the Senator a good match for his sister, but from the start Priscus could tell Otacilius Severianus had the heart of a deer. Unlike the pusillanimous Romans, the Armenian Prince Chosroes had a justifiable reason for riding up with only a thousand men at his back, not ten thousand. Another Persian army, led by the King of Kings himself, was marching up the Araxes river towards the city of Artaxata. Tiridates of Armenia was fighting for the survival of his kingdom.

It had been April when Priscus had led the army over the Euphrates and to the East. They had gone via Batnae, Carrhae, Resaina and Amouda. They had collected small contingents of the army of Mesopotamia at each town. Manu of Edessa had brought down a levy of five hundred local bowmen. All told, the total number of combatants was less than eighteen thousand.

From Resaina on, they had been shadowed by enemy scouts. But no attempt had been made to hinder their progress. The reason became clear when the vanguard breasted a low hill and Nisibis came into sight. Sassanid banners flew from the battlements. How long it had been since the town had fallen, no one in the Roman army could say. Across the plain before the walls a Persian army was drawn up for battle. It was at least thirty thousand strong: cavalry, infantry, even camels and a few elephants. The Romans had walked and ridden hundreds of miles into a trap.

Priscus had ordered a camp entrenched. The Persians had not interfered. The next day Priscus kept his men behind the palisades. The Sassanid horsemen had spread across the plain. They had come close, and shouted abuse, but had not attacked. Having cut the supply lines, they knew the Romans could not stay there for long. Time was on their side.

The second evening, Priscus had watched the enemy streaming back into Nisibis for the night. The town gates shut behind them. Then, and only then, Priscus had summoned his high command, and some senior centurions, and gave his orders.

They had left the wagons behind. A hundred volunteers from the auxiliary cavalry, including trumpeters, stayed to keep the campfires burning and to make the calls that marked the watches of the night. Before first light, they had galloped after the rest of the army, which had stolen away like a thief in the night.

The third hour of the next day they had been a couple of miles short of Amouda when the Sassanid light cavalry caught up with them. Priscus had ordered the column to halt, the infantry to form *testudo*, the cavalry to dismount behind them. Exhilarated by their wild chase, the Persians must have thought that the Romans were dropping with fatigue, were completely at their mercy. They whooped, and charged. Through the Roman ranks the officers had repeated Priscus' instruction: no one shoot until the signal. When the Sassanids were no more than forty paces away – already reining in, their charge faltering in the face of such unex-pected immobility – a trumpet had rung out. It was picked up by others along the line. Too late, the easterners sawed on their reins. They had run into a deadly storm of thousands of javelins and arrows. Men and horses, both brightly liveried, went down, bloodied and fouled, rolling in the dirt. The sur-vivors raced away. It had bought the army time to reach the gates and cram itself into the alleys, porticos and open spaces of the small town.

Priscus had spent two days in Amouda reorganizing the order of march. He had gone through it again and again, until he was sure that everyone, from the senior commanders down to the most junior officers, even to the common soldiers, knew their part. He had read the view of the Senator Cassius Dio that Ardashir was of no consequence in himself, and that all the troubles in the East stemmed from the licence, wantonness and lack of discipline of the soldiers. He had met Cassius Dio in the reign of Alexander. What little the Senator knew about soldiering had made him a martinet. True, the troops had murdered Priscus' predecessor in Mesopotamia. But Flavius Heraclio too had understood nothing about discipline. It took great kindness as well as great cruelty. In Amouda, Priscus had visited the men in their billets, had distributed his own private supplies to the army – choice delicacies and expensive wines – and had had a couple of would-be deserters flogged to death and their corpses strung up over the gates to deter any with similar thoughts.

Well handled – as Priscus knew any force he led would be – the Roman army in the East was still a potent weapon, even in adversity. The problems lay elsewhere. Too many men had been taken away to the wars in the North. And Cassius Dio was wrong: the Sassanids were far more dangerous than their Parthian predecessors. The Persians might marry their daughters, granddaughters – even their mothers – they might kill their wives and sons with impunity, they might throw out the bodies of their relatives to be eaten by dogs, but they could fight.

On the third morning the army had marched out and formed up in a hollow square, with the baggage animals and servants in the centre. Julius Julianus commanded the vanguard with the thousand men of his 1st Legion Parthica, the thousand-strong detachment of 6th Legion Ferrata from Syria Palestina and five hundred auxiliary archers. Porcius Aelianus held the right flank with his thousand men of 3rd Legion Parthica, the two thousand from 15th Legion Apollinaris from Cappadocia and a thousand bowmen. Priscus had entrusted the left to his brother. Philip commanded a thousand legionaries of 4th Scythica from Syria Coele, two thousand auxiliaries armed with spears and five hundred with bows. Manu of Edessa and his levy of five hundred bowmen were also stationed there. The rear consisted of two thousand from 12th Fulminata and a thousand archers, all from Cappadocia, and led by the legate of the legion, Caius Cervonius Papus.

Both flanks of the square were backed by a thousand riders from Hatra. Those on the right were under Prince Ma'na; those on the left a Hatrene nobleman called Wa'el. Prince Chosroes supported the rear with his thousand Armenian horsemen. The final troops – five hundred auxiliary cavalry and the same number of infantry, all from Mesopotamia – Priscus himself led, behind the leading edge of the square.

It was a cumbersome, slow-moving formation, but Priscus had been unable to think of anything better. The close-order infantry could fend off armoured cavalry, and the bowmen could shoot back at horse archers. As slingshots were more effective than arrows against the metal armour worn by Sassanid noblemen, he had called for volunteers. Some two hundred men, porters and sutlers, as well as soldiers, had claimed skill with a sling. These were distributed in small packets all around the army. The Hatrene and Armenians could shoot over the heads of the men on foot. The order of march was far from ideal, but it would have to serve.

The first attack had come within an hour of setting out. Groups of Persian light horse had raced in towards the column. About a hundred and fifty paces out, they had started shooting. Some fifty paces short of the line – well outside the cast of a javelin – they had wheeled around and galloped away, all the while plying their bows over their horses' tails. One charge had succeeded another almost without cease.

Each foray had slowed the march and claimed a few of the dead and wounded. The former, if they were fortunate, had a handful of earth sprinkled over them and a coin for the ferryman put in their mouths. Beyond that, there was nothing to do but leave the dead where they fell. Those too injured to walk were carried to the centre and mounted or strapped on the mules. Soon the path of the army was littered with the bodies of men and animals and strewn with abandoned baggage.

Progress had been agonizingly slow. Even on half rations, food had run short. It had taken two days to cover some twenty miles to the first unnamed river, another two to cover the same distance to the Arzamon, and a fifth to approach the Chaboras. At the first two crossings the Persian armoured cavalry had feinted a charge as the army struggled through the water, hoping to disrupt the lines enough to press home the attack. Priscus and the other officers had patrolled the column, shouting themselves hoarse. Somehow, panic was held at bay, cohesion maintained. The Sassanid nobles had turned their horses and, in good order, cantered away.

The Romans would have to face down their fears again before they gained the far bank of the Chaboras. Many more men would die before they reached the temporary safety of Resaina. The futility of it all dragged at Priscus. They should have accepted the offer of Ardashir, handed over Singara and Nisibis. Of course, it would have been unpleasant for the inhabitants, and the truce would have been temporary. The Sassanid was committed to conquering as far as the Aegean, and Rome would have had to try to retake the cities, and exact revenge besides. But it would have given the armies of the eastern provinces time to send an expedition west, and place Serenianus on the throne. Maximinus was bleeding the empire white for his unwinnable northern war. Priscus had served on the Rhine. There were many tribes in the North. You used money and the threat of the legions to keep them at each other's throats. In the East, there was just the King of Kings. You could set all the other rulers of the Orient on him – the Kings of Armenia and Hatra, the Lords of Palmyra, any other petty potentates you could find – and Ardashir would defeat them all, and still unleash his horsemen on the *imperium*. The real threat to Rome was the house of Sasan.

Priscus prided himself on clear-sighted realism untrammelled by sentiment. Last autumn, even his brother had been horrified by his proposal. That was why he had left Philip in Mesopotamia, when he had gone to Samosata. Priscus accepted he had mishandled that meeting. He should have known the sloth and cowardice of Junius Balbus and Otacilius Severianus would not be moved by appeal to patriotism or advantage. Even his friend Timesitheus had not spoken out. Now the opportunity had gone, and all that was left was the residual danger of denouncement.

'Infantry ahead.'

Priscus realized he was tired, his mind wandering.

The front line was less than a couple of hundred paces from the Chaboras, almost in effective bowshot.

'Archers ready.' Priscus called.

As they trudged forward, the auxiliaries notched arrows, raised and half drew their bows.

There was something strange about the line of men under the wide-spaced trees on the far bank. Those at the front were without shields or arms.

'Gods below,' a soldier said, 'they are ours!'

The murmur rippled through the ranks like wind through a cornfield.

'It is the garrison from Nisibis.'

He was right. Priscus could see men in Roman undress uniform, two hundred or more of them. They must be from the detachment of the 3rd Legion captured at Nisibis. Their hands were bound. Sassanids stood behind them.

A flight of arrows arced up from behind the human shield. The legionaries raised their shields. The auxiliaries lowered their bows, ducked into cover. Sporakes covered Priscus. The shafts whistled down. Someone nearby screamed.

'Draw!' Priscus pushed Sporakes away. 'They are dead men. Draw, unless you want to join them.'

Only a few bowmen obeyed.

Another squall of Persian arrows fell. More men howled in agony.

'All of you, draw!'

More – but far from all – did as they were told.

'Release!'

A ragged volley. There were near four hundred bowmen still with the standard, but no more than half that number of shafts sped away.

Most of the arrows struck harmlessly into the trees. But Priscus saw a captive legionary transfixed. Then another tumbled down the bank, and another.

The Sassanids were hacking down the defenceless men.

An animal roar of hatred rose from the Roman column.

'Draw! Release!'

This time, without hesitation, all the auxiliaries used their weapons.

All the prisoners were gone by the time the front rank reached the river. In their place stood a wall of big wicker shields. Dark-bearded easterners peered over the top.

The banks of the Chaboras were stony and sloped gently here. The legionaries poured down and splashed through the shallow water.

Priscus held up his hand and halted the auxiliaries. The order was relayed back. The whole column shuffled to a standstill. Too many men would breed confusion. The legionaries could clear the way. No eastern infantry could hold legionaries. Not legionaries who had just seen their comrades murdered.

The men of 1st Parthica and 6th Ferrata swept up the far bank in a terrible tide of steel. Priscus saw Persians running from the rear of their line before the clash. You could not call them cowards. Unarmoured, with inadequate shields and next to no training, the Persians who stood had no chance. They fell like wheat before the blades of the legionaries.

Priscus looked away, back across the rest of the army. Through the clouds of dust raised by innumerable hooves, he could see troops of Sassanid noble cavalry, the dreaded *clibanarii*, moving up to the south and east. Thank the gods there was no sign of the elephants.

'The way is clear,' Sporakes said.

On the far bank, Priscus could see Julius Julianus spurring his horse, shouting, gesticulating. The centurions were dragging men drunk with the violence of vengeance away from the mutilation of the fallen easterners and back into line. The legionaries were fanning out, creating a bridgehead.

Priscus gave the word to advance, told the Prefect commanding the Mesopotamian cavalry to take over the infantry as well, and pulled his Horse Guards out of the line.

Philip and Porcius Aelianus kept the flanking columns in reasonable order as they went down into the river. It was just as well. The baggage train degenerated into terrible confusion. Although there was little current and the water was not above thigh deep, the wounded men and lame and injured animals began to flounder. Some slipped and fell, obstructing or bringing down others. Soon it had ground to a flailing, staggering halt. The armed men guarding the flanks halted. Priscus sent one of his *equites* after Julius Julianus to make sure the vanguard did not continue and open a gap between the bodies of troops. At the rear, the Armenian horse and the infantry of Cervonius Papus had been turned about, and faced back the way they had come. Beyond them, out on the plain, the *clibanarii* were arrayed in a wide crescent stretching from the east to the south further down the river. They were ready, should any opportunity present itself.

When, finally, the last of the non-combatants scrambled and crawled up the far bank, the flank guards moved off. Chosroes and his Armenians wheeled about and thundered across in a cloud of spray. From the rear, Cervonius Papus sent his foot archers jogging after them.

The legionaries of 12th Fulminata were the only troops still on the far side. They were tired and hungry. They had been hard handled throughout the retreat. No more than fifteen hundred remained under the standards, many of them with minor wounds. Men in the rear ranks were looking over their shoulders, eying their retreating fellow-soldiers and the delusory security of the river.

A drumbeat rolled across from the Persians.

The first individuals began to edge back from 12th Legion.

Priscus knew what was going to happen; a lifetime in the army left no doubt. Shouting an order to a guardsman to ride and halt those on the far side, he put his boots into his horse's flanks.

The Sassanid heavy horse was walking forward.

Small groups – three or four at a time – were breaking away from the legionary phalanx and running towards the river. Centurions and junior officers grabbed some, manhandled them back into place. More broke away. The first threw down their shields the better to run.

The drumbeat quickened. The Sassanid horse were moving into a slow canter.

Priscus brought his horse up across the flight of a gaggle of legionaries. He shouted at them to stop. Ignoring him, they swerved out of his way and ran all the harder.

Flamboyant heroics were not in Priscus' nature. A Roman

general was not Achilles. Priscus tried to think calmly, take everything in, weigh up the options. Abandon the legionaries to their fate, ride back to Chosroes, get his Armenians drawn up along the far bank? No, the fleeing legionaries would disrupt their line. In the confusion, they would all be swept away. Once a panic starts in an army, it spreads like fire across a parched hillside. Sometimes even a general has to stand in the line and fight. It was the only rational thing to be done.

The *clibanarii* were picking up speed.

The legionaries were bunching together, their line contracting, gaps opening. It was worst on the right, away from Cervonius Papus and the eagle.

Priscus spurred his mount across.

'Stand firm! Hold your line. No cavalry will ride into a formed line.'

The men looked at him, uncertain and afraid.

The Sassanids were closing fast, The noise of their charge drumming in Priscus' ears.

Swinging a leg over the horns of his saddle, he dropped to the ground. He turned his horse, drew his sword and brought the flat across its rump. The animal clattered away.

'We will stand and fight together. Stand with your general.'

Priscus shouldered his way into the ranks. He took a standard bearer by the shoulders, propelled him to the front.

'Spread out. Give yourselves room to use your weapons. Not too far. Shield to shield.'

When Priscus looked up, the *clibanarii* were no more than a hundred paces away; a solid wall of steel and horseflesh.

'Stand, and they will not charge home.'

Priscus braced himself; left foot forward, right heel digging in.

'Level your weapons.'

He could not take his eyes off the Sassanid bearing down directly at him. The tall, glittering helm, flowing silks. The wicked point of a lance. The huge charger, mouth foam-flecked, hooves pounding.

Priscus shut his eyes, braced for the impact that would smash him to the earth under the hooves.

Screams, shouts, an incomprehensible wave of noise.

The Sassanid was almost on top of him; halfway up his horse's neck, clinging on, unbalanced. Further down the line a maddened animal had crashed into the line. Others were trying to push into the opening it had created. But the rest had refused. There were unseated riders on the floor. Loose horses bored into those still mounted.

'One step for victory!'

Priscus jumped forward, brought his sword down into the thigh of the unbalanced rider. The edge bit through the scale armour. The Persian gripped the wound. The horse leapt sideways, crashing into another animal. In the chaos, riders yanked the heads of their mounts around, fought to get away.

'One more step!'

Blades rose and fell, red with retribution, as the legionaries around Priscus stepped forward.

CHAPTER 30

Rome

The Forum Romanum,

Two Days before the Nones of August, AD237

Pupienus was not listening to his son. Africanus had said it all before and, most likely, he would say it again.

The heat was overwhelming. It seemed to radiate up from the pavement, and reflect back, intensified and blinding, from the marble-clad walls of the Flavian Amphitheatre. It was August, but no one in Rome could remember a heat-wave of such intensity. The superstitious were linking it to any number of prodigies; a huge red wolf had been seen slinking through the Campus Martius in the dead of night; the paintings of Maximinus by the Lake of Curtius were said to have sweated blood; a woman in Aquileia had given birth to a child with two heads. The latter at least was true. The infant had been brought to Rome. To expiate the portent, the Senate had ordered it burnt alive in the Forum, and the ashes thrown into the Tiber.

Stifling in the heavy folds of his toga, Pupienus looked with longing at the Sweating Post. Water ran down the tall cone and splashed enticingly into the pool at its base. This had all come at a bad time. Pupienus had just returned from Volaterrae and was suffering the usual emotions of guilt and relief, the latter bringing additional levels of remorse.

'The plebs are always restless in hot weather,' Crispinus said.

'This is not some minor unrest.' Africanus spoke sharply. Since he had been *Consul Ordinarius*, with the Emperor as colleague, the previous year, Pupienus' son had showed less respect than he should for his elders.

'No blood has been shed,' Crispinus said. 'With proper handling, this can be ended without violence.'

Pupienus was glad his friend had returned from Achaea. Their friendship went back many years. Like himself, Crispinus was a *novus homo*. He had risen from the equestrian order through hard work and talent. The opinions of a Senator such as Crispinus carried weight.

'The imperial commands are unambiguous,' Africanus said.

'The orders came from Vitalianus, not Maximinus,' Crispinus replied

'The deputy Prefect of Praetorians speaks for the Emperor.'

'As Prefect of the City, your father is responsible for public order in Rome.'

Pupienus sighed. New duties piled up on the old before the old were finished and, as more links were added to the chain, he saw his work stretching out further and further every day.

'If the Urban Cohorts do not disperse the mob, Vitalianus will send in the Praetorians,' Africanus said. 'There is nothing to be gained by misplaced clemency. There is no time to waste.'

'There are Senators in the temple,' Crispinus said.

'By their own volition. Three or four troublemakers – let them suffer the consequences of their demagoguery.'

Africanus turned to his father. 'You must send in the troops.'

'Gods below, boy, this is Rome,' Crispinus said, 'not some barbarian village.'

As Africanus bridled, Pupienus knew he must step in before their discussion became more heated.

'I will talk to them.'

'Talk will achieve nothing,' Africanus said.

'Your father is Prefect of Rome, not you.' At Crispinus' words, Africanus lapsed into a bristling silence.

'Send a herald,' Crispinus said. 'They may be in an ugly mood.'

They went and stood in the shade until the herald returned, then walked across the square.

The temple of Venus and Rome towered above them. At ground level, the doors to the storage rooms were locked and chained. A dense crowd looked down at them from the terrace. Gallicanus was easy to spot. He stood with Maecenas and two other men in togas with broad purple stripes.

'We are doing no wrong,' Gallicanus called. 'We have come to worship the deities and to guard their treasures.'

'It is beneath our *dignitas* to shout at each other in the street like slaves.' Pupienus had commanded armies; he could make his voice carry. 'Come down, and we will talk elsewhere.'

'Duty forbids me to abandon the goddesses.'

Sanctimonious fool, Pupienus thought. 'Give me safe conduct, and I will come up.'

Gallicanus spread his hands to encompass the crowd. 'We are law-abiding citizens of Rome. You need no safe conduct. The temples are open to everyone with no evil in their hearts.'

Infernal gods, the man was insufferable. Pupienus turned to the others. 'I will go alone.'

As one, Crispinus and Africanus said it was not safe, they would go with him. Pupienus was adamant. They were all bound by man's mortality: only the memorial of right conduct could set one free; everything else was fleeting, like man himself.

Pupienus took the narrow steps to the right. There was a makeshift barricade halfway up, on the landing where they turned to the left. Suspicion, if not outright hostility, was evident on the faces of the plebs who part dismantled it to let him through. They had piled stones behind it, and a few, in defiance of the law, openly carried weapons. Pupienus let that pass, and continued to the top.

The toga Gallicanus wore looked as if he had weaved it himself. His thick brown hair was wild and his forearms uncovered. He reminded Pupienus more than ever of an ape.

'I am delighted you have come to join us,' Gallicanus said.

Pupienus paid no heed to what he took to be a heavy-handed attempt at humour. He greeted Maecenas and the other two Senators, who he now recognised as ex-Quaestors called Hostilianus and Valens Licinianus.

'Your honour, position and reputation are all at stake,' Gallicanus continued.

'Can we talk in private?'

Gallicanus swung around, arms wide, as if he intended physically to embrace the closest unwashed plebeians. 'An honest man has nothing to hide, not from the people of Rome, not from the gods.'

With an effort, Pupienus controlled his rising anger. 'This has to stop now. I have an order from the Emperor to clear the temple.'

'So his creatures can steal the temple treasures, melt them down to give to his pampered soldiery,' Gallicanus said.

'Wars have to be fought,' Pupienus said. 'Maximinus has announced that the gods have offered him their possessions for the defence of Rome.'

Gallicanus drew himself up, and bellowed, 'Sacrilege! The plebs of Rome will not stand by and see the gods despoiled.'

The crowd murmured its approval. Pupienus looked coldly at the nearest men. They fell silent. He turned back to Gallicanus. 'You know as well as I do it is the cutting of the grain dole which has brought the plebs out, that and fewer shows. They have no concerns beyond bread and circuses.'

The noise of the throng swelled, angrier than before. Individuals towards the back called out insults and threats. Pupienus thought his words might have been ill judged.

'*Quirites*, you hear yourselves denigrated—'

'Enough.' Maecenas interrupted Gallicanus. Surprisingly, the latter stopped.

The crowd still shouted, its indignation rising.

'Come,' Maecenas said to Pupienus. 'I will escort you back.'

As he walked down, Pupienus could hear Gallicanus again haranguing the mob.

'You will send in the Urban Cohorts?' Maecenas asked.

'If I do not, it will be Vitalianus and the Praetorians.'

'You must do as your conscience dictates, but it will be a bloodbath.' Maecenas stopped, took Pupienus by the arm, leant close. 'Maximinus cannot last. The plebs will follow any alternative.'

'Even Gallicanus and his restored Republic?'

Maecenas did not respond to the sarcasm or answer the question. 'Maximinus may have married his son to a great-granddaughter of Marcus Aurelius, but the Emperor's other descendants will no longer serve under him. Claudius Severus and Claudius Aurelius have left Rome and withdrawn to their estates. The nobility are abandoning Maximinus. Too many have been condemned. The soldiers alone cannot keep him on the throne for ever.'

Pupienus was sweating, not just from the heat of the day. He had to choose his words with care. The future was always uncertain. He had not risen so high by being careless in the enemies he made. 'I do not wish you or Gallicanus any harm, but you know that any Senators caught inside the temple will have to be arrested for treason. There will be no choice.' It sounded weak to his own ears.

Maecenas released his arm, and turned and went back up the steps.

Having issued the necessary orders, Pupienus walked up the Sacred Way along the south side of the temple. Crispinus was silent, wrapped in his own considerations. Pupienus asked his son to be quiet. He needed to think. The street was like a furnace, and his head ached.

Massive and built of stone, the temple made a natural fortress. Apart from the two constricted staircases at the east, there was one easily blocked entrance on each of the northern and southern sides. The only practicable place to force a contested access was from the west, and that was up a steep flight of eleven marble steps.

Emerging from the Arch of Titus, Pupienus found his men already drawn up in the Forum. A squad doubled past to prevent anyone escaping from the southern door. An officer informed him that others were on their way to seal the other exits.

Pupienus knew there was truth in the things Maecenas had said. But the man was a fool if he gave any credence to Gallicanus' insane ideas of restoring the free Republic. This was all the fault of the yapping Cynic dog. Of course the plebs were restive – they had reason to be, who did not? – but it would not have led to this if Gallicanus had not whipped them into a frenzy. Pupienus should have handed him over to Honoratus on the evening of Maximinus' accession. He should have ignored the oath he had given the hairy, posturing philosophic ape. The gods knew, he had thought about it on the day his first son took the Consulship. Now it was too late. He would have to unleash soldiers on to the civilian population, or his own head would be displayed in front of the Senate House.

A tribune saluted, and said all was ready.

Pupienus gave him new instructions.

'We will do what is ordered, and at every command we will be ready.'

As they waited, Africanus remonstrated with his father – it was not enough, too lenient – but Crispinus said it was a good political compromise, a Tacitean middle way. When all was ready, they moved back next to the House of the Vestals to be out of range.

A trumpet sounded and the soldiers of the Urban Cohorts hefted their shields. The front rank crouched behind theirs; those in the rear held them above their heads. The trumpet called again and the phalanx edged forward. The men beat on the insides of their shields in time with their slow, measured tread.

Up on the podium, the boldest plebs ran to the top of the steps. They moved sideways, as if dancing. Their arms whipped forward, and the first missiles flew. Pupienus saw an eddy in the formation, where a soldier must have been hit. Most of the bricks and bits of masonry bounced off the shields.

The phalanx reached the foot of the steps and began to ascend, like some ponderous amphibian beast going up a beach. More projectiles rattled down. There was no order among the rioters, and no sign of Gallicanus.

The trumpet rang out a third time. With unexpected suddenness, the carapace of the phalanx broke apart. The leading ranks bounded up the remaining steps. Surprised, the mob turned to run. Some slipped on the marble paving, scrabbled desperately to get away. With the bosses and edges of their shields, the soldiers knocked the laggards to the floor. The clubs in their right hands cracked down on skulls, shoulders and arms.

In a moment, the crowd had vanished into the echoing

gloom of the temple. The soldiers chased after them, all except the rear two ranks, who drew up at the top of the steps as a reserve. One or two rioters lay prostrate at their feet.

The sound of running feet, hobnails on stone. Pupienus and his companions swung around.

'What in Hades do you think you are doing?' Vitalianus shouted.

Pupienus met the furious gaze of the deputy Praetorian Prefect, but said nothing.

'Your men are watching the traitors escape from the other doors.'

'My orders were to clear the temple, not instigate a massacre.' Pupienus spoke clearly, wanting everyone to hear.

'We will never find the ringleaders. This is your fault.'

'My orders were to clear the temple. We will do what is ordered, and at every command we will be ready.'

'Do not bandy words with me.' Vitalianus jabbed a finger at Pupienus. 'Maximinus will hear of this. You have done yourself no favours with the Emperor, no favours at all.'

CHAPTER 31

Africa
Carthage,

the Kalends of September, AD237

The ring was set under a big tree. Sunlight dappled the sand. Gordian took another drink, and offered a wager on the black. Menophilus accepted, and backed the russet. Gordian was still surprised that Menophilus had come with him; it was not his type of thing. But Sabinianus and Arrian were away, and Menophilus was a good friend.

The trainers held the fighting cocks in both hands, passing them in front of each other, lingering a moment when they were almost close enough to strike. At a sign from the official, the men stepped back with exaggerated theatre and, bending, gently dropped them to the ground. Released, the cocks flew at one another in a wing-beating, head-thrusting, leg-kicking eruption of animal fury so pure, so absolute and in its way so beautiful as to be almost abstract. They collided and merged into a tight, thrashing ball; a single animate thing of spurs and claws and hatred. Only when they both left the ground could they be told apart. The crowd sighed, and the black lay, alive but bloodied and not moving.

Gordian passed over the stake. 'That is the third bout running. My *genius* is afraid of yours. It fawns on you, as Antony's did Octavian.'

Menophilus put it in his wallet. 'Then be thankful we are contending for a handful of coins, not mastery over the inhabited world.'

Gordian finished his drink. 'I should have avoided your company today. Stoics are not meant to approve of cockfighting.'

Menophilus refilled their cups. 'We cannot all be Marcus Aurelius.'

The trainer picked up the vanquished black. Tenderly, he stroked and fluffed it, his hands expressing the grief his face would not. The crowd looked on, respecting his self-control.

Gordian took another long swallow of wine. The news had arrived that morning. He had never been close to his sister. There was nothing of their father in her, none of his delight in the pleasures of life. Maecia Faustina had always been disapproving; more than disapproving, she had always been forbidding. She took after their maternal grandfather. Still, she would be upset. Tomorrow, when he was sober, he would write her a letter of condolence. He felt sorry for that son of hers. A sickly, weak-looking little boy; bad enough having Maecia Faustina for a mother, but to have no father.

Frowning, he tried to work out where Junius Balbus would be now. The ship had made a quick passage from Syria to Carthage. It had left two days after the arrest. They were taking Balbus to the North by carriage. Fuddled by the wine, Gordian counted on his fingers. Most likely, Balbus was somewhere in Thrace. Was it true the prisoners were given no food and no water? The fat fool would not care for that. It was unlikely that he had any experience of deprivation.

302

Two new birds were in the ring. The official was inspecting the binding of their spurs.

Of course, it could not be true. Unless they were brought no distance, the prisoners would be dead by the time they reached Maximinus. There would be nothing for the Thracian to insult or torture. Although they said he had gloated over the head of Alexander. They said he had fucked the corpse of Mamaea.

Gordian beckoned for more wine, waved away the water. The estate of Balbus would go to the treasury. Although Maecia Faustina had seen to the running of her husband's house in Rome, she preferred to live in the *Domus Rostrata* of the Gordiani. She could remain there. The property of the Gordiani would not be confiscated. At least, not yet.

Balbus was blamed for the defeat outside Arete; the one where the Sassanids had killed Julius Terentius, the commander of the garrison. At the time, Balbus had been sitting on his fat arse in Antioch, miles away. Indolent, possibly negligent, but hardly deserving the death penalty. If the fault of Balbus was small, no dereliction of any sort had attached to Apellinus, arrested in his province of Britannia Inferior. There were rumours that the governor of Arabia, Sollemnius Pacatianus, had fallen as well. This was a reign of terror: Septimius Severus after the defeat of Albinus, Domitian in the dark last years of his reign. When an Emperor began imitating Polycrates, or whichever Greek tyrant it had been, and started lopping off the heads of the tallest flowers, it would not be long before he turned to the Gordiani, the sons and grandsons of Consuls, the owners of Pompey's house in Rome, the most palatial villa in Praeneste, and another dozen properties besides. No time at all, now Gordian's fool of a brother-in-law was a convicted traitor.

'I will bet on the scrawny speckled bird, give you a chance to get some of your money back,' Menophilus said.

Gordian fumbled for some coins and a couple fell on the

303

ground. He left them. 'My brown does not look as if it has much fight in it.'

These cocks were more circumspect. They circled, came together, reared up and struck with their spurs then backed away, circling again. Feathers fluttered across the sand on the downdraught of their wings.

Gordian looked away. The ring was low, constructed of packing cases. Except where he sat with Menophilus, isolated by their exalted status, the audience was jammed together. Men leant over the barrier, encouraging their bird with wordless gestures, shifting in sympathy with its movements, rapt in their attention. It was not unknown for spectators to lean too far, to lose a finger or an eye.

The birds were in the air. The speckled cock drove several inches of razor-sharp steel into its opponent's breast. The brown was down, the victor strutting sideways in its triumph. Somehow the brown gathered itself into a final, doomed attack. The spurs of the speckled bird hurled it back to the sand, trampling it to ruin.

'A day for Stoic duty, not Epicurean pleasure.' Gordian gave Menophilus the coins in his hand.

The crowd parted and the solid figure of Valerian approached. Menophilus called for a chair for the legate, and Valerian sat down.

'I am sorry about Balbus.'

Gordian smiled. 'Thank you.' He handed him a cup.

'Have you heard about Mauricius?' Valerian went on. 'Paul the Chain has summoned him to appear in court at Thysdrus.'

'Why?'

'Mauricius' steward went to pay the tax grain there, and the Chain told him to deliver it to Thabraca, or pay a huge transportation cost. When Mauricius heard, he rode over in a rage. He cursed Paul, told him that he had worked his way from poverty to wealth without ever submitting to extortion, and he was not going to start now. Apparently, Paul would have arrested him there and then, but he had only a couple of guards with him, and Mauricius had a dozen or more armed friends and clients.'

'This cannot go on.' Gordian spoke precisely, as he did when well on his way to being drunk. 'We need a new Chaerea or Stephanus or . . . ' He could not think of any other killers of tyrannical Emperors.

'Keep your voice down,' Menophilus said.

Their servants were out of earshot, and the crowd were shouting the odds for the next fight, but he spoke more softly. 'If we do not kill Maximinus, he will kill us – all of us.'

It was a measure of their friendship that the other two did not suspect entrapment.

'We have no legions,' Valerian said.

'Africa controls the grain supply to Rome,' Gordian said. 'No grain shipments, and the plebs will take to the streets.'

'And Vitalianus' Praetorians and the new Prefect of the City's Urban Cohorts will massacre them.' Valerian shook his head.

'Other provinces would join us.'

'Soldiers pull Emperors from the throne, not the plebs or the provincials.' Menophilus leant forward. 'Only three armies are big enough to win a civil war, those on the Rhine, the Danube and the Euphrates. It is unlikely the eastern army could win against the two in the North. Maximinus can only be brought down by those with him.'

'We must save Mauricius,' Valerian said.

'The Chain has the trust of Maximinus.' Menophilus spoke sadly. 'The thing is impossible.'

Gordian relapsed into silence with the others. His eyes followed the cockfight, but his thoughts were elsewhere. Mauricius had fought with them at Ad Palmam. He was a friend. Real friendship must take pains for its friends, run risks for their safety. A man should avoid pain, but even painful actions for a friend bring pleasure. Without friendship, there could be no confidence in the future, no trust, no ease of mind. Such a painful life was not worth living. Epicurus had said a wise man will not engage in politics unless something intervenes. When a tyrant threatens your friends, your tranquillity, the security of the *Res Publica* itself, a man cannot continue to live quietly out of the public eye.

CHAPTER 32

The Far North
The Hierasos River,

Three Days before the Nones of September, AD237

The plain was hard and flat and brown. The autumn rains had not yet come, and the grass was dusty. A line of trees marked the next river, a long way off. The camp on the near bank, all those dozens, hundreds of wagons and tents, looked tiny in the flat immensity. The vast herds stretched away on the other side. In the far distance the horses and sheep were indistinguishable, like worms crawling on the ground. You could see for miles out here, and that was good.

They would not have expected him to come again so late in the campaigning season, not so far out on to the steppe. All summer, Maximinus had hunted the Sarmatian Roxolani and their Gothic allies across the grasslands between the Carpathian mountains and the marshes of the Danube delta; march and counter-march, flying columns and cavalry sweeps. There had been skirmishes. The Sarmatians had raided the baggage train, swept down on detached units. The Romans had caught some stragglers, a few flocks. Nothing of any importance, no decisive battle. The barbarians had driven their herds up into the foothills or into the wetlands; confused terrain where the Romans would not follow. But Maximinus had learnt their ways. He had known they must come out on to the steppe for the winter grazing along the river valleys.

Late in August, a few days before the *kalends* of September, the army had crossed the Danube again at Durostorum. Maximinus had led them north. Heavy baggage and most non-combatants left behind, they had moved fast. They had found nothing at the Naparis, nor at the next nameless river. But here at the distant Hierasos they had found their quarry; banded together for protection, or delivered into the hands of their enemies, whichever the gods willed. Why, Maximinus wondered, did they not spare themselves? Why did they not submit?

He had asked Aspines. He often talked to the sophist, now that Paulina was dead. Aspines had said it was ignorance. The barbarians could not conceive of the advantages of being ruled by Rome. But it was the duty of Maximinus to conquer them. It was for their own good. Aspines had told Maximinus a story about a bull. When the bull met another, the leader of another herd, they would fight. The winner was the stronger. He took the followers of the vanquished. He could protect them better. It was the same with the rulers of men. When a King defeated another, it showed he had greater virtue, and he would give greater benefits to his subjects. Maximinus had understood. Stripped of all the fine phrases, to be a King was to give benefits, and the greatest benefit was security. A tyrant ruled for himself, a King for his subjects. Maximinus had not wanted to take the throne. He did not want to be Emperor. Maximinus was fighting for the good of Rome. He was no tyrant.

The barbarian camp, a semicircle of wagons, was not more than a mile away now. It was time. Maximinus reined in and told the standard bearers and trumpeters at his back to make the signal.

The infantry trudged past. A coin for a shave, they shouted. Maximinus had a bag tied to a saddle horn. He threw the coins from it with an open hand. Men ran to gather them, then jostled back to their places. Even the centurions seemed almost good-natured, as they cursed them for their avarice.

As the army moved from the column of march, fanning out across the plain, it raised great billows of dust. Through the murk patterns emerged. It reminded Maximinus of watching the clouds; the way they shifted and merged, forming now the image of a hound, now a horse, now the breasts and thighs of a naked woman. He had not had a woman since Paulina had died. He had not had another woman while she was alive. It had not seemed right. But now she was dead, and man was not meant for celibacy. Perhaps, if the day went well, he would have one amid the chaos of the sacked camp, one of those blonde Sarmatian bitches.

The army was stationary, the south wind blowing the dust away towards the barbarians. It was autumn, but the sun was hot. In his armour, Maximinus was sweating profusely. He wiped his brow. Squinting, he took one last look at his dispositions before he committed them all to the lap of the gods.

The centre of the first line was a phalanx of eleven thousand drawn from all the legions along the Rhine and the Danube. Five deep, it stretched for a third of a mile. Flavius Vopiscus would be reading line after line of the *Aeneid*, searching for encouragement, but Maximinus would not have had anyone else leading. If Vopiscus fell, Catius Clemens would assume command. The latter was always dabbing his nose, complaining of this or that ailment, but it was all affectation. Despite his hypochondria, Catius Clemens was a hard man.

Similarly arrayed, on each flank of the legionaries were a thousand regular auxiliary infantry and a thousand warriors brought by treaties from the tribes of Germania. This would be the last battle under Roman standards for the tribesmen on the left. As Maximinus had agreed with their prince, Froda, this winter the Angles and their leader Eadwine would return home to the distant North.

Anullinus' eight thousand Praetorians and Julius Capitolinus' four thousand 2nd Legion Parthica formed the second line. Shields grounded, they would be praying that the first assault succeeded and they would not have to fight.

The attacks would be supported by Iotapianus' archers. Tucked between the lines of heavy infantry were a thousand Emesenes, five hundred Armenians, and a thousand Osrhoenes. Maximinus had ordered the latter decimated in the aftermath of the revolt of Quartinus and Macedo, but otherwise had not treated them harshly. After one in ten had been beaten to death by his mess companions, there had been no further punishments. Of course, their numbers were much depleted, but any unit which had supported a failed pretender had to expect the most difficult and dangerous assignments.

The cavalry on the right wing consisted of four *alae* of regulars and the Persians and Parthians; three thousand in all. They waited dismounted, to spare their horses. Honoratus might look more suited to a symposium than a battle, but in the last three years he had given proof after proof of his martial abilities.

On the left, Sabinus Modestus commanded his thousand cataphracts and the thousand Moorish light cavalry. Maximinus had grown fond of Modestus. He was not the cleverest, but he did what he was ordered, was good in a fight. Intellect was not a prerequisite in an army officer.

As a reserve, Maximinus had kept around himself just the thousand troopers of the imperial Horse Guards. To move more quickly in the final approach, the bolt-shooters and their carts had been left at the marching camp, more than five miles behind. They would guard it with one cohort of auxiliary infantry and the Ostensionales. It amused Maximinus to have reduced his predecessor's favourite unit to a baggage guard.

The baggage caught Maximinus' thoughts, not in a good way. The provision of supplies had never been the same since Timesitheus had gone east. Maximinus had had Volo investigate Domitius. The Prefect of the Camp was embezzling large sums. Previously, Domitius would have been arrested straight away, his illegal gains confiscated, his head on a pike. Now, Maximinus was waiting until he found a suitable replacement. He had considered recalling Timesitheus from Asia, but he was needed in Rome. The *Graeculus* had a gift for organization. The grain dole was in disarray. When Timesitheus had put it to rights, the plebs would have no reason to demonstrate. Any that did could be cleared from the temples and streets by the Urban Cohorts of Sabinus, the new Prefect of the City, and the Praetorians under Vitalianus. Perhaps when Rome was quiet again, he would order Timesitheus back to the army. In the meantime, Domitius still commanded the camp. All the graft that stuck to his fingers would return to the treasury when he fell.

Maximinus gazed all around. There was nothing. No cover, no dust; nothing but the brown grass and the hot sun. He gave the order. The trumpets rang and the standards inclined forward. The army began its long walk.

'Enemy riders coming.'

There were two of them, cantering across from their wagons. From the leisure of their progress, most likely they were envoys.

'Have them brought to me,' Maximinus said.

Beyond the riders, the enemy were coming out of their camp. Lacking regular units, barbarian numbers were hard to judge. These were infantry. They formed a line roughly equal in length to that of Flavius Vopiscus' men. Perhaps their depth was not as great; certainly it was no more.

Maximinus was looking over his shoulder at the open grassland to his west when the envoys arrived. By his dress – a padded, embroidered jacket, trousers, a horseman's long sword and a long knife strapped to his thigh – one was a Sarmatian. The other had bones in his long hair. He was a Gothic priest.

'*Zirin*,' the Sarmatian said. It was the word that secured the safety of any on the steppe that wanted a parley.

Maximinus said nothing.

'We have come to arrange a truce.' The Sarmatian spoke in Greek.

Still Maximinus did not speak.

'If you halt your men, we will discuss terms.'

'Why?' Maximinus said.

The Goth spoke in more heavily accented Greek. 'The gods have shown us their will.' The bones in his matted braids clacked in the wind.

Maximinus knew he was scowling. 'All summer I pursued you, and you did not come to me. Why now?'

The Sarmatian smiled. 'We find ourselves in a worse position.'

'Seize them.' Maximinus said.

'*Zirin!*' They shouted, outraged, as the soldiers took their weapons, bound their hands behind their backs. '*Zirin!*'

'Take them to the rear.'

They were brave, but a man should not involve the gods in his duplicity. For once, the Romans had the advantage. Three days before, two brave and resourceful scouts had reported seeing the Sarmatian cavalry leaving their camp for the west. Yesterday, when the Roman approach was seen, they would have been recalled. They had not arrived by first light this morning. The attack had to go in before they returned.

'You acted justly, my Lord. The divine Julius Caesar once did the same when some Germans tried to temporize.'

Maximinus looked at the Consul, Marius Perpetuus. He was elegant, polished. Maximinus knew he was scowling again. The educated always found justifications, examples from the distant past. He was far from certain what he had done was just.

Aspines had told him that safety was not the only benefit a ruler should give. Justice was the other great gift, beyond wealth or honour. Many men had been condemned in his reign. Maximinus was unconvinced of the justice of all their convictions. Senators and equestrians fell over themselves to accuse each other. An Emperor knew only what he was told. He had asked Aspines how he should judge. Aspines had said the ruler should listen only to true friends. That was easy for the sophist to say. He had not sat on the throne of the Caesars. He did not realize that an Emperor has no true friends. Now Paulina was dead, no one spoke to him without some calculation of advantage or fear.

The wind was rising. It carried fine grit and the bitter tang of trampled wormwood. A few light clouds raced overhead; darker ones were gathering in the south. Perhaps the first of the overdue autumn storms was coming. The dust raised by the Equites Singulares blew ahead to mingle with that scuffed up by the boots of the second line of infantry. The vanguard and the bowmen were almost completely obscured. Of the thousands of men led by Flavius Vopiscus and Iotapianus, all that could be seen clearly were their standards and the helmets of some mounted officers.

Horns rang out from the front. The first flights of arrows arced up and fell like straight, black rain. The barbarians responded in kind. The infantry under Anullinus halted. The cavalry on both flanks pulled up next to them, jumping down to take the weight off the backs of their horses. Maximinus raised an

313

arm to halt the reserve. The Horse Guards also dismounted. Maximinus remained in the saddle; unlike the troopers, he had a spare mount.

Ahead, above the roiling dust, the sky was thick with arrows. There was something thrilling and horrible about watching the shafts plunge down on unseen victims who would not glimpse them until far too late, something godlike about watching from perfect safety as other men risked everything and died in that terrible gloom.

Maximinus looked away to the right at the eastern horizon. Methodically, he scanned around through the south all the way to the west, staring at every hollow, following the shadow of every cloud. There was still nothing but the high sun and the wind riffling the dried grass, tugging at the sideoats and the silkweed.

A terrible noise, like in the high mountains when a cliff face shifts and falls, rolled back from the north. The legionaries and barbarians were fighting in front of the wagons. Maximinus peered, trying to see through the murk by an exercise of will.

'Enemy cavalry!' Javolenus, the bodyguard, pointed.

Off to the left, a line of tapering silhouettes was coming up between the trees on the riverbank. Emerging from the dappled shade, the bodies of the horses formed a solid dark mass with thin, flickering legs below and the shapes of their riders above. The cavalry were very black above the tan earth. More and more came, until the very ground seemed to shift.

Maximinus smiled. You had to admire whoever led the Sarmatian cavalry. The riverbanks were high, tree-fringed. The river itself must be fordable; the camp was to the south, the herds to the north. Not there this morning, the horsemen must have ridden down the shallow riverbed from the west, using the only cover in the whole steppe. At least, depending how far they had come, their mounts might be tired.

'Modestus is outnumbered, *Imperator*, we must send Honoratus from the right to support him,' Perpetuus said.

Maximinus did not answer straight away. The Consul might be right. There were at least four thousand nomad horsemen facing the two thousand riders with Modestus. But that might not be all. Maximinus traced the line of the river from the west, past where it was hidden behind the infantry fighting in front of the wagons, to where it re-emerged to the east.

'No,' Maximinus said. Having beckoned two mounted messengers, he sent one to Anullinus with orders to wheel his Praetorians to the right to support the cavalry of Honoratus. The other galloped off to tell Julius Capitolinus to pivot 2nd Legion Parthica to the left to aid Modestus.

The Sarmatian cavalry were coming on at a walk, getting into a fighting formation as they moved. Maximinus' admiration for their leader increased: he was not a man to throw away his advantage with an over-hasty charge. Modestus, however, had responded well. Perhaps Timesitheus' cousin was not as slow as most judged him. Modestus had his Moors spread out in open order covering a lot of ground to his left, while he was with his cataphracts, who were packed knee to knee, three deep.

'*Imperator* . . .'

'Silence in the ranks!' Some fools always feel the need to talk.

Maximinus surveyed the rest of the field. Like the leaves of an opening gate, the men of Julius Capitolinus and Anullinus were jogging left and right. Directly ahead, the clouds of dust coiled up to the heavens where the battle had been joined. Soon, the Roman infantry would form an enormous inverted 'U'. The 2nd Legion had only four thousand men, compared with the eight thousand Praetorians. Maximinus judged that there would be gap between the right of Julius Capitolinus' men and the front line. Honoratus' troopers, back in the saddle, waited quietly on the east flank.

'To the right!' Javolenus said.

More mounted Sarmatians were coming up from the river in front of Honoratus' cavalry. These nomads were scrambling over the lip, scattered and disordered. The bank must be steeper, harder to negotiate there. Their numbers were impossible to gauge as yet but, no matter how many, it would take them some time to form up.

'Gods below, it will be another Cannae,' Maximus said.

Maximinus silenced his son with a glare. He should have left him with the civilian officials in the camp, or back south of the Danube with the whores.

The Sarmatians on the left were moving into a slow canter. About half, in a deep phalanx, were charging Modestus' heavy cavalry and a thousand or so heading for the Moors. The remainder, perhaps another thousand, were angling towards the gap between 2nd Legion and the infantry battle. Clearly, they intended to take the Roman left from the flank and rear, to roll up the line.

'Equites Singulares, mount up.'

Maximinus summoned the groom with his battle charger, Borythenes. He stepped from one horse to the other without alighting. The big black stallion shifted under his weight. The boy led the hack away.

'Form a wedge on me.' Maximinus knew exactly what was going to happen, what he had to do. In the theatre, he might not always follow the plot of the tragedies and allusions to epics often eluded him, but on the battlefield nothing escaped him: events unfolded in his mind like the rustic dances of his youth.

When the men were ready, there was no time for a long speech. Maximinus was relieved. He raised himself up and twisted in the saddle. Fierce, bearded faces looked up at him.

'Fellow-soldiers, let us go and hunt Sarmatians. A year's pay to every man who rides with me.'

The men of the imperial Horse Guard roared their appreciation. These were men like himself, the sons of soldiers or northern peasants. Vopiscus or Honoratus might have given them a line or two of Virgil, but Maximinus had given them what they wanted: companionship in danger and the promise of money. *Enrich the soldiers, ignore everyone else.*

With his knees, Maximinus nudged Borysthenes into a walk. He did not want to arrive at the crucial place too soon or with blown horses. He led the spearpoint of armed men directly towards the centre of the front line.

The left flank was filled with wheeling cavalry. Through the palls of dust, Maximinus saw squadrons of Moors now racing towards him, now hurtling back into the fray. Javelins and arrowheads flashed in the sun. The Africans were holding their own. Things were not going so well for the cataphracts. The fighting was at close quarters, near stationary. Each side was inextricably mixed with its opponent, all cohesion gone. Outnumbered, the Roman heavy horse were giving ground. So far, the movement was slow. Not many cataphracts were down yet. They were well protected, with men and horses in metal armour. These troopers were elite veterans; unless the gods willed different, they should hold long enough. In any event, Julius Capitolinus and the 2nd Legion were behind them.

A voice in Maximinus' mind screamed for him to kick on to a gallop, to get it over, one way or another. He ignored the strident urging, forced himself to be calm, to survey the field. On the right, the Sarmatians were still struggling into some order. Honoratus' men were drawn up, waiting. The Praetorians screened the coming cavalry combat from the rest of the battle. Ahead, if anything, the right and centre of the infantry battle seemed to be grinding towards the barbarian camp. But the Roman line was bending; the left was not going forward. As he looked, the first few individuals emerged from the pall, running. It was almost the tipping point.

Maximinus dug in his heels. The stallion gathered its powerful quarters and surged forward. Maximinus had to hold him hard to keep him to a canter. Behind, the earth reverberated under thousands of hooves.

More Romans were fleeing from the extreme left, groups of three or four. They were from the two auxiliary units posted there.

Drawing his sword, Maximinus held it aloft. About two hundred paces behind the front line, he gestured with the blade and began to swing to the left.

'Keep together. Keep your place.'

As he thundered along behind the backs of the rear ranks of the struggling legionaries, the auxiliary units came into view. They were surrounded; Goths on foot in front, Sarmatian horse behind. Suddenly, like a dam giving way, they broke. Those who could, ran; the rest turned on each other, fighting their own to try to get clear, or dropped their weapons and held their hands up in supplication. Sarmatian horsemen leant out from the saddle, slashing their long swords down on unresisting heads and shoulders.

Further on through the tumult, a large knot of men still fought under a standard of a white horse. Hedged by their shields, Eadwine and his Angles were packed together in a circle. Sarmatians rode around, jabbing down with spearheads and sword points, probing for a gap in the shieldwall. Maximinus smiled. After this battle there might be no Angles left to make the trek back to the Suebian Sea.

'Are you ready for war?' Maximinus shouted.

'Ready!'

Three times Maximinus shouted. Each time the response came back stronger.

A Sarmatian in silvered scale armour wearing a tall pointed helm saw the Romans. He raised a horn to his lips and sounded a note that pierced the din. His warriors went to answer their chieftain's call. Goths on foot and injured and panic-stricken Romans got in their way. The riders struck left and right, at friend and foe indiscriminately, as they attempted to force their way through.

A wounded auxiliary staggered in front of Maximinus. Borysthenes did not break stride. The stallion's shoulder sent the soldier spinning to the ground. A thousand-strong, the Equites Singulares rode over him.

The Sarmatian in the silver armour rode under a dragon standard. There were three or four hundred riders with him, more struggling to join. He sounded the charge. Kicking on in time with the beat of their horses, the warriors advanced. Hunched forward, faces half hidden by their helmets, they looked bestial, like savages who killed for pleasure, who slaughtered defenceless old women and children.

Maximinus tried to spit on his chest for luck. His mouth was dry. He yelled an ancient war cry from the hills of Thrace.

The leader closed from the right. His sword was levelled at Maximinus' chest. All his concentration on the glittering steel, at the last moment Maximinus forced it wide. Something hit his shield so hard from the left only the saddle horns stopped him from being knocked to the ground. Borysthenes collided side on with the chieftain's mount. Maximinus rebounded and scrabbled upright. For a second, the two men were face to face. There were red beads braided in the Sarmatian's blond beard. Each cut at the other, but their impetus pulled them past.

In the heart of the melee, Maximinus' awareness closed to the reach of a sword. Everything was moving, screaming, shouting. The clamour stunned his senses. Through the blinding dust, blows came from nowhere. He twisted and blocked, slashed and hacked. Blood sprayed in his eyes. A blade split his shield. Another buckled the armour on his right shoulder. He struck out and felt his sword bite into something. His thighs pushed Borysthenes on.

'Keep moving!' An arrow whipped past his face. A Goth lunged at him from the ground. Maximinus smashed the spear away, kicked the man in the face. The warrior reeled, and was gone. Two Sarmatians struck at Maximinus from either side. Throwing his ruined shield at the one on the right, he took the other's blow on the edge of his blade. With his left hand, he grabbed the warrior by the throat, hauled him out of seat, and let him fall. Swivelling, he slashed at the warrior to his right, turning the blow just in time when he realized Javolenus was there.

The bodyguard was speaking. The blood pounding in Maximinus' ears stopped him hearing. There was a noise of cheering, as if from a long way away. In the choking dust, Maximinus circled Borysthenes, looking for the next threat, seeking his bearings. They were in a stand of trees with thin grey trunks.

'*Imperator*.' A soldier walked up to his horse. He was holding a severed head by its long hair.

At the bottom of the bank, the river was broad and shallow, its waters churned and fouled.

'I give you joy of your victory, *Imperator*.' The soldier held up the head. There were beads of some sort in its clotted beard.

CHAPTER 33

The East
Ephesus, Province of Asia,
the Nones of October, AD237

The view from the governor's palace at Ephesus was magnificent. To the left, the saw-toothed mountains cut down
towards the sea. Grey limestone showed through the vegetation on their upper slopes; the lower were a jumble of red
tiled roofs. At their foot stood the delicate columns of the
famous library of Celsus, up against the great square of the
commercial *agora*, and along from that, almost directly below
the palace, was the broad, monumental street which ran
west, straight to the harbour. To the right, blue with distance,
more mountains curled around, with a gentler profile. Below
them, the Caystros river curved in wide sweeps through the
broad plain which stretched to the city. Inside the walls were
the grand Olympieion and the monumental complex of the
harbour baths, gymnasium and colonnaded park, all of which
drew the eye back to the statue-lined street leading to the
harbour. Timesitheus did not want to go to the harbour. He
did not want to leave Ephesus.

It was the *nones* of October, growing late in the sailing season. The poet Hesiod had advised not to go to sea after August. Admittedly, Hesiod had been a farmer in the hills of Boeotia, and presumably vessels had become more seaworthy since his day. All the authorities that Timesitheus had ever consulted had considered that three days before the *ides* of November marked the onset of winter, after which only fools and the desperate would leaveport. If the winds were adverse, Timesitheus and his party might struggle to make harbour in Brundisium before the sea lanes closed. Although his family had owned merchantmen, Timesitheus had never enjoyed sailing. Once, a ship on which he had been a passenger had been caught in a storm off Massilia. Even though he did not believe in the gods, when the crew started praying, he had joined them. Still, if they rounded Cape Malea safely, this voyage should not hold many terrors. There was no point worrying. An imperial order to proceed by sea to Rome could not be ignored.

Timesitheus was alone on the terrace. The formal speeches bidding farewell to him as acting governor had been made by the leading citizens in the Council House that morning. The slaves and porters had already taken the baggage down to the ship. Now Timesitheus was waiting for Tranquillina and their daughter. He leant on the parapet and let his eyes rest on the theatre below.

Long ago, when Ephesus had been ravaged with plague, the holy man Apollonius of Tyana had led the citizens into the theatre. An old blind beggar had sat there with his staff and a scrap of bread. He was clad in rags and very squalid in appearance, blinking in the sunlight. Apollonius had ranged the Ephesians around him and told them to pick up as many stones as they could and hurl them at the enemy of the gods. The citizens had been reluctant to murder the miserable stranger. The aged man had wept, pleaded for mercy, but Apollonius was insistent. Once their blood was up, no one in the crowd held back. So many stones were thrown, they heaped a cairn over the body. When the stones were removed, the corpse lay pounded to a pulp, vomiting foam. No longer an old man, the daemon had the form of a Molossian dog, equal in size to the largest lion.

When Timesitheus had read this story in Philostratus, he had wondered what the governor was doing while his authority was being usurped. Perhaps he had been leaning on this parapet, looking down from his palace. Sometimes politics demanded that one stood aside, let events take their course. When the stones were scraped away, what if the body revealed had been that of a broken old man? Without divine inspiration, if you were not Apollonius, it was hard to tell the innocent from the guilty.

What level of guilt had stained the soul of Valerius Apollinaris, the previous governor of Asia? Last winter, when they had first met, just the two of them at dinner, with plenty of wine, the servants sent away, Timesitheus had expressed his condolences. No one could deny that life under the Caesars had been cruel to Valerius Apollinaris: his father had been murdered by Caracalla, his son by Maximinus. Timesitheus was not alone in fearing for the safety of Apollinaris and his surviving son. As things stood, Timesitheus, like all men of rank, feared for his own safety. The old governor would not be drawn. No complaints had escaped his lips. It was his duty to govern Asia, as it was that of his remaining son to oversee the banks of the Tiber and the sewers of Rome. Nothing treasonous for the witnesses Timesitheus had hidden to record.

Tranquillina had been furious. Timesitheus had said they should proceed no further. His wife had rounded on him. What had happened to the man she had married? Like the cat, he would eat fish but not get his paws wet. Would he live as a coward in his own esteem?

She had done things differently at the next meal. Late in the night, fixing Valerius Apollinaris with her dark eyes, she had said she did not believe that old-fashioned Roman honour was dead. The young could still be led back to ancestral virtue. They needed men of age and experience to follow. Then she had told Valerius Apollinaris of the meeting the previous year at Samosata.

Appalled by the risk she was running, Timesitheus had arranged his face. Behind its mask, he heard the scrabbling claws of his fear.

Timesitheus and Priscus loved Rome, but they were equestrians; no one would rally to them. The Senators Otacilius Severianus, Junius Balbus and Licinius Serenianus were men of probity, but on that day they had lacked resolve. If they had shown more courage, Junius Balbus would still be alive, and so would Claudius Apellinus, Sollemnius and a host of others. Modestly dressed, but her eyes shining with vehemence, Tranquillina could have been Lucretia or any stern example of a virtuous matron from a bygone age as she called on Valerius Apollinaris to free the *Res Publica*.

Then it had come out: the old governor's long-stored bitterness and ambition, both cloaked in noble sentiments of duty and the public good. More than enough this time for the covert listeners.

Suitably edited – the initiative reversed and all mention of Samosata gone – the reports had travelled the *cursus publicus* to the court. *Frumentarii* had come back – with a closed carriage for Valerius Apollinaris and an ivory-bound imperial mandate for Timesitheus to take charge of the province of Asia.

That first night in the governor's palace, here on this terrace, Tranquillina had pleasured him with her mouth. When he was near thinking he could take no more, she had lifted her skirts and bent over the parapet. Gripping her hips, he had thrust into her, revelling in his power, uncertain what in her cries was pleasure or pain. Afterwards she had told him what he needed to hear. Blood will out. Valerius Apollinaris' father had been a traitor, his son had been a traitor, his other son would prove one too. Treachery ran through them like a seam of ore in a rock. Like miners, all she and Timesitheus had done was work it and bring it into the daylight.

Timesitheus turned as Tranquillina walked out of the palace. She smiled, and he realized she knew at once what he had been thinking about. She called over her shoulder and Sabinia came out to join them. Hand in hand, without attendants, they walked away down the steep path.

Reaching the Sacred Way, they turned right. The street was lined with crowds cheering the departing governor and his beautiful wife and daughter. Some threw flowers; others called out praises of his probity, his modesty and approachability. See how they did without guards or pomp.

Fools, Timesitheus thought. The ignorant had loved the Emperor Titus, because his reign was too short for him to do much wrong. The governorship of Asia could set a family up for generations. Timesitheus had been diligent in helping the imperial agent charged with confiscating the estate of Valerius Apollinaris; after all, one quarter was to come to himself as accuser. A key discovery had been that the old Senator, for all his talk of duty and virtue, had been filling his own treasure chests with both hands. Timesitheus had set about doing the same, but with more restraint and far greater subtlety. The only shame was he had not had long enough.

They turned right again, smiling and waving all the time, then left into the street to the harbour. Still the crowds cheered. Beyond the opportunities left behind in Asia, there were many reasons Timesitheus had no desire to return to Rome. Although Catius Celer and Alcimus Felicianus were in the city, their friendship would be matched by the enmity of others. One was Valerius Priscillianus, the surviving son of Valerius Apollinaris. The duty of revenge would be strong in him. Another – less virulent but better placed – was Vitalianus. Poor Macedo had been right about him; the deputy Praetorian Prefect would know that Timesitheus had argued against his previous appointment in Mauretania Caesariensis. Vitalianus had never struck him as a man likely to forgive or forget.

More mundane issues contributed to Timesitheus' reluctance. He had been appointed *Praefectus Annonae*. His instructions were to end unrest among the urban plebs by distributing more grain, while at the same time spending less money. Unless the previous incumbent had been egregious either in maladministration or corruption, it would prove difficult to accomplish the conflicting tasks. Then there was the question of a private will. The great patron of Timesitheus' early career, Pollienus Auspex Minor, had died. Auspex's natural son had predeceased him. Shortly before his death, Auspex had adopted Armenius Peregrinus. Now Armenius was disputing the large bequest Auspex had left to Timesitheus. There were only two acceptable ways to make a great deal of money in the *imperium*. One was government service, the other inheritance. Timesitheus had done well out of the former, but little had accrued from the latter. He would be in Hades before he allowed a legacy hunter like Armenius to cheat him.

How he had been landed with the currently unenviable post of *Praefectus Annonae* was uncertain. For all their well-turned orotundity, imperial orders contained no obligation to explain their motives. A hasty correspondence with his cousin Modestus, unsurprisingly, had shed little light. Modestus had written of the great honour bestowed on Timesitheus and their family. Maximinus himself had proposed his appointment. No one in the *consilium* had expressed any doubts about its wisdom.

Could even his cousin be so dull-witted as to envisage

anyone would? How did he think the objector might phrase it? *Emperor, most sacred regent of the gods on earth, while your will is law, and you are a man of notorious savage temper and violence, a man who once tried to blind his son, may I say that with this ill-judged proposal you stand revealed as a half-barbarian simpleton.*

Modestus had written that even Domitius had approved. In fact, the Prefect of the Camp now seemed amiably disposed. They often dined together, and Domitius had become something of a friend. Thank the gods, Timesitheus had never confided to his imbecilic cousin anything more sensitive than the cold of winter or the darkness of night. It was all too easy to imagine Modestus, well fuelled with wine at one of their intimate meals, turning his moon face to Domitius and laughing. *You know it is absurd, but Timesitheus has often said his life will not be complete until he has had you thrown to the animals, or stripped naked and, to the jeers of the mob, slowly flogged to death. Many times he has expressed the hope that the earth would lie light on you. It will make it easier for the dogs to dig up your corpse.*

The street to the port was long, and the crowds had thinned. They were passing the entrance to the harbour *gymnasium*. Somewhere in there, Apollonius of Tyana had once given a lecture. Its subject was not recorded; most likely a diatribe on virtue or vegetarianism. Halfway through, words had failed him. Far from being overcome by the platitudinous nature of his thinking, Apollonius had been granted a vision. At that moment, hundreds of miles away, the tyrant Domitian was being struck down. Timesitheus could not see Maximinus lasting much longer. Samosata might not have brought it about, but someone would soon encompass his fall. The old Pythagorean Apollonius had not been such a fool. When an Emperor was killed, it was better to be walking shaded paths a long way away than in the streets of Rome.

CHAPTER 34

The Northern Frontier
Sirmium,

Three Days before the Nones of January, AD238

'By Jupiter Optimus Maximus and all the gods, I swear to carry out the commands of the Emperor and the Caesar, never desert the standards or shirk death, and to value the safety of the Emperor and the Caesar above everything.'

Iunia Fadilla watched Iotapianus say the words. The little Syrian was the last to reaffirm the sacred military oath. Under his tall, pointed helm, he looked half frozen. A few flakes of snow blew across the parade ground. The officers had taken the oath for their men. Only a detachment of soldiers represented each unit, but the wide square was packed. Wherever you looked, steel and leather gleamed and standards snapped in the wan light of an early January morning. The field army billeted in Sirmium was incomprehensively large. After three years of relentless campaigning, Iunia Fadilla could not understand how there were any northern barbarians left. But apparently there were: lots of them, many still hostile. When it stopped snowing altogether and the real cold set in, when the river froze, Maximinus would lead the army north on to the white steppe to catch the Sarmatian Iazyges in their winter encampments.

She was one of the few women present. Given the weather, most of the senior commanders and local dignitaries had let their wives and daughters remain indoors. No such indulgence was extended to a member of the imperial family. Many of the men were looking at her, the Emperor among them. She caught his eye. Awkwardly, Maximinus jerked his gaze away. Since her wedding, she had often found him staring at her. It was horribly easy to imagine the sorts of things that might be running through the huge barbarian's mind.

A gust of wind tugged at her scarf, nearly lifting it and her veil. When Iunia Fadilla and her husband had appeared, Maximinus had asked his son why she was wearing a veil; they were not Greeks. Maximus had laughed, and invoked some old Roman who had divorced his wife for going unveiled in public. The law should allow her to display her beauty to his eyes alone. If she displayed herself elsewhere, she was provoking men for nothing. Inevitably, she would become the subject of suspicion and accusation. Immorality should be smothered in the cradle. Maximinus had given his son a strange look, but said nothing.

Iunia Fadilla fixed the pins in the net with the emeralds that held her scarf and veil in place. It was time for the civilian vows. Faltonius Nicomachus, the governor of Pannonia Inferior, walked forward with a delegation of the leading men of Sirmium. Attendants led out an ox.

'Emperor,' Nicomachus said, 'we offer prayers to the immortal gods to keep you and the Caesar Maximus in health and prosperity on behalf of the whole human race, whose security and happiness depend on your safety.'

The attendants readied themselves around the animal.

'For the welfare of our lord Gaius Iulius Verus Maximinus

Augustus, and for the welfare of our lord Gaius Iulius Verus Maximus Caesar, and for the eternity of the Roman people, to Jupiter Optimus Maximus an ox.'

The axe flashed in the pale sunlight, and the beast collapsed.

Maximus, resplendent in silvered cuirass, with gilded and jewel-studded helmet in the crook of his arm, drew himself up. The breeze ruffled his dark curls. There was something feminine in the beauty of the *Princeps Iuventutis*. Certainly, Iunia Fadilla thought, no vain girl could have found more pleasure in moments like this than the Prince of Youth.

The ox was the first of several victims. A cow was led out to be offered to Juno. Beasts of the appropriate sex would follow for Minerva, Jupiter Victor, Juno Sospes, Mars Pater, Mars Victor and Victoria. Each time, the prayers would be said again.

Behind her veil, Iunia Fadilla looked at Maximus with loathing. She would not have children by him. All too often, a page announced her husband would visit her bedchamber. Maximus bothered himself with no niceties and, when he had finished, he left. Thank the gods, he was never there in the mornings. No matter how often he took his conjugal rights, there would be no children. Old Eunomia was experienced in these things. Nummius had not wanted children. The nurse had honed her skills. Eunomia mixed the old olive oil, honey and cedar resin with white lead. With her fingers, Iunia Fadilla pushed the sticky mess inside herself. Perhaps Maximus thought she was excited. If he did, he did not seem to care. When he came, she was always careful to hold her breath. When he was gone, Eunomia holding her shoulders, she would squat, try to sneeze, and wash herself. If everything should fail – and there were those nights he burst in unannounced – there were ways to get rid of unwanted children.

The cattle were lowing, alarmed by the smell of blood.

Iunia Fadilla shivered. She missed her old life: the elegant house on the Carinae, trips to the Bay of Naples, the recitals, her friends. She wondered how Perpetua was doing. Maximus had taken pleasure in telling her that her friend's husband had been arrested. A traitor could expect no mercy. Maximus had no way of knowing that Perpetua had prayed that Serenianus would not return from Cappadocia. Perhaps Gordian had been wrong: perhaps the gods were not far away, perhaps they did listen. So far, they had not answered *her* prayers. Maximus was alive and in good health.

Divorce was too easy, moralists always complained. A simple sentence spoken in front of seven witnesses – *take your things and go* – and the contract was ended. A letter carrying their seals was just as effective. All easy, if you were not married to Caesar. Who would witness such a fatal letter? Where could you go to escape the outraged pride of the deserted husband?

The final sacrifice had been made; to Victoria, a cow. A procession was formed to escort the imperial family back to the houses requisitioned to make a palace. Maximus took her arm. It amused him to pinch her flesh until he heard her intake of breath, all the while smiling like Adonis.

The snow and ice had been swept from the streets, but icicles dripped from the eaves of temples and houses. The sooner it froze hard, the better. When it was cold as the grave, the army would depart, and Maximus with it. Perhaps the gods would be kind and guide a Sarmatian arrow to his heart.

Her marriage to Nummius had been unconventional. A well-brought-up girl should have been horrified. Iunia Fadilla had not been shocked. In a perverse way, it had approached the ideals set out by the philosophers. Nummius had never forced her to anything she found repugnant. There had been companionship and concern for each other. They had held everything in common, nothing private, not their thoughts or their bodies. Such ideals were rarely met. The reality of most marriages was more brutal. To show how truly he had become wife to a charioteer, the Emperor Elagabalus had appeared in public bruised with black eyes.

At last they reached the palace, and Iunia Fadilla could retire to her own rooms. Eunomia was waiting, gave her a hot drink, unpinned the heavy gold brooch and then removed her outer clothes and the net with its emeralds, the bracelet with its sapphires and the other detested betrothal gifts. Tenderly, her old nurse rubbed lotion into the bruises. Usually, Maximus hit her buttocks, her thighs and her breasts. Usually, he took care not to mark her face. This time he had claimed he could smell wine on her breath; when a woman drinks without her husband, she closes the door on all virtues and opens her legs for all-comers. He had not stopped beating her when he took her. *Bitch! What man could kiss a mouth which had sucked so many pricks. Bitch!*

Sipping the drink, Iunia Fadilla would not let herself cry. Her eyes rested on the brooch with its garnets. *Should you come this way again . . . my name is Marcus Julius Corvinus, and these wild mountains are mine.* It was a pleasant fantasy, no more. There were no mountains in the *imperium* wild enough to offer her sanctuary. Flight was unrealistic. Unless the Sarmatians intervened, it would have to be something else. Eunomia knew her herbs.

CHAPTER 35

The Northern Frontier
Sirmium,

the Ides of January, AD238

In the biting cold, Maximinus checked with numb fingers the girths of his warhorse. If it was important, something on which your life might depend, it was best to do it yourself. Javolenus grunted as he gave him a leg up. Maximinus waited until his bodyguard was also mounted, then gave the order to move out. The town gates squealed as they began to open in front of the column. Especially in this weather, they should have been oiled. No one could be relied on to do their duty these days.

In summer, it would be two years since she had died. Time had not cauterized the wound. Most of the time it was a dull pain, and he could bear it. But every so often the loss hit him with such force that he could neither act nor speak; in mid-speech or with food halfway to his mouth. He saw no need to try to hide those moments.

The gates opened on to an ice-bound world. The road ran straight to the north, bordered as far as the eye could see with tombs. The road and the tombs and the trees were very black against the fields of ice on either side. The wind had knocked the snow from the branches. Now it was very still, and the trees were a motionless black tracery linking earth and sky.

They had not gone two hundred yards, when Maximinus felt Borysthenes go lame. Leaning out, Maximinus saw he had shed the horse-sandal on his near fore. Officers quickly offered the Emperor their own horses – they would bring his mount on after. No, Maximinus said, he would ride Borysthenes at the head of the army. That was how he had seen it in his mind; that was what he had told Paulina. The army halted. Maximinus swung down. The imperial entourage did the same. As they waited for a farrier, Maximinus held the reins of his horse. Some fools would take all this for an omen.

Diis Manibus. 'To the gods below.' The tombs varied. Some were elaborate, like houses. They had sculptures, long inscriptions. Others were almost plain sarcophagi with only a few words; a name and *'Diis Manibus'*. Sometimes they bore just the two letters: *'D. M.'* She should be buried. Everyone said so. Aspines, Vopiscus, Catius Clemens, Volo, Anullinus – all had joined the chorus. She had been an Empress, and she was a goddess. The correct rituals should be observed. She should be buried in Rome. A new mausoleum could be built for a new dynasty. Maximinus had dismissed the latter idea. All revenues had to go to the northern wars. Then, they had replied, let her join the illustrious occupants of the tombs of Augustus or Hadrian. The Emperor had not answered.

She should be buried at Ovile. He had bought most of his native village and the surrounding land, including that on which stood the communal tumulus. No man should bow to him, neither in life, nor in death. He still allowed the dead of the village to be interred there. That was where she should go. When his duty was done – and it would not be long now

– he could join her. Together, their shades would ride the high hills, drink at the mountain springs, sleep in sheltered caves. Together, they would hunt at the side of the Rider God.

Yet, for now, he could not send her away. Her ashes, in an alabaster vase packed in straw, travelled in his baggage. At night he held the precious thing in his huge, man-killing hands, and talked to her. He had summoned the druid woman Ababa. She had performed strange rites and claimed to have spoken with Paulina's shade. The words Ababa reported had not rung true. No one could be relied upon.

In a way, he was already with the Rider God. Perhaps he always had been. The Thracian god had fought and vanquished the serpent which had tried to crush the tree of life. Likewise, Maximinus had stamped underfoot those who had attempted to strangle the *Res Publica*. In the North, and far, far the worst of all, there had been Quartinus and Macedo. But before them had been Magnus and his fellow conspirators, and then so many others, from all over the empire: Antigonus in Moesia Inferior, Ostorius in Cilicia, Apellinus in Britain, Sollemnius in Arabia. They had all had been killed. Maximinus had entertained doubts about the guilt of some of the latter. The rich accused each other all the time from hope of gain or preferment, or out of malice. They were not to be trusted. Yet, although it may not have been treason, all the condemned had been guilty of something. Evcryone was guilty of something: guilty of leading a shameful life, of not being open with their Emperor, of withholding funds from the war effort.

So many had been executed, and their estates gone into the war chest, and Maximinus knew that the empire was more secure for such severity. Decius, the ancestral patron of his family, still held the West from his base in Spain. He may have executed one of their relatives by marriage, but Africa would be quiet enough under the Gordiani. No revolt would come from an eighty-year-old or his wastrel drunk of a son. Anyway, Paul the Chain would watch them, and Capelianus held Numidia. The East was more of a concern. In the cellars, before he died, Junius Balbus had denounced Serenianus of Cappadocia. Under the claws, the latter had admitted plotting against the throne, but claimed he had acted alone. No amount of ingenuity or persistence had changed his story. But the fat Senator Balbus had implicated others, among them the governor of Mesopotamia. For now, Priscus was necessary to hold the Persians, but it was good that Volo had suborned one very close to him. In Rome itself the plebs might riot, but now Sabinus had replaced Pupienus as Prefect of the City, the Urban Cohorts would amicably join with the Praetorians of Vitalianus in sweeping them from the streets. Of course, there were always those who were suspect in the eternal city. It was a shame that Balbus had named Timesitheus. An Emperor had to learn patience and duplicity. Although Maximinus liked him, once the little Greek had the grain supply running smoothly, Timesitheus would have to be sacrificed.

The farrier arrived, and Maximinus talked to Borysthenes, calming the stallion as the man worked. Not long now, he said to the horse. Ten miles to the hills, twenty to the Danube, across the frozen river, then out on to the frozen plains to hunt down the Sarmatian Iazyges in their winter grazing. We will catch them as we caught their cousins the Roxolani in the autumn. After that, in the summer, one more campaign and Germania will be conquered. And then, when his duty was done, he could lay down his armour and return to Paulina.

Maximinus inspected the fit of the horse-sandal, its leather straps and their fittings. Satisfied, he told Maximus to give the man a coin. Scowling, his son threw it deliberately out of reach. The farrier picked it out of the snow piled by the nearest tomb.

Having been helped into the saddle by Javolenus, the Emperor looked around. Ice, snow, a bleak road flanked by houses of the dead. He regarded the pinched faces of his entourage. How many of them would be talking of an ill omen by tonight? His gaze fell on the new barbarian hostage. Maximinus could not remember the name of the youth, but his father, Isangrim, ruled in the far North by the Suebian Sea. Now he was a better omen. Favoured by the gods, the army of Maximinus Augustus would conquer as far as the distant northern Ocean.

CHAPTER 36

Africa
The Town of Thysdrus,

Four Days before the Kalends of March, AD238

The pursuit of pleasure was the cause of everything. The majority would not understand. Fine wines, choice foods, sex with desirable women; there was no denying they were all pleasing. So was reading a well-written book, or owning a good hunting dog, a fast horse, a brave fighting cock. But the pleasure they brought was nothing without friendship, without the knowledge that one had done the right thing. As he watched the dawn, Gordian knew his motives would be misunderstood. Men of principal were always misunderstood.

The sky was streaked with purple and the wind had got up in the night. Down in the walled garden the dark poplars nodded and the leaves of the junipers shifted. The air, even the ground and the terrace on which he stood shone an extraordinary pink, both beautiful and somehow threatening in its unlikeliness.

He could have commiserated with Mauricius, paid some of the fine himself, secured him a temporary safety and appeared to have acted as a friend. But appearance was not the same as reality. He would have known he had not done enough. He would never have been free of the worry of being unmasked as a false friend. There would have been no ease of mind. There would always have been the fear that the same would happen again, to another friend, to himself, to his father. Men would say that he had acted from ambition, but it was not true. The things he would do were not only for himself, they were for others. No one could find pleasure in a life of fear.

The purple was gone from the sky. As the world returned to its normal colour, the wind dropped and the first of the rain hissed down. Until he came here, he had never thought it rained so much in Africa; but it was still February.

The coming things oppressed him. He was acting in the name of friendship but, apart from Mauricius, he had not told his friends. They would all be put in danger without their consent. Yet they would have tried to dissuade him. Valerian would have said it was foolhardy, and Arrian most likely pulled a face which implied the same. Sabinianus would have played the cautious Parmenion to his impulsive Alexander, and Menophilus cited Gordian's own Epicurean precepts back to him: *Live out of the public eye, live unnoticed.*

There was no point in delay. Afterwards, they would all have to admit that a man should not stand aside when something intervenes to make life unlivable. If things went badly, perhaps they could disown him. If things went well, he was going to save them all: his friends and his father – especially his father. Gordian adjusted his toga and the bandage on his left arm, then turned, walked down the stairs and, all alone, without even a slave, went out of the house.

The streets were muddy. The olive season had ended, yet they were still busy for such an early hour, full of men from the country. The rustics wore big cloaks or bulky goatskins, which would be too hot when the sun came out.

Mauricius welcomed him into his house. After some hours of talk, a group of twenty upper-class young men arrived from the town. The Iuvenes wore heavy cloaks. The greetings were brief, unsurprisingly tense. Everything was ready. Mauricius told them that, once he had pleaded guilty, there had been no difficulty in getting the Procurator to agree to a postponement for the fine to be raised in full. The three days had sufficed to get all in place.

Thysdrus was not a big town. It took no time to walk past the foundations of the new amphitheatre Gordian Senior was building and reach the basilica where the court was sitting. There were many men outside. Eight guards at the door made Mauricius' party wait at a distance with a crowd of countrymen. The Pegasus on the soldiers' shields showed they were from 3rd Legion Augusta. When eventually they were admitted, they found another eight soldiers bearing the same insignia inside.

Paul the Chain was seated on a dais at the far end, flanked by a secretary and half a dozen scribes and backed by four of the legionaries. The other four were by the door. The Chain continued to read a document, studiously ignoring the arrivals.

Gordian, Mauricius and the Iuvenes stood waiting. The bandage was stiff and heavy on Gordian's arm. He forced himself not to touch it.

'Do you have the money and the deeds?' Paul spoke without looking up.

'Procurator, may I approach and speak in private?'

The Chain looked up at Mauricius. 'Do you have the money or not?'

'Yes.'

'Then hand it to my secretary.' Paul waved one of his entourage forward and resumed his reading.

There was nothing to fear, Gordian thought. 'Procurator,

as his legate, the governor has asked me to deliver a message for your ears only.'

With no attempt to hide his irritation, Paul looked at Gordian. 'Come.' He spoke as if to an importuning petitioner or a slave.

Nothing to fear, Gordian thought.

He climbed the steps with care, holding the bandage with his right hand.

'Well?'

Gordian nodded at the scribes and the soldiers. 'It is a sensitive matter. It touches on the safety of the Emperor.'

Paul signalled them to move back.

Gordian moved closer, his fingers feeling under the bandage. Death was nothing.

'Well?' The Chain smiled. 'Whom are you here to denounce?'

Better death than a life of fear. Gordian's fingers closed on the warm leather.

'Who is the traitor?'

'You.'

Gordian drew the concealed dagger.

The Chain tried to ward off the blow with the papyrus roll. The blade cut off two of his fingers. Gordian pulled back to strike again. Paul threw himself sideways out of the chair. The dagger ripped his toga, slid across his ribs. Clutching his mangled hand, Paul started to scramble away on his elbows and knees.

The scribes were trying to run. In the uproar, they collided with each other, got in the way of the four soldiers at the back of the dais. On the floor of the basilica the Iuvenes had cast off their cloaks to get at their hidden swords.

Gordian hurled himself on to Paul's back. Yanking his head back by the hair, he plunged the blade down into the side of his neck. The first blow scraped off his collarbone. Paul tried to get up, shake him off. They were thrashing and slipping in blood. The second time, the steel went in to the hilt, like a beast-fighter finishing a bull in the arena.

Mauricius and two of the Iuvenes were standing over him. The soldiers were rooted, unsure. Gordian withdrew the dagger. Blood spurted across the marble. He climbed to his feet. The front of his toga was smeared bright red. The soldiers down by the door were surrounded by rustics wielding axes and clubs. One who had resisted was on the floor. Blows rained down on him.

'Hold, in the name of the governor.'

A sudden stillness in the room. Outside, the sounds of running feet, men shouting.

'By the order of the governor,' Gordian shouted, 'the traitor Paul the Chain has been executed.'

Everyone was looking at him.

'There is no need for further violence.'

There was a commotion at the door. One of the Iuvenes pushed his way through. He came up on to the dais, and whispered to Mauricius.

'The mob are out on the streets,' Mauricius said to Gordian. 'Quick, we must get to your father before they do.'

CHAPTER 37

Africa,
the Town of Thysdus,

Four Days before the Kalends of March, AD238

It had been a busy day, busy for a man of eighty. Gordian could not now remember a time when he had not got up in the dark, and read his correspondence by lamplight. At dawn, Valens, his *a Cubiculo*, had opened the doors of the bedchamber and admitted the governor's intimate friends. Today, only his Quaestor Menophilus and Valerian had attended him as he dressed. The latter was a dutiful man. Gordian did not blame his other legates for not appearing. Sabinianus, Arrian and his son were young men. Their pleasures were more demanding, and the young needed more sleep than the old. In any event, they were all upset at the ruin of Mauricius.

At the third hour, Gordian had held court. The tutor Serenus Sammonicus had joined Menophilus and Valerian as his assessors. Gordian had always had a tendency to doze in court. It had grown worse as he had got older. Nowadays, Serenus Sammonicus was ready to nudge him. It had not been necessary this morning. It had been a case of disputed identity.

A local landowner claimed that on a visit to Hadrumetum he had recognized a stevedore on the quayside as a slave who had run some ten years before. The defendant was adamant that he was free born. Certainty proved unattainable. Gordian, as usual, had taken the path of clemency with generosity. He had declared in favour of the dockworker, but awarded the landowner the price of an able-bodied slave from his own funds. Wealth only existed to be spent.

He had heard only the one case. Afterwards, Serenus Sammonicus had remained, and they had worked on Gordian's biography of Marcus Aurelius. When he was young, Gordian had composed his *Antoniniad*, an epic poem on the dynasty in thirty books. He had written many other works beside. Now he found it increasingly difficult to hold many different things in his mind at once.

Serenus Sammonicus was a brilliant man of letters. His *Opuscula Ruralia* stood comparison with any contemporary poetry, and his *Diary of the Trojan War* was a masterpiece of prose invention. Gordian had been a friend of his father, the author of the *Res Reconditae*, killed by Caracalla. When the family estate had been confiscated, Gordian, at some risk of imperial displeasure, had appointed the son as tutor to his own boy. Under his tutelage, the younger Gordian had written some nice pieces, but he had squandered much of his talent in the pursuit of pleasure.

Gordian found little fault with his son; much of his own life had been dedicated to Bacchus and Aphrodite. His daughter, Maecia Faustina, stood in contrast to them both. From where she had inherited her censorious nature, Gordian was uncertain. Not from her mother. The character of his late wife, Orestilla, had chimed with his own. Perhaps it was from her maternal grandfather, who had always been a prig. Gordian remembered when once he had taken a seat in his own house, and Annius Severus had snapped the rebuke that no son-in-law should sit in the company of his wife's father, not until he had achieved at least the Praetorship. He had had something against washing in his presence as well.

Still, Maecia was loyal and capable. She ran the ancestral home of the Gordiani in Rome with a rod of iron. The *Domus Rostrata* had never looked better the last time he had passed through, three years ago on his way from Achaea to Africa. But recent events would not have improved her. With the execution of her husband, she would have found her share of grief. It was a pity, Gordian thought, that her son, his only grandson, seemed to exhibit the worst features of Maecia and the late Junius Balbus. If only the epicureanism of the younger Gordian had not dissuaded him from marriage. The gods knew, his son had sired bastards enough.

All too soon, his literary endeavours had faltered. In the old days, Gordian had liked to exercise before lunch. He had gone riding, wrestled, played ball; worked up a sweat and washed it off. For a long time since, he had merely ordered his carriage and gone for a drive. Today he had dispensed with even that mild outing. He and Serenus Sammonicus had bathed, eaten an early lunch and, saying goodbye to his companion, Gordian had retired for a nap.

One of the many annoyances of advancing age was sleep. Gordian felt tired all the time; he nodded off at public occasions but when he lay down to rest sleep would not come to his bed. He often tried summoning up all the animals in the huge painting that hung in the atrium of the *Domus Rostrata*. He had commissioned it to commemorate the games he had given as Quaestor back in the reign of Commodus. Two hundred stags with antlers shaped like the palm of a hand, thirty wild horses, a hundred wild sheep, ten elks, a hundred Cyprian bulls, three hundred red Moorish ostriches, two hundred chamois, two hundred fallow deer . . .

Some noise woke him. He was pleased he had an erection.

Not the aching hardness of his youth, but a definite tumescence. He had been dreaming of Capelianus' wife in days gone by. She had been wanton. Cuckolding Capelianus had added to his pleasure. For a moment he wondered whether to call Valens, have him send in some girl. There was a decadence to sex in daylight. You could see every detail of their bodies, watch the flush spread over their faces. No, it would not serve. Even as he framed the thought, he felt himself begin to go limp. For many years he had consumed aphrodisiacs; oysters, snails, wild chervil, rocket, nettle seeds, pepper, satyrion, the bulbs of the grape hyacinth. Finally, he had tried to emulate the tragedian and believe that he had been freed from a cruel tyrant.

It had rained in the morning, but now the sun was streaming through the gaps in the shutters. Orestilla would have loved Africa. She had liked the sun. When Caracalla had sent him to govern Britannia Inferior, she had been convinced the Emperor had made the appointment in the hope that the cold and damp of the far North would make an end of him. The climate had been ghastly, the winters near beyond belief, but it had not killed him, and it had revived his career. He stroked his now flaccid penis. The trouble it had caused. Although Gordian had been acquitted of adultery, Capelianus and his friends had moved heaven and earth to keep him from holding office. He had no idea why, years later, Caracalla had made him governor in Britannia. After that, his natural proclivities had stood him in good stead with Elagabalus. The strange youth had made him Consul designate, and his successor had let it stand, indeed had held office as his colleague. Gordian had had several friends on the board of sixteen Senators – Vulcatius Terentianus, Felix, Quintillius Marcellus – and under Alexander he had progressed from the governorship of Syria Coele to that of Achaea then to Africa without intermission.

There was commotion out in the atrium. Gordian rang the little bell for Valens. The *a Cubiculo* did not appear.

The door crashed open. Gordian sat up as a mob burst into the room. Although his heart was hammering, he would not betray himself. Since the condemnation of Junius Balbus, he had been half expecting this. Maximinus could take his life, but he would not let the Thracian take his *dignitas*.

'What do you want?' Gordian managed to keep his voice level.

The men stopped. They were armed, but they were not soldiers. There were three well-dressed young men with swords. Behind them were many plebs with kitchen knives and clubs, who gawped at the rich furniture and fine hangings.

Where in Hades was his bodyguard, Brennus? Where were the household troops? Perhaps he could keep the men talking.

One of them had a purple cloth in his hands. He came forward and draped it over Gordian's shoulders. By all the gods, no – he would not be trapped like that.

'Augustus!' They shouted. 'Gordian Augustus!'

Gordian shrugged off the fatal trappings. He slid off the couch, got down on his knees.

'Please—' he held up his hands in supplication '—spare the life of an innocent old man. Remember my loyalty and goodwill to the Emperor. I mean no treason. Spare me.'

One of the young men gestured for silence. He faced Gordian with his sword at the ready.

'You have a choice,' he said. 'You face two risks: one here; the other in the future.'

Gordian said nothing. Were they not agents of Maximinus?

'Put your trust in us, accept the purple and overthrow the tyrant.' The young man moved the blade. 'If you refuse to join us, then this day will be your last.'

Gordian saw the crowd behind the young man part. His

son stood there, his toga all covered in blood. No, not that! Anything but that!

His son walked forward, reached for the blade, put it down. Thank the gods, he was unhurt.

Kneeling by him, his son took his hands in his, kissed them, kissed his cheek.

'Father, the soldiers and people are tearing down the statues of Maximinus. They are acclaiming you Emperor. There is no way back. You must free the *Res Publica*.'

His son raised him up, and whispered in his ear:

'*Let me at least not die without a struggle, inglorious, but do some big thing first, that men to come shall know of it.*'

HISTORICAL
AFTERWORD

The Measure of Time

As with most things, the ways the Romans ordered time were both similar to ours and different. Like us, they divided the day into twenty-four hours. Unlike us, the length of their hours varied with the seasons. Daylight was always twelve hours, and darkness always the other twelve.

After Julius Caesar reformed the calendar (45BC) the Romans employed the months we still use. However, they did not number the days within them serially. Instead, they counted the number of days until the next significant day. There were three of these: the *kalends* (the 1st of each month), the *nones* (the 5th in short months, the 7th in long) and the *ides* (the 13th in short months, the 15th in long). Thus 14 February would be described as sixteen days before the *kalends* of March. To add to modern confusion, the Romans normally, but not always, counted inclusively (as in the previous sentence). Thus 1 February would be four days before the 5th for us, but five for the Romans.

There were many different styles within the Roman empire of designating years. Romans, as against Greeks, Syrians or whatever other nationality, usually either reckoned a year to be 'X years since the founding of Rome' (fixed after Varro at 753BC in our terms; a mythical event for us, it was historical for them) or 'the year in which A and B were Consuls' (i.e. the *Consuls Ordinarius*, the pair who took office on 1 January, rather than any of their replacements, the *Suffecti*, later in the year).

All the above, and much more, is set out with clarity in J. P. V. D. Balsdon, *Life and Leisure in Ancient Rome* (London, 1969), still the best book of its kind.

To make things easier, in the chapter headings of these novels I sometimes describe a day as being 'Y days after the *ides*' (or whatever), which keeps it in the 'right' month for us. Also, AD235 will mean more to most readers than either '989 years since the founding of the city' or 'the year in which Cn. Claudius Severus and L. Ti. Claudius Aurelius Quintianus were Consuls'.

AD235–8 – ANCIENT SOURCES

Far and away the most important ancient source for the years AD235–8 are the final two books (seven and eight) of the *History of the Empire after the Emperor Marcus* by the contemporary Greek historian Herodian. An excellent two-volume Loeb translation by C. R. Whittaker (Cambridge, Mass., 1969–1970), with introduction and notes, has long been available. Despite this, the text is little studied in the English-speaking world. Given the uncompetitiveness of the field, some might forgive the vanity of the following suggestions. Modern scholarship is surveyed by H. Sidebottom, 'Severan Historiography: Evidence, Patterns and Arguments,' in S. Swain, S. Harrison and J. Elsner (eds.), *Severan Culture* (Cambridge, 2007), 52–82;

especially 78–82. A lengthy study (full of words like 'intertextuality') is provided by H. Sidebottom, 'Herodian's Historical Methods and Understanding of History,' *ANRW*, II.34.4 (1998), 2775–836. Important studies, for those with the languages, are G. Marasco, *'Erodiano e la crisi dell'impero,' ANRW*, II.34.4 (1998), 2837–927 and M. Zimmermann, *Kaiser und Ereignis: Studien zum Geschichtswerk Herodians* (Munich, 1999).

Discussion of the series of imperial biographies known as the *Historia Augusta* (or *Augustan History*) and their mendacious, playful author is postponed until the next novel in Throne of the Caesars. The minor sources (Eutropius, Aurelius Victor, the *Epitome*, Zozimus and Zonaras) will be dealt with in the final volume of the trilogy.

AD235–8 – MODERN SCHOLARSHIP

The vital work of modern scholarship is Karen Haegemans, *Imperial Authority and Dissent: The Roman Empire in AD235–238* (Leuven, Paris and Walpole, MA, 2010). Still useful for the careers of and links between the characters is K.-H. Dietz, *Senatus contra principem: Untersuchungen zur senatorischen Opposition gegen Kaiser Maximinus Thrax* (Munich, 1980). Much can also be gained from I. Mennen, *Power and Status in the Roman Empire, AD193–284* (Leiden and Boston, 2011).

EMPERORS

The dominant modern scholarly understanding of the role of the Emperor – above all, his essentially *reactive* character – has been shaped by one monumental work of scholarship. Fergus Millar's *The Emperor in the Roman World (31BC–AD337)*, (London, 1977, reprinted with new afterword, 1991). While it is a work of almost unparalleled breadth of reading and closely focused thought, it should be noted that Millar's book looks only at certain aspects of the life of the Emperor and might be considered to homogenize into one *role* many very different individuals. An aspect, explicitly omitted by Millar, where the Emperor appears far less passive, is studied by J. B. Campbell, *The Emperor and the Roman Army 31BC–AD235* (Oxford, 1984). A recent popular study, M. Sommer, *The Complete Roman Emperor: Imperial Life at Court and on Campaign* (London, 2010), has an innovative structure and wonderful illustrations. Unfortunately, it occasionally makes empirical mistakes and gives outmoded or eccentric interpretations as if they were uncontentious.

PROVINCIAL GOVERNORS

Technically there were two types of provinces: 'senatorial', governed by Proconsuls appointed by the Senate (e.g. Africa) and 'imperial', overseen by legates (deputies) appointed by the Emperor (the latter including almost all those provinces with armies, and all those governed by equestrians). In practice, the difference was minimal. No one came to be any sort of governor without the Emperor's permission. By his *maius imperium* (overriding military authority), the Emperor could give orders to any governor and, from the beginning of the principate, we find Emperors issuing *mandata* (instructions) to the Proconsuls of 'senatorial' provinces.

One difference was length of tenure. Proconsuls might expect to be replaced after a year, while legates might hold office for several years, often at least three. In this novel, while using nearly all the office holders known to history, to avoid a plethora of minor characters I have kept both types of governors in office from AD235–8, or at least those who are not killed. While it is a fictional device, it might be justified by appeal to those times, such as the years Tiberius spent on Capri, when imperial government almost ground to a halt. Maximinus never left the northern frontiers and had no interest in civil government; both disincentives to new appointments.

Fergus Millar, *The Roman Empire and Its Neighbours* (2nd edn, London, 1981), gives a good introduction to these areas and much else.

HARZHORN BATTLE

A find by an amateur archaeologist in 2008 has led to the discovery and ongoing investigation of the site of an ancient battle in the region of the Harzhorn mountains in Germany. This incredibly important site so far is virtually unknown in the English-speaking world; although *www.römerschlachtam-harzhorn.de* has a useful summary in English and the historian Adrian Murdoch has put several pieces on his blog *adrianmur-doch.typepad.com*.

The recovery of artillery bolts and horse-sandals, neither of which are thought to have been used by German tribes, indicates that a Roman army was involved. The latest coins found are from the reign of Alexander Severus. Ancient literary sources are unanimous that the Emperor was murdered before embarking on an expedition into Germany and that the plan was carried out by his successor, Maximinus Thrax, thus pointing to a date during the reign of the latter.

The site, as the crow flies, is roughly 150 miles from the town of Mainz, where Maximinus' forces would have entered Germany. This provides a rare and very untypical instance where the *Historia Augusta* can be shown to convey reasonably accurate information which is otherwise unknown. The manuscripts record that the Emperor campaigned 300 to 400 miles beyond the frontier. Judging this incredible, all modern editors have amended the figure to between 30 and 40 miles.

We assume that the Romans won the encounter for two

reasons. First, the ancient sources, above all Herodian (see above), record Maximinus as victorious over the Germans. Second, because nails almost certainly from the boots of Roman soldiers have been found alongside bolts from ballistas, the deduction has been made that the Romans shot artillery at the area, then followed up with infantry (and cavalry also, because the horse-sandals were found in the same place).

In this novel, to explain why the Romans attacked over the ridge, I have made the Germans block the pass, where Autobahn A7 now runs, with field fortifications. Also, I have made the area less forested than in later eras, because ancient torsion artillery would have been unable to shoot through a wood. Finally, I have given the Romans larger numbers than do the excavators, relying on the statement in Herodian that Maximinus invaded with 'an enormous host' (7.2.1).

The reconstruction in chapter 17 of this novel makes no claims to be definitive. New discoveries can change our view of things out of all recognition. However, it is offered in the hope that it might provide a jumping-off point for the discussions of others.

For those who know German, an excellent starting point is *Roms Vergessener Feldzug: Die Schlacht am Harzhorn*, edited by H. Pöppelmann, K. Deppmeyer and W.-D. Steinmetz (Darmstadt, 2013), published to accompany an exhibition that ran in 2013–14 in the Braunschweigisches Landesmuseum.

HUNTING

In the late Republic the Roman elite took their idea of hunting from the courts of the Hellenistic East, the distant successors of Alexander's Macedonians. It was an activity to be done on horseback, with armies of servants, and exotic hounds that hunted by sight. It was a thing of ostentatious expense, freighted with social and ideological meaning. I know of no good systematic study, especially of the latter aspects. It would make a good doctoral thesis, or a great book, perhaps something a bit like Raymund Carr's *English Fox Hunting: A History* (London, 1976).

In the meantime, the reader can consult J. Aymard, *Essai sur la chasse romaine des origins à la fin du siècle des Antonins* (Paris, 1951), or J. K. Anderson, *Hunting in the Ancient World* (Berkeley, Los Angeles, and London, 1985), 83–153.

DIE-CUTTING AND COIN-STRIKING

No ancient literary source tells us how a die-cutter specifically, or a mint in general, went about their work. Scholars have always had to work back from the finished products. It is a province where experimental archaeology comes into its own. For the techniques in chapters 20 and 28, I draw on G. F. Hill, 'Ancient Methods of Coining', *Numismatic Chronicle*, 5.2 (1922), 1–42 and D. Sellwood, 'Minting', in D. Strong and D. Brown (eds.), *Roman Crafts* (London, 1976), 63–73.

I have accepted the traditional site for the imperial mint of Rome, under the church of S. Clemente, but there are problems with the identification; see A. Claridge, *Rome: An Oxford Archaeological Guide* (Oxford, 1998), 287.

On questions of initiative and ideology, I have broadly followed the model proposed by Andrew Wallace-Hadrill in his articles 'The Emperor and His Virtues', *Historia*, 30 (1981), 298–323 and 'Image and Authority in the Coinage of Augustus,' *JRS*, 76 (1986), 66–87: the junior magistrates in charge of the mint offer up images they hope will appeal to the Emperor, but then – in a strange reversal – when the coins are in circulation, the ideology 'what was done in the emperor's name was done by the emperor' led those using the coins to assume the 'messages' on them were their Emperor 'talking' to his subjects.

Hannibal and Scipio

In chapter 24, drink has confused Gordian. Scipio questioned Hannibal about great generals not before Carthage – in fact, their African meeting was at Zama – but years later in Ephesus.

Cockfighting

Little has been written on Roman cockfighting, gladiatorial combat being so much more shocking to modern sensibilities. It seems to have been a pastime of the raffish and the poor. In case any reader is concerned, the author has never attended a cockfight. Any number, usually from Mexico, can be viewed on the internet. The account in chapter 31 was inspired by the anecdote of Antony and Octavian and a classic article of modern anthropology: 'Deep Play: Notes on the Balinese Cockfight' by Clifford Geertz, reprinted in *The Interpretation of Cultures* (New York, 1973), 412–53. It borrows and reworks a superb line from the latter.

Serenus Sammonicus

In an influential article, Edward Champlin argues that Serenus Sammonicus, the author of the *Res Reconditae* killed by Caracalla, should be identified both with the Septimius who wrote the *Ephemeris Belli Troiani* and the Septimius Serenus of the *Opuscula Ruralia*: *Harvard Studies in Classical Philology*, 85 (1981), 189–212; this argument is summarized by H. Sidebottom in *Severan Culture*, edited by S. Swain, S. Harrison and J. Elsner (Cambridge, 2007), 60–62.

His son, also Serenus Sammonicus, the tutor of the younger Gordian and owner of a library of 62,000 volumes, most likely is an invention of the *Historia Augusta, Gord. Tres*

18.2. For these novels, I have accepted his reality and given him the latter two works mentioned above.

Quotes

The poet Ticida has not only borrowed his name from the late Republican poet Lucius Ticida but is also a plagiarist. The poem of his repeated by Iunia Fadilla in chapter 4 is by an anonymous poet under the empire preserved in the *Greek Anthology* (5.84) and translated by W. G. Shepherd in *The Greek Anthology*, ed. P. Jay (rev. edn, Harmondsworth, 1981), 324, no. 748.

When Pupienus in chapter 16 helped his son compose a speech, he must have had at his elbow the *Panegyric* of Pliny the Younger in the translation of B. Radice (Cambridge, Mass., and London, 1969).

Knowledge of literature, above all of Homer, was a badge of the elite in the Roman empire. All the lines of the *Odyssey* remembered in this novel are from the translation of Robert Fagles (London, 2006). Those from the *Iliad* are from the translation of Richard Lattimore (Chicago and London, 1951).

Previous Novels

In all my novels I like to include homages to writers who have given me great pleasure and inspiration.

When Mamaea curses her assassins, she echoes Jacques de Molay, Grand Master of the Templars, in *The Iron King*, the first volume of Maurice Druon's superb series *The Accursed Kings* (the English translation is now being republished and expanded by HarperCollins, London, 2013, and ongoing).

When Timesitheus 'arranges his face', he foreshadows Thomas Cromwell in *Wolf Hall* (London, 2009) and *Bring up the Bodies* (London, 2012). Nothing could be added to the praise already given to these novels by Hilary Mantel.

I borrowed a phrase from *White Doves at Morning* (London, 2003) by James Lee Burke. A wonderful writer, he should be far more widely read on this side of the Atlantic.

THANKS

My greatest thanks, as ever, go to my family: my wife, Lisa, my sons, Tom and Jack, my aunt Terry, and my mother, Frances. With a new series, loads of stuff to learn and lots of new characters to make up, they have put up with me working non--stop all year.

Writing a novel is an unnatural, arrogant thing to do. Without the support of both the professionals and friends around me, I am not sure I could pull it off. So, many thanks to my agent, James Gill, and my new editor, Katie Espiner; also to Kate Elton, Damon Greeney, Cassie Browne, and Charlotte Cray (all at HarperCollins), to Richard Marshall (for the endmatter, and knowing more about the novels than me) and, for the seventh time, to my copy-editor, Sarah Day. Thanks also to friends, academic and otherwise, Peter and Rachel Cosgrove, Katie and Jeremy Habberley, Maria Stamatopoulou, Michael Dunne, Vaughan Jones and Jeremy Tinton.

Various students have put up with a lot of fiction when they might have hoped for history: Jonny Riches, Olly Jones, Torsten Alexander, Fergus O'Reegan and Michalina Szymanska.

Back in the day, three senior scholars in Oxford said or did things that showed a faith in my abilities that I was far from sharing. At different times, in ways they will have forgotten, Ewen Bowie, Miriam Griffin and Robin Lane Fox gave me the confidence to write. So this novel is dedicated to them.

Harry Sidebottom
Newmarket and Oxford
February 2014

IRON & RUST:

GLOSSARY

The definitions given here are geared to *Iron & Rust*. If a word or phrase has several meanings only that or those relevant to this novel tend to be given.

A Cubiculo: Official in charge of the bedchamber, also Cubicul arius.

A Libellis: Official in charge of legal petitions addressed to the Emperor; sometimes translated here as Secretary for Petitions.

A Studiis: Official who aided the literary and intellectual studies of the Roman Emperor.

Ab Admissionibus: Official who controlled admission into the presence of the Roman Emperor; sometimes translated here as Master of Admissions.

Achaea: Roman province of Greece.

Achaemenids: Persian dynasty, founded by Cyrus the Great c. 550BC, and ended by Alexander the Great, 330BC.

Actaeon: In Greek mythology, hunter who came across the goddess Artemis bathing naked and, as punishment, was turned into a stag and killed by his own hounds.

Actium: Battle fought in 31BC that left Augustus in supreme control of the Roman empire.

Ad Palmam: Oasis on the margin of the Lake of Triton (Chott el Djerid), south west of Africa Proconsularis.

Ad Pirium: *Fortified rest house in the eastern Alps above Longaticum.*

Adlection: *Formal call to join the senate.*

Adonis: *Greek god of beauty.*

Aeaean Island: *Legendary home of the witch Circe in the epic poet Homer's Odyssey.*

Aegis: *Mythical shields or cloaks carried by Zeus and Athena.*

Aeneid: *Epic poem by Virgil, telling the mythical story of Rome's foundation. In antiquity, the most highly prized work of Latin literature.*

Aequi: *Italian tribe living north east of Rome in the Apennine mountains; conquered in the fifth century BC.*

Aetolia: *Mountainous region of Greece north of the gulf of Corinth.*

Africa Proconsularis: *Roman province of central North Africa, roughly modern Tunisia.*

Agora: *Greek term for a market place and civic centre.*

Alae: *Units of Roman auxiliary cavalry, usually around 500-, sometimes around 1000-strong; literally, a 'wing'.*

Alamanni: *Confederation of German tribes. The name probably means 'all men', either in the sense of men from various tribes or 'all real men'.*

Alani: *A nomadic people living north of the Caucasus mountains.*

Algidus: *Extinct volcano south east of Rome, site of a battle between Rome and the Aequi in 458–7BC.*

Ambrosia: *Mythical food of the gods.*

Amici: *Latin, 'friends'.*

Ammaedara: *Roman town on the eastern border of Tunisia; modern Haïdra.*

Amouda: *Town in north-eastern Syria, modern Amuda.*

Amphorae: *Large Roman earthenware storage vessels.*

Angle: *Member of a North German tribe, living in the area of modern Denmark.*

Angrivarii: *North German tribe living in the area of modern Saxony and Westphalia.*

Antioch: *Ancient city on the Orontes river in north-eastern Syria; second city of the eastern Roman empire.*

Antoniniad: *Epic poem alleged to have been written by Gordian the Elder on the Emperors Antoninus Pius and Marcus Aurelius; only the title survives.*

Aphrodite: *Greek goddess of love.*

Apollo: *Greek god of music and culture.*

Apollo Sandaliarius: *Famous statue of Apollo in the street of the Sandal-makers (Vicus Sandaliarius).*

Apulia: *Modern Puglia, the 'heel' of Italy.*

Apulum: *Roman fort in the province of Dacia; modern Alba Iulia in Romania.*

Aquileia: *Town in north-eastern Italy.*

Aquitania: *Roman province of south-western and central Gaul, in modern France.*

Arabia: *Roman province covering much of modern Jordan and the Sinai peninsular.*

Aramaic: *Ancient language spoken in much of the Levant and Mesopotamia.*

Araxes River: *Greek name for the Aras River, rising in eastern Turkey and flowing towards the Caspian Sea.*

Arca: *Coastal town in Syria Phoenice.*

Arch of Augustus: *Monumental arch in the south eastern corner of the Roman Forum, commemorating a diplomatic victory over the Parthians in 19BC.*

Arch of Germanicus: *Monumental arch built on the right bank of the Rhine at Mainz-Kastel, commemorating the German campaigns of Germanicus in the early first century AD.*

Arch of Titus: *Monumental arch between the Roman Forum and Flavian Amphitheatre, commemorating the re-conquest of Jerusalem in AD70.*

Ares: *Greek god of war.*

Arete: *Fictional town on the Euphrates, modelled on Dura-Europus.*

Argo: *Legendary ship of the Argonauts.*

Argonauts: *Crew of Jason's mythical ship the Argo.*

Armenia: *Ancient buffer kingdom between Rome and Parthia, occupying much of the area south of the Caucasus mountains and west of the Caspian Sea; much larger than the modern state of Armenia.*

Arsacid: *Dynasty that ruled Parthia 247BC–AD228.*

Artaxata: *Capital of the Kingdom of Armenia; modern Artashat in Armenia.*

Artemis: *Greek goddess of hunting.*

Arzamon River: *Greek name for the Zergan river in south-eastern Turkey and north-eastern Syria.*

Asia: *Roman province of western Turkey.*

Athena: *Greek goddess of wisdom.*

Athenians: *Citizens of the Greek city-state of Athens.*

Atlantes: *Tribe in western North Africa; gave their name to the Atlas Mountains.*

Atrium: *Open courtyard in a Roman house.*

Augean Stable: *In Greek myth, a giant stables finally cleaned by the hero Hercules by the redirecting of two rivers.*

Augilae: *Tribe of Libyans living around the Awjila Oasis.*

Augusta Vindelicorum: *Capital of the Roman province of Raetia; modern Augsburg in southern Germany.*

Augustus: *Name of the first Roman Emperor, subsequently adopted as one of the titles of the office.*

Auspex: *Roman priest in charge of telling the future from various rituals and natural phenomena, including the flight of birds.*

Auxiliary: *Roman regular soldier serving in a unit other than a legion.*

Bacchic: *Fuelled by wine; from the religious frenzy of the worshippers of the god Bacchus.*

Bacchus: *Roman name for the Greek god of wine, Dionysos.*

Baetica: *One of the three Roman provinces of the Spanish peninsular, located in the south-eastern corner of modern Spain.*

Baquates: *Nomadic Berber tribe living in the Middle Atlas mountains of modern Morocco.*

Barbaricum: *Lands of the barbarians. Anywhere beyond the frontiers of the Roman empire, which were thought to mark the limits of the civilized world.*

Basilica: *Roman court building and audience chamber.*

Basilica Aemilia: *Court building on the north-eastern side of the Roman Forum, originally built in 179BC and restored on several occasions in antiquity.*

Baths of Titus: *Built by the Emperor Titus c. AD81 on the Esquiline Hill, just north of the Flavian Amphitheatre.*

Baths of Trajan: *Large bathing and leisure complex dedicated by the Emperor Trajan in AD109, built on the flank of the Esquiline Hill overshadowing the adjacent Baths of Titus.*

Batnae: *Town in south-eastern Turkey; modern Suruç.*

Belgica: *Roman province spanning modern Belgium and north-western France.*

Bithynia-Pontus: *Roman province along the south shore of the Black Sea.*

Boeotia: *Ancient area of central Greece north east of the Gulf of Corinth.*

Boeotian: *From the region of Boeotia.*

Bona Vacantia: *Latin legal term, literally, 'unclaimed property' of those dying intestate; a major source of income for the Emperors.*

Bonchor: *God worshipped by the Numidians, equated with Saturn, Roman father of the gods.*

Borythenes: *Greek name for the Dnieper river.*

Britannia Inferior: *One of two Roman provinces of Britain, located in northern England.*

Brundisium: *Important port on the south-eastern coast of Italy, modern Brindisi.*

Bucolic: *Ancient genre of poetry dealing with rural themes, from the Greek 'cowherd'.*

Bulla: *Charm placed around the necks of children and worn until adulthood.*

Byzantium: *Greek city founded at the mouth of the Black Sea; modern Istanbul.*

Caelian Hill: *One of the seven legendary hills of Rome, lying south east of the Roman Forum.*

Caesar: *Name of the adopted family of the first Roman Emperor, subsequently adopted as one of the titles of the office; often used to designate an Emperor's heir.*

Caledonia: *Area of Britain north of the Roman provinces; roughly modern Scotland.*

Campania: *Fertile region on the western coast of southern Italy much favoured as a holiday destination by the Roman elite.*

Campus Martius: *Latin, literally, 'field of Mars'; name of a famous space in Rome; in general, name for a parade ground.*

Cannae: *Ancient village in Apulia, site of disastrous Roman defeat by Hannibal in 216BC.*

Cape Malea: *Headland on the south-eastern peninsular of the Greek Peloponnese.*

Cappadocia: *Roman province north of the Euphrates.*

Capri: *Island in the Bay of Naples, where the Emperor Tiberius spent his notorious retirement.*

Capsa: *Town in central Tunisia, modern Gafsa.*

Carinae: *Literally 'the Keels', fashionable quarter of ancient Rome on the Esquiline Hill; now S. Pietro in vincoli.*

Carpathian Mountains: *Mountain chain in Central and Eastern Europe, named from the ancient Carpi tribe.*

Carpi: *Tribe living north-west of the Black Sea.*

Carrhae: *Town in northern Iraq, scene of a disastrous Roman defeat at the hands of the Parthians in 53BC.*

Carthage: *Second city of the western Roman empire; capital of the province of Africa proconsularis.*

Castellum Arabum: *Roman fort, modern Tell Ajaja in eastern Syria.*

Castellum Neptitana: *Oasis in western Tunisia, modern Nefta.*

Castra Regina: *Legionary fortress and settlement in south eastern Germany, modern Regensburg.*

Cataphracts: *Heavily armoured Roman cavalry, from the Greek word for mail armour.*

Caystros River: *River in western Turkey, now much silted and known as the Küçükmenderes.*

Cententarium Tibubuci: *Roman outpost in southern Tunisia, modern Ksar Tarcine.*

Centurion: *Officer of the Roman army with the seniority to command a company of around eighty to a hundred men.*

Cercopes: *Mythical twins renowned for cheating, thieving, and lying.*

Cerialia: *Roman festival in honour of the goddess Ceres, celebrated on 10th April.*

Chaboras River: *Tributary of the Euphrates in southern Turkey and northern Syria, the modern Khabur River.*

Cherusci: *German tribe living in the north west of Germania.*

Chian: *Red wine from the Island of Chios; highly prized in antiquity.*

Cilicia: *Rome province in the south of Asia Minor.*

Cillium: *Town at the foot of the Atlas Mountains in eastern Tunisia; modern Kasserine.*

Cinithii: *Berber tribe living in the south of modern Tunisia.*

Civilis princeps: *Literally, a 'citizen-like emperor'; one ruling with tact and restraint rather than as an absolute monarch or dictator.*

Clibanarii: *Heavily armoured cavalry, name possibly derived from the Latin for 'baking oven'.*

Coelli: *Members of the Coelius family; their ancestors held the consulship in the Republic, making them nobiles.*

Cohors I Thracarum: *The 2nd Thracian Cohort; Auxiliary unit recruited from Thrace in the Balkans.*

Cohors II Flavia Afrorum: *The 2nd Cohort, Flavian, African; stationed in the south of modern Tunisia for much of its history.*

Cohors V Dalmatarum: *The 5th Dalmatian Cohort; in the late second century, stationed in Germania Superior.*

Cohors XV Emesenorum: *The 15th Emesene Cohort; auxiliary unit recruited from around the city of Emesa in Syria.*

Cohort: *Unit of Roman soldiers, usually about 500 men-strong.*

Colonia Agrippinensis: *Capital of the province of Germania Inferior; modern Cologne in Germany.*

Comana: *City in Cappadocia; modern Şar in central Turkey.*

Comilitio: *Latin, 'fellow soldier', often used by commanders wishing to emphasize their closeness to their troops.*

Commagene: *Small kingdom in south-eastern Turkey first assimilated into the Roman empire in AD17 and intermittently independent until AD72.*

Concordiae Augustae: *Literally 'of Augustan Concord'; a temple built in honour of the Emperor's harmonious rule was dedicated at the western end of the Roman Forum.*

Conscript Fathers: *Honourific form of address used before the Senate.*

Consilium: *Council, body of advisors, of a Roman Emperor.*

Consul: *In the Republic, the highest office in the Roman state; under the Emperors, a largely honourific and ceremonial position.*

Consul Ordinarius: *Literally 'Consul in the usual manner'; Consul who took office at the start of the year. In the Republic, a pair of consuls were elected to serve for one year, but the Emperors shortened the length of office and nominated additional consuls. The consul ordinarius remained the most prestigious position as the Romans indicated years by the names of the two consuls who entered office on 1st January. See also Suffect Consul.*

Corcyra: *Greek name for the Island of Corfu.*

Corinth: *Ancient city in the Peloponnese, notorious for its luxurious living and prostitutes.*

Ctesiphon: *Capital of the Parthian empire, lying on the eastern bank of the Tigris River, twenty miles south of modern Baghdad in Iraq.*

Cubicularius: *Servant of the bed-chamber, valet; official position in the imperial and other elite households; also a Cubiculo.*

Cuicul: *Garrison town in the province of Numidia; modern Djémila in Algeria.*

Curia: *The meeting house of the Senate in Rome; the building erected after a fire in the later third century is still standing.*

Cursus Honorum: *Literally, 'progression of offices'; the rigid career path of ranked public offices held in turn by an aspiring Roman politician on his way to becoming Consul.*

Cursus Publicus: *Imperial Roman postal service, whereby those with official passes could get remounts and a room for the night.*

Curule Throne: *Ivory folding chair, the mark of office of important Roman officials.*

Custos: *Latin, literally 'a guardian'; one would accompany an upper-class woman, in addition to her maids, when she went out in public.*

Cybele: *Eastern mother goddess adopted by the Greeks and Romans.*

Cynegeticus: *Title of several ancient treatises on hunting with dogs.*

Cynic: *The counter-cultural philosophy founded by Diogenes of Sinope in the fourth century BC; its adherents were popularly associated with dogs (the name itself is from the Greek for 'dog') for their barking and snapping at contemporary morality and social customs.*

Cyrenaeans: *Followers of the philosophy of Aristippus, who taught that pleasure should be found by adapting the circumstances to suit oneself, not submitting oneself to circumstance.*

Cyrenaica: *Roman province of eastern Libya and the Island of Crete.*

Dacia: *Roman province north of the Danube, in the region around modern Romania.*

Daemon: *Supernatural being; could be applied to many different types: good/bad, individual/collective, internal/external, and ghosts.*

Daphne: *Suburb of Antioch, famed for its oracular temple of Apollo, and its luxury.*

Demeter: *Greek goddess of the harvest.*

Diatribe: *Ancient rhetorical genre, generally dealing with the denunciation of vices.*

Dignitas: *Important Roman concept which covers our idea of dignity but goes much further; famously, Julius Caesar claimed that his dignitas meant more to him than life itself.*

Dionysos: *Greek god of Wine.*

Diis Manibus: *'For the ghost-gods', i.e. spirits of the departed; common formula on Roman funerary monuments, often abbreviated to D. M.*

Dominus: *Latin, 'lord', 'master', 'sir'; a title of respect.*

Domus Rostrata: *Home of the Republican general Pompey in the fashionable Carinae quarter; decorated with the ramming beaks (Rostra) of the pirate ships he captured, from which it took its name.*

Durostorum: *Roman fortress on the south bank of the Danube; modern Silistra in Bulgaria.*

Dux ripae: *The Commander, or Duke, of the River Banks; a Roman military officer in charge of the defences along the Euphrates in the third century AD; historically based at Dura-Europos.*

Dyarchy: *From the Greek 'rule by two'.*

Eclogues: *Title of a collection of poems by Virgil; from the Greek ekloge, 'extracts'.*

Edessa: *Frontier city periodically administered by Rome, Parthia and Armenia in the course of the third century; modern Şanliurfa in southern Turkey.*

Egnatii: *Members of the senatorial Egnatius family.*

Eleusis: *Greek religious centre; home of an extremely ancient cult of Demeter that required worshippers to undergo various secret initiation ceremonies.*

Elysian Fields: *In Greek mythology, the heaven that awaits the souls of heroes and the virtuous.*

Emesenes: *Inhabitants of the city of Emesa and surrounding area, modern Homs in Syria.*

Ephesus: *Major city founded by Greek colonists on the western coast of modern Turkey.*

Epicureans: *Greek philosophical system, whose followers either denied that the gods existed or held that they were far away and did not intervene in the affairs of mankind.*

Equestrian: *Second rank down in the Roman social pyramid; the elite order just below the senators.*

Equites: *Latin, 'horsemen', 'cavalry'.*

Equites Singulares: *Cavalry bodyguards.*

Equites Singulares Augusti: *Permanent mounted unit protecting the Emperor.*

Equites Singulares Consularis: *Mounted unit raised to protect a provincial governor.*

Erinyes: *Greek mythological deities of vengeance.*

Esquiline: *One of the seven hills of Rome, rising east of the Roman Forum.*

Esuba: *Ancient village in North Africa, location uncertain.*

Europa: *Phoenician princess in Greek mythology kidnapped and raped by Zeus.*

Exi! Recede!: *Latin, 'get out, go away'.*

Exemplum: *Latin, 'example'; has connotations of model virtue, something or someone to be followed.*

Falernian: *Very expensive white wine from northern Campania, particularly prized by the Romans.*

Familia Caesaris: *The household of the Emperor, comprising both servants and the imperial bureaucracy; largely staffed by slaves and freedmen.*

Father of the House: *Most senior member of the Senate.*

Feliciter: *Latin, 'good luck', 'hurrah'; cried by guests to newlyweds.*

Fides: *Latin, 'good faith', 'loyalty'.*

Fiscus: *Imperial treasury.*

Flamen Dialis: *The Roman high priest of Jupiter, subject to numerous taboos.*

Flavian Amphitheatre: *Giant arena for gladiatorial fights seating 60,000 spectators; now known as the Colosseum, in antiquity known after the Flavian dynasty of Emperors who built and dedicated the structure.*

Floralia: *Roman festival to the goddess Flora, held between 28 April and 3 May, featuring obscene mimes.*

Forum: *Central square of a Roman city, site of the market-place, and government, judicial and religious buildings.*

Forum of Augustus: *Built by the Emperor Augustus north of the Roman Forum, backed by a high wall to act a barrier against the frequent fires affecting the slum quarter behind.*

Forum Romanorum: *The Roman Forum; oldest and most important public square in Rome, littered with honourific statues and monuments going back to the early Republic. Surrounded by temples, court buildings, arches, and the Curia.*

Frumentarii: *Military unit based on the Caelian Hill in Rome; the Emperor's secret police; messengers, spies, and assassins.*

Gades: *Roman port; modern Cádiz in Spain.*

Gaetuli: *Berber tribes living on the fringes of the Sahara in North Africa, beyond effective Roman control.*

Ganymedes: *In Greek mythology, the hero Ganymede, the most beautiful man among mortals, attracted the erotic desires of Zeus, was abducted by the god and made immortal.*

Garamantes: *Berber tribe living in south-western Libya.*

Gedrosian Desert: *Disastrous route taken by the army of Alexander the Great retreating west from India; desert in modern Baluchistan.*

Genius: *Divine part of man; some ambiguity as to whether it is external (like a guardian angel) or internal (a divine spark); that of the head of a household worshipped as part of the household gods, that of the Emperor publicly worshipped.*

Georgics: *From the Greek georgicos, 'agricultural'; famous books of poems on rural themes by Virgil.*

Germania: *Lands where the German tribes lived; 'free' Germany beyond direct Roman control.*

Germania Inferior: *More northerly of Rome's two provinces of Germany; mainly confined to the west bank of the Rhine.*

Germania Superior: *More southerly of Rome's two German provinces.*

Gordiani: *The Gordianus family; in English, the Gordians.*

Goths: *Confederation of Germanic tribes.*

Graeculus: *Latin, 'Little Greek'; Greeks called themselves Hellenes, Romans tended not to extend that courtesy but called them Graeci; with casual contempt, Romans often went further, to Graculi.*

Granicus: *Victorious battle fought in 334BC by Alexander the Great against the Persian empire.*

Gymnasium: *Exercise ground; formed from the Greek gymnos 'naked', as all such activities were performed in the nude.*

Hades: *Greek underworld.*

Hadrianoupolis: *Capital of the Roman province of Thrace; modern Edirne in European Turkey.*

Hadrumetum: *City on the eastern coast of Africa Proconsularis, modern Sousse in Tunisia.*

Hatra: *Independent city state in northern Iraq, fought over by both the Romans and Parthians in the early third century.*

Hatrene: *Inhabitant of Hatra.*

Hellene: *The Greeks' name for themselves; often used with connotations of cultural superiority.*

Hephaistos: *Greek god of the forge.*

Hera: *Greek goddess of marriage.*

Hercules: *In Greek mythology, mortal famed for his strength who subsequently became a god.*

Hermes: *Greek messenger god.*

Hierasos: *Greek name for the Alkaliya River, flowing into the Black Sea in eastern Ukraine.*

Hipposandals: *Metal plates secured under the hooves of horses by leather straps; used before the introduction of horse shoes in the fifth century AD.*

Hispania Tarraconensis: *One of the three provinces into which the Romans divided the Spanish peninsula, the north-east corner.*

House of the Vestals: *Home of the Vestal Virgins, priestesses who tended the sacred fire of the goddess Vesta; situated east of the Roman Forum and on the south side of the Sacred Way, opposite the Temple of Venus and Rome.*

Humanitas: *Latin, 'humanity' or 'civilization', the opposite of barbaritas; Romans thought that they, the Greeks (at least upper-class ones), and, on occasion, other peoples (usually very remote) had it, while the majority of mankind did not.*

Hydaspes: *Greek name for the Jhelum River in Pakistan, site of Alexander the Great's victory over the Indian king Porus in 326BC.*

Hymen: *Greek god of marriage.*

Iazyges: *Nomadic Sarmatian tribe living north of the Danube on the Great Hungarian Plain.*

Ides: *Thirteenth day of the month in short months, the fifteenth in long months.*

Ilion: *Alternative name for the legendary city of Troy.*

Illyrian: *From the Balkans beyond the Adriatic (Illyricum in Latin); vaguely applied.*

Imperator: *Originally an epithet bestowed by troops on victorious generals, became a standard title of the Princeps, and thus origin of the English word Emperor.*

Imperium: *Power of the Romans, i.e. the Roman empire, often referred to in full as the imperium Romanorum.*

In Absentia: *Latin, 'while absent'.*

Io, Imperator!: *Latin, 'hurrah, Imperator', cry of victory.*

Ionia: *Area of western Turkey bordering the Aegean, settled by Greeks.*

Iunam: *Berber god identified with Sol or Mar, the Roman sun or war gods.*

Iupiter optime, tibi gratias. Apollo venerabilis, tibi gratias: *Latin prayer, 'Greatest Jupiter, to you we give thanks; reverend Apollo, to you we give thanks'.*

Iuvenes: *Latin, 'young men'; often denoting an elite para-military organization.*

Ixion: *In Greek mythology, Ixion murdered his father-in-law after refusing to honour a wedding contract, and was punished by being tied to a fiery flying wheel for eternity.*

Juno: *Roman goddess of marriage.*

Juno Sospes: *Title of Juno, 'The Saviour'.*

Jupiter: *Roman king of the gods.*

Jupiter Optimus Maximus: *Title of Jupiter, 'Greatest and Best'.*

Jupiter Victor: *Title of Jupiter, 'The Victorious'.*

Kalends: *First day of the month.*

Laconicum: *Dry sweating room in a Roman baths.*

Lake of Curtius: *Archaic monument in the middle of the Roman Forum taking the form of a sunken pool with statuary; the Romans themselves told various stories about its origins.*

Lake of Triton: *Ancient name for the Chott el Djerid, a large salt lake in central Tunisia.*

Lambaesis: *Fortress of the 3rd Augustan Legion and capital of the Roman province of Numidia; modern Tazoult in north-eastern Algeria.*

Lamiae: *Witches thought to suck the blood of children.*

Lararium: *Roman household shrine.*

Legate: *Latin, a high-ranking officer in the Roman army, drawn from the senatorial classes.*

Legio I Parthica: *The 1st Parthian Legion, stationed at Singara in Mesopotamia (Sinjar in Iraq).*

Legio II Parthica: *Full title Legio II Parthica Pia Fidelis Felix Aeterna, the 2nd Legion, the Parthian, Eternally Loyal, Faithful and Fortunate; in this period based at Mainz in Germany, though stationed in peacetime on the Alban hills near Rome.*

Legio III Augusta: *The 3rd Augustan Legion; stationed at Lambaesis in the province of Numidia.*

Legio III Italica: *The 3rd Italian Legion; usually stationed at Castra Regina in the province of Germania Superior.*

Legio III Parthica: *The 3rd Parthian Legion; raised towards the end of the second century for campaigns against Parthia; garrisoned at Resaina in Syria.*

Legio IIII Scythica: *The 4th Scythian Legion; from the second half of the first century AD based at Zeugma in Syria Coele (Kavunlu, formerly Belkis, in Turkey).*

Legio VI Ferrata: *The 6th Iron-Clad Legion; based at Carporcotani in Syria Palestina (el-Qanawat in Syria).*

Legio VII: *Full title Legio VII Gemina, The 7th Twin Legion, stationed at Legio (Léon) in Hispania Tarraconensis.*

Legio VIII Augusta: *The 8th Augustan Legion; stationed at Argentoratum (Strasbourg) in Germania Superior.*

Legio XI Claudia Pia Fidelis: *The 11th Legion, Claudian, Loyal and Faithful; based at Durostorum in Moesia Inferior (Silistra in Bulgaria).*

Legio XII Fulminata: *The 12th Thunder-bearing Legion; in this period, garrisoned in Syria.*

Legio XV Apollinaris: *The 15th Apollonarian Legion; stationed at Stala in Cappadocia (Sadak in Turkey).*

Legio XVI: *Full title Legio XVI Flavia Firma, the 16th Legion, Flavian and Steadfast; based at Samostata in Syria Coele (Samsat in Turkey).*

Legion: *Unit of heavy infantry, usually about 5,000 men-strong; from mythical times, the backbone of the Roman army; the numbers in a legion and the legions' dominance in the army declined during the third-century AD as more and more detachments served away from the parent unit and became more or less independent units.*

Legionary: *Roman regular soldier serving in a legion.*

Lemuria: *The days (9, 11 and 13 May) when dangerous ghosts were said to walk, necessitating propitiation.*

Lesbian: *From the Greek island of Lesbos; their wine was highly praised in antiquity, and was sometimes mixed with seawater.*

Libation: *Offering of drink to the gods.*

Liberalia: *Roman festival in honour of the god Liber and the advent of manhood, celebrated with feasting and the singing of dirty songs.*

Liberalitas: *Latin, 'generosity', a characteristic of good Emperors.*

Libertas: *Latin term for freedom or liberty; a political slogan throughout much of Roman history, though its meaning changed according to an author's philosophical principles or the system of government that happened to be in power. Also worshipped in personified form as a deity.*

Library of Celsus: *Monumental library given to the city of Ephesus in the early second century, honouring the Senator Celsus Polemaeanus, who was buried in a crypt below the reading room.*

Longaticum: *Modern Logatec in western Slovenia.*

Ludi Florales: *Roman festival in honour of the goddess Flora held on 28th April, celebrated with six days of games.*

Lycaonian Bear: *According to Greek myth, the nymph Callisto from Lyconia was seduced by Zeus, transformed into a bear by his enraged daughter, and, hunted down, turned into the constellation of Ursa minor.*

Macenites: *Nomadic tribe living in western North Africa.*

Macurgum: *Berber god identified with the Roman messenger god Mercury.*

Macurtam: *Berber god identified with Sol or Mars, the Roman sun and war gods.*

Maenad: *Frenzied female followers of the god Aionysos in Greek mythology.*

Magna Mater: *Roman title for the goddess Cybele, under the Emperors a deity of imperial protection and agriculture.*

Mamertine: *Wine from north-eastern Sicily, favoured by Julius Caesar.*

Mars: *Roman god of war.*

Mars Pater: *Title of the god Mars, 'The Father'.*

Mars Victor: *Title of the god Mars, 'The Victorious'.*

Martae: *Town on the south-eastern coast of Tunisia, modern Mareth.*

Massilia: *Roman port on the southern shores of Gaul; modern Marseilles.*

Matilam: *Berber god identified with the Roman king of the gods, Jupiter.*

Mauretania: *Roman name for western North Africa, spanning modern Morocco and Algeria.*

Mauretania Caesariensis: *Roman province of eastern Mauretania, roughly corresponding to northern Algeria.*

Mauretania Tingitana: *Roman province of western Mauretania, roughly northern Morocco.*

Melanogaitouloi: *Nomadic tribe living on the northern fringes of the Sahara.*

Melitene: *City and legionary fortress in central Turkey, modern Malatya.*

Menses: *Latin, literally 'months'; by extension, the menstrual cycle.*

Mercury: *Roman god of travellers; equivalent of Hermes.*

Mesopotamia: *The land between the rivers Euphrates and Tigris; the name of a Roman province (sometimes called Osrhoene).*

Middle Sea: *Alternative for Latin Mediterraneus, sea 'in the middle of the land'.*

Milesian Tales: *Greek genre of erotic stories.*

Minerva: *Roman goddess of wisdom.*

Mirror Fort: *Latin Ad Speculum; Roman frontier fort; modern Chebika in Tunisia.*

Misenum: *Base of the Roman fleet on the western shore of the Italian peninsular, modern Miseno.*

Moesia: *Ancient geographical region following the south bank of the Danube river in the Balkans.*

Moesia Inferior: *Roman province south of the Danube, running from Moesia Superior in the west to the Black Sea in the east.*

Moesia Superior: *Roman province to the south of the Danube, bounded by Pannonia Inferior to the north-west and Moesia Inferior to the north-east.*

Mogontiacum: *Roman legionary fortress and capital of Germania Superior; modern Mainz.*

Molossian Dog: *Ancient breed of hunting dog from the south-western Balkans.*

Momento mori: *From Latin, literally 'remember to die'.*

Monetales: *See Tresviri monetales.*

Mons Ocra: *Highest peak in the Slovenian Alps, Mount Triglav.*

Moorish: *From the Mauri tribe that gave its name to Mauretania, western North Africa.*

Mycalessus: *Site of a notorious massacre perpetrated by the Thracians, who killed the entire population of the town; modern Rhitsona in mainland Greece.*

Naissus: *Roman town in Moesia; modern Niš in Serbia.*

Naparis: *Tributary of the Danube to the east of the Carpathian Mountains mentioned by Herodotus.*

Narnia: *Ancient settlement in Umbria at the foot of the Apennines; modern Narni.*

Nasamones: *Nomadic tribe living around the Awjila Oasis in the north east of modern Libya.*

Nectar: *Drink of the gods.*

Nemean Lion: *Monstrous lion of Greek mythology impervious to mortal weapons; strangled to death by Hercules.*

Nisibis: *Roman legionary fortress on the Parthian frontier; modern Nusaybin in south-eastern Turkey.*

Nobilis, plural Nobiles: *Latin, 'nobleman'; a man from a patrician family or a plebeian family, one of whose ancestors had been consul.*

Nones: *The ninth day of a month before the Ides, i.e. the fifth day of a short month, the seventh of a long month.*

Noricum: *Roman province to the north-east of the Alps.*

Novus Homo: *Latin, literally 'new man'; someone whose ancestors had not previously held Senatorial rank.*

Numeri Brittonum: *An ad hoc unit of troops outside the regular army structure recruited in Britain; such units often retained their native dress, armament, and fighting techniques.*

Numidia: *Roman province in western North Africa.*

Nymphs: *In Greek and Roman mythology, type of minor female deity associated with a particular place, often streams or woods.*

Oligarchy: *From the Greek 'rule by the few'.*

Olympians: *The twelve major deities of Greek religion, said to live on the summit of Mount Olympus.*

Olympieion: *Shrine to the twelve Olympian gods of Greek mythology.*

Olympus: *Mountain in northern Greece, home of the Olympian gods.*

Oppian Hill: *Southern spur of the Esquiline Hill at Rome.*

Opuscula Ruralia: *'Little rural works'; title of a collection of poems by Serenus Sammonicus.*

Ordinarius: *See Consul Ordinarius.*

Orpheus: *Mythical Greek musician.*

Osrhoene: *Roman province in northern Mesopotamia.*

Ostensionales: *Soldiers specially trained for parade displays.*

Ovile: *Settlement in the Thracian highlands, named from the Latin for sheepfold.*

Palatine: *One of the fabled seven hills of Rome, south east of the Roman Forum. Site of the imperial palaces; the English term is derived from their location.*

Palestina: *see Syria Palestina.*

Panegyric: *A type of ancient speech praising someone or something.*

Pannonia Inferior: *Roman province south of the Danube, to the east of Pannonia Superior.*

Panonnia Superior: *Roman province south of the Danube, to the west of Pannonia Inferior.*

Patricians: *People of the highest social status at Rome; originally descendants of those men who sat in the very first meeting of the free senate after the expulsion of the last of the mythical kings of Rome in 509BC; under the Principate, Emperors awarded new families patrician status.*

Pax Augusti: *Latin, literally 'Emperor's peace'; a good Emperor was supposed to ensure peace for the empire; usually reduced to an aspirational slogan.*

Pax Romana: *The Roman Peace; a mission statement and justification for the Roman empire; at times, such as the mid-third century AD, more an ideology than an objective reality.*

Pelion heaped upon Ossa: *In Greek mythology, two giants planned to storm Mount Olympus and carry off two of the Olympian goddesses as wives by piling the nearby mountains Pelion and Ossa on top of one another.*

Perinthus: *Town on the northern shore of the Sea of Marmara; modern Eregli in Turkey.*

Peukiñi: *Scythian tribe living north of the mouth of the Danube River.*

Phazania: *Ancient geographical region of south-western Libya; modern Fezzan.*

Phoenicia: *Where the Phoenicians lived; an area of the coast of Levant.*

Physiognomist: *Practitioner of the ancient 'science' of studying people's faces, bodies and deportment to discover their character, and thus both their past and future.*

Plebs: *Technically, all Romans who were not patricians; more usually, the non-elite.*

Plebs Urbana: *Poor of the city of Rome, in literature usually coupled with an adjective labelling them as dirty, superstitious, lazy; distinguished from the plebs rustica, whose rural lifestyle might make them less morally dubious.*

Polyfagus: *An eater of everything; the courts of several Emperors employed such people as entertainers. One is said to have eaten condemned men alive for the benefit of the Emperor Nero.*

Polyonomous: *From the Greek for many-named.*

Polyphemus: *In Greek mythology, drunken one-eyed giant blinded by Odysseus.*

Pontes: *Fort built to defend the southern end of the Roman military bridge across the Danube; the fort and settlement on the opposite shore is now Drobeta-Turnu Severin in south-western Romania.*

Porta Querquetulana: *Gate of the Oak Grove; Gate in the ancient Servian Wall of Rome, possibly located on the Caelian Hill.*

Poseidon: *Greek god of the sea.*

Praefectus Annonae: *Prefect of the Provisions, title of official in charge of the grain supply of Rome.*

Praefectus Nationes: *Honourific title granted by the Romans to allied tribal chieftains.*

Praeneste: *Favoured hill resort of the Romans on the edge of the Apennines in central Italy; modern Palestrina.*

Praetor: *Roman magistrate in charge of justice, senatorial office second in rank to the Consuls.*

Praetorian Prefect: *Commander of the Praetorians, an equestrian; one of the most prestigious and powerful positions in the empire.*

Praetorians: *Soldiers of the Praetorian Guard, the Emperor's bodyguard and the most prestigious and highly paid unit in the empire. Unfortunately for the Emperors, their loyalty could be bought with surprising ease.*

Prefect: *Flexible Latin title for many officials and officers.*

Prefect of Egypt: *Governor of Egypt; because of the strategic importance of the province, this post was never trusted to Senators (who might be inspired to challenge the Emperor) but was always filled by equestrians.*

Prefect of the Armenians: *Commander of an auxiliary unit recruited originally in Armenia.*

Prefect of the Camp: *Officer in charge of equipment, supply, and billeting.*

Prefect of the City of Rome: *Senior senatorial post in the city of Rome, commander of the Urban Cohorts.*

Prefect of the Watch: *Equestrian officer in charge of Rome's Vigiles.*

Priapic: *Like the Roman rustic god Priapus; always portrayed with a huge erection.*

Primus inter pares: *Latin, 'First among equals'; supposed equal status claimed by the Princeps with the Senate; a boundary not overstepped by good Emperors.*

Princeps: *Latin, 'leading man'; thus a polite way to refer to the Emperor.*

Princeps Iuventutis: *'First among the youth'; title bestowed on imperial heirs.*

Principate: *Rule of the Princeps; the rule of the Roman imperium by the Emperors.*

Proconsul: *Title of the senatorial governors of some Roman provinces.*

Procurator: *Latin title for a range of officials, under the Principate typically equestrians appointed by the Emperor to oversee the collection of taxes in the provinces and keep an eye on their senatorial governors.*

Prometheus: *Divine figure, one of the Titans; variously believed to have created mankind out of clay, tricked the gods into accepting only the bones and fat of sacrifices, and stolen fire from Olympus for mortals. Zeus chained him to a peak in the Caucasus, where an eagle daily ate his liver before it grew back each night.*

Pythagorean: *Follower of the philosophy of the sixth-century BC Pythagoras, who laid stress on the mysticism of numbers and reincarnation.*

Quaestor: *Roman magistrate originally in charge of financial affairs, senatorial office second in rank to the Praetors.*

Quantum libet, Imperator: *Latin, 'whatever pleases, Emperor'.*

Quinquatrus: *Roman festival in honour of Minerva, held from 19th to 23rd March.*

Quinquegentiani: *Literally, 'people of the five tribes', nomadic coalition living on the margins of the Sahara in western North Africa.*

Quirites: *Archaic way of referring to the citizens of Rome; sometimes used by those keen to evoke the Republican past.*

Raetia: *Roman province; roughly equivalent to modern Switzerland.*

Ravenna: *Base of the Roman fleet on the Adriatic Sea in north-eastern Italy.*

Res Publica: *Latin, 'the Roman Republic'; under the Emperors, it continued to mean the Roman empire.*

Res Reconditae: *Literally, 'obscure matters'; title of a lost antiquarian work by Sammonicus.*

Resaina: *Town in northern Syria, modern Ra's al-'Ayn.*

Roman Forum: *See Forum Romanorum.*

Romanitas: *Roman-ness; increasingly important concept by the third century, with connotations of culture and civilization.*

Rostra: *Speaking platform at the western end of the Roman Forum; took its name from the beaks (rostra) of enemy warship with which it was decorated.*

Roxolani: *Nomadic Sarmatian tribe living on the Steppe north of the Danube and west of the Black Sea.*

Sabine: *From the Sabines, an Italic tribe of central Italy which merged with Rome soon after the foundation of the city in the eighth century BC.*

Sacramentum: *Roman military oath, taken extremely seriously.*

Sacred Way: *At Rome, a processional route running below the northern flank of the Palatine and passing south of the Temple of Venus and Rome, ending at the Roman Forum to the west; at Ephesus, main road paved with marble passing the Library of Celsus and leading down to the major shrines of the city.*

Samosata: *City on the right bank of the Euphrates in south-eastern Turkey protecting an important crossing point; now flooded by the Atatürk Dam.*

Sapphic: *From Sappho, Greek female poet from Lesbos who wrote love poetry to women.*

Sarcophagi: *From Greek, literally 'flesh eater'; a stone chest containing a corpse and displayed above ground, often highly decorated.*

Sarepta: *Settlement on the Tyrian coast, famed for the production of expensive purple cloth using a dye from the Murex sea snail, worn as the prerogative of the Roman elite; modern Sarafand in Lebanon.*

Sarmatians: *Nomadic peoples living north of the Danube.*

Sassanid: *Persian, from the dynasty that overthrew the Parthians in the 220sAD and was Rome's great eastern rival until the seventh century AD.*

Satyrion: *Ragwort, common ingredient of ancient aphrodisiacs; named from the licentious Satyrs.*

Satyrs: *In Greek and Roman mythology, half-goat half-man creatures with excessive sexual appetites.*

Scythians: *Term used by the Greeks and Romans for peoples living to the north and east of the Black Sea.*

Sebasteia: *City named after the Greek translation of the Emperor Augustus's name in central Turkey; modern Sivas.*

Senate: *The council of Rome, under the Emperors composed of about six hundred men, the vast majority ex-magistrates, with some imperial favourites. The richest and most prestigious group in the empire and once the governing body of the Roman Republic; increasingly side-lined by the Emperors.*

Senator: *Member of the senate, the council of Rome. The semi-hereditary senatorial order was the richest and most prestigious group in the empire.*

Serdica: *Roman town; modern Sofia in Bulgaria.*

Sicilia: *Village in Germania near Mogontiacum; possibly modern Sicklingen.*

Silentarii: *Roman officials who, as their title indicates, were employed to maintain silence and decorum at the imperial court.*

Simulacrum: *Latin, 'imitation'.*

Singara: *Highly fortified eastern outpost of the Roman empire in northern Iraq; modern Balad Sinjar.*

Sinope: *City on the southern shore of the Black Sea at the eastern end of the Roman province of Bithynia; modern Sinop in Turkey.*

Sirmium: *Strategic border town in Pannonia Inferior; modern Sremska Mitrovica in Serbia.*

Sophists: *High status teachers of ancient rhetoric who often travelled from city to city giving instruction and delivering speeches for entertainment.*

Sortes Virgilianae: *Popular method of divining the future by choosing random lines from Virgil's epic poem, the Aeneid, and interpreting them to suit the situation.*

Speculatores: *Roman army scouts and spies.*

Spintriae: *Latin, 'male-prostitutes'. From the Greek term (anal) sphincter.*

Stoa: *Pavilion by the agora in Athens where the Stoics first met, giving its name to their philosophy.*

Stoic: *Followers of the philosophy of Stoicism; should believe that everything which does not affect one's moral purpose is an irrelevance; so poverty, illness, bereavement and death cease to be things to fear and are treated with indifference.*

Stola: *Roman matron's gown.*

Subura: *Poor quarter in the city of Rome.*

Suebian Sea: *Ancient name for the Baltic.*

Sufes Pass: *Roman name for the Kasserine Pass in the Atlas Mountains of eastern Tunisia.*

Suffect Consul: *One of the additional consuls appointed later in the year by the Emperors during the Principate; less prestigious than the Consul Ordinarius.*

Symposium (plural Symposia): *Greek drinking party, adopted as social gathering of choice by the Roman elite.*

Syracuse: *Greek city on the south-eastern shore of Sicily.*

Syria Coele: *Hollow Syria, Roman province.*

Syria Palestina: *Palestinian Syria, Roman province.*

Syria Phoenice: *Phoenician Syria, Roman province.*

Tacape: *City on the south-eastern coast of Africa Proconsularis; modern Gabès in Tunisia.*

Talassio!: *Tradition cry at Roman weddings; its origins were obscure to the ancients themselves.*

Taparura: *City on the eastern coast of Africa Proconsularis; modern Sfax in Tunisia.*

Temple of Peace: *Monumental building with planted courtyard north east of the Roman Forum.*

Temple of Tellus: *Temple dedicated to the earth goddess Tellus; prominent landmark of the Carinae quarter, sited on the flank of the Esquiline Hill.*

Temple of Venus and Rome: *Temple designed by the Emperor Hadrian with back-to-back shrines for Venus, Roman goddess of Love, and Rome, a deified personification of the city. In Latin, Roma (Rome) spelled backwards is amor, love. Situated east of the Roman Forum on the north side of the Sacred Way.*

Temple of Vesta: *Circular temple in the south-eastern corner of the Roman Forum, housing the sacred flame of Vesta, goddess of the hearth.*

Tepidarium: *The warm room of a Roman baths.*

Terra Incognita: Latin, 'unknown, unexplored land'.

Testudo: Latin, literally 'tortoise'; by analogy, a Roman infantry formation with overlapping shields, giving overhead protection.

Thabraca: Coastal town in north-eastern Africa Proconsularis, five day's journey from Thysdrus by the fastest (sea) route; modern Tabarka in Tunisia.

Thelepte: Town in the centre of northern Africa Proconsularis; modern Medinet-el-Kedima in Tunisia.

Theveste: Town in northwestern Africa Proconsularis; modern Tébessa in Tunisia.

Thiges: Roman fort on the edge of the Sahara in southern Africa Proconsularis; modern Henshir Ragoubet Saieda in eastern Tunisia.

Thrace: Roman province to the north-east of Greece.

Thracians: People from the ancient geographical region of Thrace, the south-eastern corner of the Balkans.

Thusuros: Oasis on the southern fringe of Africa Proconsularis; modern Tozeur in eastern Tunisia.

Thysdrus: Town in central Africa Proconsularis, five days' journey from Thabraca by the fastest (sea) route; modern El Djem in Tunisia.

Tibur: Ancient town north east of Rome popular as a hill resort; modern Tivoli.

Tillibari: Roman fort in southern Tunisia; modern Remada.

Tisavar: Roman military outpost in southern Tunisia; modern Ksar Ghilane.

Titan: First generation of gods; defeated by the Olympians.

Toga: Voluminous garment, reserved for Roman citizens, worn on formal occasions.

Toga Virilis: Garment given to mark a Roman's coming of age; usually at about fourteen.

Transpadane: Literally, 'Beyond the River Po'; ancient geographical area of northern Italy.

Tresviri Monetales: Literally, 'Three men of the mint'; board of junior magistrates responsible for the coinage.

Tresviri Capitales: Board of three junior magistrates in charge of prisons.

Tribune: Title of a junior senatorial post at Rome (see Tribune of the Plebs) and of various military officers; some commanded auxiliary units, while others were mid-ranking officers in the Legions.

Tribune of the Plebs: *A powerful office in the Republican government, originating as a champion of the people to prevent the domination of the senatorial nobility. Under the Principate an honourific appointment awarded to junior senators by the Emperor.*

Tripolitania: *Ancient geographical region of central North Africa, at the eastern extremity of Africa Proconsularis.*

Triton: *A Greek sea god.*

Triumvirate: *'Three men'; term made notorious by two pacts to share control of the Roman government between three leading citizens that precipitated the end of the Roman Republic and ushered in the Principate.*

Troy: *Legendary city in Asia Minor; the story of its siege by the Greeks is the subject of Homer's Iliad.*

Tutor: *Guardian legally necessary for a child, imbecile or woman.*

Ubi tu Gaius, ego Gaia: *'Where you are Gaius, I am Gaia'; Roman wedding formula, its origin, and even meaning, were sources of speculation in antiquity itself.*

Ulpia Traiana Sarmizegetusa: *Legionary fortress and capital of the province of Dacia; now abandoned, the site lies in western Romania.*

Urban Cohorts: *Military unit stationed at Rome to act as a police force and counterbalance the Praetorian Guard.*

Utica: *Coastal town of Africa Proconsularis north west of Carthage.*

Vadas: *Nec victoriam speres, nec te militia tuo credas. 'Go, neither hope for victory, nor trust your soldiers'. According to the Historia Augusta, words of a prophesy offered to Alexander Severus.*

Valerii: *Members of the Valerius family.*

Varissima: *Berber goddess identified with Venus, Roman goddess of love.*

Via Aurelia: *Road running along the Italian coast north west of Rome.*

Via Egnatia: *Roman military road running east–west across the southern Balkans, ending in the east at Byzantium.*

Via Flaminia: *Road leading north from Rome, crossing the Apennines, and terminating on the Adriatic coast.*

Via Labicana: *Road leading south east from the centre of Rome.*

Via Popilia: *Extension of the Via Aurelia leading north into the plain of the river Po.*

Victoria: *Roman goddess of victory.*

Vicus Augusti: *Town in eastern Africa Proconsularis; modern Sidi-el-Hani in Tunisia.*

Vigiles: *Paramilitary unit stationed at Rome for police and firefighting duties.*

Vihinam: *Berber goddess associated with childbirth.*

Viminacium: *Provincial capital of Moesia Superior; modern Kostolac in eastern Serbia.*

Vir Clarissimus: *Title of a Roman Senator.*

Volaterrae: *Town in central Italy; modern Volterra.*

Votis Decennalibus: *Latin, 'vows of the tenth year'; common legend on coinage announcing the loyal vows made by the populous for an Emperor's safety in the coming decade.*

Zeugma: *City on the banks of the Euphrates guarding a bridge of boats; now submerged by the Birecik Dam in southern Turkey.*

Zeus: *Greek king of the gods.*

Zeus Philios: *Title of Zeus, 'The Friendly, Hospitable'.*

Zirin: *Cry of the Scythians, said by Lucian to signal a person's status as an emissary and prevent the caller from being harmed, even in the heart of combat.*

IRON & RUST:

LIST OF CHARACTERS

The list is organized alphabetically within geographic regions. To avoid giving away any of the plot characters usually are only described as first encountered in *Iron & Rust*.

THE NORTH

Ababa: A druid woman patronized by the imperial court.

Agrippina: Wife of the general Germanicus, she died in AD33.

Alcimus Felicianus: *Gaius Attius Alcimus Felicianus*, an equestrian official with a long record of civilian posts, including administering the inheritance tax; a friend of Timesitheus.

Alexander Severus: Born AD208, Roman Emperor from AD222.

Ammonius: An equestrian officer commanding a unit of Cataphracts.

Antigonus: *Domitius Antigonus*, a Senator, governor of Moesia Inferior.

Anullinus: An equestrian officer commanding a unit of Armenians.

Apollonius: Of Tyana, wandering Pythagorean philosopher and performer of miracles, whose life spanned almost the whole of the first century AD; according to the *Historia Augusta*, the private chapels of the Emperor Alexander Severus contained statues of Abraham, Apollonius of Tyana, Jesus and Orpheus.

Arrian of Nicomedia: Greek historian and philosopher, and Roman Consul and general, *c.* AD85/90–145/6.

Aspines of Gadara: Valerius Aspines, Greek rhetorician from Syria, *c.* AD190-250.

Augustus: First Emperor of Rome, 31BC–AD14; known as Octavian before he came to power.

Autronius Justus: A Senator, governor of Pannonia Inferior.

Axius: *Quintus Axius Aelianus*, an equestrian, Procurator of Germania Inferior, an associate of Timesitheus.

Barbia Orbiana: *Gnaea Seia Herennia Sallustia Barbia Orbiana*, second wife of the Emperor Alexander Severus from AD225, divorced and banished in AD227.

Caracalla: *Marcus Aurelius Antoninus*, known as Caracalla, Roman Emperor AD198–217.

Catilius Severus: *Lucius Catilius Severus*; member of the Senatorial inner council of sixteen advising the Emperor Alexander Severus; wears his hair long, and considered effeminate by Timesitheus.

Catius Clemens: *Gaius Catius Clemens*, commander of Legio VIII Augusta in Germania Superior; brother of Catius Priscillianus and Catius Celer.

Catius Priscillianus: *Sextus Catius Clementius Priscillianus*, Governor of Germania Superior; elder brother of Catius Clemens and Catius Celer.

Claudius Venacus: *Marcus Claudius Venacus*, ex-Consul, member of the Senatorial inner council of sixteen advising the Emperor Alexander Severus.

Clodius Pompeianus: *Ex-Quaestor*, and thus a junior Senator, descendant of the Emperor Marcus Aurelius and thus a distant relative of Iunia Fadilla.

Cornelianus: *Marcus Attius Cornelianus*, Praetorian Prefect under the Emperor Alexander Severus from *c.* AD230.

Decius: *Gaius Messius Quintus Decius*, from a senatorial family owning wide estates near the Danube, an early patron of the career of Maximinus, now governor of the province of Hispania Tarraconesis.

Domitius: An equestrian, Prefect of the Camp under the Emperor Alexander Severus; enemy of Timesitheus.

Eadwine: Chief and warlord in the service of Isangrim, King of the Angles.

Elagabalus: Nickname given to the notoriously perverted Roman Emperor Marcus Aurelius Antonius (AD218-22) who served as a priest of Elagabalus, patron god of his ancestral town, Emesa in Syria.

Faltonius Nicomachus: *Maecius Faltonius Nicomachus*, Governor of Noricum.

Felicianus: Senior Praetorian Prefect under Alexander Severus.

Flavia Latroniana: Daughter of the ex-Consul Flavius Iulius Latronianus.

Flavius Vopiscus: A Roman Senator from Syracuse in Sicily; fond of literature, especially biography, and much given to superstition.

Florianus: *Marcus Annius Florianus*, equestrian commander of an irregular unit of British infantry, half-brother of Marcus Claudius Tacitus.

Fortunata: Slave-girl owned by Caecilia Paulina.

Froda: A prince of the Angles, eldest son of King Isangrim.

Germanicus: Nephew and heir of the Emperor Tiberius, won his name from his father's campaigns in Germany; he died in suspicious circumstances in AD19.

Gessius Marcianus: An equestrian from Syria, the deceased second husband of Mamaea, and father of the Emperor Alexander Severus.

Granianus: *Iulius Granianus*, rhetorical tutor to the Emperor Alexander Severus.

Honoratus: *Lucius Flavius Honoratus Lucilianus*, a novus homo in the Roman Senate, an ex-Praetor, Legate of the 11th legion and commander of all detachments from Moesia Inferior serving with the imperial field army; a man of ridiculous good looks, others often comment on his perfect teeth.

Iotapianus: *M. Fulvius Rufus Iotapianus*, equestrian commander of the Cohort of Emesenes, and himself from Emesa.

Isangrim: The King of the Angles in the far north (modern Denmark).

Javolenus: A legionary in the 2nd Legion Parthica.

Julius Capitolinus: An equestrian officer commanding the 2nd Legion Parthica; often found making notes he intends to turn into biographies.

Julius Licinianus: *Quintus Julius Licinianus*, a Senator, governor of Dacia.

Licinius Valerian: See Valerian (Africa).

Lorenius: *Tiberius Lorenius Celsus*, governor of Raetia.

Lucius Marius Perpetuus: Consul Ordinarius in AD237, son of a past governor of Moesia Superior, father of Perpetua, the friend of Iunia Fadilla.

Macedo: *Macedo Macedonius*, equestrian commander of an auxiliary unit of Osrhoenes, friend of Timesitheus.

Mamaea: *Julia Avita Mamaea*, mother of the Emperor Alexander Severus.

Marcus Nummius Tuscus: An ex-Quaestor, and thus a junior Senator; the grandson of M. Nummius Umbrius Primus Senecio Albinus, Consul Ordinarius in AD206, the latter having been the brother of Nummius, Iunia Fadilla's late husband.

Marius: Roman statesman and general, 157–86BC; a novus homo who rose from humble origins to be Consul seven times.

Maximinus Thrax: *Gaius Iulius Verus Maximinus*, known as Maximinus Thrax (the Thracian), equestrian officer training the new recruits with the imperial field army.

Maximus: *Gaius Iulius Verus Maximus*, son of Maximinus and Caecilia Paulina.

Memmia Sulpicia: Daughter of the Senator Sulpicius Macrinus, first wife of the Emperor Alexander Severus, divorced and living in banishment in Africa.

Micca: Bodyguard of Maximinus from the days when both were young.

Mokimos: A Centurion in the Cohort of Osrhoene archers.

Nero: Roman Emperor AD54–68.

Ostorius: Governor of Cilicia.

Paulina: *Caecilia Paulina*, wife of the Emperor Maximinus.

Petronius Magnus: *Gaius Petronius Magnus*, member of the Senatorial inner council of sixteen advising the Emperor Alexander Severus.

Plautianus: *Gaius Fulvius Plautianus*, Praetorian Prefect under the Emperor Septimius Severus and accused of plotting against him by Caracalla; murdered AD205.

Plutarch: A prolific Greek writer of philosophy, biography, and history, *c.* AD45–125.

Pomponius Julianus: A Senator, governor of Syria Phoenice.

Pontius Proculus Pontianus: Consul Ordinarius in AD238; son of Tiberius Pontius Pontianus, sometime governor of Pannonia Inferior.

Pythias: A slave-girl owned by Caecilia Paulina.

Quintus Valerius: Equestrian commander of the Numeri Brittonum, an irregular unit of British infantry.

Rutilus: Distant relative of Maximinus.

Sabinus Modestus: Cousin of Timesitheus, not judged overly intelligent by the latter.

Sanctus: *Ab Admissionibus* (Master of Admissions) of the imperial household.

Saturninus Fidus: *Titus Claudius Saturninus Fidus*, a Senator; friend of the Gordiani.

Septimius Severus: Roman Emperor AD193–211.

Soaemis: *Julia Soaemis (or Soaemias) Bassiana*, sister of Mamaea, mother of the Emperor Elagabalus and aunt of the Emperor Alexander Severus; murdered AD222 with her son.

Sulla: Roman statesman, *c.* 138–78BC; resigned the Dictatorship in 81BC and soon after retired from public life, dying of natural causes shortly after finishing his memoirs.

Sulpicius Macrinus: The executed father of Memmia Sulpicia, divorced first wife of the Emperor Alexander Severus.

Tacitus: *Marcus Claudius Tacitus*, governor of Raetia; half-brother of Marcus Annius Florianus.

Taurinus: Not Raurinus; unwillingly proclaimed Emperor by the soldiers of Syria during the reign of Alexander Severus; trying to flee from his mutinous troops, he fell in the Euphrates and drowned.

Thrasybulus: Astrologer on friendly terms with the Emperor Alexander Severus.

Timesitheus: *Gaius Furius Sabinius Aquila Timesitheus*, senior equestrian official in charge of imperial finances in Belgica, Germania Superior and Germania Inferior; acting governor of Germania Superior; married to Tranquillina.

Titus Quartinus: A Senator, governor of Moesia Superior.

Tranquillina: Wife of Timesitheus.

Tynchanius: From the same village in Thrace as Maximinus, his personal attendant since early days.

Ulpian: *Domitius Ulpianus*, famous jurist, made Praetorian Prefect by Alexander Severus in AD222 but murdered by the Praetorians in AD223 for curtailing their privileges.

Varus: *Quinctilius Varus*, general who lost his life and three legions in an ambush in *Germania* (AD9).

Veturius: A Rationibus (Treasurer) of Alexander Severus.

Vitalianus: *Publius Aelius Vitalianus*, an equestrian official.

Volo: *Marcus Aurelius Volo*, commander of the *frumentarii* (the imperial spies).

Vulcatius Terentianus: Member of the Senatorial inner council of sixteen advising the Emperor Alexander Severus.

Xenophon: Athenian soldier and writer, *c.* 430–*c.* 350BC; though famed as a historian and biographer, also wrote a treatise on hunting with dogs.

ROME

Acilius Aviola: *Manius Acilius Aviola*, patrician Senator; his family claimed descent from Aeneas, and thus the goddess Venus, they first rose to prominence under the Emperor Augustus and an ancestor held the consulship in AD24; cousin of Acilius Glabrio.

Acilius Glabrio: *Marcus Acilius Glabrio*, cousin of Acilius Aviola; a young patrician, one of the *Tresviri monetales*; his father Manius Acilius Faustinus was Consul Ordinarius in AD210.

Alcimus Felicianus: *Gaius Attius Alcimus Felicianus*, an equestrian official with a long record of official posts, including administering the inheritance tax; a friend of Timesitheus.

Antheros: An acquaintance of Fabianus.

Balbinus: *Decimus Caelius Calvinus Balbinus*, a patrician Senator, claim kinship with the deified Emperors Trajan and Hadrian via the great Roman clan of the Coelli; Consul Ordinarius with the Emperor Caracalla in AD213; among his many political friends are Acilius Aviola, Caesonius Rufinianus, and the brothers Valerius Messala and Valerius Priscillianus.

Caenis: A prostitute living in the Subura at Rome.

Caesonius Rufinianus: *Lucius Caesonius Lucillus Macer Rufinianus*, a patrician Senator; Suffect Consul *c.* AD225–30; a friend of Balbinus.

Castricius: *Gaius Aurelius Castricius*, a young man of uncertain origins living a disreputable life in the Subura.

Catius Celer: *Lucius Catius Celer*, A Senator, Praetor in AD235; younger brother of Catius Priscillianus and Catius Clemens; a friend of Timesitheus.

Cato the Censor: *Marcus Porcius Cato*, also known as Cato the Elder (234–149BC), stern moralist of the Republic.

Cincinnatus: Roman statesman of the early Republic (519–430BC); later became an exemplum for twice leaving his small farm to lead Rome's armies in a military crisis and to prevent a coup.

Claudius: Roman Emperor AD41–54; deified after death.

Claudius Aurelius: *Lucius Tiberius Claudius Aurelius Quintianus Pompeianus*, descendant of the Emperor Marcus Aurelius and thus a distant relative of Iunia Fadilla; Consul Ordinarius in AD235.

Claudius Severus: *Gnaeus Claudius Severus*, descendant of the Emperor Marcus Aurelius and thus a distant relative of Iunia Fadilla; Consul Ordinarius in AD235.

Commodus: Roman Emperor AD180–192.

Cuspidius Celerinus: The 'Father of the Senate', the most senior Senator in the Curia.

Cuspidius Severus: *Cuspidius Flaminius Severus*, a novus homo in the Senate, an ex-Consul, and friend of Pupienus.

Domitian: Roman Emperor AD81–96, notorious for his tyrannical rule and paranoia.

ᴀomia: Aged nurse of Iunia Fadilla.

ᴀbianus: Visitor to Rome from the countryside.

Fortunatianus: *Curius Fortunatianus*, secretary to Pupienus.

Gaius: *Gaius Marius Perpetuus*, one of the Tresviri Capitales; son of Lucius Marius Perpetuus, and brother of Perpetua.

Gallicanus: *Lucius Domitius Gallicanus Papinianus*, a Senator of homespun and hirsute appearance, sometimes thought to resemble an ape, much influenced by the philosophy of Cynicism, his unusual views on the Res Publica appear to be shared by at least three other Senators: Maecenas, Hostilianus, and Licinianus.

Geta: Co-Emperor with Caracalla until murdered on his brother's orders in AD211.

Gordian: See Gordian the Younger (Africa).

Hadrian: Roman Emperor AD117–138; deified after death.

Herennius Modestinus: Equestrian Prefect of the *Vigiles* at Rome; sometime pupil of Ulpian and legal secretary of Alexander Severus AD223–225.

Hippolytus: Acquaintance of Fabianus.

Hostilianus: *Marcus Severus Hostilianus*, Senator and ex-Quaestor; a friend of Gallicanus.

Iunia Fadilla: Great-granddaughter of the Emperor Marcus Aurelius.

Latronianus: *Marcus Flavius Iulius Latronianus*, A Senator, had been Suffect Consul sometime before AD231.

Lucius: *Lucius Iunius Fadillus*, cousin of Iunia Fadilla.

Macrinus the Moor: *Marcus Opellius Macrinus*, Praetorianus Prefect, instigated the murder of the Emperor Caracalla in AD217, and briefly held the throne.

Maecenas: Senator and intimate friend of Gallicanus.

Maecia Faustina: Sister of Gordian the Younger, daughter of Gordian the Elder; married to Junius Balbus, governor of Syria Coele, friend of Caecilia Paulina.

Marcus Aurelius: *Marcus Aurelius Antoninus*, Emperor AD161–180.

Marcus Julius Corvinus: Equestrian landowner, and perhaps leader of bandits in the eastern Alps.

Mummius Felix Cornelianus: *Lucius Mummius Felix Cornelian* Consul Ordinarius in AD237.

Nummius: *Marcus Nummius Umbrius Secundus Senecio Albinus*, Suffect Consul in AD206, thereafter devoting himself to pleasure; husband of Iunia Fadilla, recently deceased.

Otho: Before becoming Emperor (AD69), was forced to divorce Poppaea so she could be married by Nero.

Perpetua: Daughter of Lucius Marius Perpetuus, wife of Serenianus, and friend of Iunia Fadilla.

Pescennia Marcellina: Elderly woman of wealth in Rome; benefactor of the young Pupienus, financing his early career and Praetorship.

Pinarius: *Pinarius Valens*, a kinsman who fostered the young Pupienus.

Poppaea: Wife of Otho before being forced to divorce her husband for the Emperor Nero.

Potens: *Quintus Herennius Potens*, Prefect of the Parthian cavalry serving with the imperial field army, newly installed by Maximinus as Prefect of the Watch in Rome; brother-in-law of Decius.

Pupienus: *Marcus Clodius Pupienus Maximus*, a novus homo of very obscure origins, brought up in the house of a kinsman, Pinarius Valens, in Tibur; now a patrician, appointed Consul for the second time, as Ordinarius, and Prefect of the City in AD234; husband of Sextia Cethegilla, and father of Pupienus Maximus and Pupienus Africanus. His many friends in politics include Crispinus, Cuspidius Severus, Serenianus, Sextius Cethegillus, and Tineius Sacerdos.

Pupienus Africanus: *Marcus Pupienus Africanus*, Senator; son of Pupienus, and brother of Pupienus Maximus.

Pupienus Maximus: *Marcus Clodius Pupienus Maximus*, Senator; son of Pupienus, and brother of Pupienus Africanus; married to Tineia.

Rutilius Crispinus: See Crispinus (The East).

Sabinus: Sometime Consul, connoisseur of art; friend of Flavius Vopiscus.

Sextia Cethegilla: Wife of Pupienus.

Sextius Cethegillus: Senator, father of Sextia Cethegilla, and thus brother-in-law of Pupienus.

Theoclia: Sister of Alexander Severus, wife of Valerius Messala.

Tiberius: Notoriously depraved Roman Emperor, AD14–37.

Ticida: A Latin love poet.

Tineia: Daughter of Tineius Sacerdos, married to Pupienus Maximus, son of Pupienus.

Tineius Sacerdos: *Quintus Tineius Sacerdos*, Consul Ordinarius with the Emperor Elagabalus in AD219; father of Tineia, and thus father-in-law to Pupienus Maximus, and a friend of Pupienus.

Toxotius: Member of the board of junior magistrates the Tresviri Monetales; lover of Perpetua.

Trajan: Emperor AD98–117; deified after death.

Valens Licinianus: *Julius Valens Licinianus*, a Senator and ex-Quaestor; a friend of Gallicanus.

Valerius Apollinaris: See Valerius Apollinaris (the East).

Valerius Messala: *Marcus Valerius Messala*, a patrician senator, son of Valerius Apollinaris, brother of Valerius Priscillianus, married to Theoclia, wife of the Emperor Alexander Severus.

Valerius Poplicola: *Lucius Valerius Poplicola Balbinus Maximus*, a young patrician, son Valerius Priscillianus; one of the *Tresviri Monetales*.

Valerius Priscillianus: *Lucius Valerius Claudius Acilius Priscillianus Maximus*, patrician Senator, Consul Ordinarius in AD233, son of Valerius Apollinaris, brother of Valerius Messala, father of Valerius Poplicola.

AFRICA

Aemilius Severinus: *Lucius Aemilius Severinus*, also called Phillyrio; commander of the *Speculatores*.

Albinus: *Clodius Albinus*, declared Emperor by the legions of Britain and Spain under Septimius Severus; killed in battle AD197.

Annius Severus: Father of Orestilla, late wife of the elder Gordian.

Apellinus: *Claudius Apellinus*, governor of Britannia Inferior; an inscription recording his restoration of an artillery installation survives from High Rochester, Northumberland.

Arrian: Legate of Gordian the Elder in Africa; especial friend of Sabinianus.

Aspasius of Ravenna: Orator and secretary to Alexander Severus; the biography written by his near contemporary, Philostratus, survives.

Brennus: Bodyguard of the elder Gordian; his name suggests he is a Gaul.

Canartha: Berber chief based at the village of Esuba.

Capelianus: Governor of Numidia; enemy of Gordian the Elder.

Chione: A mistress of the younger Gordian.

Egnatius Proculus: *Gaius Luxilius Sabinus Egnatius Proculus*; Senator, removed from the governorship of Achaea and given administrative posts in Italy; relative by marriage of Valerian.

Faraxen: Berber Centurion commanding a unit of the *Speculatores*.

Gordian the Elder: *Marcus Antonius Gordianus Sempronianus*, aged ex-Consul; after a lengthy, if interrupted career, now governor of Africa Proconsularis; father of Gordian the Younger, and Maecia Faustina.

Gordian the Younger: *Marcus Antonius Gordianus Sempronianus*, ex-Consul serving as a Legate of his father in Africa; devotee of Epicurean philosophy; sometime lover of Iunia Fadilla.

Herodes: *Lucius Vibullius Hipparchus Tiberius Claudius Atticus Herodes* (*known as Herodes Atticus*), wealthy Senator of Athenian ancestry and patron of Greek culture (AD101–177).

Julius Terentius: Commander of the garrison at Arete, killed by the Sassanids; his epitaph and a painted portrait survive from Dura-Europus.

Lycaenion: Carthaginian mistress of Menophilus.

Lydus: Commander of the Second Flavian Cohort of Africans.

Mauricius: A wealthy landowner and town councillor at Thysdrus and Hadrumetum in Africa Proconsularis.

Menophilus: *Tullius Menophilus*, Quaestor of the province of Africa Proconsularis.

Mirzi: Eldest son of Nuffuzi, tribal chief of the Cinithii.

Nicagoras of Athens: Athenian rhetorician and subject of a biography by Philostratus, *c.* AD175–250.

Nuffuzi: Tribal chief of the Cinithii.

Orestilla: *Fabia Orestilla*, late wife of the elder Gordian and mother of Gordian the Younger.

Parthenope: A mistress of the younger Gordian.

Paul: Known as The Chain, rapacious Procurator of Africa Proconsularis.

Philostratus: Greek orator and biographer of the sophists (*c*. 170–250AD); in the early third century, introduced at the court of Septimius Severus at Rome.

Polycrates: Greek tyrant *c*. 540–522BC; Gordian is actually thinking of the tyrant Thrasybulus (*c*. 440–388BC), who, on being asked how to secure a tyranny, walked though a field of corn chopping down the tallest stalks: i.e., eliminate the most outstanding.

Quintillius Marcellus: Member of the Senatorial inner council of sixteen advising the Emperor Alexander Severus.

Sabinianus: Legate of Gordian the Elder in Africa Proconsularis; especial friend of Arrian.

Serenus Sammonicus: See note in Historical Afterword.

Valens: *A Cubiculo* of the elder Gordian.

Valerian: *Publius Licinius Valerianus*, married into the family of the Egnatii; legate of the elder Gordian in Africa Proconsularis.

Verres: Notoriously corrupt governor of Sicily prosecuted by Cicero in 70BC.

Verittus: Centurion of the Third Augustan Legion.

THE EAST

Ardashir: The First, founder of the Sassanid empire, ruled AD224–242.

Armenius Peregrinus: *Tiberius Pollienus Armenius Peregrinus*, adoptive son of Pollienus Auspex Minor.

Bion of Borysthenes: A Cynic philosopher, *c*. 345–245BC.

Cassius Dio: Senator from Bithynia, Consul Ordinarius in AD229 under Alexander Severus; author of a history of Rome in Greek from the legendary origins of the city down to his own consulship.

Chosroes: Prince of Armenia, son of King Tiridates II; serving with the

Roman army in the east as a hostage for the good behaviour of his father.

Crispinus: *Rutilius Pudens Crispinus*, equestrian army officer risen into the Senate, governor of Syria Phoenice; friend of Pupienus.

Domitius Pompeianus: *Dux ripae*, commander of the Euphrates frontier stationed at Arete; according to a graffito at Dura-Europus, raised a Greek tragic actor as a fosterling.

Flavius Heraclio: Governor of Mesopotamia murdered by his own troops *c.* AD229.

Gaius Cervonius Papus: Legate of the Twelfth Thunder-bearing Legion.

Garshasp: A Sassanid warrior.

Julius Julianus: Prefect of the First Parthian Legion.

Junius Balbus: Governor of Syria Coele, husband of Maecia Faustina, and thus brother-in-law of Gordian the Younger.

Lucretius: *Lucius Lucretius Annianus*, equestrian governor of Egypt.

Ma'na: Son of Sanatruq II, prince of the Hatrene royal family; serving with the Roman army.

Manu: Son of Abgar VIII, titular Crown Prince of Edessa, although wealthy, left without real power after Caracalla incorporated the kingdom into the Roman empire in the early third century AD.

Otacilius Severianus: *Marcus Otacilius Severianus*, Senator, governor of Syria Palestina; brother-in-law of Priscus and Philip.

Paris: Mythical Trojan prince in Homer's *Iliad*; notably unheroic.

Philip: *Marcus Julius Philippus*, brother of Gaius Julius Priscus; born in Roman Arabia and serving as a Legate to his brother on the Parthian frontier.

Pollienus Auspex Minor: Adoptive father of Armenius Peregrinus, patron of Timesitheus; Suffect Consul and holder of various governorships under Alexander Severus.

Porcius Aelianus: Equestrian Prefect of the 3rd Legion Parthica.

Priscus: *Gaius Julius Priscus*, equestrian governor of Mesopotamia, brother of Marcus Julius Philip; born in Roman Arabia.

Rutilius Crispinus: See Crispinus.

Sabinia: *Furia Sabinia Tranquillina*, daughter of Timesitheus and Tranquillina.

Sanatruq: Sanatruq II, ruler of the Roman client kingdom of Hatra *c*. 200–240/1AD.

Sasan: Founder of the Sassanid dynasty.

Serenianus: *Licinius Serenianus*, novus homo in Senate, governor of Cappadocia; a friend of Pupienus, and Priscus; married to Perpetua.

Severianus: See Otacilius Severianus (East)

Sollemnius Pacatianus: *Claudius Sollemnius Pacatianus*, governor of Arabia from AD223.

Sporakes: Bodyguard of Priscus, governor of Mesopotamia.

Thersites: Deeply unheroic Greek character in Homer's *Iliad*.

Tiridates: The Second, King of Armenia from AD217; as a member of the Arsacid dynasty overthrown by the Sassanids, lays claim to the Parthian empire.

Titus: Roman Emperor AD79–81.

Valerius Apollinaris: *Lucius Valerius Messala Apollinaris*, a Senator from one of the great patrician families, father of Valerius Messala and Valerius Priscillianus; Consul Ordinarius in AD214, following which he spent some years in retirement after his father was executed by the Emperor Caracalla, has since returned to politics, and he is now governor of Asia.

Wa'el: Noble from Hatra commanding a unit of horsemen in the service of Rome.